Readers love the Mangrove Stories
by MARY CALMES

Blue Days

"Mary is such a solid author. I love how she develops and writes such likeable characters. I loved this story."

—Love Bytes

Quiet Nights

"Oh Mary, how I love thee, let me count the ways!"

—The Kimi-chan Experience

Sultry Sunset

"I loved the writing style, I loved the tone, I loved the humor, I loved the introductions to the new characters, I loved Mike, and I loved Hutch."

—Prism Book Alliance

Easy Evenings

"The chemistry between Lazlo and Britton leaps off the page…"

—Joyfully Jay

Sleeping 'til Sunrise

"This is a classic kind of Calmes with great dialogue, delicious heat and sexy times, and a breakneck romantic pace."

—Gay Book Reviews

By Mary Calmes

Acrobat
Again
Any Closer
With Cardeno C.: Control
With Poppy Dennison: Creature
Feature
Floodgates
Frog
Grand Adventures
(Dreamspinner Anthology)
The Guardian
Heart of the Race
Ice Around the Edges
Judgment
Just Desserts
Lay It Down
Mine
Romanus • Chevalier
Romanus & Chevalier
(Author Anthology,
Paperback Only)
The Servant
Steamroller
Still
Tales of the Curious Cookbook
(Multiple Author Anthology)
Three Fates
(Multiple Author Anthology)
What Can Be
Where You Lead
Wishing on a Blue Star
(Dreamspinner Anthology)

CHANGE OF HEART
Change of Heart • Trusted Bond
Honored Vow •Crucible of Fate
Forging the Future

L'ANGE
Old Loyalty, New Love
Fighting Instinct • Chosen Pride

MANGROVE STORIES
Blue Days • Quiet Nights
Sultry Sunset • Easy Evenings
Sleeping 'til Sunrise
Mangrove Stories
(Print Only Anthology)

MARSHALS
All Kinds of Tied Down
Fit to Be Tied • Tied Up in Knots

A MATTER OF TIME
A Matter of Time: Vol. 1
A Matter of Time: Vol. 2
Bulletproof• But For You
Parting Shot • Piece of Cake

TIMING
Timing • After the Sunset
When the Dust Settles
Perfect Timing
(Print Only Anthology)

THE WARDER SERIES
His Hearth • Tooth & Nail
Heart in Hand • Sinnerman • Nexus
Cherish Your Name
Warders Vol. 1 & 2

Published by DREAMSPINNER PRESS
www.dreamspinnerpress.com

Mary Calmes

MANGROVE
Stories

Published by

DREAMSPINNER PRESS

5032 Capital Circle SW, Suite 2, PMB# 279, Tallahassee, FL 32305-7886 USA
www.dreamspinnerpress.com

Mangrove Stories
© 2017 Mary Calmes.
Blue Days previously published by Dreamspinner Press, November 2014.
Quiet Nights previously published by Dreamspinner Press, February 2015.
Sultry Sunset previously published by Dreamspinner Press, May 2015.
Easy Evenings previously published by Dreamspinner Press, November 2015.
Sleeping 'til Sunrise previously published by Dreamspinner Press, December 2015.

Cover Art
© 2017 Reese Dante.
http://www.reesedante.com
Cover content is for illustrative purposes only and any person depicted on the cover is a model.

ISBN: 978-1-63533-444-9
Library of Congress Control Number: 2016917565
Published February 2017
v. 1.0

Printed in the United States of America
∞
This paper meets the requirements of
ANSI/NISO Z39.48-1992 (Permanence of Paper).

TABLE OF CONTENTS

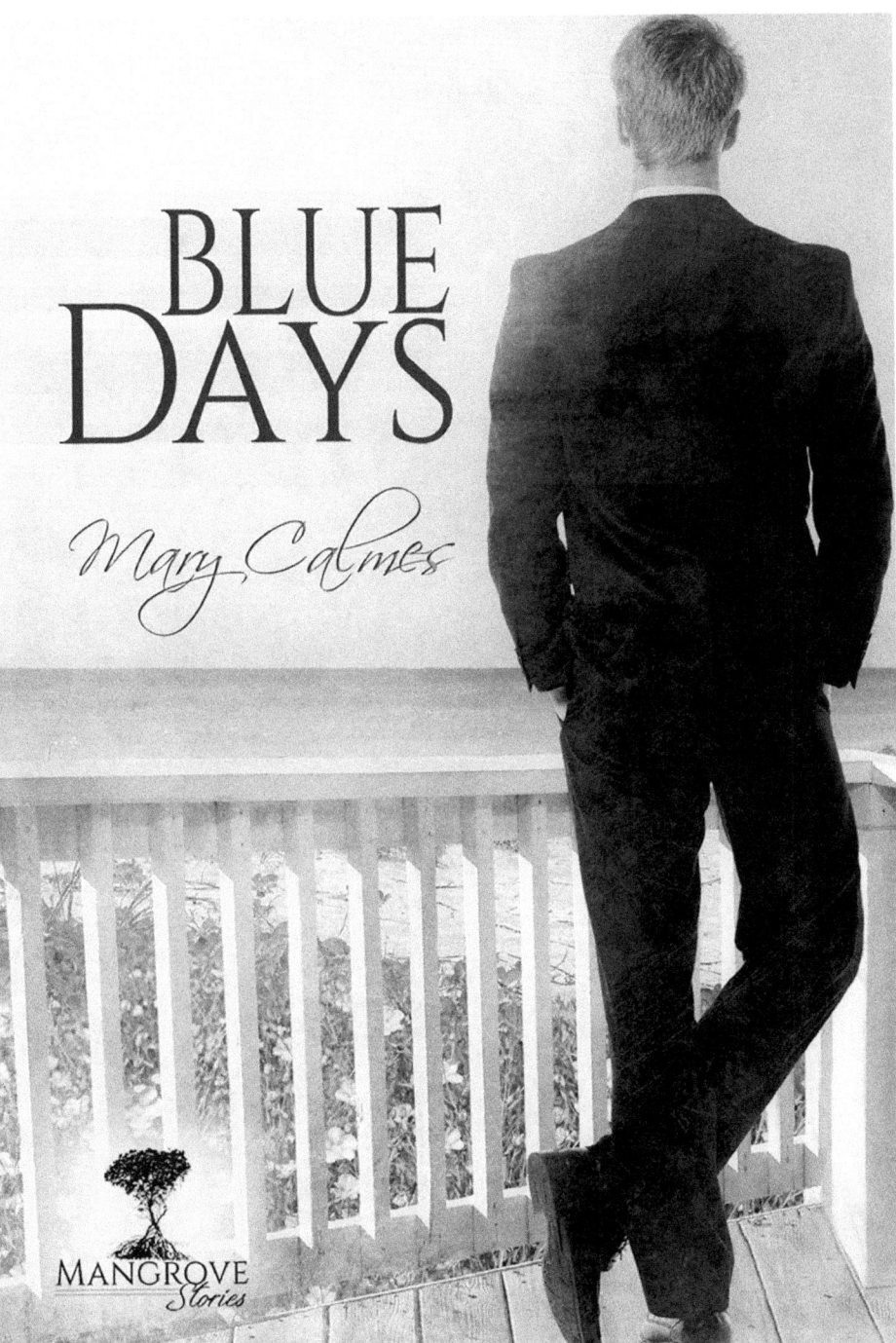

BLUE DAYS

Mary Calmes

MANGROVE
Stories

CHAPTER ONE

I HAD failed.

Epically.

But the upshot was, I was now free to go. I was never meant to sit behind a desk in an office and look at spreadsheets anyway. My dreams included sun and wind and hopefully still high-stakes sales or even number crunching—because that was the part I loved—but without the glass-walled office. It was time to take a chance on my real dreams instead of dealing with the fallout of my last career decision. I hated facing the judgmental looks every day, hearing the snickering, and knowing that every person there, even colleagues who had become friends, thought I was a screwup.

As I sat in the large conference room along with the entire firm, waiting to have an emergency meeting on a cold, dreary Monday morning in January, I contemplated my future.

We had all been sent an urgent e-mail the night before that informed us to report to work at seven sharp to hear about the "new direction" the company would be taking—and we all knew some kind of shakeup was coming—so we convened and waited to learn the future of Sakura Limited, the real estate development company we all worked for. I had stopped on the way to get coffee for the two people from my old team who were still talking to me, Shawn Ferris and Liza Cho. I was still being thanked for the caffeine when Mr. Conner Troy, CEO, came through a side door and walked directly to the podium.

"Good morning, everyone, thank you all for coming on such short notice." He glanced around the room. "The reason I called you here is to announce the immediate resignation of Managing Director Everett Connelly from the staff of Sakura Limited."

The gasp from all corners was audible, but I was not surprised. The company hadn't lost any money in the last two quarters, but neither had it made any. We were absolutely at a standstill, had been for the past year. But that couldn't have been the problem; the important thing was keeping the clients we had, not looking for new prospects. That was what had been drilled into me when my deal fell through, that I was overreaching.

"I wonder who they got," Shawn asked, turning to look at me.

"You know I don't know." I sighed. "I'm just lucky to have a job, right?"

"Don't be bitter, Dwyer," he told me. "You tried, you failed huge, but at least you gave it your best shot."

"Mr. Connelly felt," Mr. Troy continued, "that the direction he wanted for his career and the direction that Sakura would be taking would not be complementary paths."

"Which means what, exactly?" Liza asked under her breath from my right as she nudged me in the ribs.

"Just because I was inner circle once doesn't mean I am anymore," I whispered back.

Mr. Troy cleared his throat. "With that being said, we must also say good-bye to Ava Palmer and wish her the very best as she takes on her new challenges with Myer Coffman."

"Oh ouch." Liza groaned softly. "I mean, I hated her, but I would jump into Lake Michigan before I went *there* and died of shame."

Everyone knew if you couldn't make it in Chicago with one of the big three—Sakura, Sutter, or Ryerson & Wolf—you went to work at Myer Coffman.

It was painful to even hear she went there. I had told myself when I was almost fired that if I was let go, I would fall back on my minor from college and go teach art in junior college or something. No way I went from Sakura to Myer Coffman. I had too much pride.

Maybe that was bad, though. It hadn't served me all that well.

"I wonder if—" Shawn began.

"Furthermore, several members of Ava's team have also been released from their contracts."

"Oh shit." Shawn's voice edged high and Liza grabbed my hand, clutching tight.

Lots of layoffs this morning was why the conference room looked a little light. But again, it made sense—Everett had been the managing director, Ava was his right hand, and she had led a less-than-ambitious pack of development reps. They had been more interested in keeping what they had than in going after something new, because it was safe. Safe was good. Safe kept you in business. But safe didn't get you any infusion of creativity, or funds, or excitement. Safe did not show investors you were the company to watch. We showed no growth without new projects, at least in my opinion.

But after my flop of faith, I had been educated about how important it was to *not* rock the boat.

"Holy shit," Liza whispered.

"We could contemplate our losses, but instead we look to our future. As a result of these changes, Mr. Kurofuji Ryouta from our corporate office in Tokyo will be taking over the position of managing director, effective immediately. He has brought with him several key members of his team, and we could not be happier. Let's give them all a round of applause to welcome them aboard."

We all clapped and Mr. Kurofuji took the podium, the six other people he had brought lining up next to him. There were three women and three men all in suits, all looking polished and professional and perfect.

"Good morning," he greeted us. "This, of course, is only a portion of my team; the others are already at work and have been for hours."

Of course they were. His people were at the top of their game.

"I'm so fired," I groaned.

I got hit in the ribs with elbows from both sides.

I WAS sitting in the office I shared with Peter Goodman a couple of hours later when Mr. Kurofuji and two other men walked in. I had never seen the other two Japanese gentlemen, but the man in front was my new big boss. I got up, Peter got up, and remembering what I'd learned in cultural training the year before, I bowed low—since I was low man on the totem pole—and waited for Mr. Kurofuji to return the gesture.

Both he and the others bowed back, and once they did, I straightened. "Ohayo gozaimasu," I greeted, using the formal good-morning I'd been taught.

Every one of them spoke the words back to me. I couldn't help but smile.

Peter walked forward, hand out. When he was stopped by one of the minions putting an envelope in his hand, he looked confused.

"The layoffs will proceed throughout the day," Mr. Kurofuji informed him. "We appreciate your tenure here at Sakura, but your time with us has drawn to a close, Mr. Goodman. Please gather any noncompany possessions and be prepared to be escorted out in half an hour."

The other assistant handed Peter a banker's box to put his stuff in, and as he stood there—stunned, mouth open, his last check in hand—all eyes turned to me.

I smiled then and waited for my own envelope.

"Mr. Knolls, would you step out into the hall, please."

I followed, and once we were out, I realized a lot of people were leaving, trudging toward the elevators, boxes in their arms.

"Mr. Knolls," Mr. Kurofuji said crisply. "You will report upstairs to the small conference room, where Ms. Shiga Ayumi, who is the new Director of Client Services for Sakura here in Chicago, awaits you. Your new partner, Mr. Hiroyuki Takeo, is there as well."

I was confused, but I also knew that asking questions was a really bad idea. "Thank you, sir," I said as I bowed.

When I reached the small area where everyone was waiting to get on the elevators, I was getting looks. I was the only one who pressed the green Up arrow instead of the red Down one. When Liza and Shawn joined me, nothing in their hands, also waiting to go up, I was relieved.

"What the fuck?" Rob Lambert growled as he got on a car to descend. "The fuckups get to stay? How does that make any sense?"

Shawn flipped him off as the doors closed.

"Are you getting a partner?" I asked Liza.

"Yeah," she told me. "Are you?"

I nodded and looked at Shawn. "You?"

"Yeah, me too." He shrugged. "I dunno what's going on, but let's not question it."

We rode up in silence, and on the next floor, found ourselves faced with a flurry of activity as furniture and computers and people were being moved. As I walked from the lobby area down the hall, I saw a woman poke her head out of the glass door of the small conference room where we usually held morning status meetings.

"Hi, team!" she greeted us warmly, and I realized I could breathe again.

"God, I feel better already." Shawn exhaled, and when we got close, she reached for our hands instead of bowing.

Ms. Shiga's handshake was firm and her grip on my bicep as we shook was nice. Even better was her smile. It was big—huge—and made her dark eyes glint, with the high cheekbones and the way her nose scrunched up, she was like a warm summer breeze.

"Come in, sit down, who needs coffee?"

As I poured a cup from a huge pot, grabbed bagels and cream cheese, and then took a seat, I saw the whole team that used to work under me was there, along with new faces and one… really good… one.

I almost choked on my bagel. He, of course, was not eating. He was sitting up straight, like he had a steel rod for a spine, and he was just *perfect*.

All my life I had been attracted to Asian men, but holy crap… I thought only models looked like that.

"So you're all probably wondering why you're here," Ms. Shiga said. "Before we begin, let me introduce Mr. Hiroyuki Takeo."

His glossy black hair fell forward and framed his face with just wisps of it touching his long, thick eyelashes. His brows looked painted on, his nose was short and straight, and the chiseled lips were beautiful and decadent and made to take a bite of. I was seeing flawless porcelain skin, but the real thrill—what made my stomach do the flippy thing it did when I was ready to pounce—were his eyes. Fringed in long feathery lashes, they met mine, caught my stare, and flicked away. It was so fast, barely noticeable but for jet black. I had never seen eyes that color before, and I swallowed when I should have chewed and nearly choked to death. I had to grab Liza's water without asking or I would have had a coughing attack of biblical proportions.

"Hey," she groused under her breath.

"Dying," I gasped.

She huffed but said nothing more as I guzzled.

Ms. Shiga continued. "You're here because of all the development reps on staff at this office, you seven are the only ones who worked on the Wang Promenade project under Mr. Knolls."

My head snapped up and I looked over to her, because she was talking about *me*.

"Mr. Knolls." She smiled. "Had you been given the additional funding that was required for that venture, we calculated that Sakura, instead of Sutter, would have been looking at the development of the new waterfront property that has already leased out all of its available retail space."

I was stunned. "Sutter got the contract, I hadn't heard."

She nodded. "Yes, they got it a month ago, and because the property looks to be very hot, everyone jumped at the chance to be there."

"I thought—" I began, and then included everyone at the table, "We all thought that it was a good investment for Sakura."

"And it was," she told me. "Your instincts were correct even though you, and your team, did not foresee the additional costs to the company."

We were all quiet as she glanced around the room.

"The failure was not in the idea, but in the execution." She took a breath. "Now, it is unfortunate that even though Mr. Knolls missed the additional costs that were needed to fund the project, he was not given the go-ahead to complete the acquisition. The project was shut down instead. But the two hundred and fifty thousand dollar payout looks to be small in comparison to what Sutter stands to make on the deal that this office passed on."

Justified.

But after six months of hanging my head in shame, hearing people whisper, seeing them point, knowing they were talking behind my back—being told my gut had been correct was hard to hear.

"So, Mr. Knolls, you are to be reinstated as Project Manager here at Sakura with Masai Makoto as your partner and Chloe Kingman as your cost analyst. The three of you will manage the acquisitions department and report to me. Congratulations."

But hadn't Mr. Kurofuji said I was getting Mr. Hiroyuki? Wasn't he mine?

"Originally I had planned differently, but I like this approach better."

And suddenly everyone was on their feet and clapping, and I thought I was dreaming except for one small thing. The most beautiful man I had ever seen in my life was not my new partner. He was Eric Bryson's partner. There would now be two teams in Acquisitions: I was heading one group and Eric the other.

As I stood there overwhelmed, vindicated, and furious—all at the same time—I realized that not having the distraction, not nearly choking to death on coffee every morning, was probably a very good thing. I needed to focus on me, on my career and nothing else. It was for the best.

I'D THOUGHT that when I met my new partner, he would be like Takeo, so I was stunned when I walked into my new office later that morning and found a man sitting in a chair with his feet up, head back, snoring. Maybe I wasn't in the right place.

"Masai Makoto?" I asked gently.

He lifted his head and opened one eye. "Mak. Call me Mak."

"Oh, yeah, okay."

The smile he flashed me was brilliant. "You're Dwyer?"

"I am." I bristled. Who the hell was this guy, just all casual, making himself at home in the office we were going to share. We needed to be professional and—

"That's a lot to say."

I was surprised. "What?"

"Dwyer. That's a lot to say."

"It is?"

"Yeah," he said, nodding, obviously thinking about something.

"Okay," I said, chuckling, unable not to.

"So I'm going with D."

"Just D."

"Yep."

"And if I don't like that? Won't respond to it?"

He seemed to consider that. "That seems kind of a jackass way to be."

It did actually.

"Don't you think?"

"Yes," I said, already warming to the man. "So whatever you must do, g'head."

"Excellent," he teased.

"Sorry," I said, taking a breath, reminding myself that this was my new partner and I had to trust him, just as he had to trust me. "I've been so close to being out of here for so long, it's hard to suddenly have a voice again, yanno?"

He nodded slowly. "I do, actually. You wanna eat?"

"I know a really good deli."

"Lead on."

Once we were sitting across from each other at a booth, I noticed him checking out the girls at the next table.

"We could double-date, man. I just got to Chicago; you gotta show me the sights."

I needed to get this out of the way first. "Okay, so here's the deal," I said, looking directly into his dark brown eyes. They were nice eyes, kind eyes, and I was ready to try if he was. "I'm gay."

He squinted after a long moment.

"Mak?"

"I'm confused."

What was confusing? "About?"

"What does you being gay have to do with anything?"

We would be friends. "I just wanted you to know… I mean I can't very well be your wingman if I'm not into—"

"Not true," he argued. "My friend Souta's been my wingman lots of times, and he's gay, and it actually works out great because he sort of ditches out and I get lucky once the girls realize they're not gonna get him. You'd think they'd get it when he starts talking about the yaoi they all read, but they miss it every time."

I smiled wide. "I'll be your wingman."

"That's good," he said, grinning back, tipping his head toward the two women smiling over at him. "Because this relationship is all about me."

CHAPTER TWO

MAK AND I were seamless, not so Hiroyuki Takeo and Eric Bryson. The first time we knew there was trouble was the day Eric was escorted from the building after yanking his desk phone out of the wall and hurling it across his office. Apparently having Takeo stare at him and wait—just wait—not move, simply sit… was a bit more than he could handle.

When Eric was let go, Ayumi asked me if I wanted to be paired with Takeo after all, muttering under her breath as she put the question to me. But by that time Mak and I were a team and I didn't want a new partner any more than he did. That didn't stop me from talking to Takeo whenever I could and noting that brooding silence looked damn good on him. I was surprised, though. I had assumed, however wrongly, that at some point, even if people continually went crazy, that the source of the trouble—Takeo—would eventually get blamed. But others kept freaking out, and Ayumi continued to fire them, so Takeo more and more ended up tagging along with me and Mak.

I made up excuses to go by his office and say hi. I flew a paper airplane into his office that startled the holy hell out of him, as evidenced by his very girly shriek, before he realized I was being playful, nothing mean intended, and it wasn't some weird American cultural thing he was supposed to know something about.

At the company picnic, I made him try cotton candy, which he saw no point to and complained about it being sticky.

"Sticky can be good, Mr. Hiroyuki," I teased.

He turned and walked into a tree.

When we had an Easter egg hunt for the children of the employees, I purposely hid some in his office so he could see children up close. I wasn't sure he'd ever seen any, considering how he just stood there and smiled.

"You could interact with them," I suggested, leaning into his doorway.

He looked so lost that I finally walked over, threw an arm around his shoulders, and gave him a gentle clench. "It's okay," I soothed, and his sigh was the sweetest sound I'd ever heard.

He enjoyed the fireworks on the Fourth of July, and I didn't miss the fact that he moved from where he stood all alone on the roof of our building over to me. It was nice, we talked quietly, and I listened as much as I spoke.

When he bought an apartment and fixed it up, I was one of the only people he invited over who actually wanted to be there. He wasn't sure what to do with the orchid I took him, but he carried it around when he gave me, and only me, a tour of his home.

Because he was good with me, I figured that one-on-one interactions would be his strong suit. I was so wrong.

He would be asked, jovially, cheerfully, by clients genuinely excited to see him, "So how do you like Chicago?"

Mak would smile at him.

I would nod, like "Go ahead...."

Every single time his response was: "Oh, Chicago is fine."

Fine?

Really? Fine?

And heaven forbid he was asked a yes or no question, because that was all you were getting back, nothing more. People would come to him, bursting with enthusiasm, and he... killed it. Dead. He could suck the life right out of any room he walked into.

We went to close a deal at Hyerson Crawford for a building down close to Centennial Park, and they brought out champagne to toast because everyone was psyched and ready to revel in a job well done. But dear God in heaven, Takeo had to explain, ad nauseam, how we were all still working and so should not, in good conscience, imbibe. All jests and laughter meant to playfully get him to lighten up, loosen up, were met with persistent reminders that we were in fact, on the company payroll at that very moment. Eight full glasses were replaced on the tray, the loud clinking a signal for us all to get the hell out so the client could celebrate alone.

Ayumi was fuming.

Mak was beyond annoyed, and the other managers wouldn't even look at Takeo.

I walked beside him, absolutely charmed by the oblivious man keeping pace with me.

"What did I say, Knolls-san?" he asked.

"Nothing. You were right," I told him before we got on the elevator. "We're all still on the clock."

"Then I am missing why everyone seems so contrite."

I chuckled; I couldn't help it, and took hold of his bicep, moving him over next to me where he seemed always content to be.

When we got back, he came to my office, and when he walked in, Mak walked out.

"Why does everyone hate me?" Takeo asked.

"You just gotta learn to lighten up?"

Examining his navy suit, he appeared confused about what the color he was wearing had to do with anything.

Adorable. He was absolutely beautiful and brilliant and utterly captivating. If I thought there was even a glimmer of a chance that the man was gay, I would have swooped down on him like he was a dove and I was a raptor.

"You are the only one who talks to me, Knolls-san," he lamented. I had been pleased when he started using the honorific with me but found myself hoping to hear the "kun" or "chan" that indicated we were even closer. Or even better, my first name with nothing at all, all by itself. But so far, nothing.

"It's okay, baby," I husked.

"Pardon?"

"Nothing."

At an event for a new halfway house in Hyde Park, he interrogated the caterer to find out what exactly, *precisely*, in excruciating detail, was in the spring rolls. He wanted to make sure they were gluten-free, as had been ordered. But the waitstaff had no clue and three of them left, one girl in tears. Ayumi made me take Takeo out to the balcony and explain that browbeating people was not appropriate.

"I sought only to verify the ingredients, for our clients."

I found myself nodding a lot.

For him there was no forest, only trees. Branches. Twigs. Specifics concerned him. He was all about the small stuff. And I understood; he thought that if he paid attention to the minutiae, the big stuff would take care of itself. Whoever had told him that the devil was in the details had royally fucked him up.

Ayumi's next bright idea was to make his the face of charity events. Basically, she put him in charge of herding cats, and he tried really hard to do just that. When every single volunteer walked out ten minutes before our big event at the Four Seasons, we all had to take their places. Takeo was the master of ceremonies in his stunning Armani tuxedo, but the rest of us… the fashion show and bachelor auction had to go on as planned.

I strutted down the runway as best I could, glad that half my life was spent at the gym. Having the body of a male underwear model helped with the clothes bidding. We raffled off couture of local designers, and with me being toned and cut and hard, the jacket and chaps I was wearing fetched a nice price. The lady with the winning bid ran her hands all over my abdomen as she praised the craftsmanship of the outfit and finally explained to me that what was *in* the clothes was much more up her alley than the threads themselves. I got that she was very fond of my six-pack.

I could have defused it, stepped away, but Takeo was there, horrified by how she was treating me, putting himself between us and reminding her that I was not chattel.

Sadly, she didn't know what that meant. It only made things worse.

"I weep for the American educational system," he said snottily.

Lord.

"What did you just say to me?" she snapped, her voice rising.

"He is not a gigolo and therefore not for sale!" Takeo made clear.

She withdrew her winning bid, which meant I had to go back up on the stage, this time without the jacket, just the chaps over the tightest jeans I'd ever worn in my life, absolutely clinging to me like a second skin. The good news was that we helped raise funds. The bad news was that Takeo was banned from events.

After Ayumi finished lecturing him, I found him and thanked him for sticking up for me.

"You are the only one who really sees me, Knolls-san," he said under his breath.

And I knew I was. Others saw an egomaniac; I saw reserve. Others saw spitefulness; I saw insecurity. He was simply so dear, and no one *saw* him but me. When I tousled the glossy black hair, he leaned into my hand, eyes closed, pale pink lips parted. He had no clue how exquisite he was or how much I wanted to put marks on that perfect skin, kiss him until he was breathless and panting and just *mine*. I shivered with just the fleeting thought.

"You'll be okay," I assured him, cuffing his shoulder before I turned and walked away. It took everything in me not to drag him off into a dark corner, manhandle him up against a wall, and fuck him. My entire body grieved my nonaction.

"Why do you even talk to him?" Mak would grouse. "He's an idiot."

I once had to explain to Takeo that getting in the last word was not always the best course of action.

"Okay, so it's twelve thirty now," a client said, "let's convene back here at—yes, there in the back row."

And I knew what Takeo was going to say before it even came out of his mouth.

"It is actually twelve thirty-two," he corrected. "To be precise, sir."

And... done. He waited for the thank-you that never came.

People were horrified.

I found the whole thing ridiculously endearing because I understood the good place inside him where it had come from.

He made the correction because, in Takeo's mind, he didn't want the client to be wrong, so he brought the error to the client's attention. He didn't want the person in charge to be informing people that they had an hour for lunch if they did, in fact, only have fifty-eight minutes. It was completely logical in his mind.

His motivations were clear to me; I totally got him. Things other people simply let slip by because they weren't important enough to stop the flow of conversation for or to comment on, he pounced all over, making sure he mentioned them, because if it wasn't important, why was it in the conversation to begin with?

He didn't get sarcasm, flirting—which he was on the receiving end of, from both women and men—was lost on him, and if he didn't get the joke, he'd ask for it to be explained.

"He's just trying to be difficult," Ayumi snarled, ready to throw him off something high.

But I knew better, and instead of waning, my interest only grew with every sweet smile, darting glance, and sudden lingering touch. He was so awkward, and watching him try to figure out what others thought he should intuitively know simply made me protective. It was odd when his "Ice Prince" nickname popped up, because what others labeled conceit, I read as shyness. The problem was, no one else saw him that way.

CHAPTER THREE

"D," MAK whispered from his side of the room, and when I looked up, he pointed, like he was tapping gently, toward the glass wall of our office.

I saw her then, Karen Jennings, Hiroyuki Takeo's ninth partner, carrying her things with her as she made the long walk down the hall to the elevators.

I heard snickering and looked over at Mak. "Again? Are you kidding me?"

He shook his head. "I told you, Takeo's the kiss of fucking death."

"He's not." I defended him automatically at this point, but really, how many chances did any of us get?

"He is," Mak insisted. "But Karen was no prize either."

I remembered her, so far up on her high horse she couldn't even see us peons from where her head was up in the clouds, talking about how she and Takeo would run circles around the rest of us. Oh, the difference three months made.

Chloe came breezing into our office eating an apple and flopped down on our couch. "Isn't that eight?" she asked.

"That's nine," Mak corrected her. "In a little less than two years."

"Holy shit," she said, taking another crunchy bite of her apple. "What is that, some kind of record?"

He shrugged. "I told you guys, it was just like this back in Tokyo. He's a hardass and nobody likes him."

"Somebody likes him." I smiled at Mak, who had become a real friend. He and I, amazingly enough, were brothers raised on different sides of the planet. He was as laid-back as I was, but he knew exactly when to buckle down and get to work. With him being charming and careful and me being tenacious and intuitive, our team was doing great work. It didn't hurt that Shiga Ayumi was amazing about knowing which investment was sound versus something sketchy. She had astonishing insight, but more importantly, she trusted her group, of which I was a part. We were the top acquisitions team in the company. Our record blew by the Tokyo office in the previous quarter.

"What do you mean?" Mak asked, breaking into my thoughts.

"I mean all Takeo's partners keep getting fired and he's still here. Somebody likes him."

He scowled at me.

"What?"

"You really don't know?"

I squinted at him. "Don't know what?"

Mak turned to look at Chloe. "He doesn't know."

"Seriously?" Chloe sounded like she thought I was screwing with her.

"What?"

Mak kicked his legs off his desk, got them under him, and then leaned forward in his chair to stare at me.

"*What*?"

"Yeah, Dwyer, somebody likes him," he said sarcastically, using my full name to drive the point home. After our first conversation where Mak said he would only call me D, Dwyer had disappeared almost completely. Whereas others in my life sometimes shortened my name to treat me like I was stupid, Mak did it out of true affection. So the fact that he was using Dwyer now was a signal. "His father likes him, and he holds 51 percent of the shares in the company. *He's* the one who likes Takeo."

"What?" I'd turned into a broken record.

Mak was nodding at me.

Wait.

Chloe was shaking her head like I was an idiot… and then it hit me.

"Oh shit." I couldn't believe I had never put that together. Hiroyuki Takumi, the man whose signature was on my paycheck, was Takeo's father. "I can't believe I never put that together."

"You're so pretty," he teased.

"Fuck you."

He snorted out a laugh. "Are we eating? Because I'm gonna pass out from hunger."

"If," I nailed him to the wall with my stare, "we get to have…."

"No," he griped. "I want a burger. You and that hot pot bullshit. I should be the one that likes it, not you."

"It's cold today." I sounded whiney even to myself. "It would be perfect."

"Oh yeah," Chloe chimed in, trying to get him to see my side. "That's perfect for November. Let's go."

"God, why did I even take you guys there the first time?"

"Come on."

He grunted. "Fine, I don't care. I'm starving."

But the door opened suddenly and our boss, the lovely and talented Shiga Ayumi, stood in our office. I didn't think I had ever reported to anyone I liked better. She looked terrible, though, like she was wrung out.

"What's with you?"

She made a face.

"Oh." I winced. "Sorry, chief."

Staggering to the leather couch close to me, she collapsed onto it.

"Yeah, we saw Karen." Mak chuckled. "Another one bites the dust, huh?"

I started the riff of the classic Queen song.

"No," Ayumi barked, and so I shut up. "It's not funny."

It was a *little* funny. "Lighten up, boss lady. Just find him another one."

She whimpered, and I could not contain my smile. "Look at it this way: at least you'll keep his old man happy."

Something was mumbled into the seat of the couch.

"I didn't catch that," I said, looking up at Mak. He shrugged. "We should invite her," I mouthed to him.

Chloe shook her head no.

"No," Mak replied silently, putting up his hand.

I widened my eyes meaningfully.

He banged Chloe with his elbow, and she prepared to rock-paper-scissor me for it.

I scowled at both of them.

Mak's chin dropped to his chest in defeat. "So, chief, you want to go to lunch with us?" He offered like it was going to kill him.

She got up so fast she startled us all. "No! No food! Nobody's going to lunch! You guys are in this train wreck with me! Do you know what Mr. Kurofuji wants now?"

I was afraid to ask. Chloe winced, and Mak was bracing for the worst.

"He wants Takeo to be the new director of sales and marketing here."

We were all silent a moment before Mak came out with "Say it again."

And so she repeated the whole thing.

I was confused. Chloe tipped her head, squinting.

"Wait." I was trying to figure it out.

"There's no such thing," Mak informed her.

"What he said." Chloe pointed at my partner.

"There is now," Ayumi apprised us.

"Okay." Mak grinned at her. "Lemme get this straight. Takeo doesn't have the people skills to be a project manager, he can't work with anyone, so instead of shipping his ass back to Tokyo, they're making him head of a whole department that doesn't actually exist."

"Yes."

He looked over at me. "Well, I'm sold."

"I'm missing something."

Mak got up and moved to perch on the corner of my desk. "Explain it to us again, slower."

"Yeah, and use small words," Chloe suggested.

"Oh, for the love of God, do you know what this means!" She sounded like she was on the edge of a nervous breakdown.

"I don't," I confessed, glancing from my boss to my partner.

"Yeah, no, me neither." Mak was scowling.

"All of us"—she included us in the circle she made with her finger—"work for him now."

"Oh, bullshit," I snorted out a laugh. "Gimme a break."

One of her thin black eyebrows rose.

"No," Mak said flatly. "No no no."

She nodded.

"No." His voice kept dropping.

It was terrible that my first reaction was not either the horror of having him for a boss or how insane it was that a place was basically being manufactured for him, but sadness for me. If I worked for him, I was never getting him into bed. I never joined in on the Takeo bashing for the most superficial of reasons: I found him far too captivating. I had never been more attracted to anyone in my life. The fragility of the man called to me, the hooded eyes, high sculpted cheekbones, the way he bit his bottom lip when he was nervous… I wanted him badly. He needed to be naked under my hands, and as much as I tried to push the image from my mind, it always snaked its way back in. It had been that way for a year now.

"Oh shit," Chloe said, sitting down on my desk beside Mak. "I can't work for the Ice Prince."

"Me neither." Mak groaned, turning to look at me. "We have to get you a visa."

"I'm sorry?"

"A work visa. We can both get jobs back at corporate," he told me. "I like working with you, I'm used to it—the give and take of it—so you should come back to Tokyo with me."

He wasn't serious. "You're not serious."

"I am," he promised. "You'll love my mother. She still cooks and cleans for me."

"No she does not."

He nodded quickly.

"Mak, I don't speak Japanese."

"I'll teach you," he was emphatic. "Just… pack."

"What about me?" Chloe whined.

"Pack," Mak told her. "I got a spot for you, too, Kingman."

She clapped her hands happily. "Oh, I've always wanted to live in Japan."

"Shut up!" Ayumi yelled suddenly, and we all looked at her. "No one's leaving!"

"Why… oh," Mak said softly, watching, just like I was, as she lifted her left hand so we could see the ice rink that now adorned the ring finger of her left hand.

"Damn." Chloe whistled.

Ayumi made her eyes very big. "Bennet proposed to me over the weekend, and I will be damned if that annoying creature jacks up my future here in this city with his petty bullshit."

Right after Ayumi moved to Chicago, she had met the tall, handsome doctor at a fundraiser. He was stunning, she was stunning, together they were blinding. I wondered, because he was African-American, what her parents back in Japan thought. Apparently all they thought was *Hello, doctor*! During their last visit, they had gushed all over him as Ayumi's mother pointed out that she had put on weight. It was funny until Ayumi had whacked me on the back of the head. Delicate flower, my ass.

"He's such a little asshole!"

"Did you know she swears?" I asked Mak.

He shook his head.

Chloe yawned. "I did."

"So we're all going to go into that conference room after lunch and suck it up, you hear me?" Ayumi had actually snarled and it was a little scary.

I moaned, Mak grunted, and Chloe wanted to know if we were still going out for lunch.

We all glared at her.

"What? I'm hungry."

Food before death of dreams seemed like a good idea. The man I wanted was about to be my boss, I couldn't think of anything worse.

CHAPTER FOUR

IT DIDN'T even take a year. Six people quit: three teams of people who would rather be unemployed—or jump off something high—than work for the Ice Prince. On a Monday in September, when Mak came striding into our office, I wondered where my latte was.

"Wasn't it your turn to buy?"

"Never mind about that."

"Never mind about coffee? Are you high?"

"Dwyer, Hiroyuki just called my cell and told me to meet him in here," he said quickly, obviously agitated. "So I'm guessing it's gonna be us taking that meeting this morning."

I was confused. "What meeting?"

"Graham Deveraux for Byrd Superstore," he explained.

"We can't take that meeting. We didn't prepare anything. It isn't our pitch."

"I know," Mak snapped. "But what are we going to do if he wants us to take it? I mean, all we came up with for that meeting was just a load of crap. Everybody knew Donovan and Reddy were gonna get it because Ted knew the client's daughter. We didn't even put together a list of prospective clients!"

"No," I agreed, tired of discussing it already. Lately, and not suddenly or surprisingly, I was tired of my job and that feeling of *doneness* was starting to seep into everything. I was starting to realize that when I had prepared for the worst and geared myself up for an end, the idea of being free had been far more liberating than I'd given credence to at the time. Once I had made the decision to accept leaving, but in the excitement of being chosen to stay, I'd forgotten the rush of impending liberation.

The fact of the matter was, when years ago I'd envisioned my life in the future—where I was now—I'd seen myself as an actuary in some small lazy town in a state like New Mexico. Someplace far removed: where it was warm, without snow, a place where I would sip beer on the porch, in a hammock, in October. Lots of people lived for the thrill of the cutthroat business world; it turned out I just wasn't one of them.

"Why aren't you more worried about this?"

"It'll be okay, Mak."

"No, it won't be, and now those guys are out and I'll bet you that we're going to have to play cleanup because of it." He huffed, pacing the office.

"I already have too much on my plate this week," I commented.

"What's with you lately?"

How could I say that I wanted to quit and make that somehow sound okay?

"D?"

I would have answered, but we both went instantly silent as Takeo walked into the room.

"Good morning," he greeted us.

Irritation and snickering behind his back had changed over the past month to all-out resentment from his management staff and fear from the underlings. Even Ayumi had started walking on eggshells around the slight man now standing in my office.

"Mr. Knolls, Mr. Masai."

We stayed quiet.

"I need you to go home and pack. I am putting you on a plane to Florida tomorrow morning. We have had a situation arise with an acquisition in a small town called Mangrove. I need you to remedy the situation and secure the company a win."

"Certainly, Director," I said quickly, employing the new title he had instructed be used after he received his promotion. Others still called him by his last name upon occasion, but I never slipped up, and I knew he liked that. Where others got into trouble was asking questions first and agreeing second. He always explained... after.

"I fired Mr. Donovan and Mr. Reddy this morning."

And then would come the reason....

"Strippers," he said simply.

I waited.

"We lost face."

And waited a little bit more.

"They took the client to a strip club."

That would be an even bigger problem when it was reported back to Tokyo. "We're sorry, Director. You can count on us to make a better impression."

His jet eyes flicked to mine. "I hope so."

I smiled back.

"And what part of our vision will you impress upon the client?"

I thought fast. The concept of Sakura I learned when I was first hired four years ago was creating an aesthetic of beauty in all the business spaces. Everything we did was understated or... "Unconventional," I blurted. "We'll tell him that our approach to his needs will be unconventional but elegant."

"Good," Takeo said, turning for the door.

"Oh—" I said to stop him as I reached into my bag. "I picked you up those calligraphy pens you like. I know you enjoy writing with them even though you said it was cheating."

I pulled the box out and took it to him, crossing the room to the door, offering it with both hands as I had been taught to do.

He took it from me and bowed just a little. "Domo arigato, Knolls-san."

I bowed back. "You're welcome, Director."

He left, and when I turned to Mak, he was staring at me. "What?"

"Just you and him, it's weird."

"How'dya mean, weird?"

"You just... you get along really well, and no one could even call it brownnosing because that man would never allow anyone to kiss his ass—it's just... he really likes you."

He seemed to, by all indications, but more than others?

"You know he does. You're the only one he bothers to talk to."

Because I was the only one who talked to him.

"You guys have a good rapport."

It was true, we did.

"But I think you got sort of cemented as his favorite with the Chatsworth Corporation build. You remember that?"

We had been looking at spaces in Schaumberg and had been close to inking a deal when I noticed dead flowers and small animals on the property. Just a sprinkling of both, blackened marigolds and field mice, nothing huge, not something anyone would notice. But I asked for the soil to be tested, and what came back was horrifying. Takeo had waited until Mak was gone—and I knew he'd done it on purpose, he didn't like my partner—and then he'd taken a seat in the chair on the other side of my desk and explained how I had just saved his life.

"Some people," he said, clearing his throat, "await my failure with bated breath."

I knew that.

"You protected the company, and by doing so, me."

I couldn't have succeeded in suppressing my smile for anything. Seeing him so earnest, worried, and flushed over what he was saying to me brought out all my protective instincts. "I won't let you fail."

His eyes warmed until they were absolutely molten. "I know."

He took my breath away.

I recalled another incident when Takeo and I were at a meeting with a client and his team, and the man had leaned over and asked me to come back to his room when we were done. He said it was to look at some more contracts.

"I could order us dinner in," he said seductively. "And perhaps breakfast as well."

I opened my mouth to turn him down, but Takeo was faster.

"Why would you want to order in when Albuquerque is awash in excellent restaurants?"

The client gave Takeo all his attention.

"Unless you were insinuating that you sought to pursue sexual relations with my colleague," Takeo said dryly. "Was that your intention?"

"I—"

"He wants an assignation with you," Takeo announced to me.

I had never seen a man get up and bolt quite that fast.

"Did I say something wrong?" he asked, wide-eyed and innocent as we rose and made our way out of the meeting room to the elevator.

I shook my head.

"It was inappropriate, what he said, was it not?"

"It was."

After a moment of simply gazing up into my eyes—he always had to, five eight to my six two, he had no other option—his voice finally came out gentle and quiet. "Are you hungry?"

"I am."

It was small things, things I could string together and come up with a picture of a man who liked me. Not just tolerated me, but truly, sincerely enjoyed my company. He brought me scones I liked from a bakery close to the office, remembered everything I said—even in passing—and always, always, leaned into my office to say good morning. Taken as a whole, a pattern emerged, not an appearance of indifference like the way everyone else was treated, but actions of actual interest and concern. The clincher was the last time I was sick: he appeared at my apartment with shoyu ramen, including all the fixings—green onion, bean sprouts, pork, boiled egg, those weird long stemmed mushrooms, and fish cake—which I had no idea would be pink and white.

I was stunned.

He asked to come in.

After he prepared the soup for me and brewed and poured me green tea, he started to tidy up. When I yawned a lot, giving him the hint that I was ready to pass out, he tucked a pillow under my head and told me to sleep if I could. Four hours later, when I woke up a little after midnight, he had water for me before I went back to sleep. No one but me could have dreamed that Takeo was a caretaker.

So when Mak said Takeo liked me, after thinking about it a minute, I realized it would have been a lie to disagree.

"D?"

I coughed. "You're right, he likes me. It goes both ways."

Mak shook his head.

"What?"

"Not a thing," he said, grinning at me a second before returning to his desk. "Okay, so, let's see how much work we can get done since we're traveling tomorrow."

I groaned.

"We have to be on the plane at dawn." He laughed maniacally for my benefit.

"It's not that early," I grumbled.

"You wanna bet?"

Since Takeo didn't understand why morning flights were bad, it was entirely possible that he had Mak and I booked on the first plane out.

God, I really hated being on clean-up duty.

OUR CURRENT assignment was a doozy. Mangrove was a tiny picturesque beach town in Florida just to the west side of Seaside. We were going there to check on a build the local community was not crazy about. Normally I played the jobs card, that the town needed them, but from what we were being told, the town was more interested in keeping their coastline clear. The project was losing thousands of dollars a day because the party that had originally agreed to sell was waffling. But since the initial investment to create the superstore had been in the millions—other retailers were on board, they were talking outlet mall with an attached concrete parking lot monolith—the build was still on the "save pile" and not the "pull up stakes and bail pile," hence the deployment of Mak and me.

It wasn't odd that I was traveling. Part of being a project manager—fancy words for fixer—was that when things went bad, I was the one who appeared on-site to take care of it. When a build was behind, when they were losing money hand over fist, they sent me out, or Mak and me, from the corporate office to the wilds of wherever to put the project back on track. Normally I fired some people, hired new personnel, and occasionally, when the hemorrhaging money hurt the company, I pulled the plug, and we bailed on the building site and the community. It was a last resort, and it was difficult to tell people who needed the jobs that the development wasn't going forward so they wouldn't be employed at the superstore, resort, hotel, or strip mall. It was hard to say, in small towns, that there would be no influx of funds, that all the materials and builders and manpower were not going to happen. But the bottom line was that Sakura was in business to make money, not lose it. Sometimes walking away was the only solution.

I'd been told I walked away better than anyone. The fact that this opinion was shared by all my exes was probably some kind of comment on my inability to stay in a relationship. I never understood why all of them not being able to hold my interest for an extended amount of time wasn't the real issue. If they hadn't gotten boring and lost their luster, I would have stayed, end of story. But I was the one who always got blamed. They said I didn't stick, that I didn't have it in me. Apparently I was coated with Teflon.

The whole not-caring sort of bored, whiney can-I-leave-now thing made Ayumi smile when we worked together. She liked it when I fidgeted and doodled, when my head rolled back and I nodded off. She pretended to scold me, but I was like a poodle that peed on the carpet when it wanted to go outside. She couldn't just excuse herself and say she wanted to leave, but I could make an ass out of myself until whoever we were sitting with was so sick of me that they leapt to their feet and ordered me out of their office. Never once had I left alone. Mak loves me because he could never cause a scene either. It was all that polished Japanese business etiquette. He delighted in going with me to the kinds of places where he knew my attitude, manners, and boredom would rock the boat the most. We got the tough assignments because Ayumi knew we would get the job done but also because she enjoyed the fox in the henhouse syndrome we created. I went in and stirred things up, and Mak was there to smooth things over, thus securing the deal. It was the old bait and switch, but it had been working well.

So I was sitting in my seat in first class early Tuesday morning, wondering where the hell my favorite traveling companion was. Having left a ton of messages for Mak, I tried Ayumi instead, hoping she'd heard from him.

"Are you on the plane?" she asked me.

"Yes, ma'am." I yawned. "Now, do you know where the hell Mak is?"

"Are the doors closed?"

"Not quite yet."

"Are you hung over?"

"For once, no," I informed her. "Are you shocked?"

"A bit," she replied, chuckling.

She was right. Normally the night before I flew anywhere, I got wasted. I had no idea how it always turned out that way, even when I started out the night before thinking this time would be different.

"Well, you call me when you get there and let me know if there are any problems with the uhm… room."

Was she kidding? Did she expect me not to ask, with a lead-in like that? "What the hell was that with the not-so-subtle hint?"

"I'm sorry?" she hedged.

I felt my Spidey sense tingling. What the hell was going on?

"Just remember that I had nothing to do with this."

"Nothing to do with what?"

She huffed. "It's gonna be okay. There's a quilting festival this weekend."

I had no idea what the hell that meant. "What?"

She chuckled. "Apparently it's a big deal. The lady on the phone said that, among other things, they make blankets, both full and baby, wall hangings, tote bags—"

"Stop."

"What?"

"Why're we talk—"

"No, I swear to God." She was laughing now, ignoring me. "It's a real thing and I kind of want to go. I love that sort of seashore-style."

"Where am I staying?"

"At the Maple Leaf Bed and Breakfast."

"There are no maple trees in the panhandle."

"Yes, I know that."

"So why the hell would someone name a bed and break—"

"Just go with it."

"Are you screwing with me?"

She snorted into the phone, and then I heard muffled noises and a cackle I knew. My friend was suddenly on the phone.

"Mak, you dick, why aren't you here?"

Half laugh, half grunt before "Just buy a quilt or something."

"Mak—"

"Or one of those fisherman floats, you know, the glass globe in the macramé holder."

"That's not what it is."

He was laughing and apparently couldn't stop.

"It's not!"

More muffled noises, and I heard Ayumi losing it in the background. She was dying.

"What the hell is going on? Why aren't you here, and why aren't you returning any of my phone calls?"

He took a breath.

"Answer," I demanded.

"Okay, so I'm going to be in meetings with Bauhaus all morning to secure the funding for their new location downtown."

"And how come I'm here and not there?"

"Because you're stronger."

"You lost me."

"One of us had to go to Mangrove, and one of us had to talk to Bauhaus, and between the two of us, you're the better negotiator, D, you know you are. You pound people into submission."

"Again. Lost."

He cleared his throat. "And besides, Takeo is going with you."

I had missed something.

"No, ya didn't," Mak said, doing the mindreading thing that was freaky sometimes.

"What?" I had obviously misheard him. "I'm sorry, what?"

"No, you heard me." He sighed, so calm and collected in my moment of surrealism. "Our boss, he should be there shortly to go with you to frickin' Mangrove."

I had to process that.

"I can hear you thinking."

"You're fucking with me," I whispered into the phone.

"Really not."

"Come on."

He cleared his throat.

"No."

"*Oh*... yes."

"Why?"

"Because he didn't want you to go alone and he wants to watch you work," Mak said, listing these things for no reason I could grasp. "Honestly, we both know I have no idea, not really. I could keep throwing out ideas, but anything I come up with would sound dumb."

"Holy shit," I gasped, suddenly concerned that hiding my interest in Takeo for a full day while we were out of town together would be harder than I thought.

"It'll be fun," Mak said, talking out of his ass.

"It'll be hell." Because honestly, just me and Takeo alone was a recipe for disaster.

"Well, yeah, probably," Mak responded, obviously thinking I was trash-talking Takeo when that could not be further from the truth. "But you know, you like small towns."

I did, but that wasn't something I'd ever confessed to him. "Fuck you, since when?"

"I'm trying here, all right? I mean, what do you want me to say?"

"Throw me a lifeline."

He coughed. "Just try and have fun while you're there."

"I'll only be gone a day."

"Yeah," he hedged. "About that…."

"Mak!"

"Check your ticket; I think you're gone for three."

"Why the hell for?"

More coughing. "One of the stipulations is that whoever Hutch Crowley discussed selling with had to spend the weekend in Mangrove. He wants the buyer to get a feel for the community."

"No."

"Yes," he countered.

"I only packed enough clothes for one day!" I was indignant.

He scoffed. "We both know you packed enough for at least two. You always do."

"You did this on purpose."

"Nope. This is what you get for being top dog."

"Screw you."

"Just give it a chance. The town sounds super."

"For the love of God, stop! I'm there to do a job. I need to get there, get this Hutch Crowley to sell already, and get out."

"If you can."

I was incredulous. "Did you just say 'if I can'? When have you seen me *not* get someone to sign on the dotted line?"

He grunted.

"How many rooms at this bed and breakfast?"

"Ten."

"For fuck's sake."

"You're such a snob."

"I'm hanging up."

"Wait, listen."

I made a harsh, annoying noise in the back of my throat.

"I hate it when you do that," he scolded.

"I'm really going to hang—"

"Please don't give Takeo a reason to fuck with you, okay? Just don't. Do everything by the book."

"What's that supposed to mean?"

"Listen, Takeo is drowning, right? He's going to do whatever he has to do, to make himself look good in front of his father and the company, and that includes screwing you over."

"By doing what? Firing me? Why would he do that? I'm a goddamn asset now."

"I'm not arguing that, just watch yourself with him. He's not to be trusted, and even though you guys get along, that's not the same as being friends."

Yes, it was. "Yeah, okay."

"Just do what you have to and get the hell out of there. Don't drag it out."

"Drag it out? Are you kidding?"

"I know. You want to get back here where you're in the thick of things. You prefer handling the city builds, the midtown projects, not the ones way the hell out in the middle of nowhere."

"That's right," I acquiesced, because I didn't want him to think any different. He was my partner and he counted on me, and the very idea of letting him down made my stomach roil. If I told him that small-town life sounded like a dream, what would he say? "This is like a fuckin' nightmare," I finished, still putting on.

"Again, you do know what a huge snob you are, right?"

I did, especially when I was faking. "I just— We both know this is a waste of time and resources."

"Listen, you know as well as I do that we don't decide where a property is acquired. They do that at corporate. Our office fixes what other people let get broken. If you go there and decide it'll cost too much to get back on track, pull the plug, D. No one really gives a crap. If there's enough equipment and supplies already purchased, maybe we can sell it all back to the manufacturers for a profit. Again, who cares? You're the company's eyes and ears. You look at it; you make the determination. If the superstore can become the center of an entire outlet mall, then lean on this Crowley guy. If you look at the location and it's too remote, if tourists won't be able to find it, if locals won't make the trip out there, then we'll pull out. But you have to go and look. A spreadsheet and blurry pictures, a cost analysis, and phone conversations aren't going to help us. You have to come back with facts."

I groaned again.

"I'm sorry you're stuck with Takeo, but at least he likes you."

And I *more* than liked him. "You shouldn't worry about him dicking me over. It'll never happen."

"I wouldn't be so sure. Because when it's all said and done, he cares about himself more than anyone else. Remember, I've known him longer. I worked with him for years in Tokyo."

But I had seen glimpses of true kinship in Takeo that, as far as I knew, no one else ever had. "I'll see if I can talk him into coming home early."

"I think the whole point is for him to hang with you, see how this part of the business gets handled."

"For what purpose?"

"Your guess is as good as mine, but you could just ask him, I suppose. See what he says."

"If he ever gets here."

"Wait, what?"

"Yeah, he's not here yet."

"How is he not there? Aren't you going to take off in like a minute?"

"Yeah," I said as I watched people boarding the plane, walking toward the back. "But I don't see him."

He chuckled. "Just be careful, all right? I want you back in one piece."

"Should I bring you a quilt or a seashell wind chime or something?"

"You know that's really offensive, right? In small towns, their annual festivals are—"

"Shut up."

"Florida is actually really beautiful. I visited there once when I was a kid. Saw Miami Beach. I really liked it. Big diverse city."

"Yeah, not going to Miami now, am I?"

"Well, no."

"Maybe I'll bring you back an ibis."

"I don't even know what that is, but because of how you said it, I'm saying no."

"It's a bird, idiot. A big fuckin' bird."

"Now you're reaching. Just come back with your job."

"Why are you so worried?"

"I don't know," he said softly. "I just have this really weird feeling."

"Well, stop, because you're freaking me out."

"Sorry. Happy trails, brother."

When I hung up, I was sure Takeo would be right there.

But he wasn't when the pilot welcomed everyone aboard, and still wasn't when the overhead bins were being snapped shut, and I was getting really worried by the time he finally took the seat beside me.

I was stunned. I had never, ever, seen the man look hungover. But the weird part was that only his face looked like hell. The rest of him was flawless.

Hiroyuki Takeo was immaculately attired. Crisp and clean were the words I would have picked to describe him. His slim-fit black Lanvin suit fit perfectly, the gray striped dress shirt underneath wrinkle-free, the tie knotted expertly, and he basically looked like he had walked off a *Details* cover. But the bloodshot eyes, flushed cheeks, and tousled hair told another story. I waited for him to say something as he took off his jacket, laid it across his lap, and sat down. After he shoved his courier bag under the seat in front of him, he turned to look at me.

"Knolls-san," he said briskly, not friendly at all. "Gomen nasai."

"Director," I returned the greeting cautiously. "Not sure what that last part was."

"I apologized."

"For what?"

"Everything," he claimed. "But mostly for being so late and making you worry." His voice was going in and out on him.

"Are you all right?"

He opened his mouth to say something, but nothing came out.

"You're wasted."

"No." He coughed, which ended with a retch.

"You should go home, Director."

He lifted his hand. "On this trip, may I please just be Takeo?"

I stared at him.

"Onegai shimasu?"

God, he was pretty, and the big, beautiful wet and pleading eyes made my stomach do cartwheels. "Yes, of course."

He nodded and gifted me with an enormous smile. "Good," he said, jerking up suddenly like he'd almost fallen asleep. "Domo arigato."

"Are you—"

"I wanted to be here on time to talk with you, but I was late getting home."

I waited to hear the rest.

"I… I was not actually at my home—my father is in town, and he… I have been with him at a hotel."

That made zero sense. "Why wouldn't he stay with you?"

"He says that my home is too poor."

I cleared my throat. "Takeo, you live in Waterfront Plaza off the lake. You had the entire office over when you got your promotion. Your home is stunning."

He glanced down at his hands. "That is very kind of you to say, Knolls-san, but I—"

"Do me a favor."

His gaze lifted to my face.

"If I'm calling you Takeo, I get to be Dwyer, okay?"

"Hai, Dwyer-san."

It was as close as it was going to get, apparently, at least for now. "Okay. So listen. About your home, I'm not just being nice. It's fantastic. I mean, just the wall of windows in the brick bathroom that look out on the Miracle Mile…." I sighed. "Gorgeous."

"Thank you," he said sincerely, and I noticed his red-rimmed and watery eyes.

"I understand you renovated everything when you got there. Designed it all."

"Hai, so desu."

I knew "hai" was "yes," which meant he was agreeing, so I plowed on. "You have a real flair for it. Your home is beautiful."

He nodded quickly. "You are much too kind."

I was quiet as the flight attendant appeared and took his suit jacket.

"Mizu o kudasai," he said to her. That one I knew because the last time Mak was drunk off his ass at my house, he'd said the same thing.

"Pardon?" she asked, looking to me to translate.

"He needs a glass of water," I explained.

"Oh, of course."

She was efficient and back with the beverage in moments.

"I am never late" was the next thing he uttered after taking a sip.

We were back to apologies. "It's fine," I promised. "Really."

"No. Truly. Never."

"I know," I soothed. "I work with you, remember?"

"Yes," he sighed, leaning back in his seat and closing his eyes.

"I'm sorry your dad won't stay at your place."

"It is to be expected," he mumbled, yawning. "He hates me."

I opened my mouth to ask what that meant.

"After all," he said before I got the questions out, "I should have been the one to die, not my brother. He will never forgive me for living."

I held my breath, waiting, shocked, having no clue what I was supposed to say to that. Holy fuck! It was like he tossed me a hand grenade out of the blue, and I just had to hold on to it and wait. Because he had to explain—I needed to know, had to… *hoped* to.

Hoped for more.

I wanted to know everything about him, had wanted to know from the moment I first laid eyes on him, and now, right this second, maybe I was about to be trusted to see behind the mask.

And yes, lust had ridden me hardest of all, but beyond that, from the little I had seen each and every day, the more I longed to truly know him. He was worth knowing.

If I allowed the silence to continue, he'd close up. I didn't want to push—not a scrap of his confession was any of my business—but Hiroyuki Takeo was important to me. "Living?" I prodded gently.

His eyes were closed and out from under them, wetting the lashes, came tears. My heart hurt just looking at him. How ripped up did he have to be to cry in front of me?

He murmured something in Japanese that, due to the slurring, I didn't catch any part of. "What'd you say?"

He was quiet a moment. "I am a bit drunk," he replied softly.

"Oh, I know," I replied gently. "That's okay. Just tell me the story."

He cleared his throat. "We were in a boating accident," he whispered. "I was not the strongest swimmer. Jiro was better, but one doesn't have to be best to tread water. Simply patient."

"Sure."

He was quiet again.

"Tell me what you did?"

"I tried to hold on to him."

"But?"

"But he would not be held up."

"I'm so sorry."

"It was a long time ago."

With some things, though, time didn't matter. "So you're the second son."

"I am."

He had not been born to lead. He was the spare who had become the only. "How long were you in the water?"

"Two days."

Jesus.

"Were your parents happy when they found you?"

"My mother died in childbirth with me."

I couldn't even imagine what his life had been like growing up, because just this quick peek was gutting me. "I'm so sorry."

"You have a very kind heart," he said, and then stilled.

After a few moments, I realized he was sleeping. When he moved and his head thumped down on my shoulder, I let him use me for a pillow.

I was amazed that he had trusted me with his secrets and had to wonder how many people he felt comfortable enough with to do that. Considering who he was as a person—culturally, professionally, personally—I was humbled by his faith in me. At the same time, how off his game—how upset—did he have to be, to let that story pour out of him? And beyond that, again, how was I the one he chose? How was I the person he would unburden his heart to?

Everyone teased me about being the person Takeo liked, and I always volleyed the words back, figuring it was just talk, nothing really important. But what if, to Takeo, I actually was important, and not just at work?

Conversely, maybe we had no connection and because he was simply drunk off his ass and I was geographically accessible, I'd been the one he confided in.

As I sat there thinking about him, he whimpered quietly before nuzzling my shoulder. Turning my head, I whispered into his ear.

"You're okay," I said. "I'm right here."

Instantly he quieted.

Yes, he was a *bit* drunk, but that wasn't the reason he was responding to me. I made him feel safe, and wasn't that just the best feeling ever.

"Takeo?" I husked. "What do you need?"

"Could I be closer?"

Whatever you want.

After I lifted the armrest and then my arm, he pressed into my space, and when I tightened my hold from a gentle drape across his back, he tipped his head back and opened his mouth against my jaw.

Never in my life had I experienced such a surge of heat. It sped through my entire body and left goose bumps in its wake. I'd known that I wanted Takeo—he was as close to perfection as I would ever see—but it hit me all at once that between our shared moments and quiet bonding, it was very likely that I would fall in love with him if I wasn't careful.

CHAPTER FIVE

WHEN WE got off the plane at the Northwest Florida Regional Airport near Fort Walton Beach, I was informed we had to go to baggage claim. Just because everything I needed had fit in a duffel I had carried on along with my laptop bag didn't mean he had packed with the same Tetris-like efficiency. We had to pick up an upright suitcase and a garment bag.

"I am not used to traveling," he explained.

"Yeah, I got that."

After we collected his belongings on the lower level, we walked over to the Enterprise counter to pick up our rental. I received a copy of the contract along with the keys, and we walked outside to the parking lot to claim our car.

The enormous Ford Expedition handled well, so I maneuvered us out of the parking facility without incident. After putting on my sunglasses before we hit the expressway, I felt the tension drain out of me. I loved to drive, even more so at night; it reminded me of the cross-country trips in college and always had a calming effect. The music didn't, however. And while I would agree with anyone that Keith Urban was hot, country music as a whole gave me hives. I was digging in my laptop bag for my iPod when Takeo asked if he could help.

"What?"

"You should keep both hands on the wheel, Dwyer-san."

I rolled my eyes. Fortunately, he didn't see.

"What are you trying to do?"

"I need different music."

"Simply turn off the music and we will talk," he offered. "We barely held any substantive conversation on the plane before I passed out on you. Please accept my sincere—"

"We should eat," I countered, "and no more apologies, it's enough."

He nodded quickly.

"Are you hungry?" I asked hopefully. "Because I could really go for some good Mexican."

"Not in the least," he said, like maybe his stomach was iffy.

"No, I'm not talking about enchiladas or chile rellenos. All that cheese would probably kill you."

The noise he made, part gag, part choke, was not healthy.

"What I'm thinking is like menudo, something filling, a good hearty stew."

He directed me to pull over, fast, but I couldn't quite get to the shoulder quick enough. At least he got the window down.

"I FEEL like an ass," I said sincerely. "I really didn't think you'd throw up."

He said something under his breath.

"That plane ride must have been a horror with that turbulence at the end."

He made it to the brush that time.

I just needed to stop talking.

He apologized, again, as we sat outside at the restaurant the next stop down from where he'd decorated the highway. He wasn't ready to eat, but I needed some lunch. It was nice with the breeze off the ocean, just us sitting at a large picnic table.

"Maybe we should get you just some plain tortillas or something."

"No, please," Takeo replied, his voice shaky as he guzzled down the ice water in front of him. The service, even on a slow day, had been prompt. "Pay me no mind."

"Yeah, but—"

"All is well," Takeo said, swallowing hard. "Really. I am more embarrassed than anything else."

"You should lie down in the back seat when we get back out on the road," I suggested. "Take a short nap before we reach Mangrove."

"No."

"Really, it's all right. Rest. A hangover's the worst."

His knee bumped mine under the table as he fiddled with silverware he wasn't going to use. "I will recover shortly; I wish not to abandon you."

"I promise not to hold it against you," I assured him.

He visibly still wasn't sure, but when I nodded, reached out, and squeezed his shoulder, he quickly covered my hand and held tight. When I eased free, he smiled sheepishly.

"Sumimasen," he said quickly.

"You're fine."

"You have always been so nice to me."

Had I?

"Yes," he answered as though I'd asked the question aloud. "Whenever I misunderstand a situation, you explain it in a way so I do, but you never make it obvious to other people that I had no idea what was happening."

"Oh yeah?"

He nodded. "And you allow the team to laugh at you instead of me. I know this. I see it."

"Like the time you ordered all the egg rolls," I said, chuckling.

"An unfair example," he said defensively, glowering at me.

I scoffed before gently tousling his hair.

"I thought one order meant two pieces," he groaned, head dropping down onto his folded arms.

"But it was four."

"We were buried in egg rolls," he lamented, lifting his head.

I started laughing.

"And they were huge. The size of a burrito!" Takeo exclaimed. I couldn't stand it and dissolved into laughter. "It was not funny," he said, indignantly. But I could tell he was putting it on because I knew his inflections.

I was overly tired myself, just a bit loopy, and when you're like that, once you have the giggles, it's all over.

"Are you finished?" Takeo asked me drolly, unable to keep from smiling.

I tried to stifle my laughter.

"But you see," he sighed, "no one at work knew of my mistake. You told everyone that you arranged for so many so they might take them home for dinner and to church on Sunday."

"The church part, with that crowd," I scoffed, "that was the best part."

"I am trying to thank you," he pressed.

"It's not necessary." I shrugged. "I know what it's like to have people think they know you when they really don't at all. All those months, everyone thought they knew who I was and what I'd done, and it turned out they didn't."

He nodded.

"I have a unique perspective on how you get treated."

"And I know that," he said, his voice dropping. "And I feel that."

"But you're also an ass sometimes," I said.

"As are you."

I nodded.

"But you always understand my jokes."

"I don't know that you get that you're even making them sometimes."

He arched an eyebrow.

"Oh, you do? You're saying you do?"

"Of course."

Not buying it. "Uh-uh."

Sometimes he'd say something that wasn't supposed to be funny, but his delivery, so deadpan, so flat, was hysterical. I'd spit out whatever I was drinking, no one else even moderately affected, and he'd smile at me like I was the second coming. He was so happy when he made me laugh—dazzled, it seemed, just for a moment.

In meetings, he'd made it a habit to sit next to me, and people got used to leaving him a seat at my side. He once made an entire row get up and move because no one had listened to me and saved him a seat. Mak, he got. Mak, Takeo never asked to move. But everyone else, forget it. He'd order more than twenty people to shove down by one.

One time I walked into his office and threw one of those splat balls at his window. He didn't even startle. By that point, he was used to the paper airplanes, the Frisbees, the remote-controlled helicopter.

"Are you quite done?" he asked, a tiny hint of snarl in his voice.

"It's crawling down the window!" I announced, excited.

He shook his head.

"Come on, it looks like a giant ball of snot," I said, laughing. "Or an oyster."

"Does it?" His tone was patronizing.

"A booger!"

Nothing.

"You're no fun at all." I made sure he could see that I was disappointed as I trudged toward the window.

"Leave it alone," he directed, going back to whatever he was typing. "You bring your toys into my area, you don't get them back."

I huffed, turned, and stomped away. His lilting laughter followed me. We were close—we were. And better than having him ever be my partner, we had become friends.

"Dwyer-san?"

My name brought me into the present. "Sorry. You feel any better?"

He put his chin on his hand. "I do."

I cleared my throat. "I'm really sorry about your brother, but I'm so touched that you would trust me with that."

"You have always been so good to me," he whispered as I reached out to catch a stray tear with my thumb and brush it away. He was much more tenderhearted than anyone ever gave him credit for.

I cleared my throat, moving my hand from his cheek.

He caught my wrist, holding my palm to his skin. "I know why it started."

I could hear my heart pounding in my ears. "Oh yeah?"

"You felt sorry for me."

"No," I said abruptly, yanking my hand away, getting up and moving around the table to take a seat on the bench beside him. "I never felt sorry for you, not until today when you were telling me about your family."

"It is not necessary for you to say these things to me," he argued, disbelieving, head down. "You always try and make me feel—"

"No." I stopped him, taking his face in my hands and lifting so he could see me and check for himself. "I've never felt sorry for you."

He looked confused. "I do not understand, then."

"Takeo," I said, clearing my throat, because really, it all had to be out, that was fair. "The reason I was nice to you at first was that I wanted to get in your pants."

No change.

Gently, I let him go, checking to make sure no one was watching, and thankfully no one was. It was the middle of the day; the picnic area was not crowded in the least.

When my eyes flicked back to his big black ones framed in those gorgeous long and thick lashes of his, I found him still befuddled.

"How was that not clear?" I asked, unable to keep from smiling. He was so cute.

"You want me?"

I answered honestly. "Yes."

He coughed. "Even now?"

I couldn't tell if he was confused or shocked or even embarrassed. "What do you mean, 'even now'?"

"I mean now that you know me?"

I leaned forward again so I could speak softly. "I want you more now than I did when I first saw you, and that's pretty impressive."

"Why?"

"Because the first time I ever saw you, I nearly swallowed my tongue."

"Oh, how horrible," he said, aghast.

"No," I corrected, smiling because he was missing it. "What it is, is a comment about how beautiful you are."

He just stared at me and I realized how truly clueless he was.

"You find me beautiful?"

"Yes. Very."

He bit his bottom lip. "No one has ever said that to me before."

"What about the women you've dated?"

Instantly he was back to appearing confused. "What women?"

"Didn't you date women?"

"I went on marriage interviews. Is that what you mean?"

"I have no idea what that is."

"My grandmother hired a matchmaker, and the matchmaker arranged interviews."

"That sounds bad."

"It is what is expected of the heir."

"So what happened?"

"None of the women found me acceptable."

"Why? You're a catch."

"No."

"Yes," I apprised. "You're charming, funny, smart, you make a good living, you're stunning to look at... I don't see the problem."

His face flushed as the tabletop suddenly had all his attention.

"I'm sorry. I embarrassed you."

"No, I... I have never been showered with such compliments before. I am overwhelmed."

"Look at me," I demanded.

After a long moment, he finally did.

"Are you serious? No one's ever said those things to you?"

He shook his head.

"Oh, Takeo, I'm so sorry."

"Why are you sorry?"

"Because you should have been told every day when you were a boy that you were smart and kind and the owner of a wonderfully gentle heart."

It surprised me when he reached out and took my hand. "You sincerely feel this way?"

"I do."

He took a deep breath. "And you find me beautiful?"

"Yes, and I don't mean to upset you in any—"

"Anyone who could find fault in any compliment of yours is an idiot."

Our eyes locked together.

"You do not find me cold?"

He'd lost me. "Cold?"

"Yes. Most of the women who interviewed me reported back that I was frigid and abrupt and that they could not see me ever being attached to anyone, and definitely not them."

I smiled. "I don't see that at all."

"No?"

"No. The last time we had to prepare those acquisition reports and we stayed late, we talked all night. Don't you remember?"

"I do, yes."

"We're friends, and friends can talk about nothing for hours. If I thought you were cold in the least, we would have never gotten close to begin with."

"No, of course not."

"Yeah, see so—"

"Do you have feelings for me?"

The direct inquiry had me squirming, but I had to be honest. "I do, yes."

His eyes never left mine. "You are very straightforward."

"I hope you still consider us friends."

"I could do nothing else."

I took a deep breath in relief and noticed that he seemed bemused. "What?"

"You're a very odd man."

"Me?" I chuckled. "Oh buddy, do you have that wrong. I've met a lot of Japanese men and none of them act like you."

"But I am quite traditional."

I had to think of what I really meant to say. "None of them act like how you do with me."

"Well, no," he concurred after a moment. "I suspect not."

He was the most confusing man.

THE REST of the short trip proved uneventful except for remarks about how fast I drove, why speeding was both dangerous and irresponsible, and if I was really that interested in seeing the inside of a Florida jail.

We drove east along the Emerald Coast Parkway, which was a nice drive because all you saw was water. I loved the beach, and looking out at the Gulf of Mexico was a treat. When the parkway moved inland, I turned onto East County Highway 30A.

"We stopped in Destin," Takeo said as he read from the Google map on his phone. "Next we'll pass Miramar Beach, Santa Rosa Beach, Blue Mountain Beach—"

"I get it," I deadpanned. "Lots of beaches."

"Grayton Beach," he teased me, "then Grayton State Park and finally Mangrove right before Seaside at Seagrove Beach."

I turned my chin in a slow pan to him.

"I just want you to be aware of your surroundings."

"It's a straight shot," I said drolly.

His smile seriously could have powered a small nuclear reactor. He was absolutely beaming, and it was better than any scenery I was looking at. The man just annihilated me.

When we made it to the town, I realized immediately that I was overdressed. I needed to get into some cargo shorts and a T-shirt and a pair of flip flops. A beer would be fantastic as well. It was hot in Florida in September, and even the wind off the ocean, with what I was wearing, wasn't helping. My oversize Prada sunglasses were the only thing keeping me from melting.

Once inside the tiny bed and breakfast, the Maple Leaf, we found we had only one reservation.

One.

The reservation was for a single room with two beds, and *no*, there were no others, and *no*, there was not another hotel in town—but we could drive one town over to Seaside—and *yes*, they only served breakfast and lunch. For dinner we were on our own, but there were several wonderful places in town where we could grab a bite.

"Seriously?" I asked Gretchen Cavanaugh, owner of the hovel we were checking into.

She nodded kindly. "Yes, dear."

I rounded on Takeo. "I can go get dinner alone if you just want to take a shower and pass out."

"No," he said softly. "Let us leave our things and get something to eat together. I am actually starving now. Voiding one's stomach will do that to you."

"That was funny," I remarked.

"I can be funny," he retorted, scowling at me as though I'd given him some grave insult.

We took the stairs quietly, and when we got to the room and opened the door, I stood just inside the doorway silently, not moving, a bag hanging loosely in each hand.

Takeo came up behind me but didn't move by. He just froze.

"Holy 1950, Batman," I breathed.

"Huh," he grunted beside me.

It looked like we had stepped onto the set of *Mad Men*. It was all midcentury everything, from the media console in walnut to the highboy dresser to the 1950s set of nesting tables with triangular tabletops. It was stunningly preserved and absolutely terrifying.

"I don't think I want to go in," he said close to my ear, his warm breath puffing over my skin.

"Yeah, you and me both," I said, distracted. "Have you ever even seen green plush carpet in real life?"

"Actually, no," he said, chuckling. "It is really… I mean… stunning."

"Stunningly bad, you mean."

"No," he replied kindly. "Only—it takes your breath away."

"Yeah, but not in a good way." I snickered, bumping his shoulder with mine.

He shrugged. "I find it curiously quaint."

I had never seen anything like it. "It smells really good in here, though."

After inhaling deeply, he whispered, "The only thing I smell is you."

My stomach rolled up into my heart, everything feeling like it fused together for a second. It took every drop of self-control I had not to grab him, and the horrified expression on his face worried me. "You okay?"

"I… that was terribly inappropriate and I—"

"I love the fact that you think I smell good," I said, grinning at him. "You can notice anything about me you want."

He resembled a deer caught in headlights. "You smell like mint and sandalwood—do you know that?"

I squinted at him. "Is that bad?"

He shook his head. "No, it is not bad at all."

We stood there in the doorway, like statues, staring, neither of us even really breathing.

It was insane—and I knew it was—but I wanted him more than anything, and his hooded eyes, flushed cheeks, and parted pink pouty lips beckoned to me. I couldn't remember ever wanting anyone more.

"Dwyer?" he prodded gently.

I almost stopped breathing. "I've been waiting on that."

"Pardon?"

"Don't," I warned. "Don't pretend you don't understand. I've been hoping to be more than *san* to you for a long time."

"I—"

"And just my name with nothing added is more than I thought possible."

His voice cracked when he spoke. "It simply slipped out and I should not have presumed such familiarity and forgotten to use the honorific with—"

"Yes, you should have, and it didn't just *slip* out," I growled.

"It did," he contended, chewing on his bottom lip, brows furrowing in consternation.

"I don't believe you," I said, dropping my messenger bag and duffel and rounding on him.

"You have to believe—oh," he yelped when I yanked him forward into me as I took a couple of steps backward so I could slam the door shut behind him.

"No, I don't," I growled, shoving him up against the wall, holding him there with a hand braced on his shoulder. "I can believe whatever I want."

His whimper was gorgeous and carnal but completely unneeded. I was far too gone, his mouth the only thing in the world I could see.

I wrapped my hand around his throat, tipped his head back, and sealed my lips over his in a brutal kiss that was not tender in the least, instead all about claiming and taking and tasting.

Almost three years I had wanted Hiroyuki Takeo, and he wasn't getting out of the room without me showing him.

Unless....

Pulling back, I opened my mouth to get out the words I needed to hear the answer to. I was bigger than him—he was extremely slight in comparison, by no means bulked out, leaner than me. I could hold him down easily. But I didn't want to do that, not without permission.

"Takeo," I panted. "I—"

He lunged at me.

He threw his arms around my neck and pulled me down, our lips meeting for the second time, bumping, scraping in a bruising, mauling kiss that answered all my questions at once. He wanted me desperately.

I had a flash of anger—because, Jesus Christ, he could have *told me*—but it drowned in the tide of feverish, aching need.

Kissing him was an epiphany. I had no idea that another person could ever enjoy the activity as much as I did. Most men complained I was too rough, that it lasted too long, that kissing was unneeded. They wanted to get down to business. But Takeo rode the wave with me, changing from savage, urgent kisses to slow, tender sensual exploration. He moaned deeply, held tighter, ground his rock-hard erection into my thigh, and when I had to tear my mouth free to gulp air, he licked up the side of my neck to my ear.

This man was made for me. Already I knew it—had, it seemed, always known.

I tipped his head back and leaned down to suck on the soft skin at the base of his throat before biting down gently, nibbling up to his chin before kissing there and recapturing his sweet mouth.

He kissed me like he needed me to breathe, like if he didn't have me, he'd die. Never, ever, had anyone treated me like that.

Grabbing hold of his ass, I lifted him up against me and strong legs wrapped tight around my hips as he fed on my mouth, sucking on my tongue. Walking to one of the two beds, I dumped him down on it and he lay there in place, staring up at me, heaving for breath, his eyes feverish slits, his lips dark and swollen from my kisses, his beautiful pale skin blotched with stubble burns and bite marks.

"I'm gonna get lube out of my bag. You need to take off all your clothes or tell me to get the hell out of here."

Takeo immediately rolled off the bed and started tearing at his clothes, yanking off his tie and ripping at the buttons on his dress shirt as he toed off his wingtips.

That answered my question.

By the time I rose from rooting through my duffel, he was under the sheet on the queen-size bed.

"You think I don't want to see you?"

His dark eyes were liquid with heat, and it was gorgeous to see. "You first. I am not as beautiful as you."

I squinted at him.

"Your skin is gold, Dwyer. You have gorgeous hard hands, and you are so big and strong and you have all those thick muscles and—your eyes. You are the only one I know with bright sea-green eyes… they remind me of the ocean outside our window, and just seeing them always calms me and excites me all at the same time."

The rush of words and the emotion behind them drove blood straight to my cock. I was painfully hard.

"I should be embarrassed," he croaked, "confessing such things to you, but we are going to be lovers, and there should be no secrets between us. I have wanted you from the moment I first saw you but thought you would not want the attention of such a foolish man, a man who has never succeeded at doing anything but being a disappointment."

I bolted to the bed and lowered myself on top of him, pinning him to the mattress under me. "You're an idiot, but so am I."

His eyes searched mine.

"I should've just grabbed you and pulled you into my office and put you over my desk."

He arched up into me, a ragged groan torn from his chest. "Do not say such things."

"Why the hell not? I'm gonna do it as soon as we get home."

A second guttural moan. "Dwyer."

"The moment I first saw you, I wanted you, and it's only grown the more I've gotten to know you. You're beautiful on the outside, but the inside is even better. For crissakes, Takeo, your heart is the best part of you."

He grabbed me, arms wound tight around my neck, and pulled me down into a punishing, devouring kiss, his tongue acquainting itself with every inch of my mouth.

I didn't want to stop, but I'd die if I didn't get my clothes off.

He bit me, hard, when I pulled away, my bottom lip between his teeth for a moment before I sat back, straddling his hips.

"You are a tease," he rasped, then added a string of Japanese that did not sound complimentary in the least.

He wanted me, and apparently I was not moving fast enough for him. Being desired by the one you wanted most: was there anything in the world better?

I climbed off the bed and shucked my clothes. The way he watched me, eyes narrowing with heat, lips curling into a smile before he licked them, hands clenching and unclenching… *fuck*. I needed to hurry.

Once I had everything off, I bent over, grabbed the edge of the sheet, and tore it away from him, revealing his glorious body.

He was tight with muscle, toned, perfect. The soft stretch of his belly called to me, and I leaned down and pressed my lips to it above his navel.

"Oh," he sighed, hands in my hair, pushing through it, buried, tugging gently. "Come here."

But I moved lower instead, wrapping my hand around his hard length, loving the fact that he was dribbling precum already.

"Dwyer," he gasped as I licked the flared head. "I should—oh!"

I wrapped my lips around his thick cock and he went from watching me to letting his head fall back against the bed. He jerked and twitched under me as I sucked and laved, swirling my tongue over his flesh before taking him down my throat.

His language—both his languages—left him, and I heard only whimpers and whines as he reached above him for the headboard and held on tight.

I wanted him to come in my mouth. I wanted to taste him and lick him clean when he was done, but he rasped something in Japanese and I lifted my head to look at him, saliva and precum dripping from the corners of my mouth down to his gorgeous cock.

He made another noise, an aching, needy, keening sound like he was really close to dying but God, could I hurry?

"I want you to come down my throat," I told him.

"And I said, I want you to fuck me," he whispered. "As hard as you can. Other lovers, they were careful because of my stature and they thought I would break if treated roughly."

Being gentle with him had never crossed my mind. Yes, he was delicate and fragile looking, but that was only the outside. I knew he was a lion underneath.

"Your cock is huge and beautiful and I want it buried inside of me."

His command, my wish. It was all there was.

Snapping open the lube, I coated my shaft as he watched, his breath coming in little stuttering gasps that made my stomach clench in anticipation.

"Hurry," he demanded huskily.

"There's no hurry. I need to get you ready."

"I'm ready now," he growled, planting his feet on my thighs and lifting up. "Dwyer! Hamete kure!"

"What is—"

"Fuck me!"

I was not small; he had to be stretched to take me, no matter what he thought he knew.

"You are not listening to me."

And I wasn't, not really. I bent and took his cock back into my mouth at the same time I slid a slick finger into his ass.

"Dwyer!" he snarled, shoving me off him so his cock popped out of my mouth. I was so surprised. The look on his face, the anger, his narrowed eyes… it was a rush to see him so incensed. "I will have you *now*."

I reached for the lube again.

"No," he insisted. "I like the burn. Fuck me or get out of the bed and I will find someone who will."

The possessiveness that rose in me was a surprise. The hell he would! "The fuck you will! I've waited for—"

"So have I!" he yelled. "I want you more than I have ever wanted anyone in my whole life. But you have to believe what I say to you, and Dwyer… please…."

Trust.

I had to trust that he knew his body as well as I knew mine.

Grabbing a pillow, I shoved it under his ass, tilting him up, and then lifted his legs over my shoulders as I curled forward.

His hands slid up my chest as I pressed against his entrance for only seconds before I pushed inside.

"Dwyer," he gasped, and I stopped instantly, afraid I was hurting him. "I want you all."

Seeing the look on his face, like he was drunk with wanting me, I was done fighting. I shoved into the tight fist of slippery heat and felt his muscles clenching around me. "Fuck, Takeo, you feel so good."

"So do you," he murmured, bowing up against me. "Please… more. Fukaku, oku made buchikonde kure!"

I drove the rest of the way inside, and when I was there, buried in his ass, skin to skin, it clicked in my head that *this was it* and he was never getting away from me.

"Yes," he agreed breathlessly to my unspoken thought. "We will figure this out. We will."

I had known somehow, always, that if I ever got close enough, he would get me, he would be mine.

"Now move, Knolls."

I chuckled over the use of my last name before I eased halfway free of his clutching, rippling channel only to power back in.

He roared my name.

It was a big noise from such a small man, and I wanted to hear it again and again. When I hammered into him, my name, I was sure, could be heard downstairs. Other guests would know it. He was damn loud and I loved it as much as he loved the ruthless pounding he took. The way he met every thrust, arching up against me, was amazing. Never had I been in bed with anyone who let me shed all control and just take them. I would never doubt him again.

Sweat covered us as his hands tightened on the back of my neck, the top of my head pressed to his collarbone as I pistoned inside of him, harder, faster, until I felt the sizzling heat tighten my balls and spread tiny electric shocks like pinpricks all over my skin.

"Oh, fuck, I'm gonna come," I choked out, my voice broken, sounding like dried leaves being crushed underfoot.

"Deso da," he cried out as cum splattered my abdomen at the same time his muscles contracted around my cock, fisting unbelievably tight.

The pressure, the heat, just *him* under me, spread out, wanting me, it was too much. My orgasm tore through me, and I came deep inside his body, pumping, emptying, and only then did it even cross my mind that a condom would have probably been a good idea.

"Aww, shit, I'm sorry," I whispered into his sweaty hair before I brushed it aside to kiss his temple. "I forgot the condom."

His smile was brilliant, beautiful, and completely unguarded. If he wanted me, to keep, I was so his. "I did not want a condom, you ridiculous man. I have no need of one, neither of us do. We are both careful, and as long as you have me, there is no need of another lover, is that not correct?" he finished hopefully.

"That is." I was emphatic, muttering into his shoulder. I shifted to lower his legs to my sides and collapsed on top of him, wanting to stay between his thighs forever if he'd let me. When he wrapped his now shaking legs around my hips, I pressed my face into the side of his neck and kissed his soft skin.

"I cannot say what will happen when we arrive home," he said, his breath catching. "But I want you to be with me, Dwyer, and not in secret. I want everyone to see us, even my father. Do you think you would want that too?"

"Yes," I answered him without hesitation. "Absolutely."

"Your friends will laugh at you."

"My friends will get it," I assured him, lifting up as he dropped his legs, sliding free of his body. "You make me a better man, a better friend, just better. Make no mistake."

"How?"

I looked down at him, and he lifted his arms to me, waiting.

"Come back."

I returned to his embrace, laying my head over his heart. "I think of you before myself. I worry about your feelings and how something will affect you."

"I know."

"I never do that, or never *did*, before you."

He nodded.

"This has always been important to me. Us."

"I am aware," he whispered.

"I want my friends to like you and see the other side of the situation, to see the other side of you."

"It will not be easy. I am difficult to like."

"No, you're not; it's just that no one has taken the time to really know you."

"Except you."

"Except me. But my friends aren't really the issue, are they."

"I miss your meaning."

"You're my boss," I reminded him as he carded his fingers through my sweaty hair. "And even if we want this to be out in the open, it really can't be. Not really."

"We will simply explain that this is more than—"

"I won't let you be fired because of me."

"I feel the same for you, Dwyer."

"So will you call me that at work?"

"Pardon?"

"Will you call me 'Dwyer' at work? Should I call you just 'Takeo'?"

"That would not be proper," he said, absolutely scandalized.

"I know," I said, turning my head and quickly sucking his right nipple into my mouth.

He writhed under me, the mewling cry so very sweet. "You are a decadent man."

"I know, but you seem to like me anyway."

"Very much," he rasped.

"So should I think about feeding you?" I teased, kissing his chest, sliding my hand along his outer thigh and then the inner, up to his hardening shaft.

"Where?"

"I dunno, take your pick. For a tiny town, they have a ton of places to eat."

"It is a resort town." He whimpered, pushing up into my fist as I slowly stroked him. "They cater to… to… and tomorrow we need to see—*ugh*—Mr. Crowley."

"Okay," I said, loving the way he lengthened and thickened in my hand. "Takeo?"

"Whatever you are thinking," he gasped. "Please, just do."

I moved fast, rolling him over to his stomach. Instinctively he lifted for my hands, wanting more of the rough treatment. "You like being under me," I said needlessly.

The answering urgent moan left no room for confusion.

Stopping suddenly, I stared down at the trembling man. "Do you want me under you?"

He turned his head so his voice wouldn't be muffled by the pillow. "I prefer not unless you need—"

"I don't," I said quickly, because even though I *could* bottom, it wasn't my favorite.

"Perfect," he sighed, and I saw the tension roll off of him. "You are perfect for me."

That went both ways.

"I'm gonna take you like this."

"Now, yes. Hurry."

Lifting his tight, round ass in the air, I couldn't keep myself from enjoying a small bite. He jolted, and his sexy groan made me smile.

"Do it again," he begged.

I gently bit the other cheek, and he made another sweet sound that burned right through me. "We should have done this the day we met."

"Yes. Agreed. Now fuck me."

So demanding, and it was so very hot.

I put a small amount of lube on the very end of my already leaking cock and sank slowly inside of him. Watching him take me in, all of me, was absolutely decadent.

"You like that," he whispered. "I can tell from the sound you made."

"Yes," I rasped, leaning over to growl in his ear before nuzzling the back of his neck.

"Oh, Dwyer," he said, his voice trembling. "I want to do things to you, but not… I want…."

I knew without him telling me, so I slid free, dove onto the bed, and rolled over on my back. "You set the tempo; it's all up to you."

The glow in his eyes told me I was correct. Just because he liked to bottom didn't mean he wanted to give up control every time.

Rising over me, he reached behind him, took my shaft in hand, and guided me to his entrance.

I needed to drive up into him, but instead I waited, calling on reserves of patience I never dreamed I possessed as he sank slowly onto my shaft, inch by inch, until he was impaled completely. When he moved, lifting up only to slam back down, harder with each rise and fall, I gripped his hard thighs and held him still. "I'm gonna come if you keep doing that."

"No," he forbade me. "Not until I allow you."

It was exquisite torture.

Head back, eyes closed, hands clenched on my chest as he rode me, he had never been more beautiful.

"I don't think I'm gonna be able to let you go," I whispered.

"No," he gasped. "You will not."

Chapter Six

I NEVER actually *slept* with anyone; it just wasn't something I did. It was far too intimate an act for me to lower every defense and allow myself to show another person how much I wanted, needed, their company. But Takeo I simply reached for, pulled close, and held tight.

He curled into me as though he'd been doing it forever. The heat from his skin, the soft kisses along my jaw, and the quiet purr of his breathing all lulled me quickly to sleep. We never made it to dinner because everything was closed by the time we woke up from Takeo passing out and me telling myself I was just going to hold him for a moment. It was surprising that I had slept so long and hard, and even more so that the town rolled up the sidewalks at ten sharp. I discovered that after calling around and no one picking up. Takeo took great delight in showing me the hours of operation for all the places I had just tried to contact.

"This is a phonebook," he teased with a wicked smile.

I smirked back, and he dissolved into a fit of giggles. I was apparently amusing the hell out of the luminous creature in bed with me.

Dressing haphazardly, I finally went downstairs to ask Mrs. Cavanaugh where else dinner might be procured.

She looked at me oddly.

"Ma'am?"

"The kitchen is right through there," she said, pointing into the other room. "I only do breakfast and lunch, but the refrigerator is stocked for dinner and late-night snacks. It's all part of the charge."

I was supposed to cook?

"Do either of you boys know how to scramble eggs?"

"Of course."

Her smile was big. "Well, then, you're in luck. Get to it."

Thirty minutes later I returned to the room with a tray of two cheese and ham omelets, sliced avocado, blueberry muffins, cubed papaya and mango, orange juice fresh-squeezed that morning, chamomile tea, and a small pitcher of ice water.

As soon as I walked in and put the tray down on the table by the couch, I realized that from the yelling coming from the bathroom that Takeo was talking to someone on speaker. I moved quickly to the door left ajar and hovered.

"I know!" whoever it was shouted. "And perhaps if I use your precious English you will hear me!"

"In Japanese or English, my response to you will be the same as it has been for the past several minutes," Takeo replied. "You only think you understand my motivation for joining Dwyer Knolls on this trip. It was never my intention to become romantically involved with him. I asked Dwyer Knolls to come on this trip because I sought to learn to be a good negotiator and he is the best in our office. He is excellent with people."

"I am certain he is," came the snide retort.

"You belittle what you should not."

"No! Your thoughts were never pure! I know for certain why you are on the trip with that man."

"You do not know anything, Father," Takeo disputed.

I was stunned as I stood there, uncertain whether I should make my presence known.

"You are a disgrace to your family!"

My stomach curled into a cold ball of fear.

"I am not," Takeo argued, "this is simply a part of me."

"No!" Hiroyuki Takumi snarled at his son. "I do not accept that! My son would never allow himself to be used in such a disgusting and degrading manner!"

"Father, you—"

"You are an abomination!"

"I—"

"You think I know nothing of your dalliances?"

"I have never had any—"

"Your perversions?" his father roared.

"I had two boyfriends my entire time at the university," Takeo defended himself. "There were no more."

"You dare to—"

"Two men do not constitute dalliances."

"You—"

"And I assure you that Dwyer Knolls is not a dalliance," he said hoarsely. "Nothing could be further from the truth."

"Oh no?"

"No. He—"

"What?" his father challenged. "What is Dwyer Knolls to you?"

"He—"

"Yes? Speak!"

"I cannot say what he is without first asking and being given an answer, but I know what I would like his reply to be."

"This is madness!"

"*Mine*," Takeo said flatly, answering his own question.

I had never in my life been exhilarated and terrified at the exact same time. It was a very real possibility that I, who had never been enough for anyone, *could* be enough for Hiroyuki Takeo.

"What are you talking—"

He took a breath. "I would like Dwyer Knolls to be mine."

A blast of vitriol came from the phone in a loud, angry stream of Japanese. Even though I didn't understand it, the anger and hatred were undeniably clear. My heart ached for my lover, and it was more than I could bear.

Throwing the door open the rest of the way, I charged into the bathroom and snatched the phone out of Takeo's hand. "This is Dwyer Knolls," I announced loudly. "And make no mistake... I'm the one hanging up on you."

Takeo seemed stunned, considering the expression of surprise on his face as I hit END on his phone and then turned and stalked from the room. He followed right behind me, stopping me with a hand on my shoulder. I rounded on him and took his face in my hands.

"I'm sorry your father's such a prick."

He stared up at me with his deep, dark, bewitching eyes. "Thank you."

"Stop letting him speak to you the way he does."

"Is that a command?"

"It is."

"I suspect that you will not have to worry. I cannot imagine that he will ever speak to me again," he said, smiling ruefully, trying, it seemed, to reassure me even as he was dealing with his own feelings.

"I'll always worry about you," I promised.

"Yes," he murmured, lifting to his toes, wrapping his arms around my neck, and pulling me down into a hot, wet kiss.

I forgot for a moment that his whole life was changing right there in front of me, because when he kissed me, that was all I could focus on. His warm, willing body pressing against mine robbed me of every thought but the most primal. I wanted him all over again.

But he was hurting. I knew he was, so I broke the kiss to talk to him. "Come eat what I made you before it gets cold."

His smile was gorgeous, the way it fired his eyes. "You cooked for me?"

"I did."

"How very thoughtful of you."

"You have to eat," I grumbled, grabbing his hand and dragging him after me across the room to the couch and tray on the table.

"This looks wonderful," he praised. "And your presentation is so artistic."

"Knock it off. Just sit down and eat before you starve to death."

"Is that why you did this, to keep me from expiring?"

"Yes."

"No, it is not." He full-out laughed then, leaning into me, nuzzling, his hands burrowing under my T-shirt to my skin. "You did not do this because you had to. You did this because you wanted to show me something."

"Oh yeah?" I asked, taking him into my arms and hugging him tight as I rubbed my chin in his thick, silky, glossy black hair. He fit me so perfectly, the top of his head just barely notching into the crook of my neck. "What did I want to show you?"

"That you care."

I squeezed him tight for a moment before letting him go. "Will you eat already, please?"

He took a seat and I sat in the one beside him, passing him an omelet. "Can I pour you some juice? Do you want any fruit?"

"Yes, please, on both."

As I passed him a glass of water, I noticed his regard. "What?"

"This is really quite the presentation," he teased, pointing at the flower on the tray. "What is that? It is really beautiful."

"Mrs. Cavanaugh has a whole forest of them in the back yard because apparently they grow all over the property. It's called *evolvulus glomeratus.*"

"Oh," Takeo said, smiling at me. "Is there an English version of that?"

"It's a blue daze."

"What a whimsical name."

"Is it?"

He nodded. "And how romantic of you to garnish my tray with it."

I had simply seen it blooming outside the kitchen window under the dim lights and asked Mrs. Cavanaugh if it would be all right if I went out and picked one. She'd been pleased and told me that for whatever reason, in the whole town, the only place it grew was on her property. In other towns, it was everywhere; the flowering perennials bloomed along the coast all year, one of the few flowers that loved heat and the salty air.

I told Takeo she had explained while beaming at me. "If I'd been less homesick at the time I moved and more attuned to the beauty around me, the B&B might have been named after the flower instead of a tree from Vermont. But perhaps there's still time to remedy that."

"What did she mean?" Takeo asked.

"I have no idea."

"She seems very nice."

I leaned over to kiss him on the cheek instead of telling him how wonderful she thought it was that he was so loud in the sack. He would be mortified that she'd thought I must really know what I was doing to get him to yell my name over and over at that decibel.

"One of the best things in life is having great sex with the one you love," she had said with a wink. "And I could tell as soon as you two walked in here that you were mad about each other."

"Yeah, but we didn't even know," I'd told her.

"Sure you did."

"Dwyer?"

"Sorry," I said quickly, having been momentarily lost in thought. When I straightened up, I noticed that his eyes appeared to be glistening with tears. "You okay?"

He nodded.

"Then why the tears?" I asked, wiping away the few that were falling.

"You are a natural caretaker."

"I am not," I argued.

"You are of me."

I couldn't fault his logic. I did indeed want to do everything from protect and nurture him to hold him down in bed. It was getting scarier by the second.

"You are so very domestic."

"Shut up."

His bubbling laughter made me smile.

"I never imagined that you would care for me the same way I care for…."

"Care for…." I trailed off just as he had. "Finish."

He squirmed in his seat. "You know what I mean."

"Do I?"

His gaze fell to his plate.

"And don't guess about how I feel, all right?" I grumbled.

He was back to staring at me.

"I would love to belong to you. It would be my privilege," I insisted.

"Truly?"

"Truly."

He exhaled long and slow.

"So if your father asks, or anyone else, that's what you say. That I belong to you."

He nodded quickly.

"Now eat your food."

He did as he was told.

HE WENT downstairs with me when we were done eating and helped me rinse the plates, silverware, and glasses and load it all into the dishwasher. Mrs. Cavanaugh was outside watering the blue daze around the back patio and Takeo went out to talk to her while I checked my voice mail and e-mail on my phone. When I returned to them thirty minutes later, he was using the sprayer to water, listening as she directed him on how much each plant should get.

"Tell me again," she directed gently.

He pointed. "The buttercups are there, and the lantana, the pentas at the end, then the vinca on the other side, and the Mexican heather that attracts butterflies."

"Marvelous," she praised.

It was a beautiful night, warm with a breeze, and looking at Takeo, seeing him smile, hearing him laugh, I was more at peace than I could ever remember. I wondered if it was my place to shatter such a calm, tranquil place with an outlet mall. Later as I lay in bed with Takeo wrapped around me, I clutched him tight, inhaling his warm, smoky scent, and tried to think of a good reason to do my job the next day.

I shouldn't have worried.

CHAPTER SEVEN

HUTCH CROWLEY was a handsome man, and I noticed that right away when I stood in his grocery store the following morning. Blond hair, blue eyes... I was betting that if he lived in a place other than this tiny charming town, he would get laid regularly. As it was, the way he checked out every man who walked into his place—thoroughly, up and down and sideways—I was thinking he was going through a dry patch. What was interesting was that I myself had not been on the receiving end of any close scrutiny, flirtatious smiling, or suggestive leering. And while I wasn't anywhere near vain, I knew I was better looking than a few of the guys he'd checked out instead of me.

"So you don't actually want to sell," I said, needing a firm answer one way or another for the report I was going to file.

"I—" Hutch coughed, and I watched his eyes flick to Takeo where he stood at the front of the store next to a bunch of potted plants. "—wanted to move a while back but... realize now that this is my home, always has been."

"Why did you include the provision that whomever wanted to buy your property needed to visit Mangrove?"

"Because I think this place is special, and anyone who wants to build here or live here should spend some time here first and get to know the people and understand our way of life."

I nodded. "I think even when you thought you wanted to go, you obviously didn't. You were safeguarding your home."

"You're probably... right," he replied, clearly distracted.

While watching him squirm in front of me, I realized Takeo had more of his attention than I did. It would have been annoying, but Hutch's eyes were glued to Takeo—not in a "God, he's sexy" way, but more in a "I gotta watch that guy so he doesn't kill me" way. He was wary. It accounted for the fidgeting.

"Are you okay?"

"What?" He sounded scared.

I moved around in front of him, blocking Takeo from sight even though keeping anyone from looking at that beautiful man was doing them a disservice. In his black Hugo Boss suit, pale blue dress shirt, and his black Alexander McQueen gold-tip boots, Takeo was stunning. The way everything fit, I really wanted to take him back to the bed and breakfast and take it all off of him. Blowing him in the shower that morning and then fucking him up against the tiled wall had been the best start to a day that I could ever remember.

"Mr. Crowley?" I prodded. "What's the deal?"

He tipped his head, indicating the man I had in a very short time come to think of as mine. "He's kind of intense, huh?"

I squinted at him. "Sorry?"

He cleared his throat. "When you, uhm, were walking around looking at the layout of the place, and the square footage, your boyfriend there said that if I even smiled at you he'd cut my dick off."

Surely I had misheard. "I'm sorry?"

Hutch swallowed hard.

"He said *what*?"

"I guess I was sort of obvious when you walked in. I have kind of a thing for tall, strong men, and I guess he noticed and you didn't and well… he talked to me about it."

I pointed over my shoulder. "*He* did. The small pretty man behind me. He threatened you with bodily harm if you looked at me."

He nodded.

"Well," I breathed. "Isn't that interesting?"

"Actually," Hutch corrected, "it's really sort of terrifying. But I get it. If I had a man that looked like you, I'd be a little possessive myself."

I smiled at him. "Thank you, that's a very nice thing to say."

"It's true," he sighed. "And for the record, I envy your relationship with Mr. Hiroyuki. I mean, he's completely terrifying considering how perfect he looks on the outside—like an anime character—but the fact that he makes his claim known and doesn't care who knows it… I find that very romantic."

"Homicidal jealousy does it for you?"

He shrugged. "It certainly shows passion."

I couldn't argue that.

"Needless to say," he said, offering me his hand. "I'm not selling."

I was glad, even though the reason for the trip was now a bust.

"Please have your company close out my request to sell."

"I certainly will," I said, taking his hand. "Thank you."

When I turned and crossed the floor to Takeo, I saw him receiving a business card from some cute guy. I found myself vaguely irritated that Takeo was being hit on but then changed my mind. It looked more like business to me.

"Thank you," Takeo said, executing a slight bow.

"It's my pleasure." The man smiled back. "Any produce you need, just give a call." The young man had a nod for me before he turned to leave.

"Who was that?" I asked, reaching Takeo.

"Greg Chapel. He and his partner own Cypress Farms, and they provide all the produce here at the Green Grocer."

"Which matters to you why?"

"I thought it would be good to find out about some of the local vendors."

"For the outlet mall."

"Certainly."

I crossed my arms. "Why, really?"

He took a breath. "The fruit I ate last night, everything I ate this morning, Gretchen said that it was all—"

"Gretchen?"

"Mrs. Cavanaugh," he clarified.

"No, I know who she is. I was just surprised that you're calling her Gretchen."

"It is her name, Dwyer," he said, clearly patronizing me from the cackling laugh to the daring tilt of his head. Playful, teasing Takeo had me mesmerized.

"Anyway," I growled, trying to maintain my composure and realizing how badly I was failing.

Takeo chuckled. "Gretchen told me about Cypress Farms, so when I saw the truck with the name on it, I inquired as to the whereabouts of their business."

"I see."

"In case."

"In case what?"

"One never knows when one might need a produce vendor, Dwyer."

It was oddly true and somehow endearing, as I suspected everything the man did and said was. When I bent and kissed his forehead, the smile I got in return was blinding.

"What was that for?" he asked, the sweet, bemused expression on his face charming me completely.

"You were scary possessive about me with Mr. Crowley."

"Yes," he replied, matter-of-fact. "I was."

"And? Care to elaborate?"

He stepped into me, into my personal space, close enough that no one could miss that we were more than coworkers, or even friends. Much more. "I have no idea what came over me, but when I saw him looking you over like a piece of meat he wanted to buy, I was vexed."

"Vexed?"

He nodded, his face coloring just a bit with an embarrassed pink. "Yes. I needed him to understand the nature of our involvement."

"Which is what?"

"Which is do not touch what is mine and there will be no bloodshed."

I pressed a kiss to the side of his neck, and the noise I received in return, a pure carnal purr, was very satisfying. "Not that you ever have to be jealous over me, but I find your worry, just this one time, very hot."

"How hot?"

"Like come back to Gretchen's place with me hot."

I liked it when he grabbed my hand and tugged me after him.

Sex with Takeo, with him yelling my name and issuing demands, just got better. Calling into the office an hour after that was horrific.

I had to explain to Ayumi that the whole project in Mangrove was a bust. I was surprised she wasn't annoyed until she explained she needed to ask for my resignation.

"For this?" I asked calmly.

"No."

"Then what?"

"Did you sleep with Mr. Hiroyuki?"

His father certainly worked fast. "I did, yeah."

"Holy shit!" she yelled over the phone.

"Don't swear. It's not ladylike."

"Dwyer!"

"So if I just resign, what happens?"

She started hyperventilating before I heard muffled noises and then a growl of displeasure.

"Stop that."

"You fucked the Ice Prince?" Mak was incredulous.

"No."

"Oh thank—"

"I made love to him."

He gagged.

"It's the truth." And it was. Fucking didn't do what Takeo and I had become in that bed justice. It had been life-changing. "I'm a whole new person."

"Oh for fuck's sake!"

"Knock it off and just tell me what's going on."

"I hope it was worth losing your job over."

"It was absolutely worth it," I replied, cackling. "So what? If I resign do I get some kind of severance package?"

"You're taking this all very—"

"Just—what are the details?"

"One year of salary, one year of medical, done and done."

"Okay, e-mail me the paperwork. I'll sign it and scan them back to you."

Silence.

"Mak?"

"What about me?" he snapped.

I scoffed. "What about you?"

"What the fuck am I supposed to do?"

"What do you want to do?" I asked pointedly, knowing the answer. The real answer. "Don't you want to move home and open that club with your cousin Kano?"

"What?"

"What?" I echoed.

"No."

"No? Really? Are you sure?"

"Yeah," he said, sounding ridiculously unsure, his voice small for him.

"Mak?"

"I can't do that. My parents would freak."

"Only if you fail, and I know you. How could that happen?"

"But I need someone to manage the venues, pick them and inspect them and go on—"

"Couldn't I do that?"

"What?"

"Me. Couldn't I do that? I can do a lot of it from wherever I am and on-site visits, or when you decide you want to invest in something, permanent property, I could travel, right? I mean, I'm in acquisitions, you know. I am in possession of a degree in accounting as well as—"

"Yes," he said too loudly and then coughed and cleared his throat. "Yes, I mean, yeah. I would like that—love that—and maybe you could be a silent partner, too, and then… then…."

"Then we'll still be partners," I finished for him. "Which is good."

"Yes, it is. It works for me."

"And I have a severance package, so as long as you get your shit together in a year and figure out a way for me to get paid—"

"I will," he promised. "I would."

"Okay."

"Okay," he said gruffly. "Shit. Did I just figure my whole life out with you right now on the phone?"

"I think you did, yeah."

"Fuck."

I laughed. "Listen, I'll see you when I get home before you run off to wherever."

"Yes, you will."

There was a silence.

"Takeo, huh?"

"Learn to like him."

"I will, for you," he said, chuckling. "Now, lemme tell Ayumi that we're both bailing."

"Yeah, you do that."

I heard the wail in the background a second before he hung up. I was smiling like an idiot when I noticed that Takeo had taken a seat across the table from me out on the beautiful wraparound porch of the bed and breakfast. He looked sad and angry at the same time, hurt, like somebody had struck him.

"Honey? What's wrong?"

"My father fired you?"

He'd obviously been there longer than I realized. I reached for his hand and he grabbed mine tight. "It's okay, baby. I'll figure something out."

"Yes, but we just—"

"I promise."

"You know," Gretchen said as she brought out a pitcher of ice tea. "You boys both love Mangrove. Why don't you just go ahead and buy the bed and breakfast from me and stay here?"

I glanced over at her. "Have you lost your mind?"

She smiled sweetly. "Your boyfriend loves it, and so do you. Who are you kidding?"

"Boyfriend?" I choked out.

"Isn't that what he is?"

I looked at Takeo. He stared back at me.

"Yes, he's my boyfriend," I said, diving into the deep end of the pool. "You're really selling the place?"

She nodded as she smiled. "Yes. Do you think you might want it?"

Did I?

"It's a full-time job. Whoever bought it would have to live here too. Take care of guests, the land."

"The structure itself is beautiful," Takeo remarked. "It simply needs some updating."

"That's right," she agreed. "Someone would have to love it."

"Yes," he said, turning to me.

I scowled at him. "No."

"No?"

I thought a moment. "Definitely no."

He nodded. "All right, you know best."

"It's just not feasible," I said to try and convince myself.

"Of course not."

I cleared my throat. "Though, in all honesty, I have no plans, and I'm about to resign so I don't get fired for sexual harassment."

Takeo's eyes got huge.

"What else could it be? They're going to get me for moral turpitude."

"But that is not fair."

"Look at me."

His gaze lifted to mine.

"I promise you," I said, my voice low and husky. "I don't care. I'm happy to be done, but"—I gestured all around me—"this?"

"Why not?"

"Takeo—"

"Are you planning to abandon me all alone in Chicago?"

Was that even a possibility? Could I leave him someplace or watch him walk away from me? The very idea made my stomach twist in a vise of pain.

What were the chances that a man from the other side of the world would first come to the country I lived in, and then to the state and city? What kind of a signpost was I looking for that would lead me to my destiny?

"What?" I flared angrily. "Leave you? I just got you!"

"And I you," he husked, reaching across the table and grabbing my hand tight. The second our skin touched, I calmed, realizing that his presence already felt like home. "So we are together now and that will not change."

"No. It won't."

"Good."

"But here?"

He nodded.

"Oh," Gretchen sighed, "aren't you two sweet."

We were in a small town in Florida and she was cooing over us? "Dwyer?"

That fast? Just jump?

"Dwyer?" he said again.

I took a breath. "You could stay here with me."

It took a moment to process. "Really?" he gasped.

"You could."

"So you're staying here now?"

"We," I corrected. "Us."

"Us," he sighed.

"Don't you think?"

"I…. Stay here? With you?"

"Yeah," I replied breathlessly, because, Christ, I was basically asking him to marry me. It's what it amounted to, without question.

"But how can I leave the company?"

"That's your argument?" I laughed.

"You know what it is."

"Your father."

"Yes," he said, sucking in a breath.

"He treats you like shit," I told him, "and you know I'm right."

"Yes, but—"

"After this, everything with me, he'll replace you and send you back to Japan. You know he will. He'd never allow you to stay."

"That is true, but—"

"And what happens when you tell him I love you and you love me? We both know that'll be the end of you and him and you and the company."

He looked stunned.

"What? It's true. You know that's how he—"

"You love me?"

I glared at him. "Of course, don't be an idiot. Whatever else happens, we're in this. We move together as one."

His eyes were riveted on me.

"Am I wrong?"

He coughed. "No."

"No? Are you sure?"

"Do not bully me," he snapped. "Because I love you back and I do not need you to tell me how I feel. I know how I feel."

"Okay. And?"

"And I love you too!"

"Don't sound so happy about it," I groused.

"Shut up," he barked and then took a breath. "You really do love me?"

"Without question."

His smile was blinding. "How did that happen?"

"You can't plan love."

"No," he granted, squeezing my hand again. "I could tell you were upset when you heard my father yelling at me over the phone."

"I couldn't stand it," I said honestly, giving his hand a final clinch before getting up and crossing to the edge of the porch, looking at the beautiful grounds and the overgrown blue daze.

"It bothered you more than you thought it would."

"Yes, it did," I finished, turning to face him again.

"Which led you to the logical conclusion that you love me."

"It did, yes," I said softly, smiling, really looking at him, realizing that I wanted to be doing it for the rest of my life. I was ready. We simply fit; he was the missing half of me.

"Dwyer?"

"Come here."

He got up and rushed across the porch, and when he reached me, I took him into my arms. "I know it's fast, but I don't think that's a bad thing."

"It is a growing thing."

"Exactly. We're both unhappy where we are."

"Yes, we are," he said, nestling against me.

"And our lives can be wherever we want."

"Yes."

"And I have a severance, so even if your father cuts you off—"

He shook his head. "No. I have plenty of money."

"Do you?" I asked, surprised.

He leaned back and gave me a very wicked smile. "Yes, Dwyer Knolls. My mother came from a very wealthy family, and I am the only living heir."

What? "Are you kidding?"

He shook his head slowly. "No. This is why my father has given me so many chances in the company… if I quit, I walk away with half of his money and assets."

I was overwhelmed and it must have been all over my face, to cause his bubbling laughter.

"For crissakes, Takeo, why didn't you just go?"

"I never had a good enough reason."

"But you do now."

"I do, if you are serious about wanting me."

"I'm already standing in deep water with you."

"You most certainly are."

"So then?"

"So then what? Tell me what you want?"

"I want you, idiot."

"Be nice," he ordered. I growled at him. "Nicer," he said, his voice low and serious.

"I want us to buy this ridiculous place together and fix it up and own the best bed and breakfast for miles."

"I do not think that will be particularly hard," he replied snidely.

"You're crapping on my dream."

"Pardon me," he said, laughing softly.

"You're about as romantic as that table."

"Actually," Gretchen interrupted, "Mr. Cavanaugh—God rest him—that's where he proposed to me, so I'm thinking that table is actually quite romantic."

We both looked over at her.

"So, boys, would you like to make me an offer?"

EPILOGUE

WE HAD named the place after the flowers that were about to take over the yard before Takeo hired a brand new landscaper in town to make it all beautiful. We were Kelly Seaton's first clients, and he appreciated the work and the referrals that making our B&B bloom brought him. I liked him, even though he wasn't too sure about the name of our little establishment.

"Blue Days, like a takeoff of Blue Daze, right?" I was trying to explain.

"Yeah, no, I get it, but, Blue Days?" he questioned. "Sounds sad, right?"

"No, man, blue like the blue of the ocean. Spending your days in blue."

He nodded like I was an idiot.

"And besides," I told him, "in Japanese culture, blue supposedly represents purity and calmness and stability. So that makes sense for both of us."

"Yeah, I can tell that Takeo really counts on you for that. Seems like he thinks of you as home, even more than this place."

It had been good to hear.

"Mr. Knolls!"

Turning sharply, I wasn't surprised to find Margo Dayton. Again.

Her high heels scraped the cobblestones we had put in along the side of the bed and breakfast and her red Chanel suit stood out in sharp contrast to the bright blue ocean behind her. She reminded me of the actress from *The Matrix*, the one who fell for Keanu Reeves, except her face was softer, especially when she smiled as she currently was.

When she reached me, I took the business card she held out even though I already had twelve in the glass bowl on the kitchen counter. She'd left at least eight with Takeo.

"Mr. Knolls," she began. "I really need to speak with your part—"

"Ms. Dayton," I said, smiling. "I'm sure he—"

"Margo," she corrected me, "please."

I sighed. "Margo, I promise you that just as soon as he makes a decision either way that he's gonna call you."

She sucked in a breath. "Which I understand, but Mr. Sutter just wants to make sure that Mr. Hiroyuki fully grasps the extent of his business proposal."

We both understood it at this point. Billionaire used-to-be-playboy real estate developer and Sakura competitor Aaron Sutter had gotten married and his new husband had wanted to take care of the honeymoon. He picked our bed and breakfast, Blue Days, because along with being smack dab on the water, we were gay-friendly. Takeo had made sure our new status was everywhere and that ad must have caught the detective's eye.

They stayed a week, with Takeo seeing to every need, just as he did for the Murphy family there at the same time, and the Nakamuras from Kyoto. That we were fluent in Japanese was also on the ad for our business.

The thing was, Takeo being Takeo made everyone's stay flawless. Honeymooners couldn't ask for better, couples with kids—same story— and if someone wanted a quiet, peaceful getaway, he had that covered as well. It turned out that hospitality, taking care of guests, was Takeo's wheelhouse. He was fantastic at caretaking; the issue before had been that he was no good at the sales he needed to generate. Takeo didn't want to pressure anyone. He was made to help, to educate, to make everyone happy. He was a pleaser. Without the demand to motivate a team and adhere to a bottom line, he treated people like royalty, and no one, even the snarliest customers, left without gushing all over him.

Sutter had been more than impressed with Takeo's attention to detail. He wanted to hire him—he wanted Takeo to work for him like *yesterday*. When he learned who Takeo was, that he was the disgraced heir of his business rival Hiroyuki Takumi, that he used to work at Sakura, the want changed to desperation. Sutter *had* to have my partner take on the position of his head hospitality/optimization consultant. He was offering to pay Takeo to take trips to his different hotels overseas—Sutter didn't own any hotels domestically, only property—to grade the service and staff and then make recommendations. The offer was generous, the schedule light, and the thought of working for Aaron Sutter—which would surely drive Takeo's father into frothing, maniacal anger—was almost too good to pass up. But Takeo was vacillating. The idea of being away from me, even for only a week, did not sit well with him. I was his lifeline, his rock, his steady center, and the very thought of not being able to hold my hand if he wanted made him uneasy.

I had an alternative, though, that I was going to discuss with him.

"Mr. Knolls?" Margo, Sutter's personal assistant, said, bringing me sharply back to the present.

"Dwyer," I said so she'd know we were on equal footing. "Is there a time limit on the offer, Margo? Is Mr. Sutter looking at someone else as well?"

"Oh, no," she said sincerely. "Mr. Sutter has only one choice for the position, and that's Mr. Hiroyuki. It's simply that he has five hotels in Japan—three in Tokyo and two in Osaka—and would like to have them all appraised as soon as possible."

I nodded. "Well, I'll certainly talk to Takeo and find out his thoughts, which way he's leaning, and then have him get back to you."

"Please let him know that if he has any salary or benefit questions that I will be more than willing to speak to him about any concerns."

"I most certainly will."

She exhaled sharply and offered me her hand.

"This seems like such a small thing for Mr. Sutter to care about," I said, shaking her hand.

"Mr. Sutter cares about all facets of his business. That's what makes him so successful."

I certainly couldn't argue with that.

Ten minutes later, walking through the front door of Blue Days, I called out to Takeo, telling him a strange woman had just accosted me on the street.

"Again?" he asked, poking his head out of the kitchen.

"Yep," I said, holding up the card for him to see.

"She is tenacious," he commented, chuckling. "Put that one in the bowl with the others."

"What do you think you're going to do?"

He tipped his head and smiled at me. "That depends on you."

And I knew it did, which was what I wanted to talk to him about, but it would wait. There was no hurry.

"Come here."

He rushed across the room to me, and I got the kiss and hug I was used to: passionate, loving, and, most of all, hot. With all his reserve melted away, my man was an absolute furnace of want and need. I loved it more than I could say—so I'd let the rings in my pocket say it for me.

QUIET NIGHTS

Mary Calmes

MANGROVE
Stories

CHAPTER ONE

IT WAS childish, that was true, but at the moment, with my adrenaline pumping, the flush heating my body, and my heart pounding in my ears, I couldn't think of a better option.

I ran. Fast.

I had been strolling on my way to The Colonial, one of the many bed and breakfasts along the seashore in Mangrove, when I walked by the patio of Brenner Manor, one of the most exclusive B&Bs, the high end of the lot, and saw him.

It was just a quick glance, but as I would have known him anywhere, the man's features forever stamped on my memory, I'd jolted to a stop and stood there staring like an idiot. Blessedly, my brain kicked in and I got control of my muscles back. I had pivoted and run down an immaculate alley paved in brick, past white picket fences to the street on the other side. Now I flew by The Lighthouse, that good bar where they mixed handmade cocktails, then by Cuppa Joe, where everyone got their coffee all day, and around the side of Wick and Wand, which sold spells and supplies to both Wiccans and posers. When I cleared Schnapsidee, the German restaurant that made the best Jägerspätzel I'd ever had—German dumplings with mushrooms—I stopped running and ducked into another alley, this one shaded though still stunning, and leaned up against a wall.

It took long minutes for me to catch my breath and then parse what I'd seen.

Holy. Shit.

After ten years, there he was, Britton Lassiter in the flesh. What the hell was he doing in Mangrove, Florida?

The last time I'd seen him was in New Orleans. He had just graduated from college and had taken a road trip with some buddies from his home in Scarsdale, New York, down to the French Quarter before he started Harvard Law School in the fall. I learned that information walking with him while his buddies were drinking on Bourbon Street. He'd been different from the others—or so I'd thought. In the end his only agenda had been to satisfy his curiosity about being in bed with a man. What I'd taken for more—which was stupid after only two days—had been meaningless to him. I learned that the hard way when he wasn't where he'd promised to be.

Britton had asked me to go to Boston with him. But when I'd shown up, bag packed, ready to start my dream, he was nowhere to be found. At the time I thought it was the end of me, but it turned out to be only the beginning. Because, really, no one rode in on a white horse and saved you from your life; everybody had to do that for themselves. I was no exception.

The Army took me and trained me, and four years later I was out and made it to Florida as fast as I could to see a buddy who was medically discharged before I finished my tour. When my friend's mother asked me about my dreams for the future, I had an epiphany, one she was more than happy to help me with.

I heard a car close to me, but even though it broke into my memories, I didn't look up until I heard a question fired at me. "What the hell are you doing?"

Turning to the sound of the voice, I found that same friend, Cosimo Renaldi—Coz—staring at me from behind the wheel of his Crown Victoria. "Resting," I answered.

"I thought you were being chased by a hellhound or something, when I saw you blow by," he said, scowling, putting the car into Park in the middle of the street before getting out. As he came toward me, I took a moment, as I always did, to admire his height, his hard, muscular build, the V-shape of his torso and the breadth of his shoulders. I had always been an aficionado of gorgeous Italian men, and Coz was a classic in every way but for his skin, a beautiful rich bronze. I'd seen him naked enough times to know that he was a deep tan all over. It made my mouth dry just to think about it. He was sex on two legs and I never got tired of looking at him.

"I thought you had to check on the Italian cypresses at The Colonial this morning."

"Yeah," I gasped, still trying to suck in oxygen, made harder by my appraisal of his profile: the long, straight nose; lush lips; the divot in his chin; and his gleaming henna-colored eyes under dark brows. His thick black hair was coarse to the touch and only a bit longer than it had been when we served in the Army. I didn't stare at him often—it did me no good—but when I did, when I allowed myself to, I always found myself wondering what he'd taste like. It was a familiar craving.

"That's what you told me last night when you were over for dinner."

"What?"

"Dinner. Last night. Is this ringing any bells?"

"Yep."

"My mom went to Panama City for sausage and peppers."

He'd lost me. "What?"

"You told me all the things you had to do today, and so I told her and she decided to run to Panama City to pick up what she needed for dinner tonight."

"Oh, okay."

"But if you don't get all your work done, then you won't be on time for dinner, and you're gonna break her heart."

I nodded. "I won't be late."

"You will if you're fuckin' around instead of working."

He was like a dog with a bone. "I know!"

"Then why aren't you there?" he pressed, closing in on me. "You know that since my father died she's been—"

"I just need a sec, Coz," I said before inhaling deeply.

Silence, but I knew without looking that he was scowling at me. He'd done it all through basic training and continued when we were stationed together in Afghanistan. Even after the accident, when I'd crawled through the debris of his blown-apart humvee, under fire, to reach him. Even when he was full of shrapnel and missing his left arm from the shoulder down, even then, at that moment, there had been scowling.

Lifting my head, I finally took a deep breath.

"Oh," he muttered quickly, clearly surprised, if the lifted brows and concern on his face were any indication. "You actually look scared. What's wrong with you?"

I cleared my throat. "Remember that guy I told you about? The reason why I joined the Army to get as far away from my life as I possibly could?"

He nodded.

"Yeah, so, I just saw him on the patio at Brenner."

The way his eyes narrowed, I knew he was filtering my words, processing them. "No shit?"

"No shit—" I choked. "—so let me stand here and breathe, okay?"

"Huh."

I lifted an eyebrow in agreement with his assessment of the situation, the whole what-the-fuck of it all.

"And so?"

I squinted at him. "What do you mean 'and so'?" Maybe what I'd seen was *not* in fact sympathy.

"I mean, he's just a guy, right? You've fucked a ton of guys in your life."

I was being insulted and I knew it, even though it took a moment to sink in. "I'm sorry, what'd you just say to me?"

"Oh, c'mon, Kel, where is that guy on the list? Do you even know?"

"Do I *know*?" I was indignant.

He threw up his right arm and groaned loudly as he turned away from me. "Just go to work already, before my mother calls me to check up on us and has a fuckin' heart attack."

I darted around in front of him so he had to either stop moving or plow into me. "I'll have you know that your mother *never* calls to check up on me or check up on your sister. She calls to check on *you* because you're the one who's breaking her heart, not either one of us."

His eyes widened in anger, and part of me felt bad for baiting him, but he'd just called me a slut, whether he realized it or not.

"I'm breaking her heart? *I* am?"

He'd always been on a hair trigger, and losing his arm, being mad at the world, had not changed that. It had, in fact, just made it worse. I heard the frustration in his rising tone, saw the anger in the clench of his jaw, and felt the heat rolling off his sleek, hot, gorgeous frame. If he would just let me put my hands all over him, I was sure I could relieve quite a—

"How exactly am I doing that?"

"What?" It took me a second to banish my impure thoughts.

"Pay fuckin' attention! How the hell am I breaking my mother's heart?"

"Do I really need to tell you?" I asked, matching his volume. "Again?"

He waved his hand at me dismissively because he knew what he'd done.

"You nearly killed her when you took this fuckin' job," I said, gesturing at the uniform, the car, the entire officer of the law accoutrement.

"Nothing happens in this town!" he barked defensively.

"It doesn't matter," I volleyed.

"Of course it matters! Why would they make me—a man with only one arm—a policeman if they actually thought I'd have to do anything? It's a pity post, idiot."

So much annoyance colored his tone. "Then why do you have a gun?"

"Maybe because I know how to use one!"

"Or," I began, making sure I sounded just as snide as he did, "maybe the chief actually *expects* you to put yourself in danger if the situation calls for it."

"And what the fuck is wrong with that?"

"Oh, nothing, except that your mother lost her husband two years ago, and all she has left is you and your sister."

"She has you too!"

"It's not the same and you know it!" I yelled because he did. Matching his volume was one of my favorite things to do.

"It is too the same," he growled. "She likes you better than me and Mia put together!"

I stared at him and he glared back.

"Why're you still yelling?" I asked abruptly, because he was ranting like a crazy person. Normally one of us got either tired or hoarse fairly quickly.

"Because you make me crazy with this shit!"

"Okay," I began, clearing my throat, lowering my decibel level, "so you know that what your mother wanted—what we all fuckin' wanted— was for you to buy that bar and run it."

He rolled his eyes.

"It was a good idea."

"It was a boring-ass idea, and what the hell do I know about running a bar?"

"What the hell do I know about landscaping? What does Mia know about the law?"

He sniffed in annoyance, and I laughed, because, shit, that last part really was stupid. Sometimes my mouth ran on a bit quicker than my brain.

"Well, I dunno. For starters she went to law school, ya fuckin' idiot."

I snorted out a giggle that I couldn't stifle. "Yeah, fine, whatever."

His reluctant grin showed off the laugh lines in the corner of his eyes, the deep ones around his mouth, and the curl of his lip that made my stomach clench. "What does this have to do with—"

"I borrowed money from your mom for my landscaping business," I reminded him. "Mia took some when she opened the law office, but you—you had to go and be a damn lawman."

"I didn't want to be a burden on her, and I don't know how to do anything else but fire a weapon and save people."

"You could solve problems at a bar and maybe shoot someone once in a while, if they tried to rob you."

"In this town? Get robbed in this town. This is your story?"

"Seeing you in that uniform is killing your mother."

He growled. I arched an eyebrow to hammer home the point that he was, in fact, taking years off his mother's life every single day. He'd come home from serving his country with a piece missing. She didn't want him to lose any other parts—and definitely not his life.

"If you could all just open your eyes to—"

"Hah!"

His scowl was back. "Hah? That's your big retort?"

"If Mia could open her eyes? If I could? Your mom? Please. You're the only blind one around here."

"And what the fuck is that supposed to mean?"

I tipped my head sideways. "Do you ever notice any of the people who stare at you as you drive down the street, Officer? Do you ever see the people who try and talk to you or flirt with you? Do you?"

"I fail to see what any of that has to do with—"

"Getting laid," I announced. "It has to do with getting laid."

"Which again, has no bearing on what we're fuckin' talking about," he insisted.

"It has to do with your entire reasoning for taking this job, which is your perceived value."

"Oh dear God, I knew it was a mistake to take you with me to see the shrink at the VA. Why did I do that? *Why?*"

"You say you don't want to be a burden," I said gruffly, advancing on him. "So you take the only job where there is the possibility that you could get killed. Why is that?"

"I have no idea, but I'm sure you do, so please," he prodded, "enlighten me."

"Because this way, you don't actually have to live."

"I'm living!"

"You're not! You're pretending to, but you take no chances and you haven't fucked anyone in the two years since you got back."

"Just because you fuck everyone—"

"We're not talking about me," I snarled, because he always turned the tables—but not this time. "We're talking about you, and because you've stopped living, you took a job doing the only thing you could think of to help."

"And what the hell is wrong with that?"

"There's a crapton of other shit you could do where you wouldn't have to carry a gun."

"I—"

"You were gonna come home and go to school to be a teacher. Why don't you do that?"

He shook his head. "No kid is gonna listen to a guy with only one arm."

"For fuck's sake, Coz, do you even listen to yourself? Why does you not having an arm define anything about you?"

"Because it does."

"But why does it?"

"It just does!"

"And see, that's what I mean about you being blind."

"Listen, nobody wants a guy with only—"

"You're ridiculous," I snapped. "Everybody wants you."

They did. I knew so because I saw the looks he got, heard the come-on lines, and tracked the hunger in people's eyes. He missed it because he didn't believe it, didn't see himself the way the rest of us did, the way I did. It made me crazy that his missing arm had skewed his perception of his own value—but I was, for my own selfish purposes, secretly thrilled at the same time. I still had him, had my best friend in my life, in my space, but any second now he'd actually see himself and find his guy. One of these days, he was going to wake up and realize he was strong and beautiful, and whoever was there worshipping him at that moment would be in for the ride of their life.

"I love that you think my life is some big Hollywood blockbuster where bullshit like what you just said is actually true."

"You're so deluded," I said miserably.

He shook his head, not believing me, as usual.

"You're an idiot."

"Which is funny, coming from a man who just ran away from a guy he hasn't seen in, what? Ten years?"

I scowled. "Go away. Go ticket some jaywalkers or something."

"You see," he said, smacking me in the abdomen, "that's all you think is gonna happen around here. All that shit you said about me being in imminent danger, that you're worried about me getting shot—gimme a fuckin' break."

I growled under my breath. "I'll see you at dinner."

"Great."

Standing still, I watched as he stalked back to his car, got in, and drove away, flipping me off for good measure when he hit the corner.

Pivoting to run back the other way, I plowed into a woman. "Oh shit," I gasped as I grabbed hold of her so she wouldn't fall down.

"For fuck's sake, man!" The guy following her was quick to yell and would have tugged her out of my hands, but her forward lunge into my arms stopped him.

"There you are!" she announced, hugging me tight, arms coiled around my neck before she kissed my cheek. "I told this nice man that he didn't have to follow me, that you were right around the corner, that I was meeting you for breakfast, but he didn't believe me."

I uncoiled her arms from around me, took hold of her upper arms like I was going to shake her, and then glowered, going for stern. "Why were you even talking to this guy?"

I got a trace of a smile from her, because yeah, we were on the same wavelength. "I didn't. He talked to me."

"Oh really?" I asked, my voice rising.

"Yes, really," she snapped, matching my volume.

I let her go and put my hands on my hips. "Because this seems like Tampa all over again, and we know how *that* turned out and what you made me do to that guy!"

She covered her face with her hands, bursting into tears. "You went too far! Why did you have to—I told you it was nothing!"

"And I told you I didn't care!"

"We had to move," she cried. "So you wouldn't have to go back to jail."

I crossed my arms, glaring at her before lifting my gaze to the man hovering close. Never in my life had I actually seen color drain from anyone's face in absolute fear. It was interesting to observe.

"Hey man, I don't want any trouble."

"Too late," I replied menacingly.

He bolted, leaving the tiny sobbing woman with me.

"Wow," she said as he turned the corner. "Chivalry actually is dead."

"He totally ditched you," I said, chuckling as I turned back to her. "And clearly, I'm a psychopath, because I did something heinous to that guy in Tampa."

She laughed as she took hold of my hand. "Thank you so much. I've never had a better impromptu acting partner."

I squeezed back. "Where'd you pick him up?"

"I was running on that path along the beach and he came up beside me and started talking." She sighed. "I thought he'd get the hint from the monosyllabic answers."

"Sorry."

She coughed. "I got lost when I turned one corner, then another and another, and there was an alley back behind a restaurant that was a bit dark, and he stopped me to talk and got a little handsy… so when I saw an opening, I ran."

"Good."

She exhaled sharply, clearly a bit more shaken than she wanted me to see. "I mean, I don't think he would have done anything, but—thank you for being my knight. I needed one, and they've been few and far between here lately."

"Not a problem," I said, smiling, changing her grip on my hand so we were shaking. "Kelly Seaton."

"Olivia Lassiter," she answered, beaming at me, taking my hand in both of hers. "It's a pleasure to meet you, Kelly. You have to come have lunch with me and my family."

Lassiter? "I—"

"My whole family is here visiting," she continued excitedly. "We never have time to get together anymore, but my brother is moving here to become a partner at a law firm, and I just got accepted to graduate school at Cornell and—"

"Sounds like a real celebration," I said, extricating myself from her, needing to get out of there. "I don't want to intrude."

"You're not intruding," she assured me, grabbing me again, making sure I couldn't get free without prying at her fingers. "You saved me— you're wonderful."

"I appreciate—"

"Come and have lunch with my family," she insisted, trying to tug me after her.

Lassiter… holy crap…. "I wish I had time, but I have trees to check on and my boyfriend is expecting me for dinner so I can't eat a big lunch so I should just go."

"Boyfriend?"

Oh yes, the easy out. "Yeah, I'm gay, so I—"

"Serious boyfriend?"

What? "I'm sorry?" She was the strangest girl.

Her eyes opened wide like I was the one who was odd. "It's a simple question: is the boyfriend serious or not?"

"I—he's more a friend than… why?"

"I have a super hot brother."

Yes. I knew that. "Who's about to become a partner at a law firm here in town," I reminded her. "And I'm sure he doesn't need any distractions or—"

"No," she said quickly. "He could use a distraction."

I had my out. "Actually, I have never been a one night stand guy myself," I said flatly, pulling out of her grip. "But thanks for thinking I was trashy."

"Oh no," she blurted, "that's not what I meant at all."

"I'll see you around," I said, turning and jogging down the street, back on track to get to checking on the Italian cypresses.

"That's not what I meant!" she yelled after me.

I waved a hand in the air to let her know there were no hard feelings.

"My brother needs saving, is all!"

That was not my job. He'd have to do that all on his own. I learned that lesson the hard way. I was no one's knight in shining armor, and the days when I was looking for one were long over. I could ride to my own damn rescue.

CHAPTER TWO

YES, SOMETIMES it took me a minute to put two and two together, but as I stood in the shower that evening, washing off the dirt and sweat and grime of the day, it hit me.

"Holy shit!"

I was fuming by the time I threw open Annalise Renaldi's front door. I froze, confused, because a man I had never seen before was standing there.

"Hello," I greeted the stranger.

He was older—I was guessing midfifties—and he looked startled. "Are you another son?"

I was at a loss.

"Yes!" came a yell from the kitchen. "That's my adopted one—that's Kelly!"

"Oh," the man said, smiling, offering me his hand. "I'm Emmett Cheong."

I shook his hand, because what the hell else was I supposed to do? "Pleasure?" I couldn't help but make it into a question, because learning the man's name didn't dispel the stranger in the house thing. Who in heaven's name was he?

"Annie and I are seeing each other."

Annie? Seeing? And didn't using that word instead of just saying "dating" mean something important? I opened my mouth and closed it just as fast.

"Kel!" Coz bellowed, and because he sounded a bit off, his voice too high, scratchy, slightly frantic, I smiled fast and bolted.

The kitchen was a huge space with one of those islands copper pots hung over and a fridge just for wine, and more open cabinets and shelves than any one person should ever be able to fill. But Annalise Renaldi tried, and to that end: roosters. So many roosters, made out of everything from brass to wrought iron to ceramic to stained glass. They were supposed to be lucky, but dear God, they were everywhere.

"So she's dating," Coz muttered, then drained his wine glass as I reached him. "Did you know she was dating?"

"Nuh-uh," I said, glancing over at Mia. She had the same dark eyes and ochre skin as her mother and brother. "You?"

She inhaled deeply. "Nope."

My attention was back on Coz.

"Dating," he repeated.

I had nothing.

Mia poured Coz another glass before taking a swig straight from the bottle.

"Oh, Kelly," Annalise said cheerfully as she sauntered by on her way to the oven. "Have a glass of wine, dear."

I leaned sideways as I was trained to do, and she kissed my cheek before grabbing a pot holder and a slotted spoon and opening the door to check on the sausage and peppers. It was funny; people always thought when they met her that the sweet Southern lady would make fried chicken for dinner, but she'd spent most of her life married to an Italian man, and because she loved him, she'd learned to cook all his favorites. Slowly, insidiously, Sicilian cuisine became what she was best at and known for.

"So," I choked out as Mia put a glass down in front of me and poured from the same bottle she was quickly draining. "Dating, huh?"

"Yes," Annalise sighed as Emmett came into the room. "Isn't it wonderful?"

I coughed, took a big gulp of wine, and let Mia top me off before she finished up the bottle. "We need another one," she announced, walking out of the kitchen toward the wine cellar at the back of the house. "I'll get it."

"I need vodka," Coz whispered, emptying his wine glass for the second time in less than two minutes before passing it to me on his way out.

"I think we surprised them," Emmett informed Annalise as I chugalugged my Chianti.

"Yes," she said with a chuckle. "It seems so."

"How—" I gasped. "—did you guys meet?"

"Well, darling, Emmett and I met at a—"

"Wait!" Mia yelled as she rushed back into the room. She carried another bottle of wine with her, and she moved to her mother's side, facing me. After grabbing the opener off the counter, she told her mother to proceed.

"Whatever is wrong with you?" Annalise asked her daughter.

"Oh, no, nothing," Mia said with a belch. "I just want to see Kel's face when you tell this part again."

Annalise scowled at her, the very expression she had passed on to her son, the one I saw in my sleep. "As I was saying," she said, turning to me, "Emmett and I met at a tantric sex education class a year ago, because I didn't feel that just because Agosto passed on, that he wouldn't want me to explore my sexuality anymore."

I actually felt the air leave my body.

"Oh yeah, there it is, that's the same face I made." Mia snickered as she peeled the foil from around the top of the bottle and let it drop to the floor before putting the bottle between her legs to go to work on it with the corkscrew.

Annalise remained unfazed. "What began as a purely physical exploration—"

"I found vodka and bourbon," Coz practically shouted as he walked back into the kitchen.

"—deepened beyond merely extended orgasms—"

"Get ice," he demanded as Mia popped the cork out of the second bottle of Chianti and took a long pull without letting it breathe.

"—and so it became important to me that Emmett meet y'all, all my children, since clearly we were progressing from a robust physical relationship that included experimentation and shared fulfillment to—"

"Ice!" he barked at me, and I put down the empty wine glass he'd left with me not even a couple of minutes earlier. "Now!"

I darted quickly around the kitchen, first to the cabinet for the glasses, then to the refrigerator to push the lever on the icemaker, at the same time retaining supportive eye contact with his mother. I loved her, so I was practicing my active listening, even though I was pretty sure I was about ready to pass out.

"—a journey that we're taking together of mutual love and renewal," she finished, beaming at me.

"Here," I muttered, shoving two tumblers full of ice at Coz.

"So, of course, I felt like it was time to let y'all in on our relationship."

Coz poured fast, splashing a bit of the pricey Belvedere, which was a shame, but truthfully I had no time to lament—I needed the alcohol *in* my system.

"He's also my gynecologist," she added cheerfully. "He says I have the vagina of a forty-year-old woman."

The vodka went down the wrong pipe, and for a long moment, I really thought I was going to die.

Coz thumped my back as I did my very best Gollum impersonation and tried to bring up a lung.

"Oh, honey, are you all right?"

"Same"—I rasped—"hole."

She nodded kindly, then went flitting around the kitchen, pulling first a Greek salad out of the fridge and then a pecan pie out of the oven.

Once I straightened up, Coz threw back the rest of his drink and poured us each another double as Mia took a gulp from the wine bottle.

"Did you want to let the second bottle of wine breathe?" Emmett asked her.

"Maybe later," Mia answered, pouring him a glass before taking yet another healthy swallow. "Sorry about that, I swear I'm germ-free."

"Oh, so am I," he said kindly, gazing over at Annalise. "And just so you know, your mother and I both got tested so we could have safe sex."

It was Coz's turn to choke.

"So, uhm," Mia began, but then she glanced over at me, her eyes scrunched up, begging.

I knew what she wanted to know, because I did too.

"No," Coz said hoarsely, his voice burned from the alcohol. "No-no."

"So," I choked out, "since it was a class where you met and all, did you guys have sex in front of other people?"

Coz's whine was loud.

"Well, yes, sweetheart, of course."

"Pass me the bourbon," Mia demanded loudly, gesturing at me.

"You want ice?"

"No, just—pour."

But Annalise finally realized the three of us were well on our way to alcohol poisoning and made us sit down at the table.

Coz needed brain bleach first.

"I'M CONFUSED," Mia said as she served herself a third plate of sausage and peppers, much to her mother's delight.

"Save some for the rest of us," I groused, which earned me a pat on the back from Annalise as she poured me another glass of wine. We'd finished the Chianti and moved on to Shiraz with our food. I took two more pieces of bread from the bowl Coz held out for me.

"There's enough here to feed a small army," Mia volleyed, her voice louder than usual from all the liquor sloshing around in her system. "I don't think you're gonna starve."

"Well, some of us actually work outside in the sun and don't sit on our asses all day long."

"Oh? So because I don't toil all day, I don't get to eat?"

I shrugged and Coz said, "Yeah."

She flipped us off one after the other.

"Children," Annalise admonished. "No more!" After we all went quiet, she turned to me. "Now, angel, tell us about this blast from your past that you ran into today."

"What?"

"Coz said you had an event happen today."

It was nowhere near the excitement of tantric lovemaking in front of a roomful of people. "Yeah, I—wait."

"Tell me what happened," she insisted.

But I remembered my epiphany as I turned from Annalise to Mia.

"What?" she asked as I glared at her, feeling betrayed for no logical reason. If I was right, she had no idea what she'd done. "Why are you lookin' at me like that?"

"Your friend from college, the one you went to Harvard with... what was his last name?"

"Oh." She closed one eye, concentrating. We were all loaded. "Uh, Lassiter. Why?"

"Crap, I knew it," I grumbled, dropping my face down onto my folded arms.

"Oh, that's the guy," Coz trumpeted, just as drunk as me and Mia. "Your guy, the guy, who ditched you and left you crying in your beignets…. Lassiter. He's Mia's new partner."

I sighed loudly. Had the beignet thing really needed to be added?

"What?" Mia asked as I lifted my head so I could meet her gaze. "Oh… the guy, the one, that was Britton? Holy shit, what a small world!"

She knew the story just as well as her brother did; it was one of the first things Coz had—much to my horror—shared with her. It had been the whole "Guess what, Mia, Kelly gets shafted by guys too" declaration. He'd wanted us to bond, and we had, just not over that. Mia and I were close because she was the big sister I had always wanted, the one who loved you unconditionally and would annihilate anyone who tried to hurt you. I was counting on it now.

"Could you, pretty please, ditch him?" I begged. "For me?"

"Who are we speaking of, sugar?" Annalise asked.

I made a noise of disgust as I leaned my head on my fist and regarded the matriarch of our family. Did I have to confess that I knew him in the Biblical sense?

"He's the lawyer who's going to be sharing my practice, Mom," Mia answered. "We've been friends since law school and"—her gaze shifted back to me—"I'll tell him it's not going to work out."

I sat there staring at her, awestruck, as she reached across the table and took my hand. That she would make that sacrifice for me… but of course she would. She was my sister.

"Are you actually gonna do that? Is that the kind of man you are?" Coz sounded disappointed.

I groaned as he smacked the back of my head.

"Cosimo!" Annalise scolded, rubbing where he'd hit me.

But he was right, and even drunk, I knew that. "No," I sighed. "No, Mia, don't do that."

"I will."

"I know, but you shouldn't. Coz is right, that's crap."

"You're sure?" She was hedging. "I don't want you pissed off at me later."

"Yeah, I'm sure."

She nodded.

"Am I missing something? I thought you told me your new partner was married," Annalise chimed in. "Whyever did I think that?"

"I told you he was divorced," Mia explained. "And I guess from what he said, it not only messed up his home life, because he and his wife's family were so tight, but his practice as well. His wife's father is the managing partner at his law firm."

"Ah," Annalise reasoned. "That explains his need to move."

"Yes, it does."

"How long was he married?" Coz wanted to know.

"Five years or so," she said, visibly searching her memory, slower than usual as she had to do it through the alcohol. "It's only been like a year or so that he's been divorced."

"Did you know his wife?"

"Trudy," Mia said with a shiver. "Sadly, yes. She was always scary, I never liked her. None of us did. You could see her claws underneath the kitten exterior."

I nodded.

"And boy, is it lucky his father made him sign a prenup, or he would have had nothing to invest in another business."

"So the Lassiters are—"

"Rich," Mia finished. "Yeah. The filthy kind. They're old country club, 'would you like to buy a horse farm and some diamonds' money."

Perfect.

"So why'd he choose here?" Coz prodded as Mia poured him and me another glass of wine.

Mia shrugged. "He wanted to get away from Manhattan where he was practicing and just start over. I mean, I got the feeling that there was more to it than that, but I didn't want to pry."

"Okay," Coz said brightly before turning to his mother. "So, I'm drunk enough to talk about *you* now."

One of Annalise's thick, perfectly shaped eyebrows lifted as she regarded her son. "And what is it we're discussing?"

"This," he grumbled, pointing at her and then Emmett and making a circling motion that meant everything.

"What else is there to talk about, my darling?"

"So," he began, taking a fortifying breath. "How long have you and Emmett here been shackin' up?"

"Six months," she answered smoothly. "But as I said, it started as merely sex but has blossomed from there."

Mia whimpered and thumped her head down on the table.

Annalise started chuckling, and Emmett—who was actually a very handsome man, now that I was looking at him—joined her.

"Did I not call it? I told you they would all come apart at the seams."

"You did," he agreed, "though it might have been a bit of your delivery."

"Whatever do you mean?"

"You're very blunt, my dear."

"But they're used to that, for goodness' sake."

The way he was looking at her… I liked. And from Mia's soft grunt, I was thinking she might too.

"I mean, I know everything there is to know about *their* sex lives."

"Oh dear God," Coz moaned, letting his head fall all the way back. "Who's having what and with whom."

"It's like a horror movie," Mia groaned softly. "And it won't stop."

"These two," she said, indicating me and Coz, "are gay. Mia's straight, though experimentation with a woman might be a good thing."

"So Mia's the one who'll be giving you your grandchildren," Emmett chimed in.

Her slow pan to him was confusing, I could tell from the look on his face. His brows furrowed and he leaned in close. "I like you ever so much," she said softly, smiling at him. "But darling, do you honestly believe what you just said, or did you simply speak without thinking?"

He sat back and was quiet as he took a moment and reviewed what he'd said.

You couldn't beat Annalise Renaldi, originally Annalise Sherwood, from Savannah, Georgia. She was a sweet-tempered, iron-willed Southern debutante who after one meeting with Agosto Renaldi—at a fair when she was eighteen—walked away from her life and into his. She immediately married the Italian transplant who was only a year older than her, with zero prospects and no money. They moved to Chicago where she waitressed and he got a job as a plumber's assistant. Nine months later, Miranda—Mia for short—was born, and a year later, Cosimo. While Agosto moved up, first becoming a journeyman and then joining the union, Annalise went to school at night and followed her dream of becoming a teacher. It was, by all accounts, a match made in heaven. When they were fed up with the city and the cold, they moved the family to Mangrove to start over. That they wouldn't grow old side by side was never an eventuality either considered, but stomach cancer had come along and blindsided them.

After she lost Agosto, Annalise devoted her life to her children and carried his spirit with her into everything she did. So when one of them told her he was gay, she decided to keep on loving him even though it wasn't the path she would have chosen. When that same son brought home his gay friend, I became to her merely another child to love. I would be forever grateful to Annalise for accepting me into the fold, for giving me a family to replace the one that rejected me when I came out to my biologicals, and for raising a son who would become my best friend in the world. I was part of the Renaldi family and that was, so far, my greatest blessing.

"Oh," Emmett said softly, bringing my attention back to him. "I see. You're wondering if I thought that Cosimo and Kelly, being gay, can't be fathers."

She nodded.

"Oh, no, of course not," he assured her, taking her hand in his. "I wasn't thinking—thank you for pointing that out. It was a silly thing to say. Both your sons can give you grandchildren, my dear."

She was very pleased with him. I could tell by the way her eyes brightened, and she gently squeezed his hand before she leaned sideways and kissed his cheek. Emmett's face glowed in response. They were very sweet together.

"And now," Emmett announced, giving me his attention, "let's hear about this Britton fellow. Why on Earth would you run from this man?"

All eyes on me and all of a sudden I was nervous. "I'm sorry, what?"

"Mia says he's a nice, smart man," Annalise reminded me. "So why are you running from him? That seems odd."

"I—"

She prodded her daughter. "Is he a good man or not?"

"He is," Mia promised her. "A very good man."

"And is he out to his family?"

"Yeah, see, that's the thing," she replied with a burp. "I had no idea he was gay, and he was married, like I said."

"So he's bi, then," Coz offered.

"I actually thought he was straight."

"Oh, well, I see the issue now," Annalise surmised, glancing around the table. "That's why you ran from him, because he's not out and proud."

"Mom, he might not even identify as bi or gay," Coz explained.

Mia squinted at me. "I still don't get why you'd run from Britton. The thing between you two was ages ago."

"Running implies that I was scared, and I'm not," I defended. "I was more circumventing him to avoid any unpleasantness."

From the looks on all their faces, no one was buying my explanation, including Emmett, who didn't even know me well enough to judge.

"He probably doesn't even remember me."

"Because you're so forgettable?" Annalise smirked.

"You just think everyone will fall in love with me because you love me."

"No," she countered, "it's because you're beautiful inside and out."

"Oh, I'm gonna throw up," Coz commented.

"We were young," I explained, ignoring him.

"What does that have to do with anything? Youth is no excuse."

Annalise wasn't going to let it go. "I just mean, he invited me to go to Boston with him, and then the day we were supposed to go, he never showed up."

"Pardon me?"

"That's what happened."

"Oh!" She was horrified and turned on Mia. "Your friend broke Kelly's heart. You certainly can't go into business with such a man."

"Mom—"

"For heaven's sake, Mia." She was aghast. "The man's a cad."

Mia made a pained sound. "We already settled this. Were you even listening?"

Her mother tsked in that judgmental way she had.

"Stop looking at me like that," Mia muttered.

"I don't like him."

"Mother!"

"Don't ever bring him to my house!"

"Oh, that's just great," Mia mumbled as I smirked at her. "How do you know he didn't have a phenomenal explanation for ditching Kel?"

"Like?"

"I don't know," Mia said dejectedly.

"Dead," Annalise said flatly. "I would accept *dead*."

Mia threw up her hands.

"Maybe he does have a good excuse," Coz said to me, yawning. "And maybe you'd get to actually hear that reason if you ever allowed him to see you."

"No thank you," I replied petulantly.

"Oh yeah, no, of course not," Coz returned snidely. "Then you'd have to, like, have closure or something." He shivered dramatically for my benefit as he shoveled food into his mouth. "That sounds horrible."

"Leave him alone," Mia defended before her gaze slid to meet mine. "It's hard to know things sometimes. You want to and you don't, all at the same time."

And she was right. While half of me wanted to hear why Britton Lassiter had not shown up, the rest of me didn't want to know.

She shrugged. "Maybe you just let sleeping dogs lie."

"Or," Coz said, clearly annoyed with both of us, "you walk your ass over to where he's staying and ask if he remembers you, and if so, inquire as to the explanation of his whereabouts on the day in question, which was what—ten years ago now?"

"Oh God," I whined, thunking my head down on the table again. "I need to drink more."

"I think y'all have drunk enough," Annalise stated. "Let's go into the living room and I can tell you about the nude beach Emmett and I went to."

"Where's the rest of the vodka?" Mia asked her brother.

CHAPTER THREE

I SERIOUSLY could hear the grass growing, and even with a baseball cap on and my dark-lensed aviators, too much light was still getting to my eyes. When I staggered in through the back door of Blue Days, a bed and breakfast toward the end of the beachfront property, one of the two owners was in the kitchen.

"Oh," Dwyer Knolls said softly, scrutinizing me. "Are you all right?"

He was a nice guy; he and his partner had been some of my first customers, the first people to put faith in me and back it up with money, so I always made certain their property looked fantastic. Dwyer's partner, Hiroyuki Takeo, did most of the watering, and he'd had the idea to take out the fence on the north side of the property and put in bamboo as a barrier. I hadn't been sold on the idea, but it had turned out gorgeous, and now with how thick and lush the bamboo was, no one could see through it to the back patio. That had been Takeo's whole plan: he wanted that area for him and his husband alone.

"Kelly?"

I lifted my head so I could see him without opening my eyes any wider. "Yeah?"

"Are you okay?"

"Yeah, why?"

"Because you're actually *gray*."

I staggered over to the kitchen table and sat down.

"Dwyer, do you—oh," Takeo said as he breezed into the room. "Kelly-san, good morning."

"He's hungover," Dwyer explained, reaching for Takeo, who moved quickly to his side and pressed in close. They were just gorgeous together, and seeing the love wafting around them normally put a smile on my face. But I had nothing in my stomach, my head was pounding because the Tylenol also hadn't stayed down, and I knew I was dehydrated.

And all Takeo and Dwyer were doing at present was reminding me that I had no one to take care of me but a surly policeman who was as hungover as me.

"I see," Takeo said, smiling kindly at me. "I will make you some ginger tea, and Dwyer will make you some eggs."

"I'm making eggs now?"

"Yes," Takeo answered him dryly.

"Why am I doing this?"

"Obviously, he needs the protein."

I made a retching sound. "I can't eat any eggs."

"You can," Takeo replied cheerfully. "You'll see."

I wasn't convinced, but I did as I was directed, and the ginger tea, with some honey in it, did actually kill the nausea. He put a few drops of peppermint oil on a cool washcloth and pressed that to my forehead as he gave me a banana to eat. The fluffy eggs and plain toast—no meat, no grease—filled my stomach, and the water after that hydrated me. On my way out, Takeo gave me a fruit punch Gatorade and what I thought was a painkiller but turned out to be a B12 vitamin.

"Hydrate," Takeo ordered as he retreated into the house.

"I actually came over here to check on the yard," I told Dwyer as we stood together on the front porch.

"It's okay," he said affably. "I can promise you that he enjoyed that more than talking about the flowers."

"He's a natural caretaker, huh?"

"He is, yes. But you should go before he remembers that he wants to grill you about the new lawyer in town."

I coughed, which hurt. "Why would he think I would know anything about him?"

"Because he's the new partner of your best friend's sister," Dwyer explained slowly, likely in deference to my depleted state.

"Oh yeah." I groaned. Takeo truly enjoyed playing matchmaker, and so far in Mangrove, he had two successful marriages under his belt: one straight and one gay. "So what, he's gonna find the new guy a mate?"

He shrugged. "You never know."

"Ask him to find a guy for Coz; he needs the help more." The look I got was odd, like I was talking out of my ass or something. "What's with—"

"The officer is not on Takeo's radar at all. His latest vic—project," he corrected himself, chuckling, "is Hutch Crowley."

"I think Takeo should hook him up with Coz," I said to make conversation, because truly, the idea of my beautiful friend with the sexy grocer made my stomach flip over with anxiety and it was finally feeling a little better. The only one Coz belonged with was… me. But since that wasn't in the cards, it was useless for me to worry about it.

We were friends, brothers almost. To throw that away because I wanted him, however desperately, was the worst idea ever. He was so beautiful, tall and dark, and he haunted my dreams. Always it was us, together, in bed, and he was insistent, demanding, and I was gentle like I never was, and giving and…. but what was the point of that? In dreaming? In wanting? Because in the daylight hours, I longed to be closer to him, and if that desire turned to anger and eventually bitterness, it would become this wall between us. I feared that more than anything. It was better for me to pretend to be happy for him, to urge him to date, because if I actually saw him happy, I could be happy for him. I loved him more than myself, so I was almost certain I wouldn't come unglued at his wedding and make the scene of the century. Mostly sure.

Dwyer scoffed. "No, the grocer has no designs on *your* policeman."

"What?"

He turned to me. "Were you even listening? What did I say?"

"Yeah, I heard… but, you know he's not my—"

"Of course he is," he said dismissively. "Don't be stupid."

"I—"

"So apparently Hutch has confided in Takeo, now that they're friends," he barreled on, ignoring my protests, "that he's tired of fucking anything in a tight pair of jeans and is ready to settle down."

God, what was it with all the honesty about sex in the last twenty-four hours? "When," I began after clearing my throat, "weren't Takeo and Hutch friends?"

"When Takeo thought Hutch was interested in me."

It made sense. Anyone in their right mind would be interested in Dwyer Knolls. He was tall, golden god perfection, but how in the hell anyone would ever extricate him from his even more breathtaking partner was beyond me. "And when was that?"

"When we first came here."

"Which was right before me," I said, smiling—but I stopped because it hurt.

"Yes."

I had to know. "So Takeo is interested in the new lawyer for Hutch Crowley?"

"That's my theory, yes, but this *is* Takeo we're talking about. I could be completely misreading him. He said something about Mike Rojas the other day, too, but I wasn't listening."

"Huh."

"What?"

"No, nothing."

He studied me a moment before he smiled. "Try to stay somewhat in the shade today, and please, remember to hydrate."

I thanked him again before I headed for my ancient rolltop Jeep. I was about to start my girl up when I heard the blare of a siren behind me. Looking over my shoulder, I was surprised to find Chief of Police Farley Porter parked behind me. Waiting as he got out and walked over to me, I twisted around in my seat to face him.

"Chief."

His smile was warm as he stopped in front of me. "I need a favor."

This was new. "Name it."

"I need you to stop pissing off my officer and telling him to quit!" he barked, his demeanor changing instantly.

"Oh, for fuck's sake."

He crossed his arms. "You and I both know that this town is not as sleepy and tiny as people tend to think. I need Renaldi because he's military-trained and people respect him."

"Yeah, but—"

"And I need Hadjian because he's loyal and approachable. I need my men to complement each other, and they do now, but not if you keep screwing with my monolith."

I sighed heavily. "He can't get shot. Think of his mother."

"I can't promise he won't, but he's safer with me and Arad than he'd be anywhere else."

That was true.

"But when you say something to him, he takes it to heart like he doesn't with anyone else."

"Oh, that's such crap," I groused.

He put a hand on my shoulder. "You have no idea."

I leaned back in the seat. "I don't want him to get hurt—I can't live through him being hurt again."

Coz had been lying in the shell of an exploded humvee bleeding to death, and I'd crawled through what I figured hell looked like to reach him. I hadn't thought of the others as I did it, didn't visualize the remains of men as being friends of mine at the time. Only later, in the hospital, holding his hand, barfing and hyperventilating in rapid succession, had my mind made that connection. Only then had I realized that the blood on me was not only Coz's and mine.

"He needs to be good, do you understand me?" I rasped, my voice gravelly and low, the memories thick around me. I had visited each of the homes of my fallen friends before I returned to Coz's side in Mangrove. First, before anything, when I got back to the world, I had paid my respects to their families. Small tokens that I had from all of them— knickknacks, insignificant things, a bookmark, a keychain, whatever it was—had been joyously, graciously received.

"Kelly?"

"Do you get it?" I pressed, because it wasn't only important, it was *vital* that he understood.

"I do, son."

"Oh, don't fuckin' *son* me," I growled. "Just—make sure. Have Arad be sure. Both of you—our family doesn't work without Coz."

He nodded like he was actually hearing me.

It was hard to explain, but I felt it whenever I was around Coz and Mia and their mother. I had never met Mr. Renaldi, but Agosto had been there long enough and had loved hard enough that they all carried him with them and their hearts were bigger because of it. But if they lost Coz, if Mia and her mother faced going on without him… I wasn't sure they could.

"Or you."

"What?"

He sighed. "The family doesn't work without you either."

"No, you—"

"Coz always says how important you are to all of them, especially him. You should give yourself more credit for what you did. You saved his life in more ways than just the one," the chief insisted. "Coz never forgets to tell people that."

"Well, he shouldn't. He was the one who was—"

"He should," the chief asserted. "He says, without you he was screwed over there. You had his back the whole time, and all he had to do was look at you and he'd know everything would be all right."

"That's a crock of shit."

He shrugged. "What does it matter, as long as he believed it?"

I couldn't argue with that.

"And it's the same way now, which is why your opinion is the most important. What you think about what he does has the most weight. Do you understand?"

"I guess."

"So can you lay off my officer?"

"Maybe."

"I'll take that."

If you went in for ruggedly handsome men who, at first, you missed were hot but who, upon second and third meeting, you noticed had great veins in their forearms, crooked smiles, and hard, heavy muscle covering their bodies, then the chief was the man for you.

I'd missed really seeing him the first few times we'd met, but now the swagger, the golden red hair that always looked like he'd just rolled out of bed, and the ever-present stubble made me smile. He looked like a cowboy; the only things missing were the hat and spurs. All the rest, the jeans, the boots—wait.

"Why don't you have your uniform on?"

"'It's my day off. I'm taking my daughters fishing."

"Of course."

"You think I would stalk you while I'm working?"

"No, of course not," I said sarcastically. "So are you supposed to be driving around the Crown Vic, then?"

"I can do whatever I want. I'm the chief of police."

I rolled my eyes as he gave me a wicked shit-eating grin before heading back to his car. I caught the wave, heard the horn he blew at me, and watched him drive away.

Sitting there in the Jeep, both hands on the wheel, I wondered if anything he'd just said about Coz was true. Of course, I knew that during our time in the Army that I'd been my best friend's touchstone, but still? Now? It was easy to understand why he was the grounding force in my life—before him, there was nothing and nobody. He was the rock I clung to; he was earth beneath my feet; he was the lifeline, the shelter in the storm. I thought of Coz and he *was* home. But not once, not ever, had I thought he'd believed the same of me beyond what we'd been when it was just us.

As I drove toward Gaia's Garden, the tree nursery and greenhouse on Euclid, I realized I was putting too much store in what the chief had said. I was important when we were in a foreign country fighting a war; it was not the same at home. He'd needed me there; he didn't need me at home. He had his family now, and soon, because it would happen any day now, he'd spot the man for him. It was only a question of when.

I WAS looking for bird of paradise for a client's backyard, walking up and down the outdoor aisles, when I turned a corner and plowed into Mia. "What the hell are you doing here?"

"Don't yell at me," she snapped even though I had certainly not raised my voice. It would crack my head in half.

I couldn't help my grin, which caused her to smile back.

"I need a plant for a housewarming gift."

"Get an orchid," I told her.

"Yeah?"

"Come on," I said, taking hold of her hand.

People turned to look at us, and I got why. There I was in my work boots, jeans, untucked T-shirt with the name of my company on it: Seaton Landscaping—terrifyingly original—and Coz's worn White Sox ballcap. In contrast, Mia was clad in a tan Chanel suit and matching heels, a long strand of pearls hanging down the front, and carried a Dior handbag that she never let either Coz or I even move off a chair.

We passed the orchid aisle and walked around the side of the building to the greenhouse. Tugging her after me, I went inside and was surprised to find Olivia Lassiter there with two older couples and... of course... finally... Britton.

Reflexively, I tightened my grip on Mia.

"Oh my goodness!" Olivia greeted me loudly, gushing. "There you are!"

"Miranda?" Britton addressed her, moving quickly to reach her, passing his sister. "I thought we were meeting in an hour."

Mia's eyes narrowed as I let go of her hand. "We are," she said softly. "I came to pick you up a housewarming gift and ran into my... brother."

He turned to me then, blue eyes I remembered swallowing me as he looked and didn't recall me. Even a little.

I waited for *something*, a flicker of connection, of recognition, but none came. The man had no clue who I was.

When his eyes flicked to Mia, she introduced us. "Britton Lassiter, this is my brother Kelly Seaton."

"Different last name?" he asked her as he smiled wide and offered me his hand.

"He's adopted," she whispered, her head tilting to me almost robotically. "I—"

"Pleasure," I said, taking a step back, holding up my hands for him to see. "I'm filthy; I don't wanna get you dirty."

"It's fine," he said gently, advancing on me.

"It's not." I was adamant, stepping behind Mia, using her as a shield. Slipping past the rest of the people with him and his sister, I reached the door to another part of the greenhouse and went inside.

And again I had counted myself more memorable than I apparently was. What to me had been life-changing, he didn't even recollect.

How pathetic was I?

Pulling it together, I walked deep into the dark, wet corner and retrieved the orchid I was after. Most people didn't venture into the Rain Room where Callie Anderson kept her spiders—garden spiders, nothing poisonous—and unique flowers.

Taking a breath of the warm, humid air, I walked out to find Mia right there, waiting by the door. Everyone else was as well.

"What is—oh," she gasped, seeing the orchid in my hand. "Kel, what is this?"

"It's a ghost orchid," I told her, holding it out. "And they're rare and make a really good gift."

She nodded, mesmerized, before her gaze met Britton's. "How about you pick whatever you want from here, put it on the company tab, and I'll take this."

He chuckled. "It's a deal."

I moved by as Mia said her good-bye to everyone, and in moments we were at the exit. A younger girl in a Gaia's Garden T-shirt stood there with a walkie-talkie and I told her I was taking Casper with me.

"Bill it, Kel?"

"Yep," I called over, taking hold of Mia's elbow and steering her out. "So that was anticlimactic, huh?"

She rounded on me. "What the hell?"

"It's a ghost orchid," I explained. "That's why Callie has them listed as Casper, so if you get—shit!"

She'd pinched me hard. "I don't care about the goddamn plant; I want to know what the hell that was back there!"

I reached for the pot. "Give it back, then."

"No! I love this, it's gorgeous."

"I thought you—"

"Kelly!"

I groaned and tried to turn away from her, but she moved remarkably fast in heels and was in front of me again, barring my path.

"Explain to me what that was back there."

"I dunno! I guess maybe when I fucked him, he was either really drunk or really stoned or hopped up on God knows what and—why're you making that face?"

"I—"

I crossed my arms, staring at her, waiting.

"You—" She coughed. "—topped?"

I scowled.

"*What*? He's taller than you and—I mean, you're more muscular, and yours are from lifting things and digging up crap and his are from the gym, but still… I just thought that the taller guy tops. How am I supposed to know?"

"You're assuming because you have no idea."

"I just said that—kind of."

"You need to watch more gay porn."

"I agree," she said excitedly. "Tell me when you're ready for a marathon and I'm there."

I snorted out a laugh. "So, yeah, whatever, I always top. I can't see that ever changing."

"I would too," she teased, patting my cheek before her smile fell away. "I'm sorry he forgot you, honey. You want me to rescind my offer to him? We haven't signed any contracts yet. We're supposed to do that later today."

I put my hand over hers. "No. This actually works out better, right?"

"How does it?" she asked as I turned my head, kissed her palm, and then moved away, heading back toward my Jeep. I could return to the nursery later, when I was certain it was closed to the public so I wouldn't run into ex-lovers who didn't remember being in bed with me.

"Now there won't be any weirdness. He has no idea who the fuck I am," I called back over my shoulder.

She nodded. "You're sure you're not upset with me? I don't want you to feel like I didn't take your side or that I wasn't loyal. You mean more to me than he does—more than most people, and I never—"

"I swear, I'm good. I told you last night and I meant it," I said firmly. "And I love you back."

Her smile, much like her brother's, was blinding. "I'll see you at dinner. Oh, remember—we're going to Wrecked."

"Why?" I whined.

"Stop that! Mom wants us there to meet his son, Landon."

My lashes fluttered like I was having a seizure.

"I am not going alone and Coz already bailed because he has a date." Suddenly I had no air even though I was outside.

"He finally got up the nerve to ask Hutch Crowley out."

I had the incredible urge to go back to Blue Days and yell at Dwyer and Takeo. Neither one knew what they were talking about. Coz and Hutch were going out, so the whole Hutch-and-Britton thing was clearly off the table.

"Are you listening to me?"

"Yes," I said after a moment. "And yes, I'll be there. What time?"

"Seven thirty."

"Okay, see you then."

"Are you sure you're okay?" she shouted because of the distance. "You look weird."

"I always look weird," I yelled back before I got into my Jeep. It was too bad I'd done so much drinking the night before, because damn, I was ready to do some more.

CHAPTER FOUR

I WAS pissed. My best friend was keeping secrets from me, the guy I thought I'd been in love with ten years ago didn't even fucking remember me, and Arad Hadjian, the other policeman in town, was parked in my driveway when I got home after the rest of my hellacious day.

"Move your goddamn car!" I yelled as I stalked up my lawn, furious that he was sitting on my next door neighbor's porch sipping what looked like homemade lemonade.

"I'm not in your driveway; I'm in Mrs. Sorrel's!" he roared back after stilling the rocking chair and leaning forward to glare at me.

"This is mine," I bellowed, making the hatchet gesture with both hands so he'd know what I was talking about before turning to do the same thing to the next driveway over—on the other side of her white-fenced lawn. "That's hers. Get your car outta my way!"

"Why don't you come have some lemonade," he coaxed in an obvious attempt to soothe me.

I flipped him off, waved to Mrs. Sorrel, and then charged around the side of my small wood shingle-and-stone craftsman home to my back fence.

Before I could get it open, Arad was there, grabbing my arm and wrenching me around to face him.

"Dude, what the fuck?"

"Just move your car! Is that too much to ask?"

"No," he said, letting me go slowly.

"It's my house, not yours. I'd like to put my own car in my own driveway."

"Oh," he said, drawing the word out. "This is about Renaldi's date."

I growled, pivoted, opened and closed the fence, and jogged to the back door.

"You should talk to him instead of just being a dick to everyone!"

The idea that everyone thought I was in love with my best friend was horrifying, and I saw only one way to change that perception. I needed to get laid.

BEFORE LEAVING that evening, I smoked a bowl with my neighbors on the other side of my house, Greg and Candi Morrison. They were the nicest people who always offered to share their weed since I kept an eye on their backyard and made sure it looked good. They rented the house from her parents, and that was a stipulation of their continued residency. The inside was immaculate, and they only smoked the bong pipe outside on their back deck.

Normally I didn't take them up on their proposal, but my stomach was still iffy and I needed to take the edge off without hitting the tequila in my cupboard. So I crossed the lawn, reminded them that the officer might still be on Mrs. Sorrel's front porch, and climbed the stairs.

"The wind's goin' the other way," Greg explained as he passed me the bong shaped like an elephant. "We're good."

Candi then told me where they had picked up the pipe we were currently using. They had an extensive pipe collection from all over the world—they were both freelance journalists. She was the photo kind and he was a writer. It was nice that they loved each other and worked together, which I told them often.

Greg interrupted her story. "You want a glass of wine?"

I shook my head. "I'm supposed to be hydrating."

He brought me an orange Gatorade instead. It was good of him. Electrolytes and pot—I was sure to be in good shape after that.

Walking toward Wrecked, where I was meeting Mia, I was aware I was moving slower than usual—courtesy of the weed. As I passed by the patio of Delarosa, the Cuban restaurant that made the Champola de guanábana I liked, I saw Coz and Hutch Crowley waiting in line outside. I was going to cross the street so they wouldn't see me, but that seemed childish, and since I was stoned, and pretty darn calm, I stayed my course.

"Hey," Hutch greeted me warmly, and I was annoyed, baked or not, that he checked me out, up and down, since he was with the greatest guy on the planet. He shouldn't have been checking *anyone* out when he had a six-foot-two carved specimen of manhood standing beside him.

Coz was mouthwatering. The long-sleeved navy shirt set off his dark hair and eyes, the black dress pants clung to his muscular thighs, and he'd worn the new monk strap ankle boots we'd bought the last time we were in Miami. He had his suit jacket draped over his arm and had pinned the shirtsleeve up, and even though I knew he thought his missing left arm was the first thing people noticed, it wasn't true. Any connoisseur of beauty noticed Coz's gorgeous black eyes first, then his broad, strong shoulders, long legs, and perfect ass. My throat closed up just looking at him.

"Wow, Kel, look at you," Hutch said smoothly, reaching out to touch the collar of my pale blue dress shirt. "You clean up nice."

I could, upon occasion, and would have added a tie if I was eating with Coz at Delarosa. It was in no way a casual restaurant, and I was wondering how Hutch was going to get a pass with his denim. Coz was dressed up so I had to wonder why Hutch was slumming.

"Did you tell him where you were eating?" I asked Coz.

He grunted the no.

"That was shitty," I admonished my friend.

"Are you eating with us?" Hutch asked. "I mean, you're certainly dressed for it."

I was in my three-piece white suit—it was summer, after all—and the only thing missing on me was the tie. I even had a pocket square. I'd worn it to make a good impression on Emmett's son and to get noticed and hopefully laid later.

"You're on a date, aren't you?" I said snidely.

"Well, yes, but—"

"What kind of stupid question is that, then? Am I joining you," I retorted, trying not to snarl. "What the fuck?"

Hutch bristled; I could tell from the narrowed eyes and how quickly he crossed his arms. "What's wrong with you?" he snapped.

Coz interrupted our rapidly disintegrating conversation. "I think I know. Look at me."

Tilting my head back just a little to meet Coz's gaze—with me at five eleven, he had those four inches on me—I couldn't help grinning.

He squinted. "Are you stoned?"

"Just a little," I confirmed, unable to stop a sigh from escaping.

"Since when do you—oh, your charming neighbors."

I shrugged, shifting closer, unobtrusively inhaling his clean, masculine scent—soap and a trace of the cologne he wore, citrusy and smoky at the same time. "It's fine."

"It's really not."

"Why? I'm not driving or operating heavy machinery. I'm no threat to anyone."

"Except yourself."

The *psh* sound I made did not go over well.

"You should go home."

"Fuck that," I said dismissively. "After I charm the socks off of Emmett's kid, I'm hittin' Laredo."

"To dance?" Hutch asked brightly.

"To pick somebody up," Coz informed him.

My smile widened as I stared up at Coz, enjoying the proximity, the heat I could feel rolling off him, watching the muscles in his jaw clench and seeing the scowl darken. The man was truly just edible. Licking him all over crossed my mind.

"Mia called me, told me about what's his name," Coz continued.

"Mmmmm."

"You don't care?"

Trance broken, I shook my head and leaned back out of his personal space. "No, man, I don't care. I already knew I'm forgettable."

I turned to go, but he grabbed my upper arm, spun me around, and dragged me back to his side.

"You're not forgettable," he said, staring down into my eyes, his voice all quiet thunder. "That guy's a fuckin' idiot."

I licked my lips, I couldn't help it; the urge to taste him was almost overwhelming. The whimper from the back of my throat was unmistakable.

We stood there, frozen, and after a moment, when I could breathe again, I noticed his entire focus was on my mouth.

"Did you have a family thing tonight, Coz?"

It took him a second, but he turned from me, even though he didn't let me go, and gave Hutch his attention. "I do, and I'd be remiss not to show up. You should come with me since we're honestly not going to get into Delarosa, no matter who I work for."

"Yeah, I'm so sorry," Hutch said softly, tipping his head to one side. "When you invited me out, I never actually thought we'd be going to a place like this."

Coz let me go to face Hutch. "Why not?"

"Because I don't usually date, Coz. I meet people places and fuck."

"Yeah, me too," I chimed in.

Coz looked from Hutch, to me, and back to him. "Well, that's not me. I pick you up, take you to dinner, maybe even spring for dessert... we walk, we talk, and then I take you home. God only knows how many times we do that before we get around to the screwing."

Hutch smiled at him. "You really are a good guy."

"No," he countered. "Just better than the guys you've let near you."

"Meaning what?"

I could hear it in the tone on both sides. Coz was drawing the conclusion that Hutch had zero self-respect, and Hutch did not love being judged. I would have said something, but it wasn't my place to—

"You're both being dicks," I flared before my brain caught up with my mouth.

They looked startled by my outburst.

"You"—I waved a hand at Hutch—"think he's slurring your character, and he is, a little, but only because he can be a total self-righteous prick, and not because he actually thinks you're a whore. He respects the fact that you put yourself out there."

"I—"

"And you," I said curtly, indicating Coz, "want him to value himself more, but you can't help being a little bit of an asshole about it. But you gotta remember, not all of us have families that love us and good friends who think we walk on water. You've had one setback your whole life, and so regular human frailty you should give people a pass on."

They were both staring at me, wide-eyed.

Fuck.

I forgot. That's what pot did to me, made me arrogant and chatty. It was a lethal combination.

Spinning fast, I jogged away, down the street toward Wrecked.

"Kel!"

I broke into a run.

"Kelly Seaton, you better stop right there!"

Sprinting as fast as I could, I turned the corner, crossed the street, and careened into the front door of my target restaurant, making it to the hostess stand barely breathing hard. Between the gym and my job, I was in pretty good shape.

"Kelly," Didi Garretty said, smiling at me. "Are you meeting somebody?"

"Mia and her mom and some others," I answered, taking a quick breath and straightening my suit, pulling on the cuffs so I was pristine again.

"Oh, yes, we just put some tables together."

"For five people?" That made no sense.

"No, sweetie, for twelve people," she said, stepping out from behind the stand so I could see the cute gray pencil dress she had on. "I assume they counted you."

I hesitated because I didn't even want to go in anymore. And they didn't really need me. It wasn't like I was *actually* part of the Renaldi family.

A whistle caught my attention, one of those high-pitched noises you had to put your thumb and index finger into your mouth to make. It was completely unladylike. So, of course, it came from Mia. When I found her face in the crowd, the words "get your ass over here" were easily discernible.

Didi snorted out a laugh. "You better go, huh?"

"Shit," I muttered under my breath.

Of course, my party had joined Britton Lassiter's. Why wouldn't they? It just made perfect sense. I had the sudden urge to run home and change. I was outfitted for Laredo later, looking sleek in a suit for picking up guys. But here at Wrecked, which was basically an event hall restaurant, the kind people could rent to have parties, wedding receptions, b'nai mitzvah, and the like, I was overdressed. People were wearing sandals, for crap's sake.

When I was almost there, Mia came around the table and held out her arms. As I reached her, she lifted her head so she could whisper in my ear. "Not my idea—it was Britton's mother's. He came over to talk to me and she followed along and suddenly furniture was moving."

I grunted softly.

"Just so we're clear. I wouldn't do that to you, and we both know our mother thinks Britton's pond scum."

Our mother… that was nice.

I squeezed her tight, making her squeak on purpose, and then stepped back, smiling as she took hold of my hand and led me back to her seat and the one to the right of her.

I greeted the table with a wave. "Hey, everyone."

They all said hello back, and I was introduced to Landon Cheong, Emmett's son, who was very handsome, and his equally stunning fiancée, Blaire Adina. I met Britton's mother, Jacqueline; his father, Edward; his brother, Eric; and then Olivia came back from the bathroom and rushed over to hug me.

"This is the guy who saved me from the psycho the other day," she explained, which got me a handshake from her dad—who insisted I call him Ed—and a guy clench from Eric.

Britton thanked me from the other end of the table where he was sitting with Kennedy Vaughn, his girlfriend visiting from Ann Arbor.

They were in a long-distance relationship, but she was considering moving to Mangrove since it was, she said, perfectly quaint and charming.

"I'm just waiting for this man to ask me," she teased, more for his benefit than mine, bumping him with her shoulder.

Everyone immediately started in with the oohing and ahhhing and how cute and adorable they were together. It was too much for me.

Hearing the opening chords of a song I knew, I turned back to Mia, standing over her and hovering. When she tilted her head back to see me, I waggled my eyebrows for her.

"You're an ass."

"Just come on," I said seductively. "They're playing your song, baby."

She growled, and even the people at the next table overheard her. The laughter came quickly, everyone finding her amusing, even Kennedy, who, though focused on her boyfriend, clearly liked his new law partner.

Mia put her hand in mine, and I helped her out of her seat and walked her to the middle of the empty dance floor. I turned to her as the first verse of one of the most beloved ELO songs took off. I spun her around as she shook her head and then moved away just enough to give her room to get her groove on.

"This is my song?" she asked as I sang along to "Evil Woman."

I nodded as she threw away any semblance of decorum, and we danced like idiots, clearly dorking it up, having fun. When we got together, our collective age was fifteen.

Other people joined us from other tables, and when the song was over and "Tainted Love" came on—weirdest mix ever—we walked back to the table and flopped down into our chairs.

"I ordered a couple pitchers of margaritas," Eric announced, "and appetizers as well."

"Thank you," Mia said sweetly. "Though I'm thinking we're good with water."

Yes, water was very good. I still needed to hydrate more.

As I raised my glass, I noticed my drink napkin was folded up under my salad plate. When I opened it up, I saw writing in black ballpoint. The message was simple: Britton Lassiter wanted to speak to me outside.

CHAPTER FIVE

EXCUSING MYSELF from the table, I crossed the crowded restaurant, heading for the front door. When I was almost there, Coz stepped in, alone, suit jacket on, glancing around until he spotted me.

"It's not my fault you're no longer on a date," I groused as I got closer, intent on brushing by him. "So if you came here to yell at—Coz!"

He had grabbed my arm, stopping me, holding tight. "I need to talk to you."

"Britton asked me to meet him outside."

Releasing me abruptly, he just stood there, close, breathing my air.

"So," I said, exhaling fast. "Where's Hutch?"

His gaze lifted and met mine. "He went home."

"Why?"

"Because you scared him to death."

I was incredulous. "What the hell are you talking about?"

"Come here," he said, hand on my back, steering me out of the restaurant to the sidewalk. Once there, he turned to me so fast that I had to stop midstride or mow him over. "Why are you even out tonight? You're not fit company for anyone."

"I—"

"Excuse me?"

We both turned, and there was Britton Lassiter, looking like he'd seen a ghost. Yeah, he definitely remembered me now. It was easy to tell from his sort of shell-shocked demeanor that he wasn't sure what he was supposed to say.

"I wanted to speak to—"

"Sorry." Coz clipped the word. "But I need to speak to Mr. Seaton right now. It's official police business."

"No, it's not," I argued, trying to step around him to reach Britton.

Coz put his arm out, corralling me, keeping me behind him. "Yes, it is. I suggest you return to your table, Mr. Lassiter."

Clearly confused, eyes darting between us, Britton nonetheless beat a hasty retreat and disappeared back inside the always loud, always rambunctious establishment.

"What the hell was that?" I barked when Coz once again faced me.

"Like I said, you're in no condition to talk to anyone as messed up as you are."

"What're you talking about?" I asked even as I felt my heart start to pound with excitement. All of his attention was on me, and it was a rush and a terror at the same time.

"You were so jealous," he said gruffly, his voice deep, seductive, slithering down my spine. I forgot how to breathe.

What could I say? There was nothing that wouldn't sound stupid, that wouldn't give me away.

I tried to take a step back, to move away from him, but he took gentle hold of my face, and at the same time, his thumb stroked over my cheek. The throb of need in my gut made me jolt with his touch, and I saw the wicked curl of his lip in response.

"You're trembling."

Was he pleased? His smile, the pulse beating in the side of his neck, the way his breath hitched—all of it said he was, but we were in uncharted territory.

"You were insane with Hutch."

I knew I had been, and I knew why. I had actually tasted the jealousy. I was surprised neither he nor Hutch had remarked on the glorious shade of green I had probably turned at the time.

"And after you left, he asked me how blind I was."

I needed to get out of there, so I pulled free and turned from him, rushed down the street, and heard my name called out even as I slipped down an alley a block from the restaurant.

"Wait!" he roared.

I stopped, inhaled through my nose, and held it for a long moment as my best friend caught up to me.

"Jesus, I'm an idiot," Coz grumbled to himself.

His boots really were gorgeous; I knew that because I was staring down at them. Even though the alley was not terribly well lit, I could still see the workmanship.

"Stop running from me."

I nodded.

"I get it, why you never told me what you wanted."

How could I have?

"I mean, I'm all you've got, right? If you fucked us up, what else is there?"

Nothing.

There was *nothing* else. His mother, his sister, the town, all of it came back to him, to Coz, the man who gave me back my life.

"But you gotta remember, I wouldn't even be here, living this life, without you."

I stayed silent.

"The humvee was taking fire when you crawled in," he reminded me. "But you never tell that part."

I huffed out a breath.

"People think you pulled me out of a car with a flat or something, but you got carved up and burned getting me free and had to return fire all at the same time."

I knew the story; he didn't have to refresh my memory.

"And then they shelled it again, and no one could tell it had ever been a vehicle after that. It was just pieces of charcoal on the road."

I coughed softly.

"You saved my life, you stupid prick."

But my gift had only lasted moments. His was ongoing, it was everything.

He took a step forward, up against me, into my space, so I had to tilt my head back to look into those dark liquid eyes of his.

"No one looks at me the way you do."

"Of course not," I rasped, buzz gone, feeling vulnerable and self-conscious, a little light-headed as well as horrifyingly embarrassed, nervous, and starving. But more than all of that… I wanted… needed….

"Kel?"

I backpedaled, but not far, just a couple feet, so I could pivot and pace.

"Are you all right?"

God, what a mess, and it was all my fault. I should have told him years ago, been honest and bared my soul or simply taken him, jumped him, claimed him, made him mine.

"What did you say?"

I was muttering, having a whole conversation by myself as he watched me with… what? "Don't smile at me like I'm an idiot."

He shook his head. "You're not an idiot, you're adorable."

"I… what?"

"You're all flustered because I'm giving you my attention. Fuck. Why didn't I just do this a long time ago?"

Power and strength was rolling off him, and all I wanted to do was what I always did, and lean.

"Come here."

I shook my head. "You don't… you mean more to me than… and I…." God, what was I trying to say? "I don't wanna do anything to mess up."

"I know."

"I should go."

"Hey."

My head snapped up without me thinking about it, and I was again caught in his liquid gaze.

"Why would you think I wouldn't want you?"

"You could have anybody," I said quickly. "And I'm not…."

"You're not what?"

I gestured at him. "You're *you*."

He shook his head. "I should have known this was where your head was."

"Coz?"

"Right up your ass."

"*What* did you say?"

"You pick and choose what you want to pay attention to, it's how you are."

"I don't understand."

He snorted out a laugh. "It's like, I'm disfigured, right?"

"Oh, you are not!" I growled. "I hate it when you—"

"Shut up," he ordered sharply. "I am. I'm missing an entire arm and everyone sees that first, except you. Even my mother and sister try and help me, do more than I want them to, but not you. Never you."

I simply didn't see Coz and think he had any limitations. He was the same as he'd always been. All I saw was what I craved.

"When you look at me, you just want me."

My heart stopped.

"What makes you think I don't want you right back?"

Because… how could he?

"You don't see a man missing an arm," he said, taking a step toward me. "You just see *me*, and you wanna touch me."

He had no idea how badly I wanted that.

My whimper came out low and desperate as he closed the distance between us, then slowly traced up my arm with his hand. When he reached my chin, he tipped my head back so our gazes were again locked.

"No one really knows me but you. No one sees me but you," he whispered.

"What if you change your mind?" I couldn't be abandoned again. Once by my family, second by various friends and boyfriends—even Britton Lassiter had played his part.

"I won't."

I swallowed hard. "Why now? Why the change?"

He palmed the back of my head before he bent and kissed my nose. "'Cause you want me so bad you're gonna start sabotaging all my dates."

It was not beyond the realm of possibility.

"So maybe you just take me like you said, and then everyone else will be safe."

"Yeah, okay," I murmured, giving in, my skin tingling everywhere he touched. "But I won't, yanno, let you leave once we… once I… I couldn't."

"Good."

"Okay, so, follow me home," I said raggedly, my voice cracking. "Come get in my bed."

He caught his breath and I held mine until he spoke again. "You don't feel sorry for me, do you?"

"Why would I feel sorry for you?"

"Guys pity me. It's why they fuck me."

"It's not," I sighed, reaching for him, easing him down, closer with each passing moment. "You know me better than that."

"I do," he agreed before he kissed me.

It was gentle, tender, and I lost my mind.

I attacked him, mauled him, shoved my tongue in his mouth, sucked on his, tasted and licked, desperate to be closer, finally ending up plastered to his chest, hands in his hair, grinding against the thigh he'd wedged between mine. His body was so hard, his skin so hot, and I'd waited so long… I was ravenous for him.

"Jesus Christ," he panted, swallowing great gulps of air. "Why didn't you ever say you wanted me this bad?"

"Because you would have never believed me until now," I answered breathlessly before I recaptured his mouth, parting his lips as I kissed him again, deep and slow, taking my time as I hadn't the first go-around when I thought he'd pull away at any second.

His moan was dark and primal as he clutched at me. He shoved me backward into the exposed brick wall, his hand on my ass, gripping, squeezing, and me struggling to feel more of him. I needed to touch him more, everywhere, and after tugging his shirt out of his pants, I yanked and pulled until my hands slid over his hot, sleek skin.

When I started fiddling with his belt buckle, he wrenched free, gasping, hand braced on my chest to keep me still, keep me from reaching him.

I was devastated. "You don't want… you—Coz?"

The scowl, the one I recognized as a sign of annoyance, that I was talking too much, had jumped to the wrong conclusion, allowed my heart to start beating again. "Of course I want you. Everybody wants you."

For one night, maybe, but I was too much trouble to keep. My life was far too wrapped up with *him*. No one could compete with Cosimo Renaldi. "I'm no good for anyone but you—you spoiled me for anybody else."

"Oh yeah?" he asked, and I could hear how rough his voice was, both of us still recovering from oxygen deprivation.

"Yeah," I promised, putting my hands on his hips, my mouth dry just looking at his bruised lips and rumpled clothes, all telltale signs of being ravaged.

"So all this time, all I had to do was say the word, and you would have been mine?"

"Yes."

He raked his hand through his hair as he stared down into my eyes. "For crissakes, Kelly, why didn't you tell me?"

I tried to smile. "'Cause you weren't ready, and like I said, you would have never believed me. You lost your self-worth with your arm."

He took a breath. "I guess," he allowed.

"Do you believe me now?"

"It's not like that," he said hoarsely, and the sound, throaty and deep, was so sexy. "I don't trust other people but you—I mean, you're what I know. You're who I think of telling shit to, who I miss even when I'm busy doing something, and you're who I want to roll over on top of in the morning."

I had to concentrate to keep my heart in my chest.

"Every morning," he insisted, leaning in, kissing me like I never had been, before him, devouring, our lips melded together, his tongue rubbing over mine, him holding me close, so tight that it would leave bruises.

I loved it, succumbed to the feelings of his ownership and dominance, and still the kiss went on, the sensations, the fireworks swimming through my veins back to my heart, making the love swell even greater with hope. His words had given that to me. He wanted me to stay, and that was what "every morning" implied. When he woke up, I would be there.

"You're the only one I want to fuck me," I confessed, and even though my words weren't as eloquent as his, I saw the heat and hunger infuse his gaze.

"You've never bottomed?"

I shook my head.

"You're gonna give me a heart attack," he whispered, lowering his face to mine, smiling as I reached for him.

"I don't wanna do that. You need that to love me with."

He arched an eyebrow as though I needed him to point out how cheesy that was.

"Just—"

"Dumbass," he grumbled. "I've loved you since always."

His words sent a surge of electricity through me, and the resulting tremble was impossible to hide.

"Liked that, did you?"

I nodded like an idiot.

"Yeah, so," he said in his sultry growl, running his hand over the top of my head, fingers fluttering through my hair. "This is only a little longer than it was when we served."

"You wanna talk about my hair?"

"No, I just—I don't wanna make a mess of things."

"Messy's okay," I teased, hand stealing around the back of his neck. "It's why I have a white suit. No cum stains."

"Oh for crissakes," he groaned. "Can you be serious, please? What if—"

"There's no 'what if,' there's no 'when,' there's no 'stop.' It's just us being us, together, like we are now—quiet nights at home, just better."

He scoffed. "You are awfully confident alluva sudden."

"Shouldn't I be?" I asked pointedly. "You just told me you love me. That's my dream right there. And I know you, if you say it's one way, it is."

His eyes were so shiny as he stared at me.

"So since I trust you, and you told me everything I've ever wanted to hear... what other way would I be but ecstatic and confident?"

"You're right; you be confident. I like you like this."

I was sure I was beaming at him.

"But how could things be better than they are now?"

I laughed at him. "Well, for instance, wouldn't it be better with you buried to your balls in my ass?"

He swallowed hard. "Yeah," he finally answered before grabbing my hand, turning, and nearly jerking me off my feet. "That would be. Come on."

It was a big fat turn-on watching the man I loved hunger for me and want me back. I would follow him anywhere he wanted.

A couple of minutes later, as we walked toward the town square, I glanced over at the ancient mangrove tree that the small coastal community was named for. There were, of course, many of those trees around, but that one was special. I had never seen one before I arrived and had been impressed when Coz first pointed it out.

During the holidays, the tree was covered in lights; it was decorated on other holidays, too, like Halloween, with pumpkins placed between the branches. It sat smack dab in the center of town and everyone who was new—

"Oh shit," I gasped, stopping.

He turned to me, and it was nice that when he did, he didn't let go of my hand. "Oh shit, what?"

"Your mother."

He smiled warmly. "You're carrying my jacket."

"Yeah, and? How are you supposed to hold my hand if I don't? There are better things for you to do with that hand than to carry shit."

He snorted out a laugh. "You're the only one I know who doesn't give a crap how I would take that."

"Because there's only one way to take it. I want you to touch me."

"Which I wanna do right now, which is why I already called my mother when I was chasing you down the street and told her that neither one of us would be back and that I was going home with you."

"You did?"

"I did."

I was absolutely charmed by that. He'd told his mother, simply confessed that which had ended everything with my biological family. "What—" I coughed. "—did she say?"

"She said it was about fuckin' time."

I was stunned. "Your mother swore?"

"No, my mother didn't swear!" he yelled. "It was hyperbole to prove a point!"

"What point?" I asked calmly.

"That apparently everyone but you and I knew about this and thought it was a good fuckin' idea."

"Yeah? Everyone? Like for certain your mother?" Because she was the most important, after him. "You're positive she liked the idea of us?" How amazingly wonderful would that be?

"Yeah."

"You're sure? She was happy?"

"She is."

"Mia's gonna be pissed we didn't tell her."

"We didn't know," he murmured, lifting my hand to kiss my knuckles.

"I knew."

"Next time, share. Actually, no, there isn't going to be a next time. Once I'm in your bed, you're not getting out."

I stopped walking so he'd have to as well. "That's it, huh? You're just moving in?"

"I have a crappy little apartment that I hate—would living with me be so bad?"

"Of course not, but come on… you don't even know if this is gonna work."

He squeezed my hand tight while at the same time I put my other one on his cheek, caressing him.

"This has already been working. It's been five—almost six—years already. This is happening. Do you understand?"

"Yeah," I conceded as he pulled me close. "I do."

I kissed him breathless, and when he had to pry me off so he could breathe, it clicked in my brain that he needed to get me off the street before I begged him to take me right there.

"Nobody's ever wanted me like this," he said when we started walking again.

"Of course not," I agreed. "I'm the only one for you."

"You don't—" I heard the hesitation infuse his voice. He was a worrier, my man, and of course we were to that part of the program. "—I mean, you don't think we're changing things too fast, do you?"

"I dunno?" I replied instead of answering.

He was clearly deep in thought, not even paying attention to where we were going as I steered us down a side street that would lead to my house. I needed to shock the worry away and get back the guy who wanted to do sexy, dirty things to me.

"Maybe we are moving too fast," I mused, dropping his hand, putting space between us. "We should date instead; go slow like you were telling Hutch," I finished cheerfully.

"Fuck," he groaned, retaking my hand, lacing our fingers together. "Really?"

I shrugged, smiling at him.

"We both know we've been dating since you moved here. We just didn't recognize it."

"Yes, dear," I agreed.

"We belong together."

Just as long as we were clear.

CHAPTER SIX

I TOLD him filthy things on the way home: things I'd done, chances I'd taken, how wild and promiscuous my past was. I knew why, of course. Because I wanted him to think that sex was no problem for me, that I was experienced and kinky and could rock his world.

By the time we got to my front door, he was laughing.

"What's so funny?" I snapped, shaking as I tried to open it.

"You manwhore," he said, cackling. "Are you done telling me how deviant you are, or should I hear about the time you fucked the varsity football team in high school?"

It wasn't funny. I was a textbook case of once the family was gone—meaning home and security—I'd tried first to drown myself in sex, since that's what I'd given the parents and sisters up for, and second looked for a knight in shining armor in every loser I crossed paths with.

It was a damn inconvenient time to have an epiphany. "Oh shit," I groaned as Coz took the keys from me, opened the door, and shoved me through.

Locking the door behind him, Coz hung my keys up on the hook right beside it before flipping on the lamp. I was surprised by his expression when he rounded on me.

"You just figure out that Britton's been playing the part of a villain all these years for no good reason?"

I could only stare at him.

He took his jacket from me and laid it across the back of the couch before reaching for my face.

I leaned into his hand, closing my eyes with the swell of emotions coursing through me.

Easing me close, he tucked me against his chest, stroking my hair as we stood there and breathed.

"You've told me that story about Britton and how you realized years later that no one rides in and saves you from your life," he crooned, tipping my head back so he could see my face. "But did it ever occur to you when it was happening that you heard words or intentions that were never actually there?"

"Not until just right now," I admitted.

"I think the reason Britton never showed that day was because what you heard and what he said were not the same thing."

I had wanted to be white-horsed so badly that I'd created the whole scenario in my head.

"Not that he didn't wanna get in your pants, and I have no doubt that he told you what you wanted to hear," he assured me. "But now you'd know it was bullshit when it came out of the man's mouth."

Yes.

"But back then, you took it as gospel."

Dear God, I had. "How could I have been so stupid?"

His laugh was deep and resonant and I liked the sound. "You were just a baby. You were only eighteen—what the hell did you know about anything?"

"Fuck."

He gave me a smile that said I was dumb and dear at the exact same time.

"Man, Britton Lassiter must think I'm a psycho," I muttered, pulling away from him to walk around the couch and flop down on it. "Not to mention you."

He chuckled as he followed, and I watched as he took a seat beside me, loosened his boots, one after the other so he could toe them off, and then finally stretched out on the other end of my couch, pushing at me with his socked feet until I had to stand up.

"What're you doing?" I asked, my mouth dry, looking at him rumpled and comfortable sprawled below me.

"Take off the jacket and the vest and the shirt," he ordered gently.

I followed directions quickly, and he watched intently until I was naked from the waist up, shoes also off, hovering over him

"Now lie down here," he finished, patting his chest so I'd know where he wanted me.

I crawled over him and he didn't move, letting me settle, drape my body over his, press him down under me. My head over his heart, I heard how fast it was beating, like a drum, even though his voice flowed like syrup on a warm day.

"So I need you to forgive Britton, since he was actually innocent of being a dreambreaker," he mused, nuzzling his face against my hair, lifting his knee, wedging his thigh between mine as he grabbed a handful of my ass to bring me even tighter against him. "Douche bag, yes. But he was not Prince Charming in the flesh."

"Why're you caring about Britton?"

"Because I don't want anything or anyone between us," he explained as he tilted my head up so I could see him. "I want to be the only one in your head and in your heart and… just… you know."

"In me?" I teased.

His glower was hot. "I'm trying to have a fuckin' moment here and—"

"Shut up," I said affectionately, smiling as I stared at him, memorizing every line on his face, the clench of his sharp, square jaw and the mostly blown pupils. "I may have been mulling over the past, but I've been securely standing here, in the present with you, for a very long fuckin' time."

"What does that mean?" he asked, jolting under me as I sat up, dragging my ass over his groin before I straddled his hips.

"That means there's only been room for you for years."

"Yeah?"

"I promise," I said as I leaned over and kissed him, feeling lighter, freer, and more than anything, full of voracious, consuming need.

More than anyone else, I wanted Cosimo Renaldi. Britton amounted to a childhood crush in comparison. To have Coz under me, wanting me, already my best friend and poised now to become my lover, nearly overloaded me with happiness. It had to be what winning the lottery was like, except it was a win for my whole life, every part.

I kissed him hard and deep, wanting all of him, feasting, claiming, and biting when he tried to pull away even for a heartbeat.

"Fuck, I knew you'd taste good," he gasped, rolling me to my back, powering me down, letting me feel the strength in his long, muscular body before he took control and delivered one ravaging, drowning kiss after another.

I lost time because the end of wanting, of yearning, was buried down so far that excavating it, dredging it from the well of my heart made everything else fade to nothing. There was only his hot, hungry mouth and his hand tugging at my belt, working open the fastener on my suit pants and sliding down the zipper. When he slipped his hard, callused hand under the elastic of my briefs and wrapped his long fingers around my length, I bucked into his grip, wanting more.

"God, you're gorgeous," he husked, stroking me as he kissed up my throat to my jaw and up behind my ear. "Your gold skin and your big beautiful eyes that I hate to say are green 'cause that's not enough when I tell people, and your mouth and your perfect round ass."

Oh dear God, he thought I was pretty?

"I can't stand how everyone stares at you and wants to touch you because I want that to be just me. I wanna be the only one."

"Yes," I whined in the back of my throat. "Just you."

"Where's your lube?" he whispered into my ear.

I muttered the answer about the nightstand, and he unceremoniously dumped me on my side as he rolled off the couch.

"You—"

"Get up," he rumbled, grabbing hold of my hand and pulling me to my feet.

He dragged me behind him to my bedroom and shoved me down onto the mattress, my feet on the floor, as he went to the nightstand.

"What do you want me to—Coz!"

I wanted to know what he liked, if he wanted me to blow him first or if he just wanted to fuck me, but he'd grabbed the lube and returned faster than I was expecting. He dropped to his knees, shucked my unfastened pants enough to let my cock bob free, and then took my hard, leaking shaft down the back of his throat.

The movement was seamless, fluid, and the suction brought a hoarse cry from my chest, his name torn out of me.

"Fuck," I yelled, writhing under him, hearing the cap of the tube snap open and shivering with anticipation.

"We can wait," he said, his voice deep and ragged after he let my cock slip free of his mouth. "I can make you come just like this or you can fuck me. I don't care. I just wanna touch you."

In answer, I rolled to my stomach and arched my back, showing him what I wanted, needed to have.

His hand trailed down my back before his lips followed, all the way to my ass. He pushed my face down onto the bed before his fingers were at my entrance, spreading me for his tongue.

"Oh fuck," I moaned loudly, my voice decadent, filled with longing. No one had ever taken such time with me. I'd never been rimmed in my life, never experienced the soft, wet muscle sliding into my hole, swirling, pressing, the languorous licking that made me want more.

He sucked and laved and ordered me to grab my dick and pull. My words were gone, only sounds remained. When he replaced his tongue with first one lubed finger and then a second one, I began babbling, pleading, needing him before I came, the edge of my vision going white with the throb of my imminent orgasm.

I felt him at my entrance a moment before he pressed inside. The wide head stretching me caused a twinge of pain that quickly became an engulfing burn that sucked and leeched the pleasure from my body, leaving me trembling as I struggled to accept his girth, huge enough that it could rip me apart if we weren't careful.

"Wait." He gentled me as his slick hand wrapped around my cock, squeezing tight, sliding from balls to head, over and over as he kissed my shoulder and up the side of my neck.

The roll of arousal became a thrumming in my chest, spreading warmth through my body, making me shiver in his embrace, my balls drawing up tight as he pulled out an inch or so before thrusting back inside.

A second retreat, and he slid deeper into me on the return, the angle dragging him over my prostate, and I actually saw stars.

"Do it again!" I demanded, pushing back, wanting him *in*, not out, desire driving my body and nothing else.

He eased back and drove forward, hard, fast, and I gasped with how full I was, how stretched, how used.

"Please," I begged.

"I want to be in you, all the time, forever—do you understand?"

I did. "I do."

"There's only ever been me," he reminded, "and that's how it'll stay."

"Yes," I heaved out the words. "I swear."

"Do you want me?"

"Oh God, yes."

His rhythm faltered then, the pounding I was taking got wild and erratic as he hammered into me, over and over, and I became only about my aching, desperate newfound joy.

"Coz!" I thundered his name in the small room, and he bit my shoulder, laughing, the sound rushing through me as my muscles clamped down on him and I came onto the comforter, engulfed in a splintering orgasm.

He bucked into me, burying himself to the balls, his entire front plastered to my back as he pumped hot into me, grunting as he gave me his weight.

I lay there under him, pinned to the bed, semen seeping from my ass, sticky with sweat, and prayed he'd never ask me to move.

"Are you all right?"

Quick nod to his question.

"Did I hurt you?"

"No," I answered, my throat raw from yelling.

"Would you ever want to do it again?"

"Oh fuck yeah."

His exhale was sharp. "Thank God, because I'm gonna be honest and say that you have the hottest, tightest ass I've ever been in, and I think I wanna live there."

Pride filled me, which was ridiculous. He was complimenting a body part.

"But it could also be," he said, turning my head so he could kiss me, "that you trusted me to be inside you, and I want that more than anything."

"I trust you," I told him. "And I want to suck your dick and be inside of you and kiss you… please… for the rest of my life. Stay with me, Coz, live with me, belong to me."

He slid gently from my ass before rolling me to my side so we were face-to-face.

"Will you stay?" I said shyly, hopefully.

"You're so beautiful," he whispered. "You could have anybody you wanted."

"I want *you*, Coz," I entreated, wriggling closer, smoothing my thumb over one of his thick, dark eyebrows. "Only you. Please say yes."

"Well, yeah, I'm gonna say yes, 'cause I want you so bad," he conceded, leaning close, sealing his lips over mine.

There was a promise in that kiss, and because I'd never had one like that before, I felt the difference, and when he eased back, I gave him one of my own.

"I love you, Kel," he murmured between kisses.

I'd loved him for so long, it was natural to say so. "I love you too, more than you know."

"No, baby, I know. I swear I know."

And I got the feeling he actually did.

CHAPTER SEVEN

I FELT heat on my face and slowly opened my eyes. Rolling my head sideways, I released an involuntary sigh upon finding Coz there beside me, eyes closed, long lashes resting on his cheeks, chiseled lips parted, still kiss-swollen from the night before. Lifting myself on my elbows, I admired his toned, cut frame, the contrast between my white sheets and his bronze skin, and the dark hair on my pillow. I wanted him badly, and it was my first thought even as I squinted at the morning sun streaming into my bedroom. I had not remembered to draw the curtains, which were now lifting and billowing like sails in the breeze. As I focused my vision, I realized I was not the only one admiring the prone man in my bed; my neighbors were also quite interested. Mrs. Sorrel was on her back porch with a pair of binoculars, probably checking out my boyfriend's gorgeous naked backside. I immediately covered him up with the sheet, and I was certain I heard her swear.

Sitting all the way up and looking to the window on the other side of the room, I saw Greg and Candi out on their deck with cups of coffee. God, I really needed to plant a hedge.

"Nice goin', bagging the police officer!" Greg called over.

I groaned and fell back down beside Coz.

"What're you doing?" he grumbled, because I'd jostled him.

It was an excellent question: what precisely was I doing? Did I have any idea what was going on with me and Cosimo Renaldi?

"Are you breathing, baby?"

What if we didn't work out? What if he figured out that I was messed up, more so than he already knew about? I could make a million mistakes to drive him away from me and—

"Stop," he yawned before I caught an elbow in the ribs. "I can hear your brain working."

I was going to start hyperventilating, and he thought it was time for jokes?

"We're good," he said with a sleepy smile.

"How do you know?" I asked, getting worked up and scared, having tiny heart palpitations just looking at him.

God…. Coz in my bed….

"What?" he grunted.

His eyes were soft and warm as he stared at me, the stubble on his cheeks was sexy, his tousled hair, languid sprawl—all of him just breathtaking.

"I have dragon breath or something? What's wrong with you?"

"You're in my bed," I marveled.

"Yeah? So?"

"So?" I repeated. "It's a really big deal, Coz."

"It's just the first of always," he assured me. "After more days and nights, they'll all start blending together."

"I just—I don't wanna do anything to—"

"Knock it off," he ordered, shoving me over onto my stomach and pinning me under him. "Have a little faith in me."

"In you? Are you kidding? I have all the faith in the world in you."

"Well, see, there ya go." His voice became a seductive chuckle. "I feel the same about you."

I looked over my shoulder at him. "You do?"

"Yes, baby," he said, sliding off me, only his hand remaining to cup my ass.

"Close the curtains, will you?"

"Why would I wanna do that?"

"So you can have me again before breakfast," I said, arching an eyebrow for his benefit. "Unless, of course, you want everyone to see."

He rolled quickly out of bed, much to the disappointment of Mrs. Sorrel, who didn't get her binoculars back up in time, and to Greg and Candi's glee—they had a few extra seconds for an eyeful before he had us cut off from the outside world.

AFTER I showered, I made coffee and had started breakfast when I heard a knock on the front door. I answered in sleep shorts with a dishtowel over my shoulder and a mug of French roast in my hand because I figured it was one of my neighbors come to leer at my very hot new boyfriend/old best friend.

"Good morning."

I was stunned to find Britton Lassiter on my porch.

"May I speak to you, please?"

Opening the door wide, I stepped sideways so he'd have room to come in.

"Thank you," he said when I closed the door behind him.

It took me a second to remember my manners. "Oh, would you like some coffee?"

"No," he said quickly, glancing around. "What a beautiful home you have—the very definition of a seaside cottage."

He sounded stilted to me, overly rehearsed. "Thanks."

"I wish my place caught this much breeze."

I nodded because all the pleasantries were going to kill me. "So listen, about last night, I'm so sorry that Coz and I were figuring things out when you were trying to—"

"Oh, no, it should be me apologizing," he rushed out, moving closer. "I didn't... remember you at first, and that must have made you feel like crap."

I shrugged.

"No, I—I'm really so sorry. We had a wonderful couple of days, and I even offered you a ride to Boston, and I didn't follow through."

A ride.

He'd thought he was giving me a lift; I'd understood that he wanted me in Boston to be with him. It was exactly what Coz had said: I'd heard what I wanted to, and when I didn't get it, I turned Britton into the guy who used me.

"I'm so sorry."

"No," I soothed. "I'm the one who should be sorry."

He looked confused, brows furrowed, scrutinizing me. "For what? You were nothing but good to me."

What could I say? *I feel like an ass for thinking you were a bastard all these years?*

"You taught me so much about myself over that weekend. You showed me what I could have if I found the right guy."

And that person was never going to be me. I had never blipped on his radar as husband material, but whereas before now that would have made me sad, now I just felt bad for him and that he was still looking for his Prince Charming.

"You know, even after I slept with you and figured out what the big deal was about sex, I still decided to hide who I was for close to a decade before my life finally imploded."

I had no idea what the protocol was for hearing confessions.

"I came clean with Kennedy last night," he explained to me. "She was decidedly—"

"Who?"

"My girlfriend," he reminded me. "You met her at the restaurant."

"Oh, sorry, yes."

"I told her everything, and she was so angry, but as pissed off as she got, I was madder at myself," he sighed. "I mean, I'm gay and I'm still hiding it from my parents, my colleagues, and everyone back in my old life but my sister," he rambled, his gaze settling on me, waiting.

"Keeping secrets is hard" was all I could think of to say.

"It is, but now that I've moved here, I feel like I can have a second chance at a new life," he finished, raising his head, smiling at me. "Do you think that maybe I can count you among my friends here?"

I had no idea what I was supposed to say.

"Or will it be too weird for you?"

And then suddenly I did know. Extending my hand, I smiled at him. "No, I think I can do that."

The relief washing over his face made me realize that even though I wasn't important to him in the way I'd thought I should be, in a romantic vein, I still had a part to play in Britton's life, as a friend.

Coz came out into the living room as I was closing the door behind my new friend.

"Who'd I miss?"

"Britton."

He stopped moving. "I'm sorry, what?"

"You heard me," I called over to him as I walked back to the kitchen. I was surprised that he followed me so quickly, and even more so when he gently turned me around to face him. "Yes?"

"Listen," he began, and I heard the wariness and fear in his tone, neither of which had ever been present before. "I don't want that guy around here."

"No," I agreed, reaching up and wrapping my arms around his neck. "The only one who'll be around here, in this house, sleeping in my bed, will be *you*, Officer."

His smile told me how pleased he was.

"We'll have lots of days like this and long, quiet nights."

"At home," he clarified before he wrapped his arm around my back and bent and kissed me. "Just you and me."

It was all I'd been waiting to hear.

SULTRY SUNSET

Mary Calmes

MANGROVE
Stories

CHAPTER ONE

IT WAS always beautiful in Mangrove. Even on gray, overcast days when it rained cats and dogs, even when the wind whipped through the trees and you could hear chimes ringing up and down the street, and even when nothing moved or stirred and it was simply a hot, sticky, humid mess, no one could look around and say the view wasn't stunning. Having grown up in International Falls, Minnesota—before I moved to Boston for school and then to Buffalo to work—I appreciated the entirety of Florida but loved the sleepy little coastal town I called home. The days were warm, the nights were filled with stars, and I made sure to make time to watch the sun go down. Being outside should have made anyone happy, so hearing crying when I walked out my back door caught my attention.

Peeking over the side of the fence that separated my backyard from my new neighbors', I checked to see who was doing all the bawling, and it was then that I saw the girl. She was sitting on her back steps, face in her hands, with sobs absolutely racking her slight body.

I didn't want to be nosy, but when I turned away, she did the staccato breathing thing and began all over again. There had to be more from me than walking away. One did not leave a weeping, obviously needy angel.

"Hey," I called over to her.

Her head snapped up and she almost choked on how much water she was producing.

"Are you all right?"

"Oh, I'm sorry," she said, her voice thick with tears. "I didn't mean to bother you."

She was adorable. Huge brown eyes, cute little button nose, dimples, and even though I couldn't see it at the moment, I knew when she smiled that her face would light up rooms.

"Honey, you're not bothering me," I soothed. "I just wanted to make sure you were all right, is all."

She nodded quickly.

I smiled. "Anything I can do?"

Quick shake of her head.

"No?"

"No, but thank you," she said, which was nice.

"Are you sure?"

She bit her bottom lip.

"Could I try, maybe?"

She thought about it for a moment.

"You can tell me whatever it is, I promise."

She took a deep, shaky breath, deciding all at once. "Okay, so… my dad's in Miami closing up his office all this week; my cousin Debbie who was supposed to be watching me until he got here just left because she got a part in a TV pilot in Los Angeles; my aunt Genevieve who Debbie thinks was on her way here to take her place is actually in London on business; my mother died six months ago; and I think I just started my period."

Oh dear God.

She hiccupped.

I would not show any outward sign of concern, which would be no help at all, and now was not the time for sympathy. Crisis mode was needed. "Okay."

"So—" She started crying again. "I don't know what to do and I can't even get in the stupid house 'cause Debbie closed the door on accident but she was in such a hurry to leave that she forgot to give me the key and… I have no money and"—she sobbed—"I have no idea what I'm supposed to do about the blood!"

But I, youngest of four with only sisters, that part I knew all about. After hopping the low fence easily, I started across her overgrown backyard with Benny, my black Labrador, trailing after me.

Upon seeing the dog, she instantly caught her breath.

"Oh," I said, stopping, and Benny froze with me. "Do you not like dogs?"

She sniffled and shook her head, wiping at her leaking eyes. "No, I love them. My dog, Rounder, he died last year."

Jesus Christ on a cracker. Poor kid was getting screwed coming and going.

I reached her, held out my hand, and she instantly took hold. "My name's Hutch Crowley."

"I'm Ivy Dodd."

"Nice to meet you, Ivy Dodd," I said, smiling at her.

She tried to smile for me, calming just a little.

"So I live right there, as you probably guessed," I said, pointing to my back porch, which she could easily see. "And did you notice that you have a dog door?"

It was an odd change of topic, so she visibly had to process for a moment, but once she did, she whipped her head around and stood up so she could see the back door of the Craftsman bungalow.

Most of the homes in Mangrove were the same except for a few Victorians, summer cottage styles; some Tidewater designed ones; and one or two like mine that were Spanish colonials. So whereas Ivy's home was a single story, mine was two.

"Oh yeah, I saw that when we moved in. My dad said we could get a dog first thing as soon as he got back."

I waited for her to get it.

"What?"

"It's a big-ass dog door, right?"

She nodded.

"Mrs. Colby, who used to live there, had a Saint Bernard."

She still wasn't following me.

"His name was Chowder and I never really got that. Mike said it was because the dog was always eating, but that seems rude."

Apparently she was no longer listening. She reached out for my dog, and Benny—a slave to any and all kinds of affection—bolted forward, up into her arms so she could pet him and hug him and he could shove his wet nose into her eye socket, under her chin, and into her ear. The giggling was instantaneous and made me smile.

"So?" I prodded as she leaned her head on my dog and just stood there, savoring the contact.

"Yeah?"

"Do you wanna maybe use the doggy door?"

She still wasn't getting it and probably because she'd never had to crawl into a house by way of one of them, drunk, at 3:00 a.m. I did not have that luxury.

I arched an eyebrow for her. I knew I did it well because my brows had a natural tilt to them to begin with, which I always got lots of comments about. People just assumed I was a smartass.

"Benny," I addressed my pet.

He stopped mauling my new friend and looked up at me.

"Go inside."

After slipping around the girl, he bounded up the stairs and entered the house through the dog door. I did a slow pan to her.

"Oh." She drawled out the word. "Duh, I see."

"Okay," I said as Benny came loping back since neither of us was in the house and he bored easily. "This is what you're gonna do. You're gonna go inside, wash your face, change your clothes, grab some paper towels, and make a pad out of them."

She was listening intently, which was kind of cute.

"Then you shove that in your underwear, come back out here, and I'll walk you to my store and we'll get you what you need, all right?"

Her brows furrowed.

"Now, if you want, I'll call the police, and one of the two deputies will come over and either follow us in their car or walk with us. I don't want you to be scared, but again, I am your neighbor and my dog just slobbered all over you."

"Yeah, he did."

"And I'm saying we'll go for a walk; I didn't invite you over."

She nodded.

"I don't want you in my house anyway."

"Why not?" She sounded a bit offended.

"'Cause it's a mess right now," I said honestly. "My cleaning lady only comes Monday and Thursday."

She seemed surprised. "You're a grown man—you can't clean your house by yourself?"

"I could," I assured her. "I just don't want to."

"That's a little bit lazy, isn't it?"

"Why don't you mind your own business?"

"You didn't mind yours."

She had a point.

"Okay, so, what, are you coming or not?"

"Yeah, okay," she agreed, getting up.

"Don't do me any favors," I groused.

"Aww, c'mon. I didn't mean it."

I grunted. "So do you want Benny to go with you back in the house?"

She gave me a real smile. "How come you named him Benny? That's not a dog's name."

"People always say that kind of stuff to me. Like pets are supposed to have names like Fluffy and Spot and crap like that. But tell me Benny doesn't look like a Benny."

She scrutinized my dog, and he tipped his head sideways because she stared so long without doing anything else. When she laughed, he barked and I felt my chest untighten.

"Yeah, he looks like a Benny."

"Told you."

They crawled through the doggy door one after the other, and once they were inside, I heard her scolding him. First there was "Ohmygod, Benny, don't eat that!" followed quickly by a command for him to get off her bed, and "Put that pillow down!" They were going to be friends, I could tell already.

I waited, and fifteen minutes later she came back outside in jean capris, a Lionel Messi T-shirt, and white Keds.

"I like him too," I mentioned, gesturing at her shirt as she met me on the stairs.

"Yeah? You watch soccer?"

"I watched the World Cup," I told her. "My best friend, Mike, is really into it, and he made me sit there with him day after day and explained the rules."

"It's different when you get it, huh?"

"Yeah, it really is," I agreed. "So I find myself turning it on all the time now. Is he your favorite? Messi?"

She nodded. "Yeah. Most of my friends are all about Ronaldo, but I like Messi better."

"Do you play?"

"I used to, back in Detroit, but I couldn't get on the team at my new school in Miami and now that we had to move again—I mean, does Mangrove even have a girls' soccer team?"

"Of course," I told her. "What kind of backwater burg do you think this is?"

She gasped. "That was so patronizing."

"Oooh, big word."

And she laughed.

It was a good sound.

I WALKED her the fast way to my store, the Green Grocer, and gave her a quick rundown, promising to take her back by Cuppa Joe for an iced latte after we picked up her supplies.

"Mike always just has coffee in there. Don't you think that's weird? Like the people who stand in line at Starbucks just to have regular coffee?"

"You're such a snob."

"What?"

"And who's Mike? You talk about him a lot."

I did not. "I do not."

"You said you guys watched the World Cup together."

"So what?"

"And you smiled when you were talking about him."

"Hardly."

"No, not hardly," she corrected, "like really. You smiled."

"Yeah, so what? Talking about your best friend, thinking of them, should make you happy. Don't you get that way when you talk about yours?"

She thought about it for a moment. "Yeah, okay, I guess that's sound logic."

"Well, I'm so glad my thinking meets with your approval."

"Kinda sarcastic, aren'tcha?"

I ignored the question.

"And for the record, I'm a girl, and I don't talk about my best friend as much as you talk about yours. Just so we're clear."

"I'm liking you less and less," I assured her, but the sound of her scoffing made me chuckle.

"Doesn't matter, you're stuck with me now."

The confidence was good.

I showed her Wick and Wand, the store where she could get special teas, tarot cards, and spells and amulets.

"I think I might need to cleanse the house of Debbie," she told me.

"We'll pick up some sage to burn," I promised.

She was excited over that idea, as evidenced by the way she took hold of my hand and squeezed it. I was surprised when she didn't let go.

"So what does your dad do?" I asked, to make conversation.

"My father's a fireman," she explained. "Your chief retired and my dad is taking over."

I squinted at her. "Your father was a fireman in Detroit?"

"He was a lieutenant and he had his own firehouse."

I nodded.

"I know what you're thinking."

I chuckled. "Do you?"

"You're thinking, 'What is her big-time father doing in this tiny town?'"

"Pretty much."

She sighed deeply. "My parents were divorced for three years before my mom died, but when she got sick, he moved back in with us to help take care of her."

"That's really nice," I murmured. "They must have been very good friends."

"They were. Even after she told him he was gay, they were all right."

I stumbled, and she turned to look at me, though she didn't let go of my hand.

"You okay?"

"Yeah, fine, good."

She nodded before continuing. "Dad had a really nice boyfriend for a while, his name was Seth. But he didn't like that Dad wouldn't tell people they were together, and then when Dad moved back in with us, he left."

Her father would kill her if he knew she was sharing his life story with me.

"I felt bad because I could tell my dad really liked him, but I mean, if he loved him, he would have told people about him, right?"

I cleared my throat. "I can't speak for your father, sweetie."

Her face lifted. "What should I do?"

"About what?"

"Everything," she whimpered. "Did you even listen to what I told you before?"

"Well, yeah," I said, making sure I was condescending, for her benefit. "Dad's stuck, cousin's MIA, aunt is late, Mom's dead, and you just got welcomed to womanhood. I was listening. I always listen."

She stopped walking and just stood there staring at me for a long moment.

"Should we maybe get to my store so we can take care of at least one of your issues?" I asked as I started walking away.

"Yeah," she agreed, moving quickly to remain at my side, slipping her hand in mine again. I would guess that normally, being as she was a teenager, hand-holding with an adult was not her deal, but at the moment, she needed comfort.

As we turned onto Sunset, she let out a snort of laughter.

"Yes?"

"What kind of name is Sunset for a street?"

"I think it's pretty good. Ever hear of the Sunset Strip?"

"Well, yeah, of course, but this ain't that," she said snidely.

"How do you know? It could be just as exciting."

She scoffed. "Yeah, right."

"You're awfully cynical for, what, thirteen?"

"Fourteen," she corrected. "And wouldn't you be?"

"Yeah, okay," I admitted. "Now come on, let's get in there."

"So which store... is... holy cow!"

She, like most people, figured that a town like Mangrove, with a year-round population of only 11,200 people, was too small to have the supermarket I'd made. "You thought what? That I was taking you to a farmer's market or something?"

"Well, yeah," she said, clearly in awe as the automatic doors whooshed open and we entered a tropical rainforest. She did a slow turn and then walked forward, deeper into the floral department, where one of my employees greeted her and welcomed her to the Green Grocer.

"Thank you," she murmured, clearly amazed.

After the walk in from the parking lot, the floral department at the front of the store offered cool air for your skin and a treat for your nose. All the flowers smelled fantastic. When I'd redesigned the space after I bought it, it was one of the first things I'd changed.

As we moved through the produce section, she took off her oversized bedazzled sunglasses and put them on top of her head. I loved the scalp-trimmed black hair; it looked great on her, made her resemble a pixie. "This place is amazing, Hutch," she sighed. "You've got a soup bar and a hot bar and sandwich depot—how cute is that—and ohmygod, cheese!"

We passed by the olive bar/olive oil station, the fresh-made hummus in every flavor you could want, the meat section with the fresh catch of the day, and the salad bar that was simply ridiculous. It ran the length of an entire aisle.

"I'm a vegan," she squealed happily. "This is fantastic."

I chuckled as I pointed out the bakery.

"That whole thing is the bakery?"

It was.

"Is that cherry?" Her voice wobbled as she looked in the case. "My mom made cherry."

I tugged on her hand to get her moving, not wanting any more tears.

"Is it okay if Benny is in here?"

"Benny's my dog," I explained. "I allow Benny and service animals. It says so on the sign outside."

"It does not say Benny." She laughed.

"Oh yes it does. I'll show you when we leave."

She beamed at me. "That's awesome."

I pointed to the health and beauty aids. "Now you go get what you need, the bathroom's in the back, and—"

"How do I know what to get?"

She asked me like I should have known, and by all rights, I shouldn't have, but I did because I had sisters. All three of them were older, and I'd spent my entire childhood with them in every nook and cranny of my life, prying and oversharing, dragging me places, dressing me, smothering me with love and devotion. That had made coming out a nonevent in my house, and yes, I knew about times of the month. My sisters had informed my life. They explained the birds and the bees and sat with me, all three of them, when I told my parents I was gay. And they hugged my parents, just as hard as I did, when Mom and Dad said, yes, fine, whatever, gay was great, as long as I was happy, and did I know about protection? God. Of course I knew—I had *sisters*.

"Hutch?"

"Sorry," I said softly, feeling suddenly sentimental. "I need to call my family."

"Right now?"

"No, not right now."

"So, then, will you come with me?" she asked in a small voice.

"Of course."

We went down an aisle I was truthfully never on, and I grabbed what I thought was best. She had questions and I answered, and then I sent her off to the bathroom while I waited at one of the tables in the café. Benny sat politely beside me, tail thwapping the floor, happy to see everyone walking by.

My employees started wandering over one by one, and I greeted them, smiled, laughed, and finally my assistant manager, Mike Rojas, came swaggering up and flopped down in front of me, giving me the blinding grin he'd just started showing off lately.

When I first hired him a year ago, he was quiet, reserved, and sullen. He'd lost his wife in a car accident two years before while he was out of town on business. He never got to say good-bye. It haunted him, and he left his job as a day trader in San Francisco, sold his home in Pacific Heights, packed up his life, and drove around from place to place—crisscrossing the United States—and finally ended up in Florida. I met him when he was sitting on the back deck of Blue Days. I'd gone to take my friend Takeo, who owned that particular bed-and-breakfast, a case of snail egg caviar he'd ordered from me. Takeo shoved me out the back door to the patio and told me his newest guest needed a job.

Mike was stunning, drop-dead gorgeous, but that wasn't what I noticed first—instead it was the pain etched on every part of his face.

"Hi," I blurted.

He scowled.

"I'm in need of an assistant manager at my grocery store, and Takeo seems to think that you want to stay here in Mangrove. Any experience in retail?"

I could tell he was going to thank me and say no, but I crossed my arms at that exact moment and squinted, waiting.

"I don't want to waste your time," he said softly.

"Then don't," I said flatly. "Just tell me what you can do."

He had to think.

"Is there anything?"

"I'm not sure," he answered honestly, his voice cracking.

"Start at the beginning."

So he did.

And I sat.

We talked the afternoon away. Takeo fed us, and I had no idea why, but every time I said he didn't have to, he hushed me, patted my shoulder, and left.

"He's a weird guy," Mike—never Michael, because that was who he'd been to his wife—said, watching Takeo retreat into the house. "I feel like he's trying to read my mind."

"He probably is," I agreed, "and has. He tries to take care of everyone."

"My wife, Janey, was just like that."

He went on and told me his whole life story. He needed to tell it and I wanted to hear it. About midnight, when Dwyer, Takeo's husband, came out to tell us he was taking the help to bed and that we had to be quiet and get our own damn coffee from then on—Takeo had never brought out any alcohol—I turned and offered Mike a job.

He promptly accepted. A week later, I offered him my guesthouse until he found a place to live, and after a year, he was still there.

"Seriously? Are you listening at all?"

Returning sharply to the present, I looked into the mahogany-brown eyes that had just recently started to sparkle and shine. I loved watching women, the same ones who had been looking at the man for the past year without really seeing him, suddenly swivel around and stare. The trudging walk had become a fluid, rolling stride; there were dimples under the beard that had been shaved off; and his smile was simply traffic-stopping. His laugh was infectious, a deep, rumbling thing, and more than anything, he spread warmth from one end of the store to the other. Every person adored him and I was thrilled, because that meant I had more time to work on my new project to supervise the renovations on the community center. It was my baby, my gift to Mangrove, and now that the store had Mike, I could really focus my energy on that gift.

"Yes," I teased as he petted Benny. "I am absolutely paying attention."

He shook his head.

"What?"

"Your builder," he said with so much annoyance that I had to work really hard not to laugh, "had the mayor's car towed this morning."

I scoffed. "I'm sorry?"

His sigh was long and pained. "You know how he insists on parking that boat he drives in front of the gate where the construction crew goes in and out?"

It was also where all the deliveries of building supplies were made. "I do, yes."

"Well, this morning Leya had enough and she had the car towed."

"Wait. The tow-truck operator—"

"Alicia Davis," he interrupted me.

"—yeah, Alicia, she moved his car?"

"Yep."

"But she works for him."

"No, she—"

"I mean, for the city, so technically, she works for the mayor."

"Not anymore," he informed me. "Now she works under Farley."

Farley Porter, our chief of police. "But he also reports to the mayor."

"No," he corrected me. "By the new town charter, Farley reports to the town council now. The chief of police and the new fire chief, who just got hired, both report to the city council."

"When was this decided?"

"Last night at the town meeting," he answered, yawning. "We were going to walk over there together after dinner, but you got that call you didn't want to tell me about."

"Yeah, I know." I grimaced.

"Oh, now you have to tell me."

Leaning forward, I dropped my voice to a whisper. "The new lawyer, Britton Lassiter, he invited me out for a drink."

Mike squinted at me. "Wait. I thought I saw him with a woman."

"You did."

"But he's gay."

"Yeah."

"Wasn't he married before, too?"

I nodded.

"So he got a divorce… why?"

"Because he's gay."

"Wait—"

"Just forget it," I directed, raking my fingers through my hair, pulling it out of my face. I needed a haircut fairly soon. "It'll give you a headache."

"No, let me get this straight." Mike reached out and took hold of my wrist so I couldn't sit back. "He divorced his wife because he was gay and then got a new girlfriend who he just broke up with because—still gay."

"She was his beard with his parents."

"And did she know she was a beard or did she think it was real?"

"Real."

"Okay." Mike grinned, his thumb sliding back and forth over the underside of my wrist. "So what now? Does he plan to date more women here or is he going to come clean with his folks and be out and proud?"

"I think since he's so far away from them now that he can be what he wants."

"Good," he murmured, letting go of my hand only to slide his chair over close. "So what were you two doing that you couldn't make it to the town-hall meeting?"

I wasn't sure I understood the insinuation until I saw his lifted brows.

"What?"

"Were you sleeping with him?"

"How is that your business?"

"Because I live with you," he said tersely.

"Does a 700-square-foot guesthouse on my property count as us living together?"

"It does, yes."

"We just talked," I assured him. "He has a lot to work out."

"And did you explain that town-hall meetings are mandatory for business owners?"

"Miranda told him that he didn't have to attend since she was going."

"Ah."

"I think it would be weird since she always sits with Coz and Kelly, and since Kelly and Britton slept together—"

"Oh? When was this?"

"Ten years or so ago."

"What?"

"I'm just telling you what I know."

"So Kelly slept with Britton Lassiter ten years ago."

"Yes."

"Okay, so did Britton not know he was gay then?"

"He was confused."

"I see." Mike nodded. "And you know all this from your talk with Britton last night."

"Yes."

We were silent a moment.

"So did you bail on me thinking you were going to get laid?"

"I did, yes," I replied honestly.

He chuckled. "Well, I understand."

"You're my best friend. You have to understand!" I said flatly. "It's not a question."

"So," he prodded.

I groaned.

"Was there screwing?"

"No."

"No?"

"Yeah. No."

"Why not?"

I shot him a look that I hoped conveyed my annoyance.

"Where's the explanation? He's your type."

"My *what?*"

"Your type," he repeated. "Tall, handsome, that's your thing. He's not as muscular as I normally see you drool over, but he'll do."

"Drool over?"

"It's better than saying spring wood over."

I shook my head.

"So what? How come you're not making it with Britton Lassiter?"

There was friendship, and there was oversharing. In the course of talking to the lawyer, I understood very quickly that Britton Lassiter wanted—needed—to bottom, and since I shared his desire, us being lovers was not workable.

"Just—it's not in the cards."

"Okay." He shrugged. "Keep your secrets, but you need to tell me who the cute kid belongs to."

"My new next-door neighbor, the new fire chief's daughter."

"Interesting."

"What is?"

"She's black."

This was new. "And? Why does this matter?"

He shrugged. "No reason. I just never thought they'd hire a black man to do that job."

"What?" I glowered at him. "What did you just say?"

"Oh, give me a break," he said dismissively. "I don't see color any more than you do."

"Then what's with the whole 'she's black' comment?"

"All I'm saying is that the town council is made up of elderly uptight white people, so I wouldn't have thought that a man who wasn't would have a shot."

I shook my head at him.

"What?"

"Just because you're from San Francisco does not give you the right to look down on us."

He snorted. "Oh yeah, right, like this town should be on a poster for cultural diversity."

I opened my mouth to argue.

"And just because you have one of everything here does not make this a United Colors of Benetton ad."

I gave up. "You're hopeless."

He was chuckling when Ivy joined us, looking the best she had all morning.

"So are you hungry now? Because by now Benny and I are usually eating."

"Yes, please," she said, beaming at me.

"This is my assistant manager, Mike," I said, making the introductions.

It was funny to watch her turn and notice him and nearly swallow her tongue. Clearly, she was smitten. Not that I didn't get it, the man was definitely worthy of drool.

"Pleasure to meet you," he said, standing and holding out his hand to her.

She took it quickly, her gaze steady on him at first and then taking the tour, missing nothing from his wide shoulders to his muscular athletic build, to his warm copper-colored eyes. She whispered something under her breath as she released his hand, and we both watched him walk away.

"Hey."

She turned slowly from looking after him, finally dragging her gaze back to me.

"Did you say yummy?"

Her gasp made me laugh, and she desperately tried to convince me that I was hearing things. It was already the best morning I'd had in a long time.

CHAPTER TWO

I BOUGHT Ivy one of our many recyclable shopping bags—there were no plastic ones anywhere in my store and every container was made of biodegradable material. We had a huge variety of them and we found one she loved. More importantly, no one had any idea what the bag held.

We had breakfast burritos and freshly squeezed orange juice, and then I walked her back to Cuppa Joe, where she had an iced peppermint mocha and I had a cappuccino. When I took her into Wick and Wand, she was thrilled to meet the owner, Sophia D'Amato, who was putting out a Help Needed sign.

"Oh honey," Sophia sighed, taking hold of Ivy's hand. "I'm so sorry. I lost my mom when I was about your age too."

I never, ever, wondered anymore how Sophia knew things. I had stopped trying to figure it out years ago. She loaded Ivy up with hand-poured all-natural soy candles that had roots and herbs in them, gave her a bottle of different essential oils, and lastly offered a peppermint one that had a completely different label than the others.

"What does that do?" I asked.

"That's for bugs," she explained, chuckling. "Kelly told me to order that, and he was right. It's been a steady seller."

Kelly Seaton was a landscaper—gardener, actually—who was now in a relationship with Cosimo Renaldi, one of the two police officers in town. I'd known they were together before anyone else because I had been there the night their friendship combusted and became so much more. And even though Coz and I had been on a date that night, once he saw his best friend and they finally talked, I had become just a memory. I really should have been more upset, but as much as I lusted after Coz, in truth I was not certain that he'd ever have believed me when I told him that him having lost his right arm in an attack while in the military did not diminish my desire for him.

I was sure some men saw Coz's missing limb as a detractor from his beauty, but all one had to do was take inventory of the whole of him, the shoulders and long legs, and the powerful, muscular body, and the lack of an arm would be found of no consideration. But the only person Coz ever really believed about anything was Kelly Seaton, so it made perfect sense that they were now living together in Kelly's Craftsman bungalow.

"What do you do with the peppermint oil?" I asked Sophia.

"You put some in a spray bottle, add water, and then just go around the doors and windows of your house. Spiders hate it and so do mice."

"Really?"

She nodded, smiling at me. "Kelly told me, and he's right, it works."

"Okay, then."

"So that one is for the house," she explained to Ivy. "The rest are for your mind and body. And if you get cramps, you let me know."

Ivy flicked her gaze to me and because I was smiling, she did as well.

"Some women never get them. Maybe you dodged the bullet."

Ivy nodded.

"So," Sophia said softly, looking between us. "I need you both to keep an eye out for someone who needs a job, all right?"

We agreed.

"And Hutch, be nice to her father."

"Of course."

She gave me a look.

"What?"

"Just—he's been through a lot. The whole family has. Don't judge."

"When do I judge?"

I got a second look, and then she went to help some other customer pick out a scrying crystal.

"That store is awesome and I love Sophia," Ivy told me once we were out on the sidewalk. "I so want to work there when I get old enough."

"I think that's a great plan."

"Can we walk over to the high school so I can see it?"

"Sure, but first I have to go by the construction site for the community center and look in on my construction manager. It sounds like she might need me."

"That sounds like fun," she said excitedly. "Can I wear one of those hard hats?"

"I don't think so."

"But maybe—oh wait, that's my dad." I chuckled as I took the hemp bag full of goodies she'd been given by the nicest Wiccan I knew so she could pull her phone out of her pocket.

I was interested to hear what she was going to tell him. From what I knew already, she was logical and smart and had a way with words. But somehow, when she spilled it all to her dad over the phone, he didn't get that at all. She reminded me of me and my first boyfriend, of all things. All our interactions had always been made to sound worse than they really were so that Dad could figure out a way to ride to my rescue. It was like she was suddenly Little Girl Lost and needed her daddy to save her.

I whacked her shoulder to get her attention.

"Owww," she whined.

"Gimme the phone."

"What?"

"Gimme the phone. You're gonna give him a heart attack."

Once her iPhone was in my hand and I was about to say hello, the growl tore through me. "Are you insane? What if he's a psychopath! I'm calling the police."

I coughed. "There are only three policemen in town, and I'm friends with all of them."

"Who the hell is this?"

"Hutch Crowley, the psycho."

"Mr. Crowley?"

"Yes."

"How dare you take my daughter anywhere without informing me first!"

"What was I supposed to do, Mr. Dodd, leave her on the back steps of your home crying her eyes out?"

"You should have talked to me!"

I wanted to land all over him, but Sophia's weirdly timed words hung in the air. *Be nice to her father…* so I stopped, took a breath, and changed direction. "I'm sorry I didn't; I should have thought of that first. I should have called and asked permission," I said gently, turning and walking a few feet away from her. "But she was crying and she was rambling about everything with her mom and her aunt and she just started her period and—"

"I'm sorry, what?"

"Her period," I repeated. "She's a woman now."

"What?"

Poor man, his voice went out on him and he sounded terrible. I rounded on her, pressing the phone to my chest. "You didn't tell your father you started your period?"

She was mortified. "Oh God, no, we don't talk about that stuff."

"What do you talk about?"

"As little as possible," she groaned.

"That's not healthy," I volleyed.

"You want to give me advice right now?" She snickered.

"Young lady," I began. "You—"

"My dad's having a seizure at the moment, so could it wait?"

I grunted.

She smiled and gestured for the phone. When I passed it back, she took a breath. "He's an angel straight from heaven, Dad, I swear to God." She listened for a moment. "No. He's as old as you, I think—" She put the phone over her heart. "What're you, like, fifty?"

"I beg your pardon?"

She cackled. "Come on, Crowley, how old?"

"I'm forty-four, you witch," I retorted indignantly.

Her laughter came bubbling out of her. "Oh, I wish I was a witch." She cackled again and then told her father about wanting to be a Wiccan because they were peaceful and kind. She went on to tell him that I was, apparently, only a year younger than him. "And he's hot for being old."

I threw up my hands as she started laughing again. "Gimme the phone," I demanded, and when I had it again, I said kindly, "Mr. Dodd, I can assure you that I'm not any kind of path—psycho, socio, or otherwise. Your daughter is safe with me until you or her aunt—"

"She's laughing."

She was, mostly at me. "I'm sorry?"

"She's laughing," he repeated hoarsely as I watched his daughter root around in the bag of supplies she had taken back from me.

"Yes, sir, she is," I agreed. "It took a bit, but she's been doing that most of the day."

He took a breath. "It took you most of the day? It's only a little after one, Mr. Crowley."

"Well, yeah, but—"

"She hasn't laughed since her mother died. Not once. I didn't know when, or if, she ever would again."

"Oh."

"And one afternoon with you, and I can hear that husky giggle she's been giving me since she was a baby."

I stayed quiet.

"So," he sighed. "Mr. Crowley."

"Yes?"

"Please tell me… what are you doing for your next miracle?"

It seemed like he was actually interested, and charmed, and I knew it was only because of his daughter, but his deep, sexy voice did weird, unexpected things to my stomach anyway, just the same way Mike's did. I really needed to get laid.

I coughed to hide my embarrassment. "I'm taking her to a construction site because I have people I need to talk to there, and then we're going to take a tour of the high school and see if we can meet with the girls' soccer coach, and finally, I was going to offer her my guest room until either you or her aunt shows up. Does that work?"

He made a noise of disgust.

"No?"

"Oh, no," he rumbled. "Your plan is good. I just hope I show up before my wife's sister does. Genevieve will make a very big deal about me not being there and about my niece bailing on Ivy."

"Oh, I see."

"The 'unfit' thing has been tossed around since I came out."

"That must be hard."

"Between being gay and being a fireman, I'm not sure which she hates more."

I had no idea what to say to that, except to make a joke. "Homosexual or death wish: must be hard for her to choose."

He sighed heavily. "I'm sorry. You didn't ask to be involved."

"Of course I did," I corrected him. "I went to her, not the other way around."

"She did tell you I was gay, didn't she?"

"Yes."

"And apparently that hasn't alienated you, so I'm thankful, as you're the only one close enough to take care of my child."

"Well," I said, chuckling, "making you feel alienated for being gay would be awfully hypocritical of me since I am as well."

It was quiet on his end.

"Mr. Dodd?"

"I didn't—she didn't tell me you…. Jesus, I wouldn't have been so blunt had I known."

"Why?"

"I don't know. I would have been less open."

"Less?"

"I just—I promised myself I would focus on Ivy from now on, so I can't date, and I thought that certainly you were straight and so perhaps I could have a friend."

"We can't be friends since we're both gay?"

"No."

"Why?"

"It's the same premise that men and women can't be friends unless one of them is gay. There's always the potential for more."

"I disagree." I snickered. "But if you don't want to be my friend, Mr. Dodd, that's okay. Neighbors will be enough."

"Now you think I'm a lunatic."

"No. Now I think you're an egomaniac. I have a very specific type, Mr. Dodd, and I assure you, you're not it."

"Oh? Don't date black men?"

"Firemen," I teased.

I finally heard where Ivy got her good laugh from.

"Touché."

CHAPTER THREE

A WEEK later, Ivy and I had fallen into a routine. She normally got up first, fed Benny, turned on the Keurig, made herself a vanilla latte, and went out into my backyard and threw the ball for my dog while she sipped her coffee. I would come stumbling down, get my coffee, make breakfast, and we would get on our iPads and read the newspaper. The Mangrove Gazette was cute but not particularly informative unless you missed a town meeting. And even though I had, there was another one every Monday night at eight.

"Why don't more people come to this?" Ivy had asked, sounding bright and cheerful as we sat down together in the second row.

I had grinned at her, and Sophia—who flopped down on the other side of her—and Arad Hadjian—the other police officer in town besides Coz—who also joined us, both rolled their eyes. Mike came in right before the meeting began and took the seat beside me that I always saved for him. After being there for twenty minutes listening to the mayor read the minutes from the last meeting, Ivy said *Oh* like she suddenly understood the meaning of life.

"It's a snoozefest," she whispered.

"Yep," I yawned, getting as comfortable as I could in a metal folding chair and jostling Mike from his dozing.

The town was simply too small to need a meeting every week. There was no "breaking news" that everyone didn't already know. Eleven thousand people just didn't generate that much news. There were high school football stadiums that held more people than lived in Mangrove.

"Remind me to not come with my dad when he gets here."

Normally after breakfast she did the dishes while I took a shower, and then I called the store and checked in while she showered. Together we left my house, walked to hers, opened it up so it could air out during the day, and then she took Benny and did something, either met up with a new group of friends at the beach, went for a bike ride, went to Wick and Wand and visited Sophia, went to the movies—where Benny was also allowed—or tagged along with me to the construction site. She would have done the latter most every day because, as she said, she enjoyed watching Leya and Oren "go at it."

The mayor of Mangrove and the owner of the only construction company in town were going to kill each other. Ivy was certain they were madly in love, but I did not actually live in a romantic comedy, so I knew that it was just a matter of time before their story would be on one of those true-crime shows on primetime.

As the mayor, Oren Adler wanted to know what was going on with everything. Most people found his interest sometimes annoying but mostly benign. Leya Naidu found him insufferable, and because he was also the richest man in town, she refused, on principle, to do anything he asked. Ever.

He asked if the community center could have more of a Shingle Style look when it was redone so it would match the buildings downtown, but she and I had agreed on a French Colonial style, and even if I had been fine with changing it, she was not. I just stood there watching them yell at each other, like it was a tennis match.

That was the first of many battles that raged between them, from her having his car towed to him having her office rezoned so she needed all new paperwork refiled before she could even enter her building, from his parking lot repaved *around* his car to her house declared a biohazard area by the health inspector. I told both that they needed to be grownups. His priority was the total aesthetic of the downtown area. Her priority was to deliver on her promise to her customers. It was exhausting just being around them.

"Seriously," Ivy simpered, just besotted with them. "When they kiss, it's gonna be epic."

I groaned and took her for ice cream at Sprinkles On Top. Her favorite flavor was chocolate swirled with macadamia nuts and fudge. Then after our midmorning ice-cream social, I went to the store to check in with Mike.

"So how many pools will the new—is it a rec center or a community center?" Mike asked as we walked the store together.

He had a point. It would be a place where seniors could take dance lessons and teenagers could cluster, and where mothers could bring their children for playdates. Classes would take place morning, noon, and night; there would be a dojo and two Olympic-size pools, plus rooms for dance like ballet with the barre installed and one with a stage where performances could be put on. I was excited about what the center would be once it was completed, and I looked forward to hiring a staff, but what I was actually going to call it was still sort of morphing in my head.

"Hutch?"

"I have to think about that."

He chuckled.

"What?"

"Nothing. You guys want burgers or chicken or kebabs tonight?"

"Oh, are you grilling?"

"Yeah. You and Ivy have to make sides, but I need to know what you want."

"Kebabs," I answered, turning to actually look at him and not simply have a conversation as we walked.

"Why am I being scrutinized?"

"I just realized something."

"Which is?"

"Since I met you, we've only had two dinners apart."

Mike stopped moving. "Is that right?"

"Yeah. Once when your parents came to visit and once when I went out on that date with Coz," I recounted.

"You can't count that as a date," he instructed me quickly. "You were home like a half an hour later."

True. I had returned and was making myself a roast beef sandwich when Mike came through the back door and into my kitchen. He helped himself to a beer and then took a seat on one of my barstools and waited for me to explain.

"Coz and Kelly finally got their shit together."

He smiled as he sipped the Corona in his hand. "That's good."

"So it won't be me and the officer."

Mike snorted out a laugh. "It was never going to be."

And he was right; I had just needed the diversion and had hoped to get laid. "Hey, did you see there's a new lawyer in town?"

He waggled his eyebrows before he asked me to make him a sandwich too.

"Which?"

I came back to the present and gave him all my attention. "What?"

"I said, you should make either basmati rice or we can cook potatoes on the grill. Which one do you want?"

"Potatoes," I told him.

He pointed. "Go to Produce and pick them up. I'll be home around five thirty; I have to stop by and see Mia Renaldi about my wife's life insurance policy."

I instantly took hold of his shoulder. "Is everything okay?"

"Oh yeah, fine," he said softly, his copper-colored gaze meeting mine. "My wife had taken out a policy that I didn't know about because she used a different lawyer than our regular one. Her folks want the money, but I want to give it in Janey's name to the hospital where they did everything they could to save her."

"I don't understand. Aren't you the beneficiary?"

He nodded. "I am unless I can be proven unfit, and they think that traveling around for two years after Janey died shows that I'm a nut job."

"Are you serious?" I asked hotly, suddenly angry. "How dare they question *your* grief for *their* daughter? That's sick!"

Mike shrugged.

"No, really! How long did they grieve?" I yelled.

Taking hold of my bicep, he tugged me close and put his hand on the side of my neck. "You never get upset."

He was right. I was normally very steady, but that was more a product of not caring about a lot of things than of being meditative. He was the difference here, and about Mike Rojas, I cared a great deal. He had become very important to me, very quickly. Even though we'd known each other only a year, it felt as though it had been a lifetime. I would find myself talking to him about things I was sure he knew about, only to have him remark that whatever it was had happened two years ago or ten or even longer. I recounted talking to other people and I'd be certain we'd both heard the same conversation. Mike would smile, shake his head, and prod me to tell him the story.

"They—shouldn't question your love," I said, suddenly breathless.

His gaze was warm as he looked at me before he pulled me into a hug. I inhaled deeply because he always smelled so good. There was mint in the soap he used, and somehow the mix on him, his skin specifically, clean, male, always caused the same reaction—I wanted to breathe him in.

As usual, the second I felt the now-familiar yearning to keep him, I squashed down the feeling as fast as I could. Not only was he my friend, but he was my very *straight* friend, and that half second when my heart stopped because he was holding me was time I spent first scolding myself and then doing the gentle reminding of the gaping hole he'd leave behind in my life if I did anything to push him away. I'd never had a best friend before him; I certainly wasn't going back to not having one, especially when it would be me trying to create something out of thin air.

"I'll be fine, but I appreciate the worry," he rumbled into my hair. He let me go and I moved quickly, not wanting to ever make him uncomfortable with any kind of closeness.

"Okay," I responded.

"I'll see you at home later," he said before he walked away, but somehow when he turned around, almost at the front door, I was still watching him.

His wave made me self-conscious, like I was standing there staring as I would have if he was my lover. Correcting fast, I spun around to go grab what we needed for dinner.

MIKE WAS outside at the grill, and Ivy and I had the music up in the house, so neither of us heard anything until I dipped her and we looked up. Her father stood there at the back door with a woman I assumed was her aunt.

"What's going on here?" the woman asked over The Spinners.

Ivy cracked up, and I put her on her feet before she dashed across the kitchen to her father. I turned down the music with the remote.

"Daddy!" she squealed, leaping at him.

He caught her in his arms and hugged her, his face down in her shoulder. They held each other so tight, and the woman who had come through my door ready to do battle visibly deflated.

"Everybody ready to eat?" Mike announced as he walked in behind them, carrying a platter of kebabs. "We've got steak and chicken and lots of veggies."

Mr. Dodd put his daughter down, and she wiped her eyes quickly before grabbing her aunt, who was stunned at the reception as evidenced by her gasp and open mouth.

Ivy hugged her too, kissed her cheek, and then took her hand and pulled her over to me. "This is Hutch and Mike."

Genevieve Davis was a tall, stately woman immaculately dressed in a white-and-silver overcoat, a sheer white T-shirt, and white palazzo pants. The jewelry was understated, as was her makeup. She was a stunning woman.

"Hi," I greeted her cheerfully, offering her my hand.

She grabbed hold, clearly still overwhelmed by the reception from her niece.

"And Hutch, this is my dad."

I turned to Mr. Dodd and was not surprised to find him even more handsome in real life than he was on Ivy's phone. The man also was massive. He was at least six four, broad shouldered, narrow hipped, with muscular legs straining against the denim encasing them. His features were sharp, as was his square jaw, but what you noticed first was his eyes, a gorgeous dark bistre, so brown they were almost black.

"Pleasure," I said, smiling, holding out my hand. "It was a privilege to take care of your daughter. Thank you for trusting me and Mike."

"I didn't do anything but cook," Mike let me know, pressing in beside me, one hand on the small of my back as he offered his right to Mr. Dodd.

He shook both our hands, and he, too, looked a bit flummoxed.

"Sit down," Ivy directed her father and aunt as my dog came in from outside and bolted over to her side. "Oh, Daddy, this is Benny. Isn't he pretty?"

Her father dutifully petted my dog before meeting her gaze. "We should go, honey," he said. "We don't want to intrude."

"Oh, you're not intruding," she said dismissively, giving him an imperious wave of her hand. "But you both probably want to wash your hands and stuff, so if you go down the hall to your left, it's right through there."

Genevieve left to use my bathroom, Ivy ran back outside where Mike sent her to grab the second plate of kebabs, but her dad stayed there and washed his hands in the kitchen sink before turning to me.

"So I don't think I ever—would you both please call me Essien?"

"I don't know." I scowled at him. "Chief Dodd sort of rolls off the tongue."

His smile was bright like his daughter's. "It's wonderful to meet you both. I'm sorry my daughter's invaded your home, but I so appreciate you taking care of her."

"She hasn't been any trouble at all," I assured him. "She's an angel."

"Thank you."

"All she's been talking about night and day are all the things she's looking forward to doing to your home. After being here with me she's ready to start decorating."

"Is she?"

I chuckled. "She's taking a little bit of my style and none of Mike's and—"

"Pardon me?" Mike chimed in.

"What?"

"None of mine?" He was indignant.

I gestured toward the guesthouse. "What is there to take from that? You haven't done anything to it since you moved in."

"I was supposed to do something?"

"Yeah. You were supposed to make it your own."

"Really?"

I shook my head.

"Wait," Essien interrupted. "I thought you two were together."

I scoffed. "No, we're not a couple. Did Ivy say we were?"

"No, but I… I just got that impression from things she said."

"Huh," Mike grunted.

"Well, for the record, Mike lives in my guesthouse and we work together at the Green Grocer."

"Oh," Essien said, clearly embarrassed, nodding as Mike smiled at him.

"We only sound like an old married couple," I explained.

"That's right," Mike agreed, putting a hand on my shoulder. "Now finish setting the table, honey. We have guests."

I laughed and so did Essien, and when Genevieve came back and Ivy walked in with Benny in tow—since he followed her everywhere—it was time to sit down and eat.

It was funny to watch Essien and Genevieve look at Ivy like she had grown another head. They were both clearly amazed, but I had no idea why. She chatted, keeping up a steady stream of conversation as she explained about her talk with the soccer coach and how she had a tryout with the team as soon as school started.

Genevieve tried to bring up the idea of Ivy visiting her in Philadelphia, but her niece simply shut her down over and over.

"You should just plan on coming here," she told her aunt. "I mean, hello, Florida."

There was really no argument.

After dinner, Mike gave Essien his second beer and walked him around my—our—property. Technically it was mine, but Mike lived there and he was in and out of my house all the time, had a key—as I did for his place, of course—so it seemed strange to say mine when he was a fixture there. As Ivy and I cleaned up, Genevieve talked to us.

"Hutch," Ivy said as she moved up on my left, watching Mike and her dad outside. "Do you realize that both my dad and Mike have lost a wife? Isn't that sad?"

It was.

"Maybe they'll get to be friends."

And while I hoped they did—I wanted Essien to be happy in Mangrove—I had an unfamiliar twinge in my chest while watching the two men talk in the backyard, and I didn't like it at all.

CHAPTER FOUR

OVER THE next couple of months, I enjoyed seeing Ivy settle into her life in Mangrove, was pleased that her aunt left feeling secure that she was happy, and tried to keep track of the number of dates Mike went on. It was like the mourning period had officially ended and he was making up for lost time or something.

It was early on a Friday morning in October, and I was having coffee on my back porch with Essien. Both of us were early risers, and he'd gotten into the habit of walking from his back door to mine, and by the time he'd open the screen door, I'd have a cup of French roast to pass him. Then we would stand in my kitchen and wait to see the walk of shame from my guesthouse.

"Oh-oh, who do we have here?"

"That's—wait, wait," Essien stopped me. "Don't tell me. It's the lady from the witch place my daughter likes."

"Wick and Wand," I offered. And sure enough, there was Sophia D'Amato, walking very quickly across my grass, shoes in hand. "I guess Wiccans have needs too," I yelled after her.

"Screw you, Hutch," she yelled as she walked by my screened-in back porch.

It was odd to see Mike doing so much serial screwing. He'd gone from seeing nobody to seeing everyone in a few short months.

"He's going to have to start on tourists, because he's running out of residents," Essien commented, sipping his coffee.

"Has he talked to you about it?" I asked. "Because all I'm getting as the reason for the man-whoring is that he wants to start living his life again."

"Yeah, he told me he's finally in a good place."

"Which is good," I said sincerely, "but maybe remind him that the condom is his friend."

"Yes, it is," Essien agreed.

"You're awfully cavalier about it," I quipped. "Just imagine if he catches something and your daughter starts asking questions, as we both know she will. Are you ready to have that talk with her?"

"I've had the sex talk with my daughter."

"Yes, but have you ventured into STD realm?"

"Please stop," he groaned.

What was funny was that none of the dates started until *after* dinner. All of Mike's dates started with drinks or a movie or dessert or something, anything, that could be done in the later evening. He was still having dinner with me every night. It was so odd.

"You can take these women out on a proper date, you know," I suggested.

"It's just casual," he explained.

But I didn't get it. "Don't you want to date any of these women?"

"I'm not ready to do that," he informed me. "And they don't want me exclusively either."

I shook my head.

"What?"

"I think you're wrong," I apprised him.

"Oh?"

"Anybody in their right mind would want to keep you."

"And why's that?"

"You're a good man."

"I don't know about that."

"I do."

"You and Janey—you're of similar minds on the subject of me. I think you're both a bit too lenient."

I shook my head. "From everything you told me about her, I think we're both terribly smart people."

His deep rumbling laughter made my stomach tighten unexpectedly.

"You're both blinded by my charm."

"I see."

He gave my cheek a quick pat. "I have nothing to offer anyone."

"That's not true," I said, stopping him before he turned away, taking hold of his hand and holding tight.

"Yes, it is," he argued, but he didn't pull away. "Who wants a man with a broken heart?"

"It's not broken anymore. It was wounded and now it's stitched up. You're ready to start watching sunsets and holding hands again."

Eyebrows raised, he nodded like I belonged in the loony bin.

"I'm serious," I snapped, letting him go. "You should think about some monogamous dating."

But as of yet, he had not heeded my advice, as evidenced by the string of beautiful women trying to slip away unseen in the early morning light.

"You have to wonder what he's trying to prove," Essien said out of the blue.

"What?"

He gestured with his coffee mug at my guesthouse. "Mike. Why the sudden need to sleep with every available woman in town? What happened?"

I realized I had no idea.

"He's your best friend. Shouldn't you maybe find out?"

He had a point.

"SO WHY aren't you asking?"

I turned slowly to look at Kelly Seaton, who had joined me in my lean against the railing at the community center. He was doing the landscaping, and when he saw me, he had just put in the flagstone walkway that would hopefully keep people off the grass and out of the water of the small mangrove forest he had installed.

By all accounts, we should not have been friendly. But as he and Coz Renaldi sank deeper and deeper into couplehood, I found him far more grounded and approachable. So when he'd sauntered over and asked what was going on, I had unloaded about Mike and how he was sleeping with every available woman in town and how Essien had brought up the fact that maybe he was compensating for something and how half of me was debating about getting into it with him and the other half was not and how I wanted to know but how I also didn't want to pry.

"What can I actually ask as a friend?"

"But you're not just friends, right?"

"How do you mean?"

"I mean, clearly you're more than that."

My heart stopped. "What do you mean?"

"I *mean*, he's your best friend, and you want him to be more, and that's why you're jealous."

It took me several seconds to process. "I'm sorry, what?"

"You're jealous."

"Well, yes," I agreed, "just not how you think."

"Oh? How do I think?"

"I'm not jealous because I want Mike; I'm jealous because of the time he's spending with this multitude of women, nothing else."

"And how are those two things different?"

"I'm just used to having Mike around, is all. It has nothing to do with me wanting him," I explained, clearing things up for him.

"Uh-huh."

"No, really, it's perfectly—"

"Stupid. You have no idea what you're even saying."

"No, I—"

Kelly snickered. "You're so clueless that you don't even realize that you're snapping and snarling at everyone."

"I am not," I groused.

He batted his eyelashes at me, and I remembered how much of a wiseass he was.

"It's just that… see, Mike and I… we're like—"

"God," he sighed, "I shouldn't have ever been jealous of you."

"I'm trying to explain something to you," I complained.

"Yeah, I know."

I pushed off the railing and pivoted to face him instead of staring at his profile. "I have no idea what you're talking about. Would you rather tell me or just stand there and piss me off?"

Kelly had the nerve to smile. "I thought you were interested in Coz, but it's actually Mike."

"What? No," I protested.

"Yes," he volleyed.

"No, it's—"

"How long has it been Mike?"

"We're friends," I retorted, "and that's all. Just because you and Coz were buddies and then lovers doesn't mean that all relationships follow that same course of—"

"I think it does."

But that couldn't be right. Mike and I were never going to be romantic, because he was straight and maybe even still grieving. "You really don't know what you're talking about."

Kelly was going to argue; he opened his mouth to say something but stopped suddenly when someone yelled his name. We turned and found Lazlo Maguire walking toward us, and I, for one, was thrilled. I always enjoyed looking at him.

On first glance, people thought Lazlo was either a front man for a rock band, a model, or some international playboy slumming it in Mangrove. Because of his medium-length hair that went everyway at once and stood on end in an unkempt mop, the perpetual squint, the enduring stubble he let become a beard and mustache after a few weeks at home, thick black brows, and even darker eyes, I got the impression of slumber, like he'd just woken up and would love to go back to sleep. I never understood the term "bedroom eyes" before I met him, but that man simply dripped sex. He looked decadent, and he sounded even more so with his deep whiskey voice and rumbling laugh, and everything he did, he did at his own pace. I had never seen him move quickly. The man had a fluidity about him that, coupled with the occasional wicked smile, turned almost everyone who knew him into a puddle at his feet.

Finding out what he did for a living had kept me from making a move. Six months out of the year, he lived in Mangrove and ran On The Breeze, his store that sold handmade wind chimes. He made the kind that hung and the kind that went into the ground, and they were all welded pieces of art that flew out of his store. The thing was, even at some exorbitant pricing, even if he sold everything in the shop, he wouldn't be able to keep the place open. So to help, the other six months of the year, he was a highly paid escort in New York.

It was not my place to judge, and if I had his beautiful face and gorgeous toned, cut body and I was twenty-two with no obligations, I might be an escort too. But the issue was that every now and then, someone followed him home. It was easy to get attached to him and his sensual hedonism, but once he was here, he wasn't that guy.

Here in Mangrove, he was Laz, the laid-back shop owner with his place beside the tea shop, Steep. He was not the same guy he was in the big city, but clients didn't know that. Every so often, Laz would have to file a restraining order against a particularly insistent admirer, and it was always a hassle for either Coz or Arad to enforce.

"What?" He yawned as he strode over to us, board shorts and tank top on, cigarette in one hand, 32-ounce fountain drink in the other.

"Why are you barefoot?" I asked, utterly horrified. "You could step on a piece of glass or something."

He was scowling as he reached us. "The only thing on the pristine white sidewalks or the red brick driveways around here is white sand that looks like sugar, so I'm not worried."

I shook my head, and Kelly told him to get rid of the cigarette. "You know smoking in public places is against the law in Mangrove."

Laz groaned and put it out on the railing, then tossed it into the garbage can. "Which is ridiculous by the way," he added. "Who gets exposed to secondhand smoke when you're outside and the wind is blowing and you're right next to the fuckin' ocean?"

We both shot him a look.

"It's stupid."

"Whatever," Kelly said dismissively. "I want to know about you and Britton Lassiter. Why did he take out a restraining order against you?"

"How do you know about that?"

"I live with one of the two officers in town. Of course I know."

"It was a misunderstanding."

Oh, I had to hear this.

He looked back and forth between us and finally threw up his hands in annoyance. Clearly we were both waiting.

"He was a client in Manhattan," Lazlo explained. "And—"

"Before he was divorced?" Kelly wanted to know.

"He was separated already," Lazlo replied irritably, possibly because of being interrupted. "And though normally I don't do background checks before I fuck people, I think he was feeling guilty and so gave me his whole sad 'I'm getting a divorce' story."

"Okay, sorry, go on."

"Yeah, so when I saw him here, I thought he was one of those guys who'd followed me across the country."

Kelly's laughter was immediate.

"What?" I asked, unsure of why that was funny. "I'm sure lots of people would—look at him."

"Thank you," Lazlo said with his sexy, smoky voice.

"Could we finish the story?" Kelly snapped.

"Yeah. So I go walking up to him and I start to give him the standard line, yanno, the whole 'this is my home, so whatever you thought I could do for you, I can't do for you here,' and he gets all upset like I attacked him or something."

"He was horrified." Kelly chuckled.

"How do you know?"

"He told me."

"Britton told Coz he was horrified?"

"No, idiot, he told *me* he was horrified. He and I are friends."

"Oh, so you got the story from both sides, then, mine *and* his."

"I have now, yeah."

Lazlo pivoted to face Kelly. "Then explain to me why he lost his mind?"

"Are you kidding?" he scoffed.

Lazlo was clearly confused.

"He's the new lawyer in town. He's only been here a month and he's building his reputation, and you're back a week and everyone knows he knows you."

"You know me," he said curtly. "And that doesn't seem to be adversely affecting your reputation."

"I'm not a lawyer," Kelly reminded him.

Lazlo scowled. "That's the reason? Really? I embarrassed him?"

"If I was him, I wouldn't want clients knowing I paid for sex, either," I told him. "I mean, you're a lawyer and you did something illegal. What does that say about you?"

"It's not illegal to be an escort."

"You're splitting hairs," I argued. "Everybody loves you, you know that, but do they want a guy who paid to fuck you doing their legal work?"

"Why should that matter?"

"Come on, be serious."

"Uptight much?"

"The town is open-minded," Kelly sighed, "but still small. Use your head."

Lazlo shrugged.

"Maybe you should have asked questions before you rained down righteous anger on the man."

"Yeah, maybe, but it was an honest mistake. Lots of guys follow me 'cause I'm scary hot in bed."

Both Kelly and I groaned.

"What? I am!"

I shook my head. Thank God I wasn't twenty-two anymore.

"So what now?" Kelly asked. "Are you going to fight the restraining order?"

He shrugged. "He can keep it, I don't give a fuck. What the hell would I need to see him about? Ever? It's not like what I do in New York is legal anyway, so I'm not going through some screening process to have a job or keep it. I don't care about this, and it messed with my vibe anyway."

"Your vibe?" I asked, trying not to sound condescending.

"I like to relax when I'm here. I want to create my chimes and veg. I need the downtime before I gotta hustle again."

"Laz," I began gently, "you know there are other ways to—"

"Don't start with the whole 'you can do so much more than fuck to make money,'" he mocked, shutting me down. "This is easy for me, and obviously, I'm not that bright or I wouldn't have had to do that to begin with."

I opened my mouth to argue.

"Stop. I have a sister in college who loves me and a mother in Vegas who hates me and they both need money to live. Just let it alone."

I nodded.

Lazlo's smile was seriously something, the way it made his dimples pop and curled his lip. Sexy wasn't a good enough word. Breathtaking was a better one, though my Mike could give him a run for his money.

"Who wants to have a drink to my restraining order at The Lighthouse?"

"I'm buying," Kelly announced, then started asking Lazlo about a custom-made wind chime for a customer.

We started down the street, back toward the seashore where most of the bars were, and I was enjoying listening to the two of them discuss what Kelly thought he wanted to install for a customer, when it hit me.

What had I thought?

What had crossed my mind?

It had been so fast, so fleeting, but still, the thought had been mine.

I was on the back patio of The Lighthouse when I had to grab hold of the railing for dear life.

"Wait," Kelly said, chuckling. "I think someone is having second thoughts about a drink."

"Oh man, I was only kidding." Lazlo snickered. "I can't drink in the middle of the day. I meant let's have some ice tea or something."

"Yeah, me neither," Kelly teased. "It's okay, lightweight; it's actually just about the company, not the alcohol."

What had I thought?

"Hutch?" Lazlo said gently. "Are you okay?"

"You look weird," Kelly confirmed. "Well, weirder than usual."

Had I thought…. *My Mike?*

"Maybe you should sit down," Kelly offered.

"I think he might need some water," Lazlo threw out, and then because we were all now standing at an outdoor bar, he yelled, "Can we get some water over here?"

My Mike? *My* Mike?! When had Mike Rojas become mine? And when had he gotten better-looking than Lazlo Maguire?

"You're turning gray," Kelly said worriedly.

I was going to hyperventilate.

"I think he needs to put his head between his legs," Lazlo suggested.

I let Kelly lower me into a chair and bend me in half as I thought about Mike. When was the last time I had thought of him as separate from me? Why was I really bothered about all the women coming and going out of my guesthouse? And it wasn't actually my guesthouse anymore, it was *his* residence? *Mike's* residence, and had been so for quite some time, so why was I still thinking about it as mine? Yes, it was on my property, but if I rented it out, it would still be on my property, and in the past when I'd had other tenants, I didn't think of it as mine, so what made it different now? What made the guesthouse mine again?

"Hutch?"

Unless the man inside of it was mine, and so therefore, so was the guesthouse.

"Shit," I whimpered, feeling my face flush at the same time I got goose bumps from a sudden chill.

I could not be in love with my very straight friend.

"Hutch?"

Standing up suddenly, I made a quick excuse that I was nauseated from lunch, then brushed off their concern—and their hands—and was halfway down the street headed for home when I heard someone yelling my name.

When I turned, I found Mrs. Evanston of the town council charging toward me with her assistant, Emily Chapel. Both women looked distressed.

"A word, Mr. Crowley," Mrs. Evanston called out.

I stood there, waiting, as the two of them reached me.

When people asked, I always described Mrs. Evanston as having the exterior of a sweet Southern matriarch and the personality of a Rottweiler. She was simply terrifying. In contrast, Emily Chapel only ever wore pink in various shades and even had carnation-colored cat's-eye sunglasses with fuchsia lenses—glasses she had on at the moment.

"Good afternoon," I greeted them, and Emily gave me a quick shake of her head to let me know that, without question, this was not going to be pleasant.

"What can I do for you?"

"Mr. Crowley," Mrs. Evanston began, "I regret to inform you that I'm calling an emergency meeting of the board today on the grounds of fraud."

"Fraud?"

"Yes, fraud."

I sighed. "And what does this have to do with me?"

"Well, I can promise you that directly after our meeting you will be removed from the community center project."

It was the fifth time they'd tried.

The first time they'd tried to remove me was because they said I didn't have the correct building permits. It turned out that some more fees paid directly to the town council budget cleared that up.

The second time they tried to remove me was because large trucks were not permitted downtown in the middle of the day because it messed with traffic. What traffic, was my question, but whatever, I complied.

The third time was because I violated the noise ordinance by having the trucks move before nine in the morning. I got around that by waiting until one in the afternoon and having my guys work into the night. After the second week of the klieg lights turning night into day and the sound of workmen until eleven every night, they went back to letting me move the trucks in the morning. Better to annoy people waking up in the morning than during romantic beach dinners, strolls along the beach, and other various nighttime pursuits. Everyone on the town council had a service business they didn't want impaired.

The fourth time, they didn't think my construction manager was actually licensed in the state of Florida. Leya's credentials shut them up.

So this was their fifth try. It was annoying to say the least, and I wished, as I did on occasion, that I had left the headache of building a community rec center to someone else. I'd gotten nothing but grief from the beginning. Since at this point, the outside was all built and we were at the putting in walls and toilets stage, there was no way for me to simply walk away.

I tried not to sound too exasperated. "I can't be removed from the project, Mrs. Evanston; I'm the only one with any money."

She huffed. "You can't promise free food to the rec center, Mr. Crowley."

I swear the woman was going to make me bald. Emily groaned as I raked my fingers through my hair, pushing it back out of my face and taking hold of it.

"Did you hear me?"

"I did, but I'm not really following you."

"Mr. Timmons explained to us that you would supply the rec center with free food once it was built, and as such, people would know where the food came from and would take a very favorable view of you, so that when it came time for you to either run for mayor yourself or endorse a candidate, people would be easily swayed to your side. Mr. Timmons does not take kindly to that sort of fraudulent do-gooding and neither do we!"

I was going to kill Blake Timmons. "You realize, Mrs. Evanston, that the good doctor actually wants to be mayor."

"I have no idea what you're talking about, Mr. Crowley, but I will tell you right now that I'm calling an emergency meeting of the board, and I plan to have you removed!"

"And if you have me removed, since I'm the one who financed the goddamn build in the first place, who precisely will take over?"

"I'm sure the mayor would be more than happy to—"

"You'd have to pay me for everything I've done up to this point, if you could even prove fraud to begin with, and—"

"Oh, I will! I won't let you just ramrod your way into being mayor, Mr. Crowley! You may think you can bribe the good people of this town, but I'm not going to let you!"

"I'll see you in court, you old bat," I yelled.

Her eyes got so big I thought they were going to pop right out of her head. Emily started coughing really loudly.

"Well, I never!"

I growled and turned away from the two women, then headed over to the practice of Timmons and Hammond, the two pediatricians in town. We also had two internal medicine guys, one ob-gyn, three nurse-practitioners, four midwives, and a chiropractor. I was always hoping we'd get a dentist to move into town, but so far no luck; everyone still had to drive to Destin for that as well as any and all adult mental health issues. Child psychiatrist, we had that covered, as well as lots of lawyers. It surprised me how many we actually had: six in all. But one of them was Cosimo Renaldi's sister, Mia, and I knew she'd love to help me sue the town council. But first, I was going to go beat the crap out of Blake Timmons.

He shared an office with Roark Hammond in a converted barn, and where the hay loft used to be, they'd installed a play area for kids, complete with a giant slide that curved around and dumped kids off into a giant sandbox. It was a beautiful, pristine white structure that kids and their parents enjoyed. That was lucky because there was always a wait… for Roark. Everyone in town loved Roark, who had moved to town from Detroit four years ago. No one, as far as I could tell, liked Blake, who was a legacy in town since his father, Sidney, practiced for more than forty years before him. The thing was, everyone knew Blake was a nozzle, and so no one went to see him. A town that should have been his had turned its back on him. It was so busy on Roark's side that he had just hired another doctor to assist him. He'd tried coaching Blake into being nicer; we'd had many conversations about it when we used to be fuck buddies, back before

Mike moved into my guesthouse. Then it became weird to be running off to get laid when Mike was home, alone, and needing a friend.

As I charged up the wide whitewashed steps to the enormous wraparound porch that was filled with rocking chairs and an outdoor checkers set, various people greeted me before I walked in. Blake was out front, eating an apple and leaning on the reception desk, when I slammed the door behind me.

He did the jolt of recognition thing and ran.

"You ass!" I yelled, bolting after him.

I slid around the corner—the polished oak floors were slippery and I was wearing wingtips—and had to grab at the archway molding to not go careening into the other room.

"Hutch?" Roark said as he walked out of his office with a patient.

I ignored him in favor of racing after Blake, grabbing hold of the banister to help launch me up the stairs after him, following him down the hall to his office, and then wedging my foot into the doorway before he could slam the door shut.

"You se-seem upset," Blake stammered through the three inches of space my foot was allowing between us.

"You fuck!" I roared. "How dare you try and screw with my building! I'm doing this for the community, you selfish piece of shit!"

"Hutch!" Roark shouted from behind me as I leveraged my weight against the door, trying to get in, while Blake pushed with both hands, trying to keep me out.

"Stay out of this, Roark," I barked. "It's between me and your gutless partner!"

But he was suddenly there beside me anyway. "How does it look, you, a pillar of our community, trying to beat the crap out of a doctor?"

"I don't really give a shit," I snarled, shoving the door open wider, wedging my shoulder through the crack. "He's putting my community center at risk with his petty bullshit!"

"Listen," Roark soothed, hand on my side, stroking over my hip. "Why don't we—"

"You're acting like a child, Hutch!" Blake shouted from the other side of the door. "Think about how this must look."

"You started it," I growled back, giving a hard push that almost knocked him free.

"Hutch," Roark said softly, hands on my sides. "Let go of the door, and I'll have him come out and talk to you."

I stopped pushing and Blake stopped resisting.

"I promise he'll be right here."

Straightening from my leveraged stance, I took a quick breath to try to calm down. "Let go so I can pull myself free," I ordered roughly, the anger still vibrating in my voice.

"Okay," he agreed from the opposite side of the door.

It opened just wide enough so I could step back, and then it closed delicately in front of me.

"There," Roark said, smiling, turning me around so he could see my face. "See? Diplomacy works."

I wasn't convinced.

"You look good, by the way," he said, his gaze roaming all over me.

Roark was pretty much stunning, himself, but I was not there for him and I was too annoyed to flirt as I stepped sideways and kicked the door. "Come out here, Blake, so we can settle this. I expect you to go talk to the council."

I clearly heard the slide of a window opening.

"Sonofabitch!" I bellowed before I kicked the door open and saw Blake's foot disappear outside. The bougainvillea trellis went from the second story to the ground, but I certainly wasn't following him down that way.

Yanking free of Roark, I darted back to the top of the stairs and took them by threes. At the front door, I nearly collided with Essien.

"Hutch," he said, surprised, automatically reaching for me.

"Hold on to him!" Roark called from behind me, but I guessed Essien thought he knew me better than Roark, so he let me go. I ran out onto the porch and leaned over it.

Blake hit the ground and started running.

"You better stop!" I threatened.

He didn't even hesitate, just ran, which looked odd in his white coat, and I bolted by Ivy on the way down the steps.

"Do you need help?" she called after me.

"No, baby, I'm fine," I answered before I took off in a sprint after Blake.

I could only imagine what the two of us looked like. How often, unless you were watching some kind of law enforcement drama, did you see a grown man chasing another down the street?

"Calm down, Hutch!" Blake called back over his shoulder.

I growled at him and he ran faster, trying to put more distance between us, but I was stronger and so started to close. We ran across town, behind buildings, down alleys, through backyards, around pools, through a cute house people were moving into, and finally, down the boardwalk.

I knew at that point that he was trying to reach city hall, but he swerved at the last moment to go to the police station. Since I didn't want to be arrested, I leaped and caught him in a flying tackle. We flipped over the railing and fell hard down into the sand ten feet below.

I was winded, he was winded, and so we both lay there and tried to push air through our lungs. Soon after, I became aware of all the people above us and groaned.

"I'm so"—Blake huffed out—"pressing charges."

"For what? Making you run?" I panted.

"You're such an asshole, Crowley," he heaved out. "And I'm going to make sure that you're never mayor."

"Who told you I wanted to be mayor?"

He rolled his head to look at me. "Don't you?"

I smacked his abdomen with the back of my hand.

"Crap, Oren said you did."

"Oren is paranoid, you stupid ass," I gasped.

He looked genuinely surprised, like our current mayor's mental state was not something he had ever thought of before.

"This is such small-town bullshit," I muttered as Arad Hadjian suddenly appeared beside us.

"Gentlemen," he said dryly.

"This is all Crowley's fault," Blake was quick to offer.

CHAPTER FIVE

As JAILS went, Mangrove's was where you wanted to be incarcerated. The floors were made with the resin finish that looked like it had glitter underneath, the interior of the cells was washed with a lovely jade, and the bars were more of a hunter green. The bench I sat on was padded, and at the moment, I was listening to a sort of bouncy bossa nova beat piped in through the audio system. It was like being put in timeout at an amusement park.

"I can't believe this," Blake complained from the next cell over. "How come I'm in here too?"

"Because it's called disturbing the peace, you stupid prick," I muttered as I lay down, lifting my knees so I could stretch my back.

"What about you trying to kill me? Attempted homicide and all that?"

I grunted.

"Hutch!"

I sat up as Mike came rushing into the room, slipping around Arad to make his way into the holding area.

"Hey," I sighed, really happy to see him.

He rushed up to the bars and grabbed hold of them, staring in at me. "Are you all right?"

"Yeah, I'm fine."

"Come here."

I got up, felt a twinge from where I'd flipped over the railing, and pressed my fist to the small of my back.

"What's wrong?"

"I went over that railing from the boardwalk down to the sand," I replied, smiling as I thought about it. "Not the smartest thing I've ever done, but you know—heat of the moment and all that."

He nodded as I reached him, taking hold of the bars on either side of his hands.

"So what was this all about?" he asked, scrutinizing me, checking me over.

"Blake screwed with the community center."

"You're having another problem with that?"

"I know, right? I mean, when are they gonna stop?"

He cleared his throat. "You need to hire Mia Renaldi and have her on speed dial until this thing is over."

"Agreed. Will you call her for me and see if she'll take the job?"

"She'll take the job, and I really like her. She got the money with my in-laws all squared away."

"Oh yeah?"

He nodded. "Yeah. She explained to them that trying to prove I'm nuts, though easy, would take a lot of time and well… money."

I chuckled. "Nice."

"So yeah, she's on a roll. I'll give her a call as soon as we get home."

"No, call her now. I don't think I'm gonna be out of here for hours yet."

"No, you're getting out right now," he insisted. "All you needed was someone to take custody of you. Roark's coming to take Blake home, and I'm here for you."

"Oh, that's great," I sighed, smiling at him.

He reached up and threaded his fingers through my hair. "You have sand in this. You gotta take a shower when we get home."

"And after that, I'm gonna put a heating pad on my back. I feel like I'm bruised."

"Turn around and let me see."

I did as he instructed so he could reach me.

He gently lifted the lightweight Henley I was wearing, and when I felt his warm palm slide over my bare skin, the sound I made was carnal and not friendly in the slightest.

"Okay, get him out!" Mike yelled, startling me with his fury.

I pivoted to face him and watched as he swallowed hard.

"I need to talk to you," he whispered. "We need to go home right now."

"Yeah. I need to talk to you too."

"Oh? About what?"

I grimaced as Arad reached the cell and unlocked it.

"Speak," Mike ordered as the door rolled sideways.

"I think it might be time for you to move out."

He nodded like he was taking that in. "Okay."

I was surprised. "Okay?"

"Yeah, sure. I'll move out of the guesthouse and into your house, no problem," he said, following Arad out the door and into the main area of the police station.

I stood there, confused, then turned to look at Blake through the bars.

"Mike's moving in with you?" He appeared as befuddled as I felt. "Why did I think he was straight?"

"Because he is."

"Clearly not," he said dryly. "He wants to live with you."

"That makes zero sense."

"I'm probably not the one to be discussing it with," he said, pointing after Mike.

"Yeah… I…."

"And I won't press charges for you making me run."

"You're really a prick, Blake."

"As are you, Hutch."

We left it at that and I went after Mike.

I was only a few moments behind him, but by the time I reached the booking area, Mike already had my possessions and was standing at the door waiting for me. I thanked Arad for some stupid reason, like being on autopilot, and was outside seconds later.

"So let's talk," Mike said, grabbing hold of my wrist and dragging me around the side of the building, into the bushes where no one could see us.

"What's going on with you?"

"A lot," he said right before he crushed me into the stucco wall and then covered me with his hard, muscular body.

I caught my breath, and he stared at me, into my eyes, and as we were both six foot tall, there was nowhere else to look but at each other.

"I have a theory," he said gruffly before he leaned in and kissed me. Everything stopped.

My heart, my pulse, the blood rushing through my veins, everything in me stilled and savored and coalesced into one aching, drowning, devouring need.

I wanted Mike Rojas desperately.

He pulled back, and I saw the look of confusion come over his beautiful sharp features, and it hit me that in my discovery of the meaning of life, I'd forgotten to kiss him back.

"You…," he began hesitantly.

"No-no," I corrected quickly before I took hold of his face and kissed him, hard, so he could feel it down to his toes. I mauled him, opening him up, used my tongue to explore his mouth, all of it, missing nothing.

The sounds he made, the husky moans, made it impossible not to touch him, pull at his clothes, tug the button-down oxford shirt out of his jeans, and get my hands on his hot, sleek skin. I traced over the bumps and dips of his chiseled abdomen as I stroked his tongue with mine, taking and tasting, coaxing him forward into me, until he was the one with his back against the wall and I had him there, at my mercy, as one hot, wild kiss became another and another.

"Fuck," he growled, shoving me off him, panting hard, dragging in air.

All I could do was stand there, taking deep breaths as I waited to hear if the swearing was a good or bad development.

"Couple months back," he said hoarsely, "I was standing in the backyard at the grill, and I looked up and you waved to me and I had this feeling that I used to get when I walked into the house and saw Janey… like I was home."

Anything I said would be wrong, so I stayed quiet.

"And I was pissed, right, because what the hell? You're not her. You can't take her place! If she hadn't died, I'd still be there in San Francisco with her, so what the fuck?"

I nodded.

"But that's not what happened. She died and I lived, and we used to talk about it all the time and back then I thought—" He took a breath. "—my wife is crazy maudlin."

I would have probably thought the same.

"But now I gotta wonder if somehow she knew. She was always so sure we were never going to have kids, so sure we'd never grow old together… and I always said you're nuts, this is forever, you and me, but…."

I put a hand on his cheek, and he turned quickly and kissed my palm, my skin feeling branded by the simple press of his lips.

"I told her if I died she had to find a man to love her as much as I did, and she always said she'd find a *person* to love her. *A person.* And I'd tease her and say, you're going to become a lesbian, and she said she didn't know, couldn't say for certain. Because maybe it would be a woman, after me, that would fill her heart, and maybe it would be a man for me."

His wife was an angel and I'd always have to remember that.

"I used to laugh at her," he husked. "A man… for me… are you high?"

God, I really hoped it would be a man for him. "And what did she say?"

"She'd say, whoever loves you with their whole heart, don't turn them away."

"Yeah," I whispered. "Don't do that."

He grabbed hold of my face and pulled me forward, into him, and his mouth settled hard and hungry over mine.

I kissed him back as passionately as he kissed me, over and over, until I could feel the trembling excitement of need wash over me. I shook with it, with the idea of what I could have from this man, what I could take and give in return.

We parted gently the second time, each caught in the other's gaze.

"I thought maybe I just needed to get laid," he confessed.

I grinned at him even though he was trying to be so serious. "I see. Now all the women make sense—you were running away from me."

"I was trying to see if I was just lonely."

"Or you hoped that if you slept with enough of them, you wouldn't think about sleeping with me anymore."

"That too."

"And what did you figure out?"

He inhaled sharply and I saw the fear on him. "That sleeping around isn't going to help me when the only person I want to be with is you."

"How come?" I pressed.

The scowl was adorable.

"Mike?"

"'Cause you love me, right? I mean, you do."

"Do I?"

"Yes," he said quickly, irritably. "I don't see you lighting all up when other people smile at you or touch you. There's a difference."

Yes, there was. "Clearly," I agreed, stepping into him, my hands around his neck as I attacked him again, in the bushes, kissed him breathless until the sweet, urgent moans made me ready to get on my knees in the dirt.

We tore free of each other, and he pointed to the parking lot. When we emerged—flushed, hair tousled, clothes rumpled, lips swollen—Coz and Arad were there talking, leaning against their cruisers.

"I thought you two were gone," Arad stated in his superserious cop voice.

"We're going," Mike informed him, taking my hand and tugging me after him.

"You're not worried about this?" I asked Mike as we started for home, squeezing his hand, not wanting him to pull away from me.

"Worried about what?"

"You're holding my hand."

"I am."

"And what if people see?"

"I suspect that most everyone who does see will say the same thing that Kelly Seaton did when I passed him on the way to the jail."

"Which was?"

He started walking faster. "He asked me, 'Are you going to the jail to get your man out?' and I said, 'Yes, I am.'"

He was going to kill me with how possessive he was being.

"And he said, 'Once you get him out, you keeping him?'"

Kelly Seaton was both a blessing and a curse.

"And I said, 'Yeah, I'm keeping him,' and he said, 'That's good, because pretty soon, somebody else will.'"

"That's crap," I said with a chuckle as I started jogging to keep up with how quickly Mike was moving. "Nobody wants me; I'm a joke in this town."

He stopped so suddenly, I almost got whiplash.

"You're not a joke," he snarled, hands on my face, making sure I couldn't move as he glared at me. "You're smart and funny and so fuckin' sexy... I mean, do you even know what you look like when you grin when you're tired? Or how husky your voice is when you first wake up in the morning?"

I couldn't have spoken to save my life. No one ever noticed anything about me. Not me. I was the guy who hit on everybody; I was available and desperate and no one took me seriously.

"You think you're like this sad little man who everyone just humors, but Jesus Christ, Hutch, do you ever actually look in the mirror and see yourself?"

"I don't—it doesn't matter," I told him. "What do you see?"

"I see everything I want," Mike said raggedly. "My heart stops when I look at you."

I nodded. "Okay, so… let's go home."

"Why do you think I'm hurrying?" he replied grumpily, glancing around, figuring out where we were since I was too out of it to know where the hell I was, and yanking me after him.

No one ever manhandled me and I found that I liked it quite a bit.

It was hot that, when he got to the front door of my place, he used his key, opened the door, showed me through, and then ordered me not to move while he put Benny outside.

I stood there in my own living room at four in the afternoon wondering what I should be doing.

When I heard him coming back, I turned in time for him to gently take my face in his hands and kiss me.

It was different now that we were in the house—more intimate, of course, but also there were no rules. We could combust and become anything we wanted to be.

I whimpered when he kissed me back into the wall, shoved my arms up, and then yanked my Henley over my head and off. Our lips parted for mere seconds before I recaptured his, nibbling and licking, ravaging, wanting all of him.

He spoke to me in broken whispers as my hands clutched at his broad back, slid into his thick, coarse hair to hold him close, anything I could do to keep kissing him, to prolong the feel of him, his taste. When he wrapped his arms around me so tight, clutching me to his heart with his bare skin plastered to mine, I gave up any concerns I had about air.

He broke the kiss, and I saw it then, the lust all over him.

"You want me," I whispered.

"More than anything," he vowed before he dragged me off the wall and started kissing me, hungrily, all over again.

We went down the hall, unbuckling belts, hopping on alternating feet to pull off shoes—his steel-toed work boots that he wore when he was moving pallets in the warehouse nearly made a hole in my floor—

bumping into walls, knocking things over, and repeatedly making pictures rattle until we stumbled through the doorway of my room and crashed into my bed.

When he lifted free to laugh, I followed, not wanting my mouth parted from his, but he bent to help pull my left wingtip off so my jeans and briefs could follow.

"Here, lemme help you," he said under his breath, moving his hands down my thighs to my knees, then gently over my calves to my ankles and feet.

He was massaging, his hands creating circles of welcoming heat, and I was quivering as I never did, wanting to drink in each touch, absorb it into my body.

"I've seen other men and thought they were handsome before," he said, kicking his jeans away before taking off his briefs and adding them to the pile of discarded clothes. "But I've never wanted to hold another man's dick in my hand."

"I was at the right place at the right time," I informed him, reaching out and taking his hard, heavy uncut cock in hand and stroking him from balls to head.

His gasp of pleasure made me bold, and I pulled harder before I went to my knees.

"No," he practically yelled, grabbing my arms and powering me up beside him before he shoved me down on the bed. "That's not what I want for the first—you don't even understand how much I…. Hutch."

I turned and looked at him over my shoulder.

"God, look at you."

It was him, though, not me. His body was a work of art, powerfully muscled under the deep, dark tanned skin. I wanted to touch all of him. "Holy crap, Mike, you're—"

"Michael," he corrected, and when his gaze slowly and with difficulty lifted from his perusal of my form and locked with mine, I understood how I had wanted to be looked at in bed from the very first time. That… how he was doing it… like he wanted to both devour and cherish me at the exact same time—was it. That was how your lover was supposed to stare, where you could feel the heat and desire and dangerous, razor-edged longing rippling just there below the surface. "No more Mike."

He was Michael to me now, as he'd been to his wife, as he was to his family, and I was included, the circle extended to me because I was part of them, the sacred trust he shared with only a few.

I rolled over on my back, sprawled out and ready for him to do with as he pleased, and when he climbed onto the bed, I reached for him.

"I've dreamed about this," he told me as he crawled over me, lying down between my legs, his hard, leaking shaft sliding along mine as he pinned me under him.

"Oh yeah?" I asked, my voice barely above a whisper.

"I dream about all kinds of things with you," he rushed out, wrapping his arms under me and burying his face in the side of my neck.

His jolting shiver made me smile.

"You needed me."

"Like fuckin' water—yeah."

Michael's answer made me brave. "You were wasting your time on anyone who wasn't me," I said as I pushed his thick black hair out of his face, savoring the feel of the cool texture against my suddenly hot skin, trailing my fingers up and down his spine, wanting to hold him tight, never let go, willing myself to not show him how frantic my desire was.

"I know."

He knew!

"I won't do it anymore."

"Your family—what will they think?"

"They'll think 'If he loves him, then so will we.'"

Michael loved me.

It wasn't right place–right time, it was simply me.

Me.

He loved me because I'd been the one to drag him back into the light.

I was the one who'd insinuated myself into his life, under the tripwire where everyone else got trapped, and danced around inside of his dreams.

I was the one who made him care about food again and take pride in its preparation, which touched on his childhood and his family and was the reason he was back on the phone with his mother asking for recipes.

All roads led to me.

I was it, the man he loved.

"Did you hear me?"

The tears were ridiculous; I never cried over anything, ever, but there they were, because I didn't have to tiptoe around what I wanted, what I could say.

"I want your mother to lose her mind over me because mine is gonna adore you," I sighed, more happy than I could ever remember being.

His smile was so warm as he lifted for my kiss. "We'll go see them, my family, as soon as you sort out your latest community center debacle."

"Oh, you heard about that," I growled, because *of course* he had. The stupid town was only so big, and he had picked me up in jail, after all.

He laughed and scrambled free, flipping me over on my stomach and hauling me to my hands and knees.

"Well, now, Michael, what is it you want?"

He kissed down my spine and I shuddered beneath him, letting my head drop as he kissed over my right cheek and his hands spread me open.

"You should let me shower or—"

"No, I like the way you smell… and taste."

The strokes over my puckered hole went from tentative to teasing to deliberate so very fast. "You've been thinking about me for a while," I said, nearly vibrating with happiness. The idea that I had occupied his thoughts made it hard for me to even form words.

"Yes" was all he said before his thumb slipped inside, eased by the saliva dripping between my cheeks.

"Michael!" I yelled, pushing back against him. "Get the lube."

"Where?"

I pointed at the nightstand and he stretched for it, pulled the drawer out, dumped it but got the lube. We could collect the television remotes, mechanical pencils I did the Sunday crossword with, and lip balm later. The only thing I cared about at the moment was having Michael Rojas inside me.

"Did you fuck anyone without a condom?" I was afraid of the answer, and also, there was suddenly a niggling doubt in the back of my head. I didn't know what about, I was just anxious.

"No, sir," he answered, his voice low and guttural as he snapped open the cap.

"If you sleep with anyone other than—"

"Oh no," he cautioned. "I'm made loyal. It's gonna be just us."

"You're going to break so many—" I gasped as he slid two lube-slicked fingers into my ass. "—hearts when they find out."

"Nope," Michael said, withdrawing fast, rolling over on his back, lying down beside me. "No hearts involved 'cept yours and mine."

He was breathtaking, stretched out on my bed, in my room, in my house, in my life… he was mine, and my brain had not caught up with where my heart already was.

"I know you," he mentioned.

"What?"

"You were thinking, he may love me, but when it comes down to it, I'm not a woman and the only way he'll be able to be inside me is from behind."

"No, I—"

"Yes," he stopped me, as he slicked his enormous, engorged cock with lube. "But I promise you: I know you're a man—a very strong, handsome, beautiful man who I want more than anything to watch fuck himself on my dick."

He knew me so well, all those nights together, the endless conversations, the constant banter, and the complete, unconditional support. We'd been in the middle of our relationship before either of us even knew we'd begun.

"Come here."

I leaned into him, and he kissed every part of me he could reach. Face, neck, shoulders, stomach, until I couldn't think, and he didn't seem to want to stop.

"Please touch me," he moaned. "I wanna come all over you and your bed."

"You're killing me," I moaned hoarsely.

"Me?" Michael rasped. "God, Hutch, do you have any idea what you look like right now? Could you please just put your hands all over me?"

I could do better.

Straddling his thighs, I lifted over him only to sink slowly down, inch by inch, the lube and the rimming allowing for the steady breach as I stretched around his considerable girth, until I was finally and completely impaled on his shaft.

"Oh fuck!" he snarled. It was primal and dark, and his hands on my thighs would leave bruises. I was not going anywhere. Since no one else had ever laid claim, I was content in a way I'd never been before.

His hips rolled under me as he pushed up to meet my downward thrusts, a smooth retreat followed by the thrum of us coming together, the rhythm increasing quickly, driving, pounding, as I grabbed hold of my cock and tugged to the same tempo.

"Jesus, Hutch, you're so fuckin' tight, you feel so—Hutch!"

His words were pushed aside by his roar as he suddenly came, exploding with a cry, shivering hard with his release, pulsing deep within my body.

I spattered his abdomen seconds later, no way to avoid it from where I was, head back, eyes closed, riding him to my completion, feeling my muscles clamp down around him, not ready to let him go.

"Goddammit."

My head snapped forward, and I checked to see why the first word out of his mouth after the best sex of my life was a curse.

"We just blew the dog's mind."

I turned to look for my dog, and there was Benny, sitting in the doorway, head tipped, looking utterly confused. "You should've locked the doggie door so he couldn't get back in."

"Yeah, now he's messed up for life, poor bastard."

I snorted out a laugh.

"It's like he's never seen you in bed with someone before."

Ridiculous man, ridiculous ruse.

Leaning over, hands on either side of his head, still with him buried to his balls in my ass, I kissed him deep, with lots of tongue.

"No one's ever been in this bed but you, Michael Rojas."

"Well, now," he sighed, clearly very pleased, very smug. "That's very good to hear."

"Is it?"

"Oh yes," he murmured, reaching up for my face. "And I plan to keep it that way."

That was excellent news.

CHAPTER SIX

WE TRIED to talk, but we were too warm, too sated, and so fell asleep in the sweaty, sticky mess we made of the bed. When I woke up a couple of hours later with the man wrapped around me, I sighed happily, leaned my cheek in his hair, and passed out again.

The second time we woke up, Michael wanted to know if he'd hurt me.

"No, baby, you didn't hurt me at all."

"And you're not hurt from your fall, right? You're okay?"

"I'm better than that."

"Yeah?"

"Oh yeah," I murmured, reaching for him.

He sank into my arms like he'd been snuggling up to me for years.

The third time, Michael woke up with me, and before either one of us could get up, we started laughing about Benny, that we'd probably have to get him some therapy and how much was that going to cost and how in the world would we know if it was even working or not. When we heard people moving around down the hall, we both fell out of bed and scrambled around for clothes.

"You guys better get out here!" Ivy called from the kitchen, and I cursed the fact that while the other bedrooms were on the second floor, the master was on the first. "You promised to make dinner tonight, and I want to hear all about Hutch getting incarcerated!"

We had our clothes pulled on when a deeper voice came right after hers. "And the grownup wants to know if you two are finally calling yourself the couple that everyone can see that you are."

We both leaned out the door to see Essien standing at the opposite end of the hall, beaming at us.

"She's back outside," he informed us, "so you can both take a fast shower before you come out. Having dinner with you guys while you smell like jizz—not that appealing,"

"How do you know we smell like—"

"Did you see your dog? Something in here traumatized him—only so many things it could be."

"You could just, you know, take your kid out for pizza," Michael groused at him even as he started rubbing the back of my neck.

"Nope. Me and Ivy both want to hear the story, and I can tell you about Blake Timmons taking back that absurd trumped-up fraud charge and how much fun it was to watch Mia Renaldi work him over."

"How did you see that?"

"Jail, city hall, fire department… seriously, what are they, fifty feet away from each other?"

I couldn't stifle my soft laughter. "We'll be right out."

"Hey, what's the story on the hot doctor?"

I ignored him, bolting for the shower, wanting to be the first one under the hot water. But Michael beat me to it when he went in without taking his clothes off. I had to strip them off before lathering up my mesh sponge.

"What the hell were you thinking?" I laughed as I peeled him out of his jeans. "Now you're all wet."

"I was thinking that you having to get me naked did not sound like it had a downside."

Shaking my head, I soaped his gorgeous cock, which, even flaccid, was impressive. "You know we really have to figure out a way to get them out of here."

"Hey, Hutch."

I lifted my gaze.

"I love you. I'm going to make you very happy."

And I knew that. He already did.

I grabbed him, hugging him tight, and he did the same, the two of us breathing together under the warm spray.

"I love you back," I whispered. "Never doubt it."

"No," Michael promised. "I never would."

EASY EVENINGS

Mary Calmes

MANGROVE
Stories

CHAPTER ONE

I DIDN'T like lying to my friends, but it was necessary. When Hutch and Kelly asked me about the restraining order Britton Lassiter, the new attorney in town, served me with, I said I didn't care. I told them that since it didn't affect me or my business in Mangrove, Florida, he could leave it in place, for all I cared.

The problem, though, was that I really did care. I cared quite a bit.

As a rent boy in Manhattan, I had hundreds of clients, all different, all with different sorts of kinks. But the straight-laced attorney had distinguished himself because of the trust he'd placed in me from our initial meeting. We'd met as equals, just two guys, and because of that, ours had never become a relationship in which he paid me. Britton knew what I was, but he was excluded from having to know anything about my business. When we met, he put himself in my hands, did everything I asked, and was truly submissive in bed. It was the missing component from all of my other encounters. I had never been entirely trusted before. He was the only one I truly ever saw.

People thought the yearly masquerade shindig was really just a big orgy, but it wasn't. The Halloween party I met Britton at—it was a far more upscale event than that. There was wait staff, alcohol, and whatever the hell kind of drugs you were into. The warehouse in Tribeca had been all done in a gothic theme, which I myself found ridiculously cheesy but apparently got people in a certain mood. There were black birdcages everywhere—with candles burning inside them as well as inside the faux fireplaces in the rooms set up with moveable red-painted walls. The furniture was all black: a Belle de Fleur sofa, a carved mahogany Louis XV Bergère armchair, an Absolom Roche chair, as well as the chandeliers, sconces, antique lanterns, and the many bookcases. The place was draped in black velvet, damask, and red satin. I felt like I was going to a party at Tim Burton's house—or Dracula's—but more upscale and Hollywood, less 7th grade Halloween dance.

I was invited as a party favor, paid to be there as one of the pretty people who lured others deeper into the maze, fucked them, and then moved on to the next. It was all for bragging rights, having the party everyone wanted an invitation to year after year.

It started out as billionaire Aaron Sutter's New York Masquerade Ball, and he flew in from Chicago to host it. The jet set and the glitterati would have died to be seen at that ball. Now it was run by Geneva Grace, a socialite whose father built casinos all over the world.

It was a sordid affair, the masks given to everyone only adding to the illusion of fun without consequences. Obviously some people at the event would not be fucking in private rooms—two at a time, three, maybe four—if they weren't hopped up on something or didn't have their faces covered. So with the masks, no one would be able to pick out anyone in a lineup later, even if a life depended on it.

I was prowling around when I spotted him: tall, built like a swimmer, broad shoulders, a wide chest, the whole V-shape, long legs, and a perfectly tight, round ass. Even through the black lace mask, I could tell his eyes were a stunning shade of brilliant ocean blue. I was immediately drawn across the room, and the closer I got, the more I realized how ridiculously uncomfortable he looked. In the middle of all the debauchery going on around him, he had a tightness to the set of his mouth, an obvious hesitancy, and most of all, more than anything, he was intimidated. It made no sense; he was the focus of three stunning men and they were all pawing at him and letting him know in no uncertain terms that any of their asses were his for the taking. As I reached them, I heard the dry sound of his laughter and realized it was forced. He was trying to scramble free of their hands, push the one guy off his lap and slip away, get out as fast as he could.

I didn't want him to go.

"Move," I commanded the long, leggy twink in the assless red leather chaps wiggling around in his lap. It was obvious he was hoping to grind over a cock straining to get free of dress pants, but the man in question was not hard in the least.

"Oh, sweetie, I'm not going anywhere."

"You will if you want your nose to stay as perfect as it is now," I warned, my voice going low and scary.

He climbed off, and I removed my mask and waited.

"Oh," the twink purred, hands on my black Armani suit jacket and then under it to the black dress shirt seconds later. "Maybe you want to play?"

"Not now. Maybe later," I said, dismissing them all with a wave of my hand before flopping down beside the beautiful man.

"Thank you," he said after a moment, his sharp exhale not lost on me. "I didn't want to hurt anyone, but they needed to go."

I nodded and did a slow pan to him. "Can I get you a drink?"

His eyes were shiny, and he licked his lips. "I already had a few, thank you."

"We should move so no one else comes along and attacks you."

He scoffed. "I don't think that's going to be a problem now that you're here."

"No?" I fished.

He cleared his throat. "No. You're, uhm, clearly the pretty one between the two of us."

"You think?"

Quick nod.

"That's very flattering."

He caught his breath, and I felt the nervous tension rolling off him before I leaned sideways into his personal space so my lips hovered close to his.

"May I?"

The whimper was sweet, and I turned into him and took what I wanted.

He tasted like champagne and strawberries, and faintly of chocolate, but more than anything, more than the part that was him alone… he tasted like desire.

His hands clenched in my suit jacket, holding me close, tight, and when he opened for me and I ravaged his mouth, all hot and wet, the tremor that immediately tore through him told me everything I needed to know. The man was not about to fuck anyone; he would be the one spread out and begging for me.

Slithering out of his grip, I rolled into his lap, straddling his hips, and took his face in my hands, nibbling along his jaw as he let his head fall back against the loveseat, giving himself completely over to my care.

It was surprising; men didn't normally let themselves go in my presence. I'd been watched while I performed, been asked to keep kinky secrets, dressed up in costumes, tied people down, and had been given cash and drugs and even jewelry to carry, but not once, not ever, had anyone just let out a deep, languorous, lion stretching in the sun sigh and put themselves in my hands. It turned me on big time.

I sucked and licked my way up to his mouth and then recaptured his lips, parted them, and began my assault anew. My hands were everywhere, tugging on his shirt, yanking it free, burrowing until I hit skin.

"Oh, you're gorgeous under these clothes," I whispered as I smiled, taking in the sight of the washboard abs and smooth, muscular chest before pinching his nipple with one hand as I worked open his belt with the other.

"I shouldn't—"

My tongue shut him up, shoving into his mouth, tasting, pushing his around, showing him who was boss, the kiss savage without a hint of tenderness and easily, obviously, what he craved. He was hard under my ass, moaning as his hips jerked involuntarily, his dick straining to reach me through two layers of cloth.

"You want me to suck your cock?"

"I—no, I—I could… you."

The man was in desperate need of direction. "Get up and come with me," I commanded, climbing off his lap to stand.

He complied quickly and I took his hand, lifted it to my lips, kissed his knuckles, and then tugged him after me.

I led him down a short corridor and found an actual functioning maintenance closet, opened the door, ordered the people making out against the metal shelving to get out, and then slammed and locked up behind them.

"I thought I was going to be on display somewhere," he whispered.

I knew all the encounters in the main area were recorded; some of the beds in the makeshift rooms were either for many to enjoy or for people to mill around and watch a performance.

"Would you have preferred that?" I asked as I spun him around and shoved him up against the door so that he had to catch himself with his hands or go face first into it. Maybe he was an exhibitionist.

"No," he murmured, gasping as I kicked his feet apart, forcing him to widen his stance. "Just… alone is better."

"Good," I husked, leaning in, kissing up the side of his neck to his ear, pulling the condom from the pocket of my dress pants at the same time.

"Shouldn't we—"

"No," I told him, putting the condom between my teeth while I pressed my chest to his back and went to work on his pants.

"But I should know your—oh!" He gasped as I shucked his pants and briefs to the floor in one tug. They pooled around his ankles, limiting his movement or escape, and I instantly took his already leaking cock in hand.

I stroked fast from balls to head as I used my other hand to rip open the lubed condom and slip it on. I'd been hustling since I was sixteen, I could multitask with the best of them.

"My name's Britton," he croaked, pushing back into me, hands splayed on the door in front of him, head dropping forward, ready for whatever I was going to do.

"It's a nice name," I murmured, distracted, glancing around and seeing what I needed. "C'mere," I instructed, first helping him out of his pants so he could do what I wanted.

He moved fast, obeying, again putting himself in my hands, asking no questions as I shoved him to his knees on a short bench against the wall next to the door. I was shorter than him, but now with us close to the same level, the curve of his ass nestled right against my groin, we'd line up perfectly.

"You can just—"

"No," I quieted him, reaching back into my dress pants for a lube packet. I was always prepared with travel-size supplies.

"I don't need—"

"I know what you need," I said, clenching the packet between my teeth, then ripping it open so I could squeeze it all into my palm and slather it on my cock.

Spreading his cheeks, I angled myself to his entrance and pushed into him ever so slightly, the lube allowing me to open him a bit easier. But there would be no smooth, seamless slide.

"Oh… damn," he groaned, his voice guttural and low. "I haven't been—" He shuddered under me. "It's been a long time since I've been filled and taken."

"Why?" I asked, distracted, admiring his gorgeous, firm round ass.

"I don't— It's not something I let anyone see."

"So you normally do the fucking."

"Yes." He huffed out the word.

If there had been a sufficient amount of lube to shove past the tight muscles and breach him in one thrust, I would have, but there wasn't, and no matter what, I would not be the cause of any kind of pain. I knew what it was like, to be the one on the receiving end of that.

So I worked slowly, pressing, stretching him, screwing myself into his tight heat, all the while gentling him—my words, I'd found over the years, were as important as my actions.

"You feel good."

I knew I did, I was paid to do this, after all. "You're beautiful," I whispered, and when he lifted his head and turned his chin to look at me over his shoulder, I saw the blown pupils, heard the sharp catches of breath, and felt him shudder again.

"Just please fuck me."

"Oh, I intend to," I promised, leaning in to ravish his mouth, to suck and nibble on his delectable lips.

He jolted against me, and I understood fucking was not the only thing no one had done with him. When he'd covered up his need to be topped, he'd also hidden his craving to be dominated, to have someone else take charge. And though I suspected it was only a bedroom thing— I'd seen his type before—he yearned to submit.

Hearing a soft moan, the ragged pleading and near sob of frustration, I took hold of his hips and drove the rest of the way inside his body, burying myself to the hilt.

"Oh yes," he whimpered, shivering hard, reaching behind for me, his fingers digging into my ass through my dress pants. I had only loosened my clothes, having learned on many occasions that getting naked was not only unnecessary but could also be potentially dangerous. Being able to run at a moment's notice was sometimes critical in my line of work.

"Bend over," I directed, easing him backward enough to better my angle, needing to piston into him hard and fast.

He followed my order immediately, and I pulled out a fraction only to ram back in, over and over, setting a tempo of thrust and retreat, rucking up his dress shirt so I could curl over him and kiss his broad back. He was beautifully made, and his skin was warm and sleek over long muscles, and as I fucked him, watching his hole stretch around my fat cock, I realized his submission was not the most appealing thing about him. What was,

was that he trusted me to care for him and not hurt him, which was both sexy and sweet at the same time. That fast, I was intrigued.

"My name's Lazlo," I rumbled into his skin, licking it before I bit him.

"Lazlo," he repeated with a rasp in his voice, "come home with me."

"Why?" I asked, even though I'd already decided I would.

"I want you to fuck me in my bed."

Honesty was *hot*. "Then I will."

"I need," he whined, writhing in my grip, "I want...."

"What do you want?" I asked as I pegged his gland.

"Oh fuck," he groaned, and I heard the desperation. "I want you deeper, but I want to kiss you at the same time."

The bed made sense, then, and his desire to have me in it—he wanted to be under me, have arms and legs wrapped around me as I ground down into him.

"And what do you want right now?"

"I want to come!"

"Then do that," I growled, fisting my hand in his hair, yanking his head back, bowing his spine for me, the position allowing me to penetrate him completely on each stroke as I hammered up into him. "Come now, because I can't wait for you to ride me in your bed."

The noise he made, half cry, half yell, giving himself over to me, to his passion, was as gorgeous to hear as his release was to watch.

He spurted all over the wall, and his muscles clamped down, tightening like a velvet fist around me, and I came hard, pumping into him, my climax blinding me for just a second.

I lay against his back, letting his breathing raise and lower me, and when I realized I was enjoying the quiet communion with him that I never allowed myself, I went to move.

"No, give it another second," he requested, hand over his shoulder, fingers in my hair. "And then pull out and follow me home. I'll feed you before round two."

"I'm not a stray dog," I reminded him, and though normally I would have bristled over his comment, coming from a man who wanted to kiss me, it didn't rankle.

"No," he sighed, "you're a very beautiful man who I really want to spend the night with."

I could not say no.

I was a hustler, he turned out to be a powerful, high-priced attorney, but still, we fit—and not just in the bedroom.

He cooked for me and wanted to cuddle on the couch after. And even though nine times out of ten, the nestling turned into frottage and more, the tenth time never went any further than snuggling. He enjoyed holding me, rubbing his chin in my hair, and stroking my back.

Sometimes I'd come into his apartment after he buzzed me in from downstairs, and he'd be on his bed spread out, waiting for me.

"Please come put your gorgeous body on mine," he'd beg, "and in mine."

I never hesitated.

When I showed him my test results from my normal three-month checkup—it was important to show clients I was disease-free—he gave me his. After that there were no more condoms with him, and that, too—because I was still a rent boy and anyone who wanted to spend a grand a night could have me—was special and touched me.

His trust was overwhelming, and so when I saw him that day on the street in Mangrove and bounced up to him, happy, thrilled he was there, elated to have a do-over, it was painful to hear his anger, see his condemnation, and know it had all been a lie. He thought I was filth, and so the betrayal, since I knew better than to ever fall in love, sent me into a rage.

"What, I'm good enough to fuck you but not good enough to talk to on the street?"

That was the real reason for the restraining order.

For once, it wasn't one of the guys I'd screwed showing up out of the blue and wanting to keep paying me while I was at home. It was the guy I'd told I wouldn't give up hustling, the guy I also thought I had a second chance with.

I was wrong when I said no to him the first time, and I was wrong when I thought he was in Mangrove to give me a second chance at happiness. I really hated making a fool of myself.

CHAPTER TWO

MY PLACE, On The Breeze, sold wind chimes, both hanging and free-standing, because that's what I made. I also had ornaments, but not like scary flamingos or ducks or swans or signs for the garden, but animals, huge ones, some ten feet tall. I made giraffes and wolves—a guy in Destin ordered a whole pack of them, six in all for his backyard—lions, bears, anything really, as long as it wasn't expected. I made a pterodactyl once that a lady told me scared the crows away much better than her scarecrow ever had. I also made owls, big creepy ones with enormous jeweled eyes. One lady bought one and promptly returned it because she said it scared her Chihuahua so bad he stopped peeing in the yard and went back to doing his business in her living room. Apparently she'd just gotten him house-trained the week before and she was back to square one. So I refunded her money, because really, if the dog couldn't pee, I'd maybe done my job too well.

All my creations were made of hammered sheet metal and wrought iron, and I kept all my materials out in the converted tool shed that now doubled as my workshop. The only drawback was that when my goggles were on and the Foo Fighters were blasting from the iPod connected to some of the best speakers money could buy, there was no way I could hear anyone ringing my doorbell or even pounding instead of knocking at the front door of my craftsman bungalow. That was why when I turned, dancing, acetylene torch in hand, to find a man in a bespoke suit standing beside a tiny little girl, I was surprised.

Quickly I killed the fire and then grabbed the remote to turn off the music, but not before I noticed that the little girl had been rocking side to side to "Best of You." Torch extinguished, I placed it gently on my work table, put my goggles up, and waited.

"Mr. Maguire?" the man asked.

I squinted at him, wondering why I was being served with a subpoena. Clearly I was looking at a lawyer, but the little girl was throwing me. Who brought his kid along to work?

"Hello?" he snapped, clearly not the patient sort.

I cleared my throat. "Sorry, yes. I'm Lazlo Maguire."

Coming forward into my space, he presented me with an envelope. On the outside was my name, handwritten, and nothing else.

My eyes flicked to his face. "What's this about?"

"Please read the enclosed note," he said, his voice flat, before he looked down at the child tugging on his hand. I realized then that she had not been rocking out to Dave Grohl and the boys with me, but was instead doing the pee-pee dance. She needed to go.

"Do you wanna use my bathroom?"

"Yes," she piped up.

"She can hold it," he answered, tightening his grip.

"Owww," she almost cried, and I saw her bottom lip quiver.

"No, I don't think she can," I said, holding out my hand. "Come on, kitten, I'll take you."

She lunged for me, and only because he let her go could she grab hold of my hand with both of hers.

"Do you want to come with us?" I inquired.

His face, screwed up like he smelled something vile, and the way he shook his head disdainfully told me no before the word left his mouth. He was revolted by me and also, it seemed, by her. It hit me that this was not his child.

"We'll be right back," I said as I walked by him, out of the shed. It had big barn doors on both ends that I normally opened for ventilation and to allow the breeze to waft through. It was fortunate I was on the end of the street with no neighbors on one side, the beach on the other, so my music and the decibel I kept it at never bothered anyone.

I led her up the back steps to my porch and inside first the mud room and then the kitchen.

"Oh pretty," she sang out as the titian and mint green walls caught her eye, along with the huge oil paintings, metal sculptures, the Hacienda gated bookcase, the black amethyst Carnival glass pitcher filled with sunflowers, and the white armoire with wire mesh doors I used to store various knickknacks.

"Yeah? You like it?"

She nodded, clearly dazzled.

"Me too. I gave up traditional years ago."

"Oooh," she whispered, pointing at the Chinese lanterns hanging from the ceiling in the living room. "I like lights. I want some in my room."

"Okay," I agreed, because why wouldn't she be able to get some? That made no sense.

The bathroom with its aqua walls, mason jars with sand at the bottom and candles stuck inside, eucalyptus hanging in the shower, painted vinyl shower curtain, and shadowbox above the toilet, she loved.

"This is good," she sighed, nodding. "I like it."

"Well, go pee so we can get you back to your uncle?" I offered.

She shook her head.

"He's not your dad, is he?"

Her eyes widened almost comically. "No. You're my daddy."

It was time for *my* eyes to do the bugging out. "I'm sorry, what?"

She slipped her little hand in mine. "It's you. Camlin said so."

Camlin?

I coughed. "Maybe I should—read this letter."

"Yes," she said, beaming at me. "It's from Mommy."

"Okay," I said, exhaling sharply. "You need help or anything?"

"I'm three," she explained like I was slow. "I can potty on my own."

Good to know.

I closed the door after her, hearing her start to hum what I thought was "Brown Eyed Girl," by Van Morrison, and then ripped open the envelope and found a note inside addressed to me.

It was one page, typed, single-spaced, and at the bottom it was signed Olivet Lautner. I read the letter once, then again, and was on my third go-through when the little girl, who I now knew was named Katherine, came and sat down beside me on the small bench in the hallway. It was cute how her legs were too short to drop over the edge and dangle, but instead just stuck out in front of her, straight.

I turned to look at her.

"Camlin doesn't want me since Mommy went to heaven, but you're my Daddy, so you want me, right?"

Holy. Fuck.

"Mommy said you would."

I couldn't move air into my lungs.

"She told me it would be like Bambi when his mommy was killed by the hunters and his daddy took care of him until he got big."

Any second now I was going to pass out. Right after I stopped hyperventilating.

"I miss Mommy," she whined softly before the tears welled up in her big, dark emerald green anime eyes and then spilled over. "And Camlin doesn't want me."

The sobbing was heartbreaking, and instinctively, I lifted her into my lap and hugged her. She sobbed on my shoulder, face pressed into the side of mine, little arms wrapped around my neck.

I knew right then, whatever else happened, I was never going to let my daughter go.

Chapter Three

RESTRAINING ORDER or no, I had tried to woo Britton Lassiter. And it wasn't just because I craved the feel of his hands on my skin, or liked the way he moved, or how his smile made me feel warm and light, but mostly because I was just plain happier when he was around.

When I used to go over to his place late at night, letting myself in with the key he'd given me, sometimes he was already asleep, and just watching him for a minute before I crawled in beside him soothed me. At other times, he was ready to pounce and wanted me hot and naked right that second. Now and then, he would be reading on the couch and dinner would be warming in the oven—getting there, just being in his space, inhaling the smell of his laundry detergent on his clothes and traces of cologne on his skin, the way he lifted for my kiss, glasses on because he was reading… I would come all undone, letting my slick, swaggering hustler armor fall away and dropping down into his lap to let him hold me. Those were the moments I missed most. I'd known I would when I'd broken it off and walked away.

There had been no choice. He'd wanted me to stay. Even though he had been in the middle of a divorce, not sure where he was going to live, his whole life up in the air, the one truth he'd held on to was that he wanted me there with him—in his home, wherever that was, in his bed beside him, because I was the only one who'd ever made him *stop*.

Britton Lassiter moved fast.

He worked in a blur of activity: he wheeled and dealed, he handled and negotiated cases in the millions, and when he was done, he went immediately to the next challenge… and the next. He never slowed, his entire career—always moving forward, never back—was about precision and speed. He'd married with that same efficiency. It had been the quickest way to get his parents to stop nagging him. His ex was a decision based on the most effective use of his time, and she'd been just as devoted to success and a future and the pursuit of the American Dream as he was. They were the perfect couple doing precisely what was expected.

Where it fell apart was when it came time to have kids and Britton woke up. He came to a skidding halt, because living in hyperdrive, on the fast track, did not equal hearth and home. Children were about family and he did not want that with his wife. From what he'd told me, she'd been just as relieved as he was when he called an end to the grand charade.

After that Britton had bobbed along, trying to figure out his life, still a shark, still moving fast and dangerous, but with the extra risk of not caring who he used or who used him. When we plowed into each other at the Halloween party, he was ready for his life to start. Normally, Britton noticed no one, but me he saw clearly and that was it—he wanted me to be his happily ever after. We weren't the same—he was rich, I was not—and for me to be his everything… I would have had to live off him, because the life where I didn't was either in Mangrove, a world away from New York, or made up of the nights when I wasn't fucking someone else.

The fights were epic, and when I finally walked out and didn't go back, he replaced me with a really nice girlfriend, Kennedy Vaughn, who became the person I saw hanging on his arm every time I opened up the society page. But when I saw him in Mangrove without her, I thought he'd remembered where I told him I lived six months out of the year, and my heart had leaped and I charged over to tell him I was sorry and that if he was willing to work out a solution, so was I.

He'd looked at me like I was nuts. And then there was yelling, and the next day I was served with a restraining order.

I was devastated at first, then furious, then hurt again, then relieved, and finally just sad. I missed him terribly, but now, suddenly, bigger issues were at play and I didn't necessarily need him. But I did, in fact, need a lawyer. I wanted Mia Renaldi, his partner at Renaldi & Lassiter, but Mia was on a case in Miami and only Britton was there.

"What precisely are we doing?" Cranston Polk, the lawyer of Camlin Baylor, software magnate, asked me as he watched me pace.

"I'm having issues with my lawyer," I explained. "He has a restraining order against me."

His eyebrows shot up. "Your lawyer has a restraining order?"

"Yeah."

He coughed. "Interesting. So how do you plan to get this paperwork looked at, then?"

"I'm not—oh!" I almost shouted because I'd just had an epiphany. "You take it in and I can wave from here."

"I—"

"I'll stay here with Kitty."

"Katie," he corrected.

"I like Kitty," Katie told him. "And he's my Daddy, so he can name me what he wants."

Cranston was clearly exasperated with the both of us. He wheeled around, looked both ways before crossing the street—for God knew what reason, this was Mangrove after all—and jogged up to the small converted Cape Cod that Mia and Britton practiced law out of.

I squatted down beside Katie because she was squeezing my hand.

"What's wrong, kitty cat?"

Her face lit up over the name. "You won't not like me, huh?"

I smiled at her. "You mean, will I change my mind?"

She nodded.

"No, I won't change my mind."

"Promise?"

"I do."

"Can I have a cat?"

"Sure."

Huge smile from her. "A kitten?"

"Yes."

"Can we get it now?"

"After we talk to the lawyer."

"I hate lawyers," she said gravely, sounding very grown-up at that moment.

"Me too." I sighed, standing up as I watched Britton striding across the street with Cranston and stopping in front of my daughter and me.

"What the hell is… is…." He glanced from me to Katie and back to me. "What're you trying to pull?"

I cleared my throat. "This is my daughter. Currently she's in the custody of Camlin Baylor, who wants to give her to me lock, stock, and barrel along with a check for fifty thousand dollars so he never needs to see either one of us again. His concern is that down the road she'll contact him, or I will, and that he'll get stuck paying for something. I want her, not his money, and I want that ironclad between us. I need you to make sure that happens."

He glared at me.

"If you could do that for me, I swear to God you'll never have to see me for the rest of your life. I'll get out of Mangrove as soon as I can."

His eyes flicked to Katie again; checking, I was certain, to make sure she was an actual child and not some trick of the light I was pulling. Her scowl up at him was full of obvious judgment. She didn't care for him one bit. "I—the moving is not necessary if you simply keep your distance."

"Done," I agreed quickly.

The look on his face was confusing. I was finding it hard to tell if it was sadness, regret, anger—but really, it hardly mattered. I was in parent mode, and it occurred to me that an hour ago, I had no earthly idea what that entailed but right now was fairly prepared to say that putting the needs of someone else before myself was just the beginning.

He turned to Cranston. "Please come into my office."

"You're all nuts," Cranston retorted, clearly tired of the drama that had invaded his life.

Britton could not argue that point.

KATIE LIKED the fish tank in Britton's office, and she told him so as he sat at his desk in front of Cranston and me, reading the paperwork sent along with the little girl. A moving truck would follow in a day or two with the rest of the clothes that were not in the two large Louis Vuitton suitcases currently in the back of Cranston's car. Katie's armoire, bed, her mother's vanity table, some framed artwork—the names of the paintings and artists were listed—a hope chest that included an antique set of silverware given to Katie's mother, Olivet, on her wedding day, and an entire wardrobe box full of stuffed animals were in transit as we spoke.

"And do you have power of attorney in this matter?" Britton asked Cranston after a solid thirty minutes of reading.

"I do."

"Good," Britton said, leaning forward in that fluid way he had that made him look boneless. Watching the man move was a treat. "I have some additional provisions."

"For what?"

"In case Mr. Baylor changes his mind, wants to see the girl, or wants any of his property returned. I want the entirety of the contents of what's been promised to irrevocably remain with Katherine Lautner Maguire."

Hearing him add my name after Lautner made me smile.

"I need you to—" Britton saw my smile and coughed. "—to make sure that provision is met, so I'll need to draft that document before you leave."

"No-no," Cranston said quickly. "We agree to all contents so stipulated, and if Mr. Maguire is in earnest about refusing the fifty thousand, I'll have my firm send over a blanket release for everything listed there on the manifest that was either purchased for the child or that used to belong to her mother."

"Everything that was included?"

"Yes."

"So, being that Katherine's own previous possessions, as well as whatever was removed from the residence at Park Avenue South as belonging to Olivet Lautner, you're stipulating to all of that becoming the sole assets of Katherine Lautner-Maguire."

"Yes."

He passed Cranston the check. "Send me the blanket release for all contents, and your boss is free and clear."

Cranston looked relieved as he opened his briefcase and put the check inside. "I'll have that here in five minutes. To what e-mail would you like the form sent?"

Fifteen minutes later, Cranston was driving away, and Katie was standing with me on the front steps watching him go. From the backseat of his car, he'd produced the two large suitcases, a My Little Pony backpack, and a stuffed lamb I could tell had once been a cream color and now had matted-down fur from going into the washing machine many a time.

"What's his name?" I asked.

"Lamby."

Of course it was. "Okay, so we gotta get this stuff home," I said, thinking I might need to call a cab since Cranston had driven us over. I could walk home easily, and had many a night when I was stalking Britton, trailing after him from the office to his rented townhouse, but now I had a tiny person with me, and her legs were not as long as mine.

"I can pull a suitcase," she assured me.

I grinned at her and she smiled back, but before I could get out my phone, Britton called out to me from the porch. Katie walked up the steps with me and we stopped in front of him.

He exhaled sharply. "I had the restraining order removed since you gave me your word I wouldn't see you around any more than was necessary."

"Thank you," I said softly, sad that this was absolutely, irrevocably the end of us. There was no chance ever now; I had given my word not to pursue him. "I appreciate everything you did today, and please, send me a bill."

"That's not necessary," he said under his breath.

"Thank you again," I said, reaching out to run my fingers through his hair, seeing something caught in the chestnut waves.

He let me touch him, only leaning back after a moment, realizing, I was certain, what he'd allowed.

"Dandelion seed," I said, showing him.

"Oh."

"So, uhm, will you please have Mia call me when she gets back?"

"Of course," he said quickly, passing me a blue folder, everything bound together, professionally done. He was a lawyer, after all. Only when he reached the door and opened it to go inside did he look back and inquire about the why.

"What?" I got lost staring at him.

"Why do you still need to speak to Mia?"

"Oh, well, my mom'll probably try and sue me for not being able to take care of her anymore, and my sister might too, so I should be ready."

He waited there a moment, possibly processing, before shaking his head and coming back out to stand in front of me. Staring up at him—I had to, he was a whole head taller than me; I was only five ten to his six two—I noticed the black flecks in his gorgeous sea-blue eyes.

"Pardon me?" he asked, pained, incredulous, irritable, all of it in his voice, like: *What the hell did you just say?*

I coughed. "Well, see, back when I was younger, like fifteen, sixteen, my mom had me—" I put my hands over Katie's ears. "—turn tricks to support her 'cause she was sick, but not sick enough for us to get welfare or nothin', but—"

"I'm sorry?"

"What?" I wasn't sure where his confusion was.

"Did you just tell me that your mother had you selling your body when you were fifteen to take care of her because she was sick?"

"Yeah."

"Seriously."

"Yeah," I repeated.

"And you see nothing wrong with that?"

"She was sick, Brit—I mean, Mr. Lassiter," I corrected quickly. "She was stuck in bed and I didn't have any other way to take care of her and my sister."

He inhaled audibly through his nose. "Yes, of course, sorry, go on."

"Okay," I said, taking a quick breath. "So she drank a lot, right, and—"

"Drank a lot?"

He'd lost me again.

"She bought alcohol with the money you got from sleeping with men."

"And drugs and stuff she needed," I explained. "She was in a lot of pain."

He nodded slowly, and I took that moment to smile down at Katie, who didn't seem to mind my hands over her ears. She found it novel, it seemed, for the time being.

Lifting my head, I found Britton scrubbing his eyes with the heels of his hands.

"You okay?"

"Yep, great, go on."

"Okay, so like two years after I left home and finally got my GED, I got a call from her, and she said she still couldn't work and that she needed me to take care of her and to help with Ronnie's—that's my sister, Veronica—college tuition."

"Really," he said dryly.

"What?" I was confused. Why did he keep stopping me? I already knew he wanted nothing to do with me, and yet he persisted in interrupting me, which extended our conversation. It made no sense.

He lifted a finger to get me to wait and squatted down beside Katie. I moved my hands so he could talk to her. "Sweetheart, do you like animal crackers?"

She nodded.

"Could you go inside and get me a box of them? They're right next to my water cooler."

Her eyes narrowed.

"No?"

"I don't like lawyers."

"Is that right?"

"Uh-huh."

"How come?"

"They're mean."

His grin made his eyes twinkle and her smile in return was huge.

"I'm not mean, I promise."

She leaned in and kissed his cheek. "You know, my mommy has blue eyes just like you."

I thought "had" when she said it, but the past and present were probably a bit blurry for a three-year-old. It would take some time to fit her mother squarely into the past as Olivet was gone from Katie's present.

He hugged her, snatched her off her feet, and she molded herself against his chest, arms tight-tight around his neck, and he made the noise that you do when you're hugging a child and then let her go. Her smile for him was full of sunshine, and it was easy to see how smitten she was with Britton. She was utterly under his spell, and I understood the feeling.

He rose once she was through the door, leaving it open as she slipped inside.

"She's an angel, don't you—"

"What the hell?" he roared, grabbing my upper arms and shaking me hard. "Why didn't you tell me?"

The blue in the middle of a flame, that part that sort of glows and pulses with heat—that was what Britton's eyes looked like at that moment. He was incensed and it made me shiver.

Yes, I was a shark of a hustler, moving from man to man, devouring them and then moving on to the next. But I had stopped for Britton Lassiter, stilled, and even though he didn't know it was a big deal, for the little time that we'd been together, it had been heaven to me.

So now, with his hands on me as I'd thought they'd never be again, I couldn't hide the shudder of pleasure, the whimper from the back of my throat.

"Jesus, Lazlo," he sighed, pulling me in close against him, clutching me tight, his chin resting on top of my head. "I thought everything you did, not wanting to stop being an escort—I thought that was because you liked it too much."

It hit me hard, and I shoved out of his arms. "You think I don't like being a whore?"

"Wait—"

"You think I'm ashamed of it?"

He took a step forward and I took one back.

"You think I need you to fuckin' save me?"

He reached for me, advancing again, and again, I retreated, careful at the step so I didn't tumble down the short flight.

"I don't need anyone to save me. I told you that once, that your offer to keep me was really good for someone like me, but no thank you," I finished, whipping around him, reaching for Katie as she came outside with the box of crackers in her hand, holding it by the string.

"Just wait," he pleaded.

"I thought—" What had gone through my head? That we could get married? Raise Katie together, him and me? That he would forgive me for walking away and take me back? But mostly, forget I was a prostitute and start over? Think of me like a man and not a bird with a broken wing? "—I thought…." I sighed.

He lifted his hands. "Calm down and hear me out."

"You don't see me," I whispered.

"I do," Katie piped up, taking my hand, chin lifted so she could look up into my face. "I see you, Daddy."

And that was the whole point of my original question to him a hundred years ago when this conversation first started. "Would you please have Mia call me, because I'm gonna need to stay here full-time and that'll take every penny I've got, so my mom and Ronnie have the rest of this year and that's it," I concluded, turning my head toward the street at the sound of a horn blowing, seeing the hand lifted out of the driver's side in a friendly wave. "Roark!" I yelled, because in that moment, my friend and his car were my salvation.

The ancient 1949 Chrysler Town and Country woody wagon came to a rolling stop in the middle of the street and sat there gleaming under the sun for a moment before the driver, pediatrician extraordinaire Roark Hammond, leaned over to the passenger-side window so he could see me on the porch.

"Laz?" he called out.

"Hey," I greeted him, moving forward, Katie in tow. "Could you give me and my daughter a ride home?"

Roark got out of the newly restored to mint condition car, moved quickly around the front end, and then jogged from the path to the porch to the bottom of the steps.

"Britton," he greeted my ex-whatever-he-was.

"This isn't necessary," Britton said, stepping forward, blocking my way. "I can take them home after I talk to Lazlo."

"You're busy," I said, stepping around him, sweeping Katie up off her feet and tucking her to my chest. Her weight was so slight it didn't slow my momentum as I descended the steps to where Roark was waiting. "Could you help me with those two big suitcases?" I asked the doctor. "It's her stuff. I don't know why I didn't just leave it at my house when the lawyer was here, but my brain was just stuck on getting here to talk to Mia."

"To Mia?" Now Roark was confused, and I didn't blame him. I was standing with Britton, after all.

"I needed a lawyer," I responded quickly.

"You lost me."

"Just—help me to the car, yeah?"

"Since when do you have a daughter?"

"I'm three," Katie told him, holding out her hand.

He shook it, charmed completely, if the bemused expression on his face coupled with his smile was any indication. "I'm going to be your doctor, honey."

"Do you have sugar-free lollipops in your office like Dr. Yoshida?"

"I have fruit snacks," he answered, taking hold of both of the large suitcase handles. They were the rolling ones, so he pulled them as we walked. "Does that work?"

She nodded.

"Lazlo," Britton called to me as I moved along beside Roark.

I wanted to run but kept my pace steady.

"Laz!"

Reaching the car, I opened the door and put Katie in the back, buckled her in—the car had been restored and things like seatbelts had been added. There were no airbags, but Roark only drove it around Mangrove. He'd never get the car up over forty.

"Cearul!"

I turned for that. It was special. No one but him had ever, ever learned my middle name. He'd started calling me by my last name, Maguire, because everyone in the world called me "Laz" or "Lazlo," and he didn't want to call me what my tricks did. He'd wanted to distinguish himself, but my last name was too common as well, so one night he asked if I had a middle name.

I shrugged, but he caught my hand, turning me in his arms, lifting my chin to stare down into what he called my well-deep brown eyes. "You can't see the bottom," he said often. "It's too dark down there."

"Why don't you just watch me while I take off your—"

"No," he ordered, both hands on my face, studying me. "What's your middle name, Maguire? I want to know."

I sighed deeply. "It's Cearul."

"Oh, that's pretty."

"It's Irish. My dad named me after his father."

"Where is he, your dad?"

"He died before I was born. He was in a car accident. Everyone said he was a great guy. They said before he died, my mom was different, not the person she is now."

"Oh? What's she like now?"

I'd stopped that line of questioning with a kiss and my hands all over him, followed by my mouth. After that, though, I was only Cearul, until I wasn't anymore. I thought he'd forgotten, but clearly not.

"Don't do this."

"I don't need to be saved," I repeated and got in the car.

Roark threw the suitcases in the back, and moments later we were rolling down the street, Katie waving to Britton.

"I feel like maybe you were supposed to stay there," he said after the silence stretched on for a bit. "I didn't know you and Britton were close."

"We're not," I said tightly.

It was nice that he didn't pry.

CHAPTER FOUR

MY FRIENDS were all at my house looking at me.

Hutch Crowley, Kelly Seaton, Jenna Zaan—my best friend and neighbor both at home and downtown where my shop and her tea shop, Steep, were located—and Roark Hammond, who'd called them all because when I got home, I started to hyperventilate.

"You're a doc—" I stopped to breathe into the paper bag Hutch had brought over from his grocery store. "—tor, aren't you supposed to be able to handle this kinda shit?"

"Yes," Roark agreed, watching me pace, "but normally this kind of thing is controlled through calming down, and that doesn't seem to be happening here."

"Oh God," I groaned, whipping around to walk back in front of him as I panted into the bag.

"Lemme get this straight," Jenna said, rubbing her temples as her husband, Marc, walked into my kitchen through the side door.

"I came as fast as I could," he announced, bolting over to me, grabbing me tight and giving me the big, hard bear hug he was known for. I'd known he was good at seventeen when she first met him. All of us on the street in Brooklyn, Jenna thrown out of her house because her stepfather wanted her more than her mother, me working to take care of mine, and Marc allowed to run free because his mother was dead and his father drank. It had been bad until we found each other.

I found Mangrove when a john brought me down from the Big Apple for the weekend. I convinced Jenna and Marc to move too, and now they owned their own business. I'd been thrilled to have my best friends with me, even when they both got on me to quit hustling.

"Now what the hell's going on?" Marc continued.

"Shhhh," Kelly hushed him, "your lovely bride is about to sum up."

"Oh, okay." He crossed his arms, waiting.

"That little girl asleep on the couch is yours," she said in the Brooklyn accent I loved that I had never picked up, having been born and raised in Long Beach, California, before my mother followed some guy across the country. "That angel, she belongs to you?"

"Yeah."

"Because some rich guy who her mother was dating at the time paid you to fuck her so he could watch."

"Yeah."

She turned to Hutch. "What the hell?"

Hutch cleared his throat, eyes back on me from Jenna. "Okay, so, Katie's mom, Olivet, she has Katie, and then sometime in this timeline, marries Camlin Baylor, who's worth like a billion dollars."

I nodded.

"And Olivet has a brain tumor that no one but her knows about, but she's a smart lady, so she gets her ducks all in a row for her daughter because it could happen at any time."

"And did," I told them sadly. "The lawyer said that she got on the private penthouse elevator to go out and pick Katie up from school, and by the time she reached the bottom floor, she was dead."

"Jesus, that fast?" Jenna hissed out the question.

"Yeah."

She turned to Roark. "Do you think she suffered?"

He looked pained, his face pinched. "It's doubtful, but I can't say for certain. Either way, it was very fast."

"Poor thing," Jenna sighed.

"Yes," Roark agreed, turning back to me. "It had to be scary, not knowing how long she had, having no idea when she'd be taken from her daughter."

Jenna took a breath before her focus returned to me. "God, I feel so bad for her, but Jesus, how does she just make the decision to give you her kid?"

"Whaddya mean?" Kelly chimed in, "Katie's his kid too."

"Yeah, but she didn't know what kind of guy Laz is now."

But she'd known me enough, from our one conversation those few years ago, just as I'd been able to judge the kind of person she was.

"She knew him at some point," Kelly responded, "and so she knew she could trust him, and Katie's their daughter."

"Plus," Roark said, "from what I understand, she had no other family, no parents or siblings, so Laz was her one shot, the only other person who could love her child."

"And he will," Jenna conceded, smiling at me. "I know he'll make a good dad, but Christ on a crutch, she had no idea who she was sending her daughter to!"

"I think she did," Marc argued. "I think she knew enough about him."

"Or he was her only option."

"What does it matter?" I snapped. "She's here now."

"And we're all thrilled, honey," she soothed me. "It's just scary to think about what could've happened to Katie if you weren't the man you are."

I couldn't argue that point.

"I mean, what kind of mother just leaves something like that to chance—"

"She probably—"

"Or for that matter, what kind of mother turns her kid out and makes them whore around for her."

"Jesus, who would do that?" Hutch asked, horrified.

"Nobody," I flared. "Can we focus?"

"Yes, fine. Sorry. Focus it is."

"Okay, so this guy, this Camlin Baylor, he was Katie's father for three years?" Kelly asked.

"Two," I explained.

"Right," he agreed. "So Baylor marries Olivet when Katie is one, she dies when her daughter is three, and the first thing he does when he finds out his wife is dead, is figure out who Katie's real dad is so he can give her away so he's free again?"

"No, not exactly," I apprised him. "What happened was that Olivet sent everything I have now to her lawyer so that if she died before Katie was eighteen, Katie would come to me."

"Because she knew her husband was a selfish prick," Jenna chimed in.

"Because she knew he never wanted to be a father," I clarified. "He wanted her—he wanted Olivet—but not Katie. At least he was honest about it."

"Yeah, he's a prince," Jenna said sarcastically.

"I think you have to commend his honesty," I insisted. "I mean, lots of people would have just kept her for appearances or whatever. The man knows his limits, good for him."

Jenna rolled her eyes.

"Well, it makes sense that Olivet would be ready for the eventuality of her death," Roark explained. "She would have had no idea what kind of time she had and still made all the appropriate provisions. I think that's commendable."

"I agree."

"We all do," Jenna said with a sigh.

I cleared my throat, because thinking about Olivet made me sad. It was awful that she wouldn't get to see Katie grow up. "Okay, so, Olivet's attorney contacted Mr. Baylor's guy, Polk, who was here earlier, and all the paperwork that you read was delivered to me by them."

"So clearly, Olivet wanted you to have Katie."

"She wanted me to know about Katie and make an informed decision. If I didn't want her, there were arrangements made for her to go live with Camlin's parents."

"Camlin's parents?"

"Yeah, they apparently really dote on Katie, but Mr. Baylor Senior is in his mid-80s and Mrs. Baylor, late eighties," I informed them. "Not that it matters, 'cause I'm keeping her."

"Of course you're keeping her," Jenna half shouted.

"I would never give her up," I confirmed for all of them. "I want her, and that means the other part of my life stops now."

Jenna squealed, and then she was off her stool and in my arms a moment later. "Ohmygod, yes!" she cried, hugging me tight as Marc joined in, squeezing the both of us. "I've wanted that for you for so long."

I kissed her forehead and thought about how much I loved my dear, sweet friend. She was more a sister to me than the one I was currently putting through college.

"I knew you'd never do it for yourself, because you think that would be selfish to do because of your mother and sister, but you'd do it for your girl, and I'm so happy!"

When Katie came stumbling into the kitchen, everyone clapped, she grinned, waved, and did a little curtsey. The best part was when she walked around the others to get to me, snuggling into my arms and sighing hard. She was a sweet thing, and I promised myself that I would be her guardian angel for all time. I hoped I'd never disappoint her.

AFTER EVERYONE left, I was in the kitchen rinsing dishes, having insisted everyone leave them even though they offered, and it occurred to me that Hutch was not rushing off but instead sticking around.

"What happened, you and Mike already tired of screwing?" I asked tactlessly.

He flipped me off as he loaded the dishwasher.

I stopped and scrutinized him. "Seriously, why are you here?"

"You don't want me here?"

"Don't be a douche, just tell me what's up."

He let out a deep breath. "Mike's pissed at me."

I was surprised. "That was fast."

"What are you talking about?"

"Well, I told Kelly that you'd do something to piss him off, but I didn't think one month in and you'd be in trouble already."

"I'm not in trouble," he replied irritably. "He just—Dwyer Knolls is an asshole."

"Sure," I agreed, "but not, yanno, just out of the blue. He's normally a dick only if you push him into a corner or if you're stupid enough to do something shitty to Takeo."

"Like Takeo needs help taking care of himself," Hutch groused, "or anyone else, for that matter. Jesus, Laz, Takeo's the scary one of the two of them."

I nodded my agreement, because yes, Hiroyuki Takeo looked all sweet and pretty on the outside, but underneath the veneer of calm was a man who would gut you like a fish if you looked sideways at his man. I pitied anyone stupid enough to walk up on Dwyer with anything but pure intentions. "Okay, so what'd Dwyer do?"

"We were over there for dinner, and he told Mike that I'd been planning to sell the market a while back."

"Oh, I remember that," I said, smiling at him, returning to rinsing the dishes and passing them to him. "You thought you wanted to go live somewhere more exciting."

"Yeah."

"And I told you that you should make anyone who wanted to buy the place have to come down and stay for a few days so they could get a feel for the town."

"Yes, you did," he agreed, "and that was very good advice. I don't think I ever gave you credit, and I definitely didn't tell Dwyer you said anything."

"I don't give a shit," I assured him. "But I bet Mike was pissed when Dwyer, what, just mentioned it in passing?"

"Yeah."

"'Cause he figured you already told Mike."

"Yep."

"So did Mike have a total meltdown?"

"That's an understatement."

"Why didn't you ever tell him?"

"It just sort of slipped my mind after I told Dwyer I wasn't interested in selling, so then when it came up—"

"It was a big-ass hairy deal."

"Yeah."

We worked in silence for a few moments.

"How long you think he's gonna stay mad?" I asked, wondering.

"There's no way of telling."

I snorted out a laugh. "You wanna do errands with me and Kitty?"

"Yes, please," he said cheerfully.

KATIE, HUTCH, and I walked to the hardware store. It was called Handyman and was owned by Christopher Walsh, who I never missed an opportunity to try and talk into asking Mia Renaldi out. He'd carried a torch for so long, the poor man could combust at any second. His answer was always the same: what would a woman like that want with a guy like me? Obviously he missed how easy on the eyes he was and how much business savvy he had, but no one listened to me anyway. I was too young. So when we got there and I asked if he'd called her yet, of course the answer was the same "no" as the last time.

Hutch was going to give him crap about him being a coward, but when he saw his boyfriend, he ducked behind the lawn mower display. Katie and I had a good time watching Mike walk around the other side so when Hutch turned—*bam*—there he was. Hutch's unmanly shriek followed by the roll of Mike's eyes made us laugh, and as Mike hauled Hutch to his feet and kissed him, Katie asked me how come I didn't have a husband who wanted to kiss me.

"It's a long story," I apprised her.

Her eyes narrowed like she was twenty-three instead of just three. "Is it really?"

"C'mon," I grumbled, grabbing her hand and hauling her along behind me, which she found hysterical, considering the squeal of laughter.

"Will Hutch be okay?"

Watching him melt into Mike's kiss, seeing the two men stare into each other's eyes and smile…. "He'll be fine," I promised.

We bought many strands of white and colored Christmas lights. I also bought rope lights that I put under the bathroom cabinets so she could see where she was going at night. When I closed the door so she could see what I'd done and she saw it glowing along the ground, she was so pleased, I got kisses. She didn't love the dark, and neither did I, so the spontaneous decorating was a good thing for both of us.

I used my staple gun and lit up the ceiling in her room, putting strand after strand up there and trailing them down the walls. When I turned off the light, she said it was like having fairies in her room. I had really missed having a little girl in my life.

We had macaroni and cheese for dinner and sliced apples for dessert, and after that, since it was still really early, only after five, we walked to the beach together to look for seashells.

She talked and I listened. I heard about her mother, Olivet, about Camlin and how he was allergic to cats so she couldn't have one, and how nice his father, her grandfather she called him, was. We talked about her nanny and her chauffeur—she called him her driver—and how funny they both were, and how much crying her mother used to do.

I had to carry her lamb so he could see the ocean, though, on her orders, he was not allowed to go in.

"Don't lambs like to swim?" I offered.

She regarded me critically.

"What?"

She pursed her lips—someone's habit, perhaps her mother's. I would have to ask when she was older. "He's stuffed, Daddy," she said pragmatically, her tone and look indulgent.

"Right," I agreed.

We were quiet for a bit, and then she took my hand again. I looked down at her as she lifted her head to see up into my face. "Mommy said you were nice to her when you didn't have to be. What does that mean?"

I thought for a minute, thinking back four years to the young woman I'd had sex with instead of allowing the guy with me, Ty, to perform the act. I couldn't remember her boyfriend's name, but he'd asked me and another rent boy to show up at his party. Only when we got there did we realize that one guy was for him, the other for his girlfriend. He'd talked her into it—letting him watch her have sex with someone else—and because of the look on her face, I'd asked for it to be me. I knew Ty only vaguely, but what I did know, I didn't like. He would have been rough, and no one needed that in bed unless they wanted it. Hers was a gentle soul, and so, though it had been men most of my life—the tricks I'd been turning since fifteen had all been with guys—I had bent over and kissed her, and she drew me down into her embrace. When we were done and sitting together in the kitchen, her boyfriend and Ty still going at it in the bedroom, I had squinted at her when I noticed her regard.

"What?"

"I'm going to move out in the next couple of days."

"That's good," I told her, "since your boyfriend, like me, is clearly not bi, but gay."

Her laughter was soft and warm. "Did you just now figure that out? Were you bi before you got into bed with me? Did I turn you off women? Because if I did, I feel sorry for the other girls who'll be missing out."

I chuckled. "No, I was pretty sure that's the way I was, but I think when you have sex for a living, and when it hasn't always been your choice, that maybe along the way you second-guess who you want."

"Oh, I get it. The whole being attracted to your abuser thing and how healthy is that."

"Yeah."

"But it's not men you shouldn't love. Just the ones who hurt you and those who allowed you to be hurt."

She was right, and we'd both figured something out that night—as well as made the person standing in front of me now, waiting for an answer.

"Daddy?"

"I picked Mommy, and she picked me, and we didn't have to, but we did," I told Katie. "I think that's what she meant."

She was pleased with the answer, as evidenced by the enormous smile. "Did you love Mommy?"

"I didn't know her very well, but I'm sure I would have if I'd been given enough time."

She nodded like that was a very good answer, and we walked quietly down the beach.

IT WAS so easy to be with my daughter. Katie simply accepted me, and the fact that she was mine to mess up and spoil and influence and love without limits melted any fears I had away.

A week later, as she sang "Jingle Bells" in the shower, I sat on the toilet seat lid and listened. She peeked out to make sure I was there, and I waved. Her laugh was good, all squeaky and girly. When she got out, I dried her thick hair, not black like mine, more the color of Britton's but with streaks of dark gold and auburn. I brushed it and then got into bed with her to read her a chapter from *101 Dalmatians*, which was a better book than a movie. She'd seen the Disney adaptation and could imagine the dogs. What was nice was that because she was three, I didn't get any questions about why that particular book was in my house, so I didn't have to say that I kept a few hopeful books around because I was comforted by them.

I had loved school, was sad when I'd had to miss chunks of it at fifteen and then drop out altogether at sixteen. As a kid, my favorite part had been storytime. I'd loved being read to by teachers and librarians, and I loved reading aloud. A judge I'd screwed regularly for a while had liked to read me the laws against having sex with a minor before he in fact had sex with a minor. Even that was okay. But I was going to make a safe, happy place for my daughter to live, and that started with me reading to her every night. I had already decided that everything I didn't have, she would.

I really hoped Mia Renaldi got home soon so my lawyer could let everyone in my life know where my new priorities lay.

CHAPTER FIVE

I HAD three weeks of bliss. I took Katie to see her pediatrician, and it was Roark Hammond, of course. He requested all the medical records from her old doctor and made sure everything, including shots, was all up to date. I was in the doghouse for a solid two hours after that—no kids liked needles—but I'd saved the trip to the pound for that day because I was brighter than I looked, and we brought Bird home at lunch.

He was the smallest gray kitten I'd ever seen in my life. When we took him to the vet so he too could get shots, Dr. Korat said he took to Katie like she was his mother. Never in my life did I imagine that cats followed people around like dogs—or chirped liked birds, hence his name. Following her from room to room, inside, outside, in the attic, up on her bed, and under the covers at night, not meowing, instead chirping the whole time, he was never far from her.

"Bird is a weird name for a cat."

She squinted at me. "But he tweets."

"He does."

"I think he was a bird in his last life, so since I don't know which kind of bird, I have to just call him Bird."

"Last life?"

She nodded. "Sophia says we all have them. She was a witch in the Renance."

"Renaissance?"

"Yeah, that one," she yawned, pressing the button I'd installed beside her lamp to turn on all the white lights in her room. She called them fairy lights, and some of them were bunched in the clear glass bowl by the door, others wrapped around hooked-together half-globe wire baskets, made into giant light balls that hung, one from her ceiling and one in front of her window.

She loved her room, with her mother's vanity table in it and the reading nook with the bay window that, when she was sixteen, she could sit in and write in her diary about how much she craved killing me. I was surprised she didn't want the canopy bed that was sent, just the frame. She had been a princess before. It's what Camlin had called her, and she didn't want to be that anymore. Seeing the ceiling, the lights, and her magical room that we'd painted pale blue with big fluffy white clouds was all she wanted. She was Kitty now, not Katie anymore, not to anyone, and more than anything, everyone had to know I was her daddy. Strangers on the street, her dentist, Mia—when she came over to the house and saw us the day she got back from her trip—no one was left unsure of who I was. I'd never been so proud.

We were coming up the street from the grocery store, her sitting with the groceries in the wagon I'd bought three days earlier, me pulling as she chattered away about how Cheerios were a bad choice and how the cookie one or the candy one or any of the others really had been the way to go. The last part—"way to go"—was something I said on occasion, and it was funny hearing it come out of her. Already I was getting a lot of my inflections, word choices, and opinions about other people back at odd times, and I was continually amazed by what she picked up. I had made sure not to swear around her after a particularly embarrassing incident at the outdoor market when she asked for someone to pass her a goddamn apple.

"Cheerios have less sugar," I told her.

"Yeah, not so much," she replied snidely.

Christ. She was an extremely precocious three. How snarky would she be when she was a teenager?

"Laz!"

I wasn't really surprised when I looked up at the porch of my tiny bungalow and saw Mia there again, the third time in as many days. But I *was* surprised to see Britton with her. I had been very careful to avoid him like the plague. If he walked in someplace, anyplace, I walked out. I crossed streets to give him a wide berth, had not gone near his office, had not been out at all at night—certainly not on a date, hadn't fucked anyone or done anything remotely age appropriate for a twenty-two–year–old man since Kitty took up residence in my heart and house. I was a grown-up now, and everything else was secondary.

After rolling the wagon to the bottom of my stairs, I put my foot behind the back wheel so it couldn't move as Katie stood up and jumped out.

"Ta-dah!" she announced, and I cheered and whistled like an idiot. She was just so amazing, and I wished with all my heart that I could thank her mother for the gift she had given me, and even more so, for putting my name on the birth certificate. Olivet could have lied, named another man Katie's father, or worse, put no one's, and my sweet girl would be a ward of the state after Camlin Baylor threw her away and his parents were deemed too old. Sometimes I stood in my kitchen and just shivered thinking about the "what ifs" and how lucky I was. I was still dealing with the *holy fuck* of it all, the overwhelming, terrifying, drowning tsunami of joy the whole thing was.

Mia laughed at Kitty, and when we reached the porch, my daughter carrying a bag of three apples, me with everything else, Mia took the groceries from me and said Britton needed to talk to me.

"But you're my lawyer," I protested weakly.

"No," she soothed me. "Not really."

She asked Kitty if she could make her a snack, and my little girl checked with me to see if it was okay.

"Go ahead," I told her and watched as the two of them went inside. When the door closed, I turned to face Britton and was surprised to find him right there, having moved up beside me while I was focused on my child.

He was in my personal space, and when I went to take a step back, to give myself room, he grabbed hold of my bicep, hard.

"Brit—"

"Shut up."

My chin snapped up, and I was ready to give it to him with both barrels, but he was furious, and seeing that… deflated me completely.

His scowl was dark, the muscles in his neck were corded, he was breathing through his nose, and that jaw of his that could cut glass, sharp, defined, was clenched.

"What'd I do?" I asked breathlessly, simply overwhelmed by his anger and beauty.

It really wasn't fair that he got to look like that all the time. He was immaculately dressed: the gray suit he had on with the yellow tie and patterned pocket square hugging his broad shoulders, showing off the breadth of chest, and the pants clinging to his narrow hips and long legs. My mouth went dry as I gazed up at him, and I would have stopped staring, would have hidden the hunger for him I kept locked deep inside, but within his grip on my arm and under the weight of his stare, I was unraveling.

He pulled me closer, into him, and I swallowed hard, not moving, barely breathing as he put both hands on my face. It was hard not to respond to the pure physicality of the man.

"God, you're a pain in the ass."

This was new. "What?"

"I wondered how you could simply stop, change your whole life for a daughter you didn't know, and then it hit me."

"I don't—"

"You never wanted your life. You never wanted to do what you did," he said gruffly. "You hated it, in fact."

I tried to pull free, because, holy shit, I needed to gather up my armor and put it back on. He had to see nonchalant, swaggering hustler Lazlo, not Kitty's father, not the guy who hadn't felt alive until he was snuggled up tight beside Britton Lassiter. I would not let him see the guy who'd been dreaming about having a home and a man to share that with ever since he'd been twelve years old and discovered he wanted to kiss boys, not girls.

"I wanted you to stop for me so badly, and I was hurt and angry that you wouldn't, just devastated that I wasn't important enough for you to leave your life for—"

"Just don't—" I took hold of his wrists, planning to move his hands, but he stroked my face, then moved to my hair before slowly, gently easing me into his arms.

"—but really, it had nothing to do with me."

He was so warm and I was freezing. How, in March, in Florida, in eighty-degree weather I could be shivering was beyond me, but I was.

"Stopping for me, because you wanted me, that, in your mind, would have been selfish, that would have been quitting for you… for something *you* wanted."

I closed my eyes, trying to absorb his heat through my skin, drink him in so I'd remember this when he pushed me away again and I wouldn't get to touch him anymore.

"If you quit for me, what would you tell your mother or your sister? You'd have to explain that you wanted a different life, a simpler one, one where you couldn't afford to take care of them anymore because you wanted your own happiness, your own home, your own love."

It was way too much honesty, especially since Britton had hit the nail on the head. I couldn't stop whoring myself out for him because that would have been what I wanted in my dreams. And I would never allow him to keep me because I knew what a burden that was. But for Kitty… for her… I could stop in a second because she needed me, and that was not selfish in any way. I was a parent, and parents sacrificed everything for their kids, and in my case, my old life was not compatible with who I needed to be for her. So I was simply Lazlo Maguire, shop owner, and I would figure out what I needed to do to be that.

"I thought you didn't care enough about me to change for me."

Shoving out of his arms, I backpedaled enough to see his face. "What the fuck? Not care about you? I love you more than—"

"I know!" he shouted, pouncing on me, manhandling me into his arms, wrapping me up, bending over enough to press his head down into my shoulder. "You want me badly."

Oh God, I did, and the whimper came out before I could stop. His sigh followed the sound as he squeezed me tighter.

"We should go inside before people see you hugging me," I whispered into his throat, turning my head so I could inhale the spicy scent of his skin.

"I don't give a crap who sees me holding you, Cearul," he husked, lifting me up off my feet so I had no choice but to wrap my legs around his hips. I couldn't just hang there like dead weight. I needed to be… closer. "I'm so tired of hiding who I am, I could scream."

I could feel how hard his body was under his clothes, feel the muscles moving, bunching, and my cock noticed, too, thickening almost painfully fast inside my cargo shorts.

He chuckled warmly, one hand slipping to my ass, squeezing tight.

"Fuck," I moaned as I ground my groin into his hard abdomen. "Put me down."

"Why would I do that? I finally have you where I want you, all hot and needing me."

"I always needed you," I confessed, wrapping my arms around his neck. "I just couldn't have you."

"Because you thought it was selfish."

"And because you're too good for me."

His scowl was instantaneous, and I laughed in spite of how serious I was trying to be.

"Come on, you, you're a dream I could never have."

"No, you—"

"You're this perfect prince of a guy from an amazing family, and you're rich and successful and—"

"Yours," he said before he kissed me.

I was not a romantic. All that had been fucked out of me years ago as I'd allowed myself to be used for money, sometimes cruelly, sometimes painfully. But when Britton kissed me, *whenever* he kissed me, I felt like it was the first time and I was sparkly, shiny, and new. The difference was, I was a man, not a boy, on the receiving end.

I tried to crawl down his throat.

My tongue pushed inside, and I tasted and claimed, sucking on his lips, wanting to brand him so he'd never be able to walk away from me again.

His chuckle surprised me, and I broke the kiss to check his expression, to get a read on him.

"God, I'm so stupid."

"What?"

"All I had to do was just look past all your cocky strutting bullshit and I would've—fuck."

He only swore in the heat of passion. "Britton?"

"You want me."

"Well, yeah, of course."

He exhaled sharply. "And you love me?"

I thought hard about what to say, eyes on his Marc Jacobs tie.

"Don't think," he said, both hands on my ass, holding me against him. "Just speak."

I lifted my head to meet his blue gaze. "Yes, Britton, I love you so much I'm stupid with it, okay? You happy?"

He nodded, his smile almost blinding. "I am, yes, because I love you back, and I'm sick to death of us being apart. Please don't send me away anymore."

"No," I said before I kissed him again, harder, deeper, until he was the one grinding me against him, his breath coming out in short stutters before he tore free and set me back down on my feet.

"You—not fair," he gasped, bending over to catch his breath and get his body under control. "Every time I'm near you, I want to go to bed."

It was good information to have. "So, not that I'm not thrilled with your epiphany, but what happened?"

He waved his hand dismissively. "Everything."

"I don't know what that means."

"Let's go inside and Mia and I will talk to you, and afterwards we'll make lunch and Mia will go back to work and Kitty will take a nap and you can have me in your bed."

My whole body throbbed.

"From the noise you just made, I'm counting that as a yes."

It was definitely a yes.

MIA WAS livid. She was pacing back and forth as Kitty watched her while dipping her baby carrots and broccoli florets in ranch dressing, her pretzels in yogurt, and her apple slices in peanut butter. My girl liked to dip, and I'd found it the quickest way to get food down. She also liked veggie burgers and, now, hummus. I had explained that there was no meat in my house—I was a vegetarian, and after I explained about the cows and the pigs and the goats and the baby lambs other people ate, she was fine with giving up meat since her entire life experience consisted of hamburgers, bacon, ham, and lobster. She'd been much more concerned with the status of cheese, was it or was it not a kind of meat. Her relief over finding it was not had made me laugh.

"So I called your bit—"

"Child," I pointed out.

"—mother," Mia finished, glancing at Kitty, who lifted both eyebrows.

Britton snorted out a laugh, leaned over, and kissed the top of Kitty's head as he made himself and Mia avocado and Swiss cheese sandwiches. He was very comfortable moving around my kitchen, and seeing him there made my heart flutter.

"Laz!" Mia yelled.

"Sorry," I responded quickly. "So you called who? My mother? My sister?"

"Both!" she yelled, rounding on me. "I can't even—God, Laz, your mother… I treated her like a wife who has to reenter the workforce after being married for half her life. I was gentle and kind and… and she was… vile."

I moved quickly and put a hand on her shoulder. "I'm sorry."

She took a breath and turned to me. "She asked if you were sick, if you were dying, if you'd caught a disease or—like that was the only way she wouldn't get paid."

I rubbed circles on her back as her eyes narrowed so the tears brimming in them wouldn't overflow. Poor soft-hearted Mia, she'd never met anyone like Valerie Jessup.

"She said you were her son and you owed her and Jesus Christ, Laz, she's just… I…."

I gave her a quick hug as the tears rolled down her cheeks. Britton brought her some tissue, and she wiped her eyes and blew her nose and got herself back together before she faced me again.

"I had to go to my mother's and hug her, and then I had to go find Coz."

I smiled at her.

"Because your sister—Jesus, Laz."

"What did Veronica say?"

Mia crossed her arms, her face so sad as she tipped her head a bit to study me. "She claims to love you, but heaven forbid she comes here to meet her new niece, and when I suggested you go there—"

"Oh, no, she wouldn't want that," I assured Mia.

"That's right, she wouldn't, because she's building a life there in New Haven, and she doesn't want you to ever show up."

"She's embarrassed."

"Yeah, I got that," she said curtly. "Where the hell does she get off being embarrassed?"

I squinted at her. "You're kidding, right?"

"No, I'm not kidding! How dare she look down her nose at you! She's a hypocritical bitch who's been using you her whole goddamn life!"

I turned to Kitty, but Britton was already on it, as in his hands covering my daughter's ears.

"Don't swear in front of my girl," Britton warned her—and that quick, because he'd been possessive and used "my" in referring to Kitty, I had to grab for the counter before my knees buckled. He always thought of himself as slow to get things, unsure and noncommittal, but when he was *in*, however fast—God—he was in all the way.

"I'm sorry, I just—they're both so awful!"

I reached out for Mia, who grabbed my hand tight.

"She wanted to know if you were taking care of Ronnie," she said, like that was ridiculous, like the name left a sour taste in her mouth. "Why does Ronnie get concern and you don't? How does your mother care about her and not you?"

"I'm the whore, not Ronnie."

"No," Mia said emphatically, enfolding my hand in both of hers, staring into my face, looking for answers. "I know she's her favorite, Laz—how come?"

Britton moved his hands, kissed Kitty when she tilted her head up for it—melting me completely—and then walked over and kissed my cheek. "Tell us. How come Mom loves Ronnie best? Does it have something to do with the different last name?"

I cleared my throat and turned to my daughter. "Love, we're going to step into the living room for a just a few minutes, okay? You keep on eating,"

"You need to talk about grown-up stuff?" she asked.

"Yeah."

"Okay," she said, beaming at me for a moment before returning her attention to her veggies.

I darted into the living room with Britton and Mia trailing after me, then rounded on them once we were out of earshot of my angel. "Okay, so, Ronnie and I have different fathers. Mine was Maguire, hers was Jessup."

"Did Mr. Jessup like you?"

"No, not at all."

Britton cleared his throat. "Did he hurt you?"

"He didn't molest me, if that's what you mean. Just knocked me around a little bit."

Britton carded his fingers through my hair, pushing it out of my face.

"You have a soft heart," I said hoarsely, loving how he was looking at me, all tender and sweet with hooded eyes.

"So she put his kid out on the street to punish Mr. Maguire for dying," Mia offered, reminding me that she was there, as I had been caught up in Britton and the reaction he was having to me.

"I guess, but it wasn't like he ever knew."

"And you're trash," Britton surmised.

I shrugged. "Pretty much, yeah."

Mia took a deep breath. "Never in my life have I hated two people I've never met so much."

"Don't hate them," I instructed. "It won't do any good and it'll only end up hurting you, making you feel like crap."

She growled. "That's fine, but Lazlo, so help me, after I pay off the mortgage on your mother's condo and send twenty grand to Ronnie, that's it. No more. Done."

I nodded.

"You will not give either of them another cent, do you understand me?"

"Yeah."

"Your mother's on welfare. Your sister's school is paid up through this, her sophomore year, and she gets money for next year, and then she has to get a loan, but not from you—never from you—and I don't give a fu—"

"Kitty," I reminded her.

"Can't hear us from over there!" Mia ranted, gesturing over her shoulder toward the kitchen.

"Yeah, but I'm working on making this a swearing-free zone."

She snarled. "How's heck?"

"Heck's okay."

Her huff of air was funny. "I don't give a *heck* what she wants to do, but you will not give her anything. Nothing. At all. Ever. Do you understand me?"

I couldn't keep from chuckling. "Yes."

"Are you sure you understand me?"

"Man, you're really mad," I baited her, reaching out and patting her cheek gently.

"I have never been this mad in my life," she assured me. "I literally want to pummel these women."

"I'm sorry."

"You're a meal ticket. You're a checkbook, that's all. They couldn't give a crap if you're dead or alive. They just want the money."

"I know."

Mia shook her head. "Why?"

I shrugged for the second time. "It's how it always was."

"Not anymore," Britton promised, his voice a deep rumble as he turned me around to face him. "We're done with you being taken advantage of. Kitty needs you now."

"Yeah, she does."

"And you need to provide for only her."

There was no argument.

His grin was a surprise, warm and sexy at the same time. "I bet you really want a cigarette, don't you."

I was startled. "How'd you know I quit?"

His grin widened as he took my chin in his hand. "I've been watching, and I haven't seen a cigarette since Kitty showed up."

My small whine made him laugh.

"Rough, huh, cold turkey?"

"You have no idea."

He leaned in and kissed me, softly, barely brushing my lips. "We'll figure out something else you can do with your hands."

"Oh, get a room," Mia complained, walking back to the kitchen. "I'm going to check on your kid to give you guys a minute."

I couldn't even mutter a thank you, too intent on Britton as I grabbed hold of the lapels of his suit jacket and hung on. "It's not fair that you get to make all the choices and I make none."

"Choices like what—to come back to you?"

"Yeah."

"You're worried about the power dynamic, right?"

I was. "You can't have it all."

"I know, baby."

"Don't."

"Since when don't you like me calling you baby?"

"It's not fair," I insisted, standing my ground.

"Oh?"

"Don't say 'oh' like that," I snapped.

"How did I say it?"

"Being patronizing is not going to get you what you want."

"How do you know what I want?"

I bristled. "Is it something other than me?"

"No," he said, his voice dropping low, coaxing. "I want you desperately."

"Then say that," I whined, frustrated, not even sure what I needed from him.

"Should I go away, and come back and grovel? Would it be better if I told you how sorry I was and got down on my knees and begged for your forgiveness?"

"Yeah," I admitted.

"Because the person who makes the first move, he's the one with less power, yes?"

I nodded.

"And you want it to be me with less, so I can never hurt you again."

"It was awful to come to you that day, just to have you send me away."

"I know."

"But you did it anyway."

"I wasn't ready."

"And what, you're suddenly ready now?"

"Come here," he ordered, grabbing my hand and yanking me after him out of the living room and into the short hall. When he stopped, he rounded on me and bumped me gently backward into the wall. "I'm sorry about the restraining order. I'm sorry I was so mad. But, Jesus, Cearul—what the hell?"

I watched him as he began to pace in front of me.

"After we broke up, you got a girlfriend," I threw out, because that too had hurt.

"I know what I did."

"Why? Why not just come out?"

"I wasn't ready."

"Second time you've said that," I retorted, getting annoyed all over again. "So maybe you're still not in a place where you can be honest."

"I am!" he flared.

"Are you sure? What happens when your parents visit?"

He stopped pacing to meet my gaze. "What are you accusing me of?"

"Nothing, I'm just asking."

"What, precisely?"

I swallowed down my fear. "Will you tell your parents about me and Kitty if and when they come to visit?"

"Yes, I will."

"Why?"

"Because you're too important, and now, so is Kitty."

I searched his face for a lie, for anger, for anything that would make me hesitate to tell him everything. "Why wasn't I important enough before?"

"You were always important."

"Bullshit."

"Are you *kidding*?"

"Britton—"

"First you tell me you can't be with me anymore," he declared angrily. "Then when I finally stop being pissed and go looking for you, you're gone, vanished. And the next thing I know, you're here, in my new hometown, wanting to pick up where we left off because you've had a change of heart."

"I didn't have a—"

"I never understood why you wouldn't just live with me in New York, because we both know you weren't after my money."

"It had nothing to do with that," I snapped.

"I know that! Don't you think I know that?"

"I have to pay my own way and more, so… what was I gonna do, have you support my mother and sister too?"

"I would have fixed that."

"I didn't want you to fix anything. I wanted you to want me!"

"I did!"

"If you wanted me so bad, why were you so mad when I came up to you in town that first day when I saw you?"

"I was mad because I wanted to take care of you, I wanted you to be with me, and not only did you say no, but you left me and you left New York!" He was indignant, his tone defensive, with the same lifted chin and clenched jaw I saw whenever he felt like he was right.

"I always leave New York after the first of July."

"How was I supposed to know that?"

"You never gave me a chance to explain anything!"

"You ran away," he accused.

"I didn't run anywhere," I said levelly. "You didn't want to hear anything but 'yes,' and when I couldn't give you that, I knew you wouldn't want me around."

"I wanted you!" he yelled, grabbing my arms and again pressing me to the wall, clearly wanting me to stay put so he could make his points. He was a lawyer, after all, used to a captive audience that didn't argue back. "God, Cearul… you're the first person I've *ever* wanted in my whole life."

I threw myself at him, arms around his waist, face buried in his chest, holding tight, listening to his heart through his dress shirt.

He wrapped me up tight, rubbed his cheek in my hair, and then let out a deep sigh that released all the tension out of his body. I felt him settle around me, solid and strong.

"You can't just go and come back again, right?" I made clear.

"You left me, remember? *You* walked out on *me*."

"I didn't think I could stop. Not for me, not for what I wanted and needed."

"I know."

"I was breaking your heart, and I didn't wanna do that."

"It happened anyway."

"So now you could do it back, if I let you."

"Because why?"

"I don't—"

"There's only one way I have any power," he said flatly.

"You know why."

"Tell me."

"I already told you."

"I want to hear it again."

I had to be brave, and it was hard, but I was raising a kid now, and I had to lead by example. "I love you," I confessed.

"Not into my shirt, please."

I lifted my head, and my eyes locked on to his. "I love you."

"And I love you," he promised exuberantly, bending to kiss me, taking my mouth, letting me taste, feel, and see his feelings, hiding nothing. His passion and possessiveness were right there clear as day.

His hands were warm on the sides of my neck as his mouth ground down over mine, wanting more and deeper, tasting, taking.

I tugged off his suit jacket and yanked at the tie and dress shirt. Everything needed to be off, and even though I knew logically that I could not have him right there in the hall, the craving was ravenous, as was the kiss.

What if he hadn't moved to Mangrove? What if he'd found someone else? What if he hated kids? What if he thought I was filth after all? What if…?

They could go on and on, my questions, my heart-stopping moments of fear.

At the time, I'd walked away from him for many reasons. I was no good for him. I had nothing to offer the rich, successful attorney. I had fiscal responsibilities that could not be pushed aside simply because I was tired of whoring myself out. When I thought I had a second chance, I was so thankful, only to be devastated, and now… *now*….

I broke the kiss, panting, meeting his dark blue gaze as he breathed heavily above me. Always, passion looked good on him, and with the blown pupils, kiss-bruised lips, blotches of flush on his throat, and rumpled clothes, he was stunning.

"What if you change your mind?" I whispered, my breath still choppy and uneven, terrified to give the question full voice.

"Never," he vowed. "We're going to be a family."

CHAPTER SIX

MIA TOOK one look at Britton and one look at me when we walked back into the kitchen, made her excuses, promised to be in touch the following day, took her sandwich and bag of veggie chips, and got out of there fast. Kitty was fading, in need of her normal afternoon nap, and after we washed her hands and I promised her that Britton would be there when she woke up, I put her down to sleep.

When I trotted back out to the living room, he was gone. I found him in my bedroom, sitting on the overstuffed wingback chair in one corner beside the window. The gentle sea breeze was blowing the gauzy pale blue curtains that brushed against him, creating a charming picture. It was like it was staged, it was so perfect—beautiful man in repose.

Walking in, I closed the door behind me, locked it, and when he stood, smiling at me, holding out his arms, I took a few steps forward and then dropped to my knees.

"No," he rasped, striding forward. "I want you in your bed and—Cearul."

"I want things too," I said hoarsely, hands on his belt, working it open fast, tugging his pants to the floor, his briefs following fast so that his long, cut cock bounced free and curled toward his abdomen.

I took hold, knelt forward, and swallowed him down in a practiced move that had been a staple of the service I provided as a rent boy. I knew how to suck cock, and even more important, I knew exactly how Britton liked it done.

"Fuck," he groaned, hands in my hair, firm but gentle, holding on as he let his head fall back.

As I licked and sucked and laved his cock, I wet my fingers with saliva before curling them around his ass and slowly parting his cheeks.

"Oh God, where's your lube," he whined, bucking forward, shoving deep, hitting the back of my throat. "Please, Cearul, I don't want—"

I leaned back, letting his cock slip from my mouth, and when I spoke, my voice was husky with arousal. Tasting him always did things to me. "You don't want me?"

He snarled, but not loudly. "I would scream at you, but that'll wake up our kid, and I don't want to do that right now," he rasped, grabbing hold of me under the arms and dragging me to my feet.

"What're you—Bri!" I couldn't help the relieved laughter that bubbled up out of me, because *this* man I knew. He'd done this in the past, manhandled me into bed and made adamant, passionate demands, then fucked himself on my cock. Because, yes, he liked me to top, but more than that, he loved me to take him, but he was never docile about his wants, needs.

"Don't—" He spun me around, shoved me over to the bed, and then before I could topple over, whirled me to face him so I landed on my back. "Fight me," he ordered, his voice ragged and hoarse.

"Why would I?" I ground out.

"I forget sometimes how young you are," he groused, stalking around the bed to my nightstand. "Take off your clothes before I rip them off."

I couldn't stop smiling, and since I was already barefoot, I only had my Foo Fighters T-shirt, briefs, and cargo shorts to strip out of, which I did as fast as I could. Britton Lassiter needing me naked was a huge turn-on.

He pulled off his loosened tie, then yanked both his dress shirt and the white T-shirt he was wearing underneath up and over his head. All of it, all his clothes were strewn across the floor in my bedroom, and they looked really good there.

Moving to the center of the bed, I watched as he crawled over to me and then straddled my hips, staring down at me with equal amounts of fury and hunger.

"Have you ever fucked anyone but me without a condom?"

"No," I answered gruffly, my voice cracking from simply looking at him looming above me, shivering slightly as the warm breeze ghosted over my sweaty skin. He was beautiful, absolutely focused on me—on what he wanted and on my answers.

"I haven't either," he husked, flipping open the lube and dribbling it over my cock.

"Britton," I moaned as he took hold of me, stroking slow, my body beginning to throb. "Love… what do you want?"

His exhale was sharp before he lifted, one hand on my shaft, guiding me to his opening, the other flat on my chest for balance.

"Go slow," I cautioned, wanting to be buried in him with an urgent, aching intensity that was making it hard to breathe. "I don't want to hurt you."

"You only hurt me when you left," he huffed as I pushed between his cheeks and breached him, slowly impaling him on my length. It felt incredible, the way he took me in, inch by inch, stretching around me only to clasp tight as I pressed farther inside.

His muscles rippled around me as he sat over my groin, my balls against his ass, both hands now on my chest as he breathed raggedly, in and out, both of us waiting, giving him time to adjust.

"Britton," I said, my voice raw with emotion, wanting to move, to attack him, to roll him quickly onto his back and simply take what I wanted.

He lifted languorously and then pressed back down.

"Oh, fuck you," I groaned, "I won't last a minute with you doing that."

His chuckle was evil and filthy, and I knew I was the only one who ever heard that from him, the only one gifted with his style of submission.

I wrapped my hand around his cock and stroked fast, working him over, and when he leaned forward to kiss me, I told him to get on his hands and knees.

I missed him the second he moved, but I was on him fast, returning to his welcoming heat, laying across his back, my left arm wrapped under and around his abdomen, my right hand gripping behind his thigh, holding tight, keeping him there, for me, as I pistoned inside.

"I remember your smell," he said, straining to speak, "and the feel of your hands and the taste of your kiss."

"You missed me," I concluded as his head dropped forward, and I changed my rhythm and angle to what I knew he craved.

"It was so—short, our time, but you know me… my body and my head and… what I want and need and… I can't—you can't—leave me," he whispered harshly. "Don't leave me."

"No," I promised, the rumbling sound of my voice in my chest vibrating through his back, causing a tremble before he came.

His muscles contracted around me, squeezing tight, and I cried his name as I climaxed, pumping deep inside his body.

Neither of us moved, just stayed there, still, and I laid my cheek between his shoulder blades and breathed with him.

"I've never been able to just be with anyone but you, in my whole life," he murmured.

"Yeah, me too," I confided, because it was time. I trusted Britton Lassiter. I always had. None of my own baggage could change that. "So you should move in with me and live with me forever, okay?" I said as I lifted, shifting so I could slip gently from his body and kiss my way down his spine at the same time.

"I can move in tomorrow, but I'm going to sleep here tonight."

"You think you're gonna sleep?" I teased.

"God, I hope not," he whispered, looking at me over his shoulder.

I waggled my eyebrows at him, and his answering laugh, the warm, sensual sound of it, brought a happy sigh deep from my chest.

"Oh, he loves me," he whispered.

I *so* did.

CHAPTER SEVEN

AFTER THE conversations Mia had over the phone with my mother and sister, the one I was not privy to that Britton had with his family, and another Britton had—with Cranston Polk—that I didn't know about, I was not really surprised that people descended like locusts upon us. The timing was what did me in.

I walked Kitty to preschool, delivering with her cheese and crackers and sliced apples, and put Britton's name on her Emergency Contact Card at the same time. He was also allowed to pick her up and drop her off.

"Britton Lassiter, he's the new lawyer in town, isn't he?" Gloria Cantrell, the clerk in the front office, wanted to know.

I turned and smiled at the cluster of other mothers, the principal, and one of the teachers. "Yes, he is."

Their smiles were a surprise.

"Well done," Gloria simpered, waggling her eyebrows at me.

I grinned at her and heard a collective sigh before I was engulfed by well-meaning mothers who wanted to know if Kitty wanted to come on a playdate. The standoffishness I'd encountered at first had apparently not been them, but me. Now that I was smiling, they were too. I knew better. I had been so worried about being judged that I imagined them doing it even when they hadn't been. No one had thought, *I don't want to be around Lazlo Maguire, I don't want my kid around Lazlo Maguire's kid.* It had all been in my head. Had the opposite been true, if they really had treated me like I thought they were, I could have changed their minds. But I hadn't been thinking straight, or it would have hit me. I'd been a hustler a long time. I knew a lot about people, how to handle them, how to be charming. I just had to remember to translate that now that I wasn't trading on my body anymore.

On the way home, I stopped for coffee at Cuppa Joe before continuing on. When I reached the white picket fence around my home, I saw my mother and stopped.

It was her. I'd know her anywhere. What startled me was how old she appeared. Coz Renaldi's mother, Annalise, was older than mine, but she looked easily ten years younger. My mother, who was only forty-six, having had me at twenty-four, had aged poorly.

"You fucking whore," she screeched, charging down my front steps and rushing to the gate.

It didn't hurt much when she struck me. It was simply jarring.

"How dare you have your fucking cunt lawyer call me and give me an ultimatum," she shrieked. "Who the fuck do you think you are?"

Even with her shrieking on my front lawn, the thought of moving her inside—into my home, into the sanctuary I'd always had in Mangrove that was now sacred with the inclusion of first Kitty and now Britton—never crossed my mind. I would not share my life with her; it meant more to me now.

"Ronnie's only nineteen, you faggot piece of shit! You don't get to throw her out on the street!"

After the second round of sex last night, after our nap, after Kitty woke up from hers and came staggering out onto the back deck and climbed up into Britton's lap, yawned, and asked him for a glass of water, Britton had called Mia and invited her over for dinner to talk the whole thing out. It was nice that she came out to stand with me, beer in hand, while I grilled corn and veggie burgers and artichokes, and said she didn't know that Britton had been walking around this entire time belonging to me.

"He's the kind of man," I said as I put more corn wrapped in tin foil on the grill, "that is better when he knows where his home is."

"Aren't we all?"

"Some of us need it more than others," I assured her.

"Well," she sighed, watching him inside with Kitty, the two of them using the juicer to make lemonade. "I had no idea that Britton could ever look like that."

"How do you mean?"

She snorted out a laugh. "I've never seen him in a pair of shorts or a T-shirt—in all the years I've known him! Even at law school, or on vacation, he just was never not *on*. He was always this perfectly put-together Ken doll that his wife used to adore and his parents—I don't know who he is right now."

"Is it a good thing?"

"It's a wonderful thing," she sighed, beaming at me. "I had no idea he could smile like that."

"It's Kitty."

"It's you, idiot," she assured me, smacking my arm. "It's all you."

And when he and Kitty joined us outside and he bent close and kissed me, his mouth lingered on mine until I leaned into him, entwining my hands in his hair, and he wrapped me in his arms.

We saw Kitty put her hands together and make a little purring sound of happiness. When I laughed, she smiled big.

"You like us kissing?" I teased.

She nodded. "Now I have a family."

It made sense. She was raised by her mother and her stepfather; now she had her father and hopefully, someday, when we made it legal, whatever she would call Britton. To her a family was three, and she had that again.

I thought Mia was going to pass out from the cute, but I told her to drink her beer because we needed to talk shop.

We had gone over it all while Kitty blew bubbles in the backyard. Everything was drawn up, funds were set aside. Mia and Britton took notes, and brick by brick we planned my separation from my mother and sister and my life in New York. It was quick and easy, as I owned nothing in the Big Apple. I could simply not go back, and that was all there was to it. Any clients would easily find other playmates, and I dumped all the contacts in my phone and had my carrier change my number without setting a forwarding message.

Britton was practically thrumming with happiness, and when I cornered him inside and said it was done and couldn't be changed, he mauled me in the kitchen, kissing and groping, hands and mouth everywhere until I had a hard time recalling my name.

So now, as my mother stood there fuming, enraged at my actions, I could calmly take a step back out of striking distance.

"You and Ronnie are both set up going forward," I said frankly, my eyes meeting her rheumy blue ones. "She's paid up at Yale through the end of this semester and next year. After that she's on her own. I paid off your condo; you just have to live off your welfare money now or get a—"

"I can't work!"

"Then welfare," I said, hand on my gate, but not to open it, instead just reminding myself that it was mine. My sweet little house, my front yard, my street where I lived with my family, and my solid life that she couldn't take away, all of it reminded me of who I was now. "But at least your place is paid off."

"You don't get welfare if you own your own home, you stupid shit!"

I shrugged. "It's not my problem. I'm not going to change my mind, so—"

"I bet it will become your problem when I tell whoever cares to know that your sweet little daughter is being raised by a filthy fucking whore!"

"Everyone here knows what I used to do," I said, feeling my skin crawl, my stomach twist, and my throat get dry. "You can tell whoever you want, it won't matter."

"Oh no?" she said snidely. "I saw that rich lawyer come out of your house this morning. What do you bet his clients will care about where he's putting his dick? I should warn him before he gets a disease."

It was just so over the top. As I stood there and looked at her, I realized how many years I had lost. I'd always thought that one day she'd wake up and call me and say, "Ohmygod, Lazlo, honey, I've been so blind. You've taken care of me practically your whole life, and I love you for sacrificing your youth, I love you for stepping up and being the man of the house, but mostly I love you because you're my baby." I'd waited a lifetime, and now, finally, I was done.

I needed Britton. I needed to hear I was loved and treasured, and I needed him now.

"You should leave," I told Valerie Jessup. "And don't come back."

"This is not over, you stupid little—"

"What's going on here?"

We turned, and there was Mrs. Evanston, chairwoman of the town council, walking her two pugs, Scheherazade and Augustine. My friend Hutch Crowley always had trouble with her, and I never understood that.

She'd never been anything but lovely to me since I'd hit town when I was twenty. She fed me, took walks with me, met me for coffee, and I in turn watched her dogs for her whenever she and her personal assistant, Emily Chapel, went out of town without them, and I fished with her, and most of all, I simply sat out on her deck and sipped ice tea with her.

"Morning, Delilah," I greeted her warmly, moving to her side.

She tipped her head so I could kiss her soft powdered and blushed cheek and not get caught in the eye with the wide-brimmed lavender sun hat. She was decked out in pale purple today, with enormous amethyst jewelry all of the same hue, down to the polish on her bubble-gum toes. She'd lost her husband, a fighter pilot, in the Vietnam War and raised four children on her own on a secretary's salary. Now she had them flying down to see her all the time, grandchildren as well, and never did the whole army of them, thirteen so far, miss any birthdays or holidays with her. Even her in-laws preferred her rambling Mangrove beach mansion to their own homes all over the country. The first sculpture I ever sold was commissioned by and sold to her, a wind chime that looked like a plane propeller that she knew her husband would have simply adored.

"What is all this ruckus about?" she inquired frostily, eyes on Valerie.

"It's none of your business," she spat, rounding on Delilah. "You—"

"I have no idea who you think you are, madam, but I assure you that *everything* that goes on in this town is my business."

"I—"

"Now who precisely are you?"

"Are you important in this town?" Valerie asked, advancing on her.

"I am the most important citizen," Delilah huffed, lifting her chin, clearly ready for a fight.

"Ladies," I began, though really, there was only one there.

"Well, do you know you have a filthy whore living in your town?"

I groaned and watched Delilah's eyes widen almost comically, her face flush red, and her hands fist at her sides.

"How dare you say something so vile in my presence!"

Valerie was shocked because the response was so unexpected.

"Whatsoever my boy used to find himself having to do outside of my town is of no concern to myself or any other person in this community. The only concerns we have with any of our populace is how they comport themselves within town limits, and I can assure you that no such behavior on the part of Lazlo Maguire has ever been seen or reported here."

"He's fucking that lawyer, Britton Lassiter. Are you telling me that you allow sodomites in your perfect little town?"

Delilah took a deep breath through her nose. "I would stand here and explain that love is love, no matter the sex of the people involved, but I suspect it would fall on deaf ears."

"You—"

"So instead I will tell you that you have five minutes to remove yourself from this street and twenty to get out of my town, or I will file a stalking complaint against you and have you charged and put in jail."

"How dare—"

"You'll certainly stay overnight as a guest of our deputy county attorney, Langley Beghe, and before that, one or the other of our two lovely officers will escort you to the police station in the back of their patrol car."

"You have no right to disrespect me!"

"I have every right! You are shrieking at my boy in the middle of the sidewalk at ten o'clock in the morning on a Thursday, disturbing the peace and hurling about wild accusations. This is the very definition of disrespectful!"

"Is he screwing you too, you old bitch? Is that why you're calling him your boy?"

Delilah's catch of breath was loud. "I call him my boy because he's a part of my family, you disgusting creature! He doesn't have a mother so—"

"I'm his mother!"

And with that, Delilah stopped, gasped… and then dissolved into a fit of laughter I would not have thought her capable of.

"Ohmygod, go away," I told Valerie. "Leave and don't ever come back."

"You can't—"

"Yes," Delilah said, still chuckling as she spoke into her phone, which neither Valerie nor I had noticed her using. "I have an emergency on Sand Dollar Lane near the corner of Beach. A woman is harassing me, and she's about to hit me. If you don't hurry, the dogs might bite her." She listened a moment. "Oh my, yes, Coz, bring the pepper spray and the Tasers."

Hearing that, Valerie took several steps back as Delilah hung up and then lifted the carved staff her grandson Jerry had brought back from his tour in Afghanistan for her. She carried it every day when she walked her dogs, in case any other dogs got too close. It was no big secret that her two were overindulged troublemakers.

"Now, I suggest you run before Cosimo Renaldi gets here, because though he was a bit snide on the phone with me a moment ago, he will most assuredly take you in simply because I drive him bonkers, and he'd rather not have to speak to me," Delilah haughtily informed Valerie.

"You should be nicer to him," I suggested for what felt like the billionth time.

"No," she scolded. "He goes around with that Kelly Seaton, who cavorts with Hutch Crowley, and dear God, you know how awful that man is!"

I snickered. "Hutch is a nice guy."

"He's a menace and he will not be mayor."

I rolled my eyes.

"And you," she said to Valerie, brandishing her staff and poking Valerie in the hip with it. "Off you go now, never to be seen again!"

Valerie was dumbfounded, and I got it, I did. Delilah Evanston was chairwoman of the town council and director of the historical society; she owned Brenner Manor, the most exclusive hotel on the beach, and she had her finger on the pulse of the community. She used her shrewdly invested money to keep things small and keep big developers out, and she made sure that her favorites—including me; our new fire chief, Essien Dodd; and Hiroyuki Takeo and Dwyer Knolls, who had opened a new bed and breakfast the year before—were coddled and welcomed by the entire town. She was a force of nature, and people either loved her, like I did, for her warmth and kindness, or feared her more than the annual hurricanes. I would have to work on her with Hutch, but that was a fight for another day.

We all heard the siren at the same time.

"This will not be the last you hear of me," Valerie warned.

"Oh, I think it most certainly will be," Delilah promised. "I'm filing a restraining order as soon as Coz picks me up and takes me to the station, and Lord help you if you ever come back here. I don't allow trash in my town."

With that, Valerie bolted for her rental car, got in, and had it started when Cosimo Renaldi rolled up. The rental flew by his now parked car, and he watched it go before turning his attention to Delilah and me.

"I can't wait to hear this," he drawled.

"I tell you, I was attacked," Delilah apprised him arrogantly. "And I do not care for your tone in the least, Mr. Renaldi."

He squinted at her. "Do you need a ride, is that why the 911 call?"

"No, Mr. Smarty-pants, I'm filing a report."

"You are not putting those dogs in my car until I see them pee and poop."

"That's ridiculous," she snipped, opening the back door and cooing at her angels to jump in.

"This is your fault," Coz groused at me.

"Not this time, I swear."

His scowl was dark. "You're dead to me, Maguire."

"Until your boyfriend needs another lawn sculpture?"

"No, until tomorrow night," he grunted. "You and Britton and your cute kid are invited to Mom's for dinner. She's making fettuccine in cream, tomato and basil sauce, roasted spinach and mushroom Carbonara, and stuffed manicotti pasta shells with ricotta cheese for Kitty."

It was all vegetarian, of course, because his mother knew I didn't do meat. "That sounds great," I said, walking over to the car and putting my hand on his shoulder, squeezing tight. For some reason I found the act of that grounding. "We'd love to come."

"Oh, that does sound wonderful," Delilah said, pulling out her phone.

"Wait, no," Coz whimpered.

"Annalise," Delilah said cheerfully, smiling into the phone. "I have Coz here, and he told me about the feast you were making tomor—oh, you did? In my mailbox? That's so lovely! Calling cards are such a thing of the past, but I do adore them," she tutted, so very pleased with Cosimo's mother. "Oh yes, dear, I will, and I'll send a note just as soon as I get home and—oh? Well, yes, of course, I would be delighted to do that. Lemon meringue pie and bars for Mia. She so enjoys those, as does Lazlo."

She was right, I did, but really, watching Coz wither just hearing about Delilah in his house was hysterical. It was all I could do not to laugh, but he'd kill me if I did, so I stood there and stayed silent.

Once she was off the phone, she gave Coz a little pat on the arm and then took my arm and moved me back over to the gate that led into my yard.

"I never want to see that woman around here again, do you understand me?"

"Yes, ma'am."

"Now," she began, looking up into my face. "You do love Britton Lassiter, don't you?"

I smiled at her. "I do."

"Well, that's wonderful news. When you set a date, do let me know, and I'll make the ballroom at Brenner Manor available."

Oh dear God, she was going to marry me off to the rich lawyer. "Thank you."

"Of course, darling," she replied sweetly, patting my cheek before turning back around to Coz and announcing that she was ready.

I stifled my laughter as she got into the backseat, patted Coz on the shoulder, and then waved to me. Clearly, he was to be her chauffeur for the day.

He flipped me off as they pulled away, and I was left alone on the street to contemplate my new life for a few minutes.

Everything had changed so fast, but because of that, because of Katie giving me the impetus to leave my old life behind and Britton recognizing that I was ready to be the man he needed, I had the strength to say good-bye to my mother and finally not care what she thought of me. It had been years—my life had drowned the boy I was—but still, even after all of it, I was ready to hope and dream and love again.

The soft breeze on my face felt good, and more, felt like it was blowing through me, getting things moving. I felt light, free, and ready to see what could happen.

"Hey."

Pivoting, I saw Britton walking up the street in a pale gray suit with a light blue tailored shirt and brown belt, and wingtips the same color. He'd left my place that morning in a pair of my swim trunks and a New York Giants T-shirt, so the change was nice. It wasn't that I didn't like seeing him in casual wear, but he wore a suit really well.

I waited for him, and he reached me, hands slipping around my hips, up under the olive green pocket T-shirt I was wearing, sliding over my skin.

"Are you okay?" he asked, searching my face.

"How did you know there was a problem?"

"Coz called me after Mrs. Evanston called him. He said there was some issue at Beach and Sand Dollar, and that's right near our place."

I stepped up against him and he made a noise of pleasure.

"What?"

"I like these jeans," he admitted, glancing down my body before taking hold of my hand and leading me toward the house.

"Hey, no," I said, laughing. "I have to go to work."

"No, not after your mother was here, not after she hit you."

"It's okay," I assured him as he tugged me behind him. "I didn't expect anything else from her."

He made a noise as he used his keys and unlocked the front door, then walked me in. He closed the door, rounded on me, and took my face in his hands.

"I'm okay," I said, smiling through unexpected tears.

He wiped them away with his thumbs and bent and kissed my forehead, my eyes, my nose, and finally my mouth.

I melted into him, my lips notching perfectly with his, and he kissed me until the sadness was gone and only my joy about having him back with me remained.

"I wish I'd been here," he said after he broke the kiss, clutching me tight.

"You were," I sighed deeply. "I was thinking when she was attacking me that for once it was okay because I had you and I know you love me, and so… I'm good."

He pressed his face into my hair, inhaling deeply. "I do love you, so much, more than you know, and me, you, and Kitty are going to be so happy."

"I know."

"But you have to let me take care of you, all right? Because I'm dying to do it, and I want to, so badly. Lean on me, will you, please?"

"I will."

"I mean it, Cearul. I want you to need me as much as I need you."

"That's already happened."

"Are you sure?"

"I'm sure."

"And you'll maybe listen to me a little?"

"A lot, yeah."

"We have to make things easier on each other, easy everything, especially the evenings, just us and Kitty, happy."

"Yes, absolutely."

"And you're going to stay with me no matter what."

"No matter—wait," I said suspiciously, feeling like something was amiss.

"Nope, you already agreed."

I tilted my head up to meet his gaze. "What's going on, Lassiter?"

His grin was wicked. "My folks and my sister are coming next week to meet you. They can't wait, they're all so happy for me and that I'm finally madly in love, so they got plane tickets as fast as they could."

"Your family?" I croaked.

"I'm so excited! My whole life is coming together so perfectly, and you, baby, you're the center of it all."

"I think I'm gonna pass out."

He grabbed me, lifted me up off my feet, and twirled me around the living room. "Oh baby, I'm gonna be the very best man for you, I promise. You're going to love me so much, you won't ever be able to let me go."

"I couldn't do that now," I sighed, realizing how far down the rabbit hole I already was. He was madly in love, and God, so was I. "You're it, Britton Lassiter. I'll love you forever."

I felt the happy tremble race through him as he hugged me to his heart. "Oh man, how did I ever get so lucky? I've got my baby, and my baby has a baby. I could die happy right this second."

"No dying, only living," I replied, laughing softly and kissing him.

"Yes, living," he murmured. "Lots and lots of living."

SLEEPING 'TIL SUNRISE

Mary Calmes

MANGROVE
Stories

CHAPTER ONE

"Oooh Dad," Ivy exclaimed. "I just had the best idea ever!"

Oh God. "No."

"You don't even know what I was gonna say," she argued.

I groaned.

"What? How did I know you didn't like blonds?"

"I'm sorry, what?"

Even though I loved her, Ivy could try the patience of a saint. Since I wasn't one, I was *this* close to throttling her. The matchmaking had to stop. Even though she meant well, I was starting to cringe whenever I came home and smelled something cooking as I walked into the house.

"Craig was adorable," she cooed.

He was also, easily, twenty years my junior. And even though the school counselor had put his hands all over me when my daughter left the kitchen to set the dinner table, showing me in no uncertain terms that he was more than interested, I was not. I wasn't in the market for a boy; I was looking for a man. Or more precisely, if I was, in fact, searching for anyone, it would have been a grown-up.

"Stop trying to set me up," I enunciated for her.

"Pardon me?"

Her eyes blinking as though she were all innocent sweetness… was a crock. "Stop bringing strange men home."

She scoffed.

Jesus, what had I just said?

"I bet you didn't think you'd be saying that to me until I was eighteen, huh?"

I was horrified. "That's so not funny. Don't ever say that to me again."

Her cackle was evil. "I wouldn't have to bring home strangers if you'd just put on your big boy pants and take a chance."

I stopped walking. "I'm sorry?"

She whined, "Come on, Dad, it's time already."

It was a blessing that Ivy, who thought she missed nothing, considered me boring and stalwart and all those things a good father should be. But after my friendly, supportive divorce, I had made up for lost time after living in homosexual denial and slept with every man I found even remotely appealing. What that amounted to was more sex than I'd ever had in my life, and I became such a player that names got confused and I turned into one of those guys I hated who evaporated in the morning light, all slick come-on lines and no substance. I got really good at sneaking out of bedrooms, down fire escapes, and out back doors.

When I woke up one morning in Seth Jordan's bed, alone, I was surprised that he walked into the room a minute later with two cups of coffee as I was frantically dressing. The arched eyebrow, warm smile, and teasing tone while he asked what my hurry was threw me for a loop. It turned into one of the best relationships of my life.

Ivy continued. "I know you're all worried because Mom died and you think I've lost enough and you don't want me to get attached to people who aren't gonna stick around."

It was a lot of psychology so early in the morning. "Where are you getting—"

"I talked to Hutch, and he said that since you're the only parent at present, that you probably have unrealistic expectations of what you need to do to keep me emotionally balanced."

"You—"

"And Mike said that you're probably concerned about bringing people into my life who might not stay."

They were both dead men.

Seth hadn't lasted. Six months was all we got before Deanna's illness and Ivy needing me full-time took its toll. I'd lied to her, lied to both my girls—told them I wasn't ready to tell people about Seth and so he left me, because the real truth—that he wanted me to live with him and hire a nurse for Deanna and be less involved with Ivy—was too hard for me to say let alone allow them to hear. He'd given me an ultimatum: him or my dying ex-wife and my little girl.

Leaving Seth, his home, his bed, the circle of his arms, annihilated me. He was the first man I had ever loved, but I made the only choice

I could. I had to spend the small amount of time Deanna had left with her and Ivy as a family and make sure she was as comfortable as she could be. I had to let her know she was loved. Pancreatic cancer ate Ivy's mother up, and the end of her battle had been heartbreaking for both my daughter and me. When the end came, we were with her, my dear friend who would forever be the mother of my best girl.

When it was finally all over, I sought Seth out, only to find him happily moved on. At the time I didn't understand why I was relieved, but it occurred to me afterward, as I was leaving Detroit for Miami, that I needed a fresh start. I needed to breathe on my own for a while. I was glad to be reinventing myself, excited for Ivy to be on the adventure with me, and ready to live and simply *be*.

I hadn't clearly thought out the move to Miami. Exchanging one big city for another was not something either Ivy or I had needed. It had taken only a month of being there for me to go to my new boss and explain the situation. I was fortunate he'd been so understanding, and even more fortunate that he'd known the tiny resort town of Mangrove was in the market for a new fire chief.

"The money's crap," he told me as he stood in my office. "But it's beautiful there, and small, and maybe you and your kid—after what you just went through—could use a small, tight-knit community."

"I think that sounds great," I sighed, and his smile, in response, was warm and kind.

"I do too."

While I had stayed in Miami and closed up my office and got out of our lease and hired movers and basically undid everything I'd just gotten done doing, I sent my daughter on ahead of me with my sister's kid, who was a twenty-two-year-old struggling actress I thought was far more responsible than she turned out to be. I was lucky Ivy had found Hutch and Mike next door along with other friends in the tiny resort community.

But now I really needed them all to butt out of my love life, especially because I had no idea what to do.

Ivy was *still* talking. "But I understand you have needs."

I was lost for a second, catching up. "What?"

"*Needs*," she said, emphasizing the word, making her eyes big for my benefit.

I was about to have an aneurysm. "Please stop."

"What, Dad? It's a natural part of being an adult."

"I'll *pay* you to stop."

"You know Hutch and Mike are right next door. You can always start spending the night other places, because you know I'll be safe."

"Ivy," I began, rubbing the bridge of my nose, my voice pained.

"And c'mon, this is Mangrove. There has never been any kind of violent crime in the history of this town. Coz told me."

I groaned. All the people I knew who were trying to be helpful, and probably even thought they were, were driving me nuts.

"Not that there are a ton of gay men to choose from here, that's true," she continued, pinning me with her stare. "Don't look at me like that. Hutch said, so you know it's true."

I needed a drink.

"He's going to run for mayor, you know, just because Mrs. Evanston told him not to."

"Don't believe everything you hear."

"She hates him for no good reason."

But having known Hutch Crowley for the last six months, I was sure that Mrs. Evanston had cause. The man was definitely annoying.

"So I was thinking you should ask out Dr. Hammond, cuz he's superhot."

I did the slow pan and glared at her, and she waggled her eyebrows in response.

"Yo, Poison!"

Her head snapped up, and there was the boy, that one, the blond surfer with the hair and the dimples and the big blue eyes. She made a noise, that noise, the one my wife had made when she first met me, half whimper, half sigh.

"Don't do that," I groused.

I thought there'd be a learning curve, there normally was. I figured Ivy would need me… and she did. She loved me, of course, but she did not need hand-holding.

Except when she did.

Sometimes, not often, but upon occasion she broke into a million pieces I had to gather and hug whole. She needed her daddy when it hit her—at sometimes strange, unfathomable times—that her mother was altogether gone and all she had was me.

A lot of that pain and desolation had run through her system by the time we reached the sleepy little coastal town, but I still thought she'd disintegrate more often. She had moments of falling completely apart, and though there were hundreds in the past, once we moved to Mangrove, she suffered only a handful. I blamed the town. It wasn't Detroit, full of memories and pain for her. Instead, everywhere she looked was new and shiny and God, so very bright. I'd never worn sunglasses so often in my life.

"I gotta go," she said, brushing me off, as she ran to catch up with… Derek. I was pretty sure that was it.

"Davis!" she called, and he turned and waited and had the balls to wave to me.

I growled.

Davis, not Derek, had been on my porch the first weekend they'd met and every one after that. I'd said no, but he was relentless.

"Why are you here?" I'd asked, irritated, as I stood there in the entryway of my home.

His smile was blinding. "Mr. Dodd, you realize that I have the utmost respect for your daughter."

I sighed deeply. "I'm sure you do, Derek—"

"Davis," he corrected. "But you can call me Derek if you want."

Which was where the confusion came in. I had the kid's own permission to re-christen him. "No."

"But sir—"

"She's fourteen," I reiterated, as I'd done the last five times he was on my porch.

"And a half," he added.

"Sixteen," I told him again. "That's the magic number you're waiting for here. She doesn't get to date until she's sixteen, Der—crap, Davis."

"But we can hang out, right?"

He himself was sixteen, and I knew that because he'd told me so on a number of occasions. "Not alone," I explained, "because I don't want to have to hurt you."

"She's the only one who can hurt me, sir, by taking away her smile."

He was seriously going to make me vomit.

Ivy sighed from behind the screen door like she was a character in a Jane Austen novel, and Davis leaned sideways and smiled the smile that would serve him well later on in life when he became President.

And now he was waving, and she slipped her hand into his as they turned and walked away.

"I thought she couldn't date until she was sixteen?" Lazlo Lassiter, formerly Maguire, reformed rent boy, now full-time father, shop owner, and new husband to Britton Lassiter—they had been married at Brenner Manor right on the beach—volleyed as he walked by.

"She can't," I snarled.

He tipped his head at my girl and her suitor. "That looks like more than friends to me."

"I will kill you where you stand," I warned.

His shrug, along with a giggle from Katie, his adorable little girl he was currently walking to preschool, told me I wasn't scary in the least. "It's sweet," he assured me.

I rounded on him and pointed down at the cherub at his side. "I will remind you of this conversation years from now when she starts to date."

His eyes bugged out and he looked suitably horrified.

"Yeah, see that?"

He muttered something under his breath before tugging his daughter after him, leaving me alone on the side of the road to think about *my* daughter.

Ivy had friends, activities, she was grounded and happy. I was needed, of course, but not nearly to the extent I had been.

My job as fire chief was easy, mostly kittens in trees, CPR classes, checking fire extinguishers, and talking to Mrs. Halsey about bonfires on the beach and getting the correct permits before she and the other seniors got naked and danced around the blaze. Having a group of them all looking at me while I averted my eyes was problematic. I also helped Mr. Sutherland, the deputy mayor, talk to local businesses about fire lanes and how packing boxes in front of emergency exits was not kosher. It was tame, my life, and so I had no excuse, none at all, not to focus on my love life. Or, in Ivy's case, have it focused on *for* me.

WALKING OVER to Cuppa Joe to get my daily fix of the hazelnut latte Mike Rojas, the better half of Hutch Crowley, had gotten me addicted to, I was surprised to see Roark Hammond, pediatrician extraordinaire, the man my daughter wanted me to ask out on a date, in line for coffee, wearing a baseball cap, aviator sunglasses, and clothes that looked like they'd been slept in. Even though I knew better than to pry—it looked like a morning walk of shame to me—I simply had to know what was going on with the good doctor who normally was the epitome of style and beauty.

I liked and was impressed by all that Roark was and the fact I had really enjoyed our interaction the first time we'd met.

I was walking into city hall, he was coming out, and I held the door open for him.

"Oh thank you," he said offhandedly, rushing to get out of my way.

"My pleasure," I replied, smiling as he turned to look at me.

He froze, nearly tripping, and I reached out to steady him because he was on a step and I didn't want him to lose his balance.

That was the day I noticed his jasper-green eyes, because they were open so wide as he stared at me.

It was impossible to miss how beautiful the man was, and so I let go of the door and stepped into his space, wanting to get a name. He had to tip his head back to hold my gaze, as I was six four and had several inches on his long and lean-muscled frame, and when I heard his breath catch and saw him wet his lips, I was encouraged by the reaction. As a fireman, I needed to be in great shape, so I was. Even though I didn't really see it—I had looked like all the other guys in my neighborhood growing up—I'd been told since I hit my early teens that I was handsome, beautiful, gorgeous. And while it had never gone to my head, I hadn't heard a "no" from anyone I tried to pick up, even the married/in a relationship guys, since I turned sixteen.

"I'm Essien Dodd, the new fire chief," I said softly, offering him my hand.

He tried to answer, but his voice was full of gravel that needed to be dislodged. Coughing, clearing his throat, he took my hand as he started again, only to have the beginning of his reply come out in a low, almost yodeling sound.

I couldn't control my smug grin. Apparently the gorgeous man in front of me, squeezing my hand as he tried to get his voice to work, found me quite appealing as well.

"I'm," he began again, for the third time, his tone like dried leaves crunched under a boot, "Ra-roar—Roark, Hah-hah-hammond," he stuttered.

I covered his hand with my other and held tight. "You're the doctor, right?"

He nodded.

"I'm bringing my daughter in to see you."

"Oh?"

"Yes. Next week."

He took a quick breath. "You'll bring her or your wife will?"

"I will," I told him, taking in his long, thick eyelashes, dark curved brows, and lush lips. "I'm not married."

"Uh-huh."

"And even if I was, it wouldn't be to a woman," I added, because that needed to be clear even if I wasn't in the market for a new man in my life.

He gave me a fleeting smile, and I let his hand go but remained where I was, close, staring down into all that deep, dark green.

I was surprised when he suddenly closed his eyes and inhaled deeply before letting them drift back open.

The urge to lean forward and kiss him was overwhelming and just a tiny bit terrifying. There'd been no one since my wife died, since my ex-boyfriend in Detroit told me it was too late to rekindle our romance, not even a one-night stand, in either Miami or now Mangrove. It hadn't been a problem. I was focused on my daughter and our exodus from Michigan to Florida, and then to a new and even better opportunity in the small coastal community where we'd landed.

I realized now that, if I thought about it, the only man in town I had any interest in at all was the good doctor. And really, if it wouldn't be breaking my firmly laid-out rules, I would have been more than happy to follow my daughter's prompt to ask him out. But as it was, he—and every other available man in Mangrove—was off-limits.

"Good morning," I greeted him softly, my voice warm as I leaned in close, whispering, my breath on Roark's ear.

He shivered, and I was surprised that he kept his focus forward instead of turning to look at me.

"Roark?"

The answering whimper was sweet. He finally turned to me. "Yeah?"

Not quite the response I was expecting, but as his gaze met mine over his shoulder, and his lips parted, I found myself lost in his dark eyes. They were a beautiful green-black color, and when he laughed, which was rare, they sparkled. I knew I wasn't the only one who noticed, as often as I'd seen strangers transfixed on the street when he stopped to talk.

"Essien?"

I coughed quickly. "So why do you look like you slept in your clothes?"

He took a breath before glancing away. "I didn't sleep."

"Should I be sorry or not?" I chuckled, surprised.

"Oh, no, not like that," he grumbled. "God, I wish."

"Pardon me?"

His groan was tired.

"Roark?" The tremble that ran through his long, lean-muscled frame was noticeable. I took hold of his shoulder and turned him around to face me. "What's wrong?"

He cleared his throat. "It's possible I could be a little needy this morning."

"Because?"

"I was up all night with Mr. and Mrs. Garcia."

"I don't know them, I don't think." I had only been in Mangrove for six months, so it was possible the Garcias were people I'd missed.

"The litter was delivered early this morning."

It took me a moment. "I'm sorry?"

"I'll give you a thousand dollars if I don't have to explain," he mumbled before pivoting to face toward the counter again.

"Hold up."

His whimper was cute before he mumbled something under his breath about the town being much too small as he moved up one space. Our place in line was slowly edging toward the counter.

"Kittens?" I said to his back.

"No."

It was too good. "Puppies?"

Exasperated sigh from the man, and I found I couldn't stop smiling.

"Please let it go," he grumbled. "I can't even see straight, let alone think."

"You delivered puppies?" I snorted.

He ignored me as he reached the cashier and ordered a regular cup of coffee with four espresso shots mixed in.

"You don't think maybe sleep would be better?" I prodded.

He shushed me, paid, and stepped off to the side to wait instead of quickly darting to the other end of the bar to wait with other customers. It was surprising, because he usually bolted. If we saw each other in line for coffee, he'd pretend I wasn't there or talk to anyone but me and would certainly grab his coffee and get out of there as fast as he could. Normally he never lingered. It had actually become kind of our thing, his hurry to ditch me whenever possible. He was always in a rush when it looked like we'd get a few minutes to talk. I had no idea what I'd done to the man, but it was like he couldn't stand me. Until today. Until now.

He was staying put, waiting not just for his coffee, but for me.

Knowing he was there, that I had his attention, was dizzying, and I had no idea why.

Adam Crawford, the barista, brought my regular and passed it over.

"Here you go, Chief," he said as he did every morning, and I thanked him, paid his sister, Pattie, the perky little cashier, and then moved sideways to stand with Roark, who was still waiting on his cup.

"How come you get yours so fast?"

"I'm special," I said like it was obvious.

He smiled even though his eyes were watering. "Yeah, okay."

I tipped my head, studying him.

"What?"

"Why work today?"

"It's kind of what I do."

"Yes, but what if you diagnose something wrong? What if in your sleep-deprived state you do something really stupid?"

"I was a resident at one time, you know, so I've done without sleep for days on end. It's how doctors are trained."

"You're telling me you never made a mistake?"

"Never," he promised.

I tried another tactic. "You could reschedule and—"

"I have patients booked solid the whole day," he explained calmly. "And if I don't go in today, then all that does is make tomorrow absolutely insane."

"Yes, but—"

"People need me."

He got off on that, I could tell. People thought he was so magnanimous, but the truth was, he liked the attention. His ego was huge, and there was no way it wouldn't be, with everyone telling him he was the Second Coming. I knew that because I used to be the same exact way. The birth of my daughter changed that for me. Before she'd been born, I'd been the kind of guy who took foolish chances just to be told he was amazing. In his way, it was the same for Roark. He gave his time selflessly just to be praised. I often wondered what was missing in his life that made him seek validation from others, but we weren't good enough friends for me to ask. Maybe, though, with him stilling for a moment, actually waiting on me, perhaps I had an opportunity that had never presented itself before.

I cleared my throat. "So," I said softly, stepping in close, into his space. "Puppies?"

"There's no vet in town, and Domino, the Garcias' pit bull, was suffering."

"And so you did what? Performed an emergency C-section?"

"Yeah."

I nodded. "And how's the dog now?"

"Resting comfortably."

"And the puppies?"

"All five are good," he answered with a smile followed by a quick yawn.

"Good job, Doc," I assured him, brushing his thick hair out of his face so I could keep looking into his gorgeous eyes, red-rimmed with dark circles under them.

"Thanks," he grunted, taking a breath, ready, I could tell, to leave.

"Hey, I have a proposition for you," I offered, dropping my hand.

He coughed. "Oh? What's that?"

"How 'bout you let me come over after work and bring dinner."

"I don't know if that's—"

"Come on," I insisted, "just let me."

"But I'll be exhausted."

"That's the point. You'll be too tired to cook. Who takes care of you?"

He looked startled. "No one."

"Well, then," I said gruffly. "Allow me."

"Why would you—I mean, I'll be fine."

"That's not the point, is it. Not that you'll be fine, but that you could use the caretaking and that's who I am."

His jaw clenched. "I've heard that about you."

"Oh?"

"Yes," he assured me, firmly but gently. "And I can promise you that I don't need to be looked after."

With that he whirled around, grabbed his coffee off the counter since they'd called his name, and left the shop out the side door so he didn't even have to look at me again.

"Why doesn't he like you?"

When I turned my head, I found my neighbor, Hutch Crowley.

"He likes everyone," he said.

I just stared at him.

"Hello?"

"What?" I said irritably.

"Why doesn't the most eligible bachelor in town like you?"

"I have no idea," I admitted.

"You should maybe figure that out."

"Go away," I groused. "And stay out of my love life."

He scoffed. "Oh buddy, that ain't love."

No, it wasn't. Not yet, anyway.

CHAPTER TWO

I COULDN'T shake the feeling that I was missing something with Roark, and even after a day of lecturing fourth, fifth, and sixth graders about the dangers of matches, and extinguishing a science experiment at the high school, a grease fire at a shrimp shack on the beach, and a barbecue that almost got out of control because of the wind and the seven years' worth of petrified Christmas trees in the backyard, Roark Hammond was still on my mind.

Ivy called and said soccer practice was running late and that afterward her coach, Kahala Hill, was taking her team out for pizza. I told Ivy I'd see her at home, changed out of my uniform and into jeans, a T-shirt, and running shoes, and headed over to Roark's office. Though it was after seven when I got there, I wasn't surprised that his car—a gorgeous restored 1941 Chrysler Town & Country Woody Station Wagon—was in the driveway, not the car that belonged to Blake Timmons, his partner at work. They were both pediatricians, but while Roark was booked solid from morning to night, Blake was basically the fallback. If Roark was sick or away, you got Blake.

The office was a converted barn, just stunning inside. From the enormous double ceiling fans that extended the length of the hall to the polished wood floors and distressed white walls, it was beautiful.

Walking inside, I realized no one was there, not even a nurse or the receptionist.

The howl of pain startled me, even more so because I knew exactly who'd made it. Bolting down the hall to look for Roark, I rushed into his office and found him slumped over his desk, files on the floor, keyboard wedged against his cheek, moaning in his sleep.

A lot of the guys I'd worked with over the years had been soldiers, and since we slept at the fire station during our three days on, I learned some had been abused and still others had worries that ground away at them in their sleep. I knew the sound of a nightmare you couldn't wake up from, though I wasn't actually looking at PTSD.

Hustling around the desk, I lifted him from where he'd passed out on top of paperwork, leaned him back in his chair gently, and rubbed his upper arms.

His eyes fluttered open, but when he saw me, his eyes that had been wild softened, telling me he was more than pleased to see me.

"It's okay," I soothed, stepping around in front of him and sinking down to one knee. I took hold of his shoulders and kneaded them, moving slowly, carefully, to his biceps, getting the blood flowing, certain that he was stiff and cold from being unconscious in such a contorted sprawl across his desk.

"Why are you here?" Roark asked tentatively.

"I'm taking care of you, of course," I answered softly, smiling at him.

He wasn't really awake yet, so he couldn't hide his reaction to having me close. His pupils dilated, the black absorbing the jasper, he puffed out a breath followed by a sweet little whine, as he licked his lips, swallowing hard.

When he tentatively leaned forward as my hands were massaging his wrists, I drew him closer, into my space, and kissed him.

It was meant to be a quick peck of comfort, but the second our lips brushed, mine parted for him, and that was all the invitation he needed before he pounced.

I was more than ready to allow the mauling and returned the passion, slipping my tongue into his mouth. I tasted and savored, sliding a hand around the back of his head, fingers tangled in his thick, wavy black hair as I held him against me. I didn't want him to move. The way he responded, submitting, opening, moaning into my kiss, wrapping his arms around my neck, made it hard to not take him over the desk.

Easing him out of the chair, I lifted him off his feet and carried him, still kissing me, never breaking away, to the couch. When I sat down, I pulled free for a moment to take a gulp of air, but before his mind could clear—which would lead, I was sure, to him pulling away from me—I recaptured his soft, supple, pouty lips.

The shuddering groan was full of hunger, and when I shoved my tongue in his mouth again, he sucked on it hard, moaning deep and sexy as he bucked in my lap. Quickly, I worked open his belt buckle and got into his Dockers, the button and zipper easy to maneuver. He broke the kiss and put his hands flat on my chest, panting and shivering. "Essien, we should stop and—oh!"

I had his hard cock dribbling in my hand, and the way he pressed up into my grip, shuddering as I rubbed precum over the head with my thumb, left no doubt in my mind that stopping was definitely not what he truly wanted.

Running a hand around the side of his neck, I tilted his head down to me and took his mouth in a claiming, devouring kiss at the same time I rolled him sideways to his back under me, my hand never stopping the slide on his shaft from balls to head.

He writhed under me, his body quivering from the contact, breath stuttering as I suckled on his bottom lip a second before I abandoned the kiss and sat up.

The panting, the flush, the wide-open, trusting glazed expression in his eyes made me smile as I roughly shucked his jeans to his knees and curled over him. He yelled my name when I deep-throated him in one smooth movement.

I smiled around his cock before I swallowed down the length of him, sucking and laving as he palmed the back of my head, clearly wanting me there, holding on, his hips lifting off the couch as he fucked my mouth.

"Essien!"

I took hold of the base of his cock, squeezing tight, and he gasped, digging his fingers into my shoulders.

"I can't—you shouldn't," he moaned, low and seductive, his body bowing under me as I made the suction too strong for him to hold himself back.

He arched hard, freezing in position as he dumped down my throat, and I swallowed fast. It took several long moments for me to lick him clean, and when he was, when he slipped from between my lips, sated and spent, I leaned back and grinned down at him.

"This is a mistake," he whispered as the first tear slipped from the side of his eye and down his temple.

"Why's that?" I asked, leaning over him, hovering close.

"Because." He took a breath. "I'm no good for you."

"Again I ask, how come?"

"You've already been a caretaker once; I don't want you to have to do it again."

"Why?" I asked, studying his face.

He was beautiful, with his forest eyes, the deep laugh lines around them; the long, straight nose; full lips and chiseled planes of his face. His glossy black mop was getting long, tumbling almost to his broad shoulders. I wanted to feel his body pressed to mine. I wanted Roark Hammond naked in my bed, but he was trying to tell me something important, so I wanted to not only hear, but listen.

"Tell me," I demanded, leaning back a little, sitting beside him on the couch, admiring his long, veined dick lying flaccid against the treasure trail on his stomach.

He cleared his throat, still breathing heavily. "I have cancer."

It took me a moment to process what he'd said, because honestly, that word and I were so deeply acquainted that hearing it again, even just for a second, blotted out everything else.

Some words, some smells, even songs could rush you right back to a place in time and you were caught there, reliving a memory, stuck with no way out until the flood receded.

I saw a rush of images of tubes and machines, heard sounds of crying, but thankfully not the smell of antiseptic or worse. I rode the roller coaster for a long moment, and then I was suddenly back, present, with a beautiful man who was searching my face for a reaction.

It wasn't fair. He finally opened up to me, allowed me close, and what? It took everything in me not to yell. How many people was that fucking disease going to take from me?

"I have leukemia."

I nodded and took a quick breath, careful that he didn't see any sympathy or hear it in my voice. Straightforward, no beating around the bush, was, I knew from experience, the way to go. "Which one?"

He squinted at me. "Most people don't know there are different kinds."

"I'm not most people."

"No, you're not," he said softly, and I saw a hint of a smile.

"So?" I prodded.

"I have CML, chronic myeloid leukemia," he answered quickly. "Or chronic myelogenous leukemia… it's all the same."

"Stage what?"

Quick clearing of his throat before he said, "Leukemia doesn't— it's not like that. There aren't stages per se, as it already occurs in the developing blood cells within the bone marrow."

"Okay. Then how sick are you?"

"I'm not, not really."

"Good."

"You're so matter-of-fact about all this."

"You'd prefer I did what?"

His brows furrowed and his face tightened almost in a grimace before he glanced away, not meeting my gaze.

"It's the reason you've been avoiding me, so let's get it out in the open," I went on.

He sat up fast, squirming out from under my arm, pulling up his briefs but unable to fasten his pants because of how much I was crowding him. "I haven't been avoiding—"

"Yes, you have."

"I just—" He took a breath. "—we all know, the whole town knows… what you did for your wife."

The town was small; everyone knew everybody else's business. It was not a surprise that this, too, had been shared. "Which matters why?"

"I don't want you to have to live through that again."

"I thought you said you weren't sick," I said flatly.

"I did."

"Then how am I living through the same thing?"

"Down the road," he snapped.

"So you're planning on a down the road with me, then?"

"I—"

"Because every time I get near you, you disappear, and when I do see you out, it's always with some tourist who's gone in a matter of days."

He shoved me off him and stood up, adjusting his pants and zipping up. He didn't fasten the button, though, or fix his belt; instead he began pacing in front of me.

"Yes?"

He spun around and pointed at me. "I'm not a whore!"

"That's an interesting logic jump," I replied, leaning back, hands behind my head, looking up at him. "How did you get there?"

"You just said you see me with a different guy every—"

"You're deliberately trying to pick a fight with me so you can order me out of your office, but we just had a breakthrough and you let me suck your dick, so I'm not going anywhere."

He sneered. "Are you looking for me to return the favor first? Is that it?"

I scoffed, chuckling even as I saw the quick flush burn up his throat and cheeks. "I like these tactics, Hammond. You're really good at this."

"Just get out," he snarled irritably, his eyes filling even as he glowered at me.

"No," I said with a shrug, parting my legs, tipping my head as I held his gaze. With his swollen lips, glittering eyes, tousled hair, and flushed face, he was simply gorgeous. I wanted almost desperately to take him home. But he was used to playing this game, allowing physical contact and then pushing people away.

I wasn't going to let him win.

"What do you want?" he yelled, back to pacing.

"I think the better question is, what is it that *you* want?"

He was holding himself so stiffly, twisted into knots right there in front of me, all his energy being spent on not breaking down.

"Roark?"

"I'll get sicker," he said as he inched closer.

"Or something else could happen."

He raked his fingers through his thick hair as he eased forward. "Chances are this disease is going to kill me."

"Yes," I agreed.

"It's cancer," he almost whined, stepping into the space between my parted knees.

"But there are a lot of factors," I rumbled as he wiped his eyes with the heels of his hands before letting his head fall forward so he could stare into my eyes. "And you don't have a crystal ball—you can't see the future."

He nodded. "It's true."

"So then why worry now?"

"Because if I get really sick," he said under his breath, "then you'd be back to taking care of someone."

"I'd have to really like you to do that, wouldn't I?"

"Listen, Ess, you—"

"My mother used to call me Ess," I said, chuckling, lifting my hand, fingers splayed, seeing what he'd do if he caught the movement for the invitation it was.

He laced his fingers into mine and I drew him close, turning him so he sank down into me, on my thighs, his back nestled against my chest, head tucked under my chin.

"You shouldn't waste your time with—"

"Stop," I grunted. "Don't you like sitting here with me?"

"Yes," he breathed out. "Too much."

The honesty was a nice change.

"What do you want?" he asked, and I could feel the tension drain out of him as he gave me his weight.

"How about your time? Could I have some of that?"

He tilted his head up and I bent and kissed him. It was just a brush of my lips over his, but his sigh was deep.

"This is not a good idea," he whispered when I pulled back.

"Oh yes it is," I argued gently, my hand rubbing circles on his stomach as I kissed his forehead. "Could I take you home?"

"I'm going to pass out on you when we get there."

I chuckled. "I know."

"I would really like to"—his voice bottomed out—"see you."

"I'd like to be seen."

He sat up fast and rounded on me as he sat there, perched on my knees. "I've been so scared."

I leaned forward and cupped his face in my hands. "Because you don't want to start something serious with someone who might leave you when they learn you're sick or who you might end up dying on."

"Yes," he admitted, his voice crackly and edged with pain. "And at some point, I'm going to need you way more than you're going to need me and—"

"That's what a relationship is about."

"But you don't have to have it, you could run now."

"No I couldn't. It's already too late," I said, grinning at him. "I like you too much already."

Tears welled in his eyes. "I shouldn't—and I've worked so hard to stay away from you and not…. I mean, you're just the worst choice because what I could do to you is horrible."

It was, and I felt a tremor of panic make a knot in my stomach with the realization of the step I was about to take. "Let me take you home," I soothed him, kissing his forehead before helping him up off the couch.

He buttoned his pants and buckled his belt and then trailed after me out of his office, locking doors and turning off lights. On the porch, I asked for his keys.

"I can drive."

"You better let me," I told him, gesturing for him to hand them over. "Besides, I want to drive your baby, really bad."

His smile made his eyes glint in the moonlight. "Everybody's in love with my car."

"Can you blame us? It's vintage."

I loved his laugh, deep and throaty and real, and when he passed over his keys, he leaned sideways and kissed my cheek.

"Let's go," I prodded, not kissing him back, not reaching for his hand. I was in full friend mode now, wanting to take care of him and make sure he got home and ate and went straight to bed. "You need sleep."

He didn't argue, just followed dutifully behind me as I took care of him. It was, after all, what I did.

CHAPTER THREE

FRIENDSHIP WAS one of those odd things that could not be relied upon to make sense.

My daughter thought that since we lived next door to Hutch Crowley and Mike Rojas, and since they were both gay and I was gay, and because Mike had lost his wife and I'd done so as well, we would be fast friends. And while they were really good guys and we sometimes ate together and I trusted them with my kid, they were almost more Ivy's friends than mine. It took me a long time to open up to people, and while I shared a lot of surface things that anyone could know or that my daughter would tell them, I was not about dredging up my soul to people I'd only known for six months.

The exception was Dwyer Knolls, who ran a small but gorgeous bed and breakfast right on the beach called Blue Days. He ran it with his husband, Hiroyuki Takeo. They hadn't been in Mangrove as long as a lot of others, but while everyone sort of knew one another's business, Dwyer and Takeo were a bit more solitary. While it couldn't be said that they were standoffish in any way, neither were they like Hutch or Kelly Seaton or Britton Lassiter. They kept to themselves, and so when I ran with Dwyer in the mornings, no one ever just joined us, because he was with me. It was actually very nice.

"If I wanted to run alone, I would," he teased, easily keeping pace with me even though I was taller and my stride was longer.

"Sorry."

He grunted. "What's on your mind this fine morning?"

"Nothing."

His snort of laughter made me smile.

"Try again."

"Yeah, okay," I huffed out. "Roark Hammond."

He squinted at me. "I thought we were holding off on dating until your kid went off to college."

"Shit, I know."

"Oh, no, don't get me wrong," Dwyer said quickly. "I think that makes a lot of sense, and you and the doctor—that totally works, but it was *your* mandate, so I'm just wondering what changed your mind."

I groaned.

"Need to get laid?"

"Yes," I replied honestly. "But there's more to it than that."

"I get it, he's husband material."

"What? No."

"What? No," he repeated with a snicker. "That was so convincing, I think you should get an Oscar or something."

"Why don't you run that way," I said, pointing out to the ocean.

He bumped into me, gently, just a nudge of comradery. "Knock it off. I've seen the way you look at him, and I've seen the way he looks at you. You're both idiots."

"I—that's not—what makes you… I don't—"

"Wow," he scoffed. "All that?"

"No, it's—no. We're just talking about hanging out."

"Oh yeah?"

"Yeah, it would just be casual."

"I see," he said, his voice dripping with judgment.

"What?"

"Nothing."

"For crissakes, just spit it out."

He shrugged as he jogged along at my side. "Roark doesn't seem like a guy you do casual with."

"Are you kidding? As far as I can tell he *only* does casual."

"Because he's been keeping himself from doing anything at all with you," he concluded.

"And you know this how?"

His grin was really just filthy; it was the first thing I ever noticed about him. He had been drinking at Wrecked, a bar on the boardwalk, and no one else got near him. I'd left Hutch and Mike, and Kelly and Coz, and leaned close to him. Dwyer hadn't noticed, but I'd felt the lime wedge hit my back. When I turned, everyone at the table was waving at me to get the hell away from him. But the town was not full of gay men, they were few and far between, and when I'd smiled at him earlier, the openness of the smile I got back had made me brave.

"Can I buy you a drink?" I asked as I got close, breathing in his musky, and at the same time citrusy, scent.

He turned then and gifted me with that grin, ripe with heat and sex and daring, and the turquoise of his eyes reminded me of the ocean first thing in the morning. He was breathtaking. No other man besides Roark had me more interested.

"I would," he said, his voice a sensuous, smooth rasp that I liked. "But I'm spoken for, finally, and you know how it is when you have the guy you can't breathe without."

I sighed. "Not yet."

The laugh lines around his eyes deepened as he turned in his chair to offer me his hand. "Well, then, brother, we better get on that."

It was the best start to a friendship I'd yet to experience. As a rule, I didn't have a lot of male friends, gay or straight, so meeting Dwyer Knolls, having him steer me out of the bar and into his life, was so very welcome. Meeting his husband, Takeo, had been such a nice surprise as well. The few times I had connected with someone, the wife, girlfriend, husband, or boyfriend had either liked me too much or not enough. I was worried before Takeo breezed into the room and first bowed, then took my hand.

He was quiet and reserved, but not cold, and really funny and very quick, but most of all, his observations about people were so spot-on it was sort of terrifying. It was all the listening he did, all the secrets shared with him that he would take to his coffin, and how much taking care of you he was willing to do. When he gazed at Dwyer with all that love and adoration, it was easy to discern the depth of his heart.

They welcomed me into their cocoon, and I was happy to go there. It was a refuge, one Ivy found as soothing as I did. Not that she didn't love and adore everyone else, but now and then, she needed to decompress, and there was no one better to do that with than Takeo. The first time she was sick and he arrived with homemade shoyu ramen instead of chicken noodle soup, she was in love. Between me liking Takeo and Dwyer, and my daughter liking them as well, I finally had that best friend I'd always heard so much about.

So the fact that he was lecturing me at the moment could not simply be ignored.

"Are you listening to me?"

"Actually, yes," I assured him. "And I ask again, how do you know that Roark Hammond is pining away for me?"

"I'm sorry, when did I say pining? I said that he fucks around because he can't start something with you."

"And why is that?"

His glare made me feel stupid.

"What?"

"You told Hutch Crowley your life story."

"Correction: my daughter told him."

"Same difference," he snorted out.

"Hutch is a good guy. He didn't tell everyone my business."

"No, he told Kelly, and Kelly told everyone your business."

"What?"

"Which doesn't make Kelly a bad guy, 'cause he's not, he's just really young and—"

"Lazlo Lassiter is younger than him."

"Yeah, but Laz was never really young, right?"

We had all heard the story by that point, because when his husband-to-be Britton's parents showed up to meet him and Lazlo's daughter's mother's parents had visited, the truth had all come tumbling out of Coz's sister, Mia. I, of course, had known Lazlo used to be a rent boy—Kelly had told me—but I hadn't known the extent of his life before he was an adult, when he hadn't been the one making all the decisions. So even though Kelly's childhood had not been all milk and cookie happy either, so far Lazlo won for crappiest.

"Yeah, okay."

"So basically, when Kelly told everyone what a saint you are and—"

"What're you—"

"Stop," he placated me. "You are, don't be stupid. You're the kind of person we all hope to be when push comes to shove."

"That's a really simplistic interpretation of—"

"Just let it go," he directed. "And take the fuckin' compliment."

My groan made him smile.

"But the problem is, now you're this paragon of virtue no one wants to sully."

"I'm sorry, what?"

He coughed. "You're like a virgin."

I almost fell because my feet got tangled up midstride. Dwyer was quick to steady me and then yank me to a stop so I wouldn't hurt myself.

"What the hell did you just say?"

"Calm down."

"What the *hell*, Dwyer?"

He tried not to laugh but failed miserably. "Listen, the whole town knows you're a goddamn prince of a guy," he said, chuckling, throwing up his arms. "All the women wish their husbands were you, all the husbands fuckin' hate you and are thanking God you're gay, and all the gay men… well… no one wants to be the guy who did anything to fuck up Essien Dodd's life or his daughter's."

I stared at him.

He lifted his eyebrows.

"You're serious?"

He nodded quickly.

"Holy shit, you *are* serious."

"I mean, what's his name, the little twink counselor Ivy brought home from school for you to snack on, who clearly did nothing for you, was—"

"You know about that?"

"Aww man, everybody knows about that."

I had to sit down and started looking around for a bench, which wasn't difficult. The whole town was salted with little whitewashed benches placed on grassy knolls and under tiny arbors draped in wisteria, and all around the mangrove tree in the center of town.

"And Hutch cornered Craig Turley the next time he went in to buy groceries and, well, that's why when he sees you coming he runs the other way."

"He did what?"

Dwyer shrugged.

"He had no right to—"

"Better him than somebody not as professional, and you know everyone knows Hutch, right? I mean, he owns the only grocery store in town."

Finding a bench, I flopped down on it hard, then bent forward so I wouldn't hyperventilate from the sheer horror of having Hutch Crowley warn Ivy's high school counselor to stay away from me.

"I'm actually a grown-up, you know. I don't need everyone keeping an eye on me and making sure I don't get hit on."

"But that's the issue, right? No one wants to see you or your cute kid, get hurt. So if you want to run off to Destin or Panama City to get laid—go for it. But since everybody who's gay in this town knows everybody else—"

"You don't know—"

"Pardon me—everyone who is out and gay knows everyone else," Dwyer amended. "That okay? Not offending your delicate sensibilities?"

I flipped him off.

"Since our community is small," he said, glaring at me, "you need to come to the realization that everyone who knows you is looking out for you."

"I need to move," I moaned, leaning back on the bench. "Holy fuck."

"It's really not that bad."

I stared up at him. "How do you figure?"

"Well, for one, we're all pulling for you and Roark."

"Oh God."

"But I get why he's been ducking you."

I looked back at him. "Why?"

"He told Takeo and me that he's sick."

Deep breath. "Yeah."

He took a seat beside me. "So it makes sense that with all you've been through already that he would steer clear of you."

"But I'm drawn to him."

"Well, yeah, who wouldn't be, he's gorgeous."

"I'm sorry?"

"What? I'd have to be blind."

"Takeo better not hear you say another man is pretty."

"Like he gives a shit," he scoffed. "Takeo knows I worship the ground he walks on."

And I knew it went both ways.

"But I think Roark's decision was a sound one, considering everything."

I shook my head. "He needs to let me make my own choice."

"I know."

"I mean, Jesus, Dwyer, he's amazing."

I'd known Roark was worth getting to know after the first time I'd taken my daughter to see him. He sat beside her on the examination table, and together they filled out the questionnaire about her health history. They had a very frank discussion about her period—far more than I ever wanted to know—and he asked her, not me, if she was planning to have sex.

I was horrified and had told them both that would happen only over my dead body.

"We'll talk about it later," he assured her, scowling at me.

She was relieved, and when he took her hand, she squeezed tight.

When she told him about her mother, I was surprised, because she wasn't usually so open—unless you counted Hutch Crowley—but he listened and then hugged her afterward as she blubbered all over his midnight-blue Henley. What impressed me was that I saw a man clearly interested in my child, and not just as her doctor. He cared about her, I could tell, and that, as a parent, went a long way. It wasn't lip service, it wasn't professional courtesy. He liked kids, and he liked her.

I saw him at her soccer games, in the stands cheering, and afterward it wasn't just my kid he went down and high-fived. All the girls adored him, as did their parents. He was mobbed wherever he went.

Toddlers went charging down sidewalks to him, boys who were in that transition from adolescent to teenager would catch up to him just to walk with him a little, whispering questions I could see Roark answer in the same hushed tone so as not to embarrass them. I tried not to smile when I caught questions about hair on balls, morning wood, and waking up with wet sheets as they walked by me with him. He was that rare combination of a doctor kids trusted implicitly and parents respected. If the town had a superstar, it was him, and while he enjoyed being needed, he still managed shy and self-deprecating at the same time.

"So?"

I returned my attention to Dwyer, reining in my wandering thoughts.

"You back from your trip down memory lane?"

"Has anyone ever told you that you're a smartass?"

He tipped his head like he was actually giving it some sincere thought. "Now, what'd you ask me?"

His smile made his eyes heat. "About Roark, where are we at?"

I huffed out a breath. "I dunno."

"What do you want?"

"I don't know that either. I mean, like you said, my plan was not to do anything serious until Ivy left for college, and then I thought, maybe I could just see Roark casually."

"Like he used to see Hutch," Dwyer offered cheerfully.

"Shut up."

"You don't care that he slept with your next-door neighbor?"

"It's ancient history, according to Hutch."

"Okay. So what else?"

"Meaning?"

"Well, I figured you and Roark were gonna bond because you're from the same place."

"We're from the same state," I corrected him, "not the same area. I'm from Detroit, Roark's from Grosse Pointe. That is not the same, my friend."

"Like not at all?"

I chuckled. "Worlds apart in socioeconomic status."

"Big words," he teased me.

"Well, let's face it. He named the city to make it accessible when you asked where he was from, but he explained in more detail when I hit him up for answers."

"I see."

"Again, I'm from Detroit, from the city—he's from a very upscale burg."

"Okay, so you have no common ground at all, then."

"Not really."

He shrugged. "Then let it go. You don't need the hassle, right?"

But the question was not about what I needed, instead, what I wanted. Half of me just wanted to fuck Roark, and the other half wanted to keep him. And I was terrified that he'd die and I'd be left alone again, and Ivy would have to deal with loss up close all over again.

"I'm an asshole for even thinking about walking away just because I don't want to get hurt. That's weak."

"It's not weak, it's honest," he assured me. "You did that already, nursed someone, cared for them through the very worst time. You were the good guy, the best guy, and you honored the whole in sickness and health bit even when you'd already been let out of the promise."

Yes, I had. Just the thought of doing it again was terrifying.

"You have nothing invested yet—now's the time to run the other way."

Except that running away felt wrong. It was a mess.

"I think you should default to Ivy, right?"

I met his gaze.

"Your life isn't really yours right now—it belongs to her. That's what it means to have a kid, right? That's what prompted Lazlo to iron out his clusterfuck of an existence. He had to straighten up for his daughter; don't you have to do what's best for yours?"

"Meaning?"

"Meaning that you have to consider what the best thing is for Ivy. Is getting involved with a man with cancer in this small town where everyone knows everybody else's business really the best choice for her?"

"It might be."

"Shouldn't you know for sure?"

Perhaps.

"I bet Roark doesn't want to be a burden."

"He could never be that."

"Come on, get up," Dwyer ordered. "There needs to be more running and less sitting."

"But I haven't figured anything out yet."

"I think you have."

"Could you tell me, then?"

He grunted and started running. It took me only a few moments to catch up to him, and when I did, I realized he was right. I knew what I had to do.

CHAPTER FOUR

I WORRIED about what I would say to Roark, but I shouldn't have. It turned out he had to fly out to Grosse Pointe on family business, and he left town without a word to me. Of course I was illogically hurt because I thought that we'd bonded, but apparently it was just another blow job to him. I should have been happy that I had dodged the bullet of his illness as well as his clearly cavalier attitude toward sex, but while the first seemed horrible, the second was sad. I'd thought we were both in the market for something deeper, and to be wrong felt like my instincts were for crap. I was clearly a terrible judge of character. The only good news was that I didn't need to dwell on my failure now. I had four years to figure it all out before my daughter went away to college. I'd worry about it much later.

Ivy was having dinner with her best friend, Julia Kent, at her house because Sharon, Julia's mom, needed help making up the wedding favors for her Saturday nuptials. It was going to be a sweet, small private wedding in her backyard, where she and Fuller Denny were tying the knot. I'd met them both, very nice salt-of-the-earth types, and the gift bags going next to everyone's plates were 100-percent organic and biodegradable, as was everything going inside. Julia had pressed her best buddy into service with her, and when I called to make sure that Ivy's help would indeed be appreciated, Sharon nearly broke down thanking me. Apparently Ivy being there, excited for her, was helping Julia be a bit more accepting.

"Your daughter's a godsend," she assured me.

It was always good to hear that.

I talked to Ivy, told her I'd be over by nine to pick her up, and headed home from the office. It had been a low-key day. Only one call for sunburn, one from a woman who'd locked her poodle in her car for—gasp—at least two and a half minutes, and one from Jeremy Riley's mom, who had another emergency with him and his latest thrill ride. I had no idea how they even got the wood up onto the roof without her knowing—or the grocery cart for that matter. They were about to try the latest coaster of death when I got there and called them all down instead.

"You're making your mother crazy," I informed the eleven-year-old.

"She needs to embrace her inner daredevil," he volleyed.

"You're so grounded," I responded, shaking my head.

"Whatever Chief Dodd is telling you, you better believe it!" Candace Riley shrieked from her front door.

Jeremy groaned. "You're a buzzkill, man."

I knew that. It came with the job.

"I thought firemen were risktakers."

"Only when we're saving people," I said, setting him straight.

The second groan from him was even more pained than the first.

As I turned onto my street, I saw Britton Lassiter walking toward me with his newly adopted daughter, Katie, on his shoulders. She waved to me and he slowed. It was cute how she had her hands in his hair, holding onto his head. I had carried Ivy the same exact way.

"Hey," I greeted them.

He gave me a wincing smile.

"Jesus, what's wrong with you?"

"His mommy and daddy, my new grandparents, are at my house again," Katie announced happily. "They're going to stay the whole month!"

My gaze met Britton's. "That sounds great."

"Does it?" he snapped.

I scoffed. "Weren't they just here?"

"Uh-huh." His voice sounded so strained.

"They like the beach, do they?"

"No, not really."

I tipped my head at Katie.

"That's right," he told me. "Lazlo too."

Britton had worried—the whole town knew he had—about how his parents would take the news that he was gay. By all accounts, they were very kind people, so it wasn't a stretch to find out that they wanted only the best for their son, and as that was so obviously Lazlo—who lit up like a neon sign whenever Britton came near him—the fact that they were on board with the relationship was not a surprise. What *had* been was the revelation that along with a new son-in-law, they got their first grandchild as well. Katie, the epitome of cuteness and smarts, was a gift.

I couldn't stop the chuckle. "They seemed great when I met them at your wedding. What's the problem?"

He cleared his throat. "They like staying at the house with us instead of at a hotel."

"So you're not getting… any." I snickered.

"That's right," he said not so cheerfully.

Lazlo, former wild child, former loner, who no longer drank or smoked or did drugs or fucked for money, also refused to have sex in a house with paper-thin walls where guests could hear him make love to his new husband. No ring on his finger, even with a diamond as big as my head, would sway him.

"He doesn't want to offend them," I said graciously.

"Have you looked at him lately?"

I had, and so, I knew, had every man and woman in town. Lazlo had always been gorgeous, striking, with that smoldering beauty that made you think he should be on magazine covers, but now, loved and cherished by Britton, he had bloomed into something else entirely. The confidence that had before been all bravado and swagger was now simply *there*. He was self-assured because he was loved, and that, he'd never been before. Only the wedding ring kept people from throwing themselves at him morning, noon, and night, as well as getting a look at his husband. Britton was nothing to scoff at, himself.

"I can—" Britton cleared his throat. "—barely keep my hands off him, and my parents… are in my house, having the best time hanging out and talking."

"And he loves being part of a family," I surmised. "Am I right?"

He grunted miserably.

"Well, they have to go home eventually."

"They're looking into getting a house here."

I nodded, trying not to laugh.

The noise of disgust he made as he walked around me heading for home was funny. Katie waved back at me and then leaned over the top of Britton's head. No matter what he said, he was happy to have his family there, too, even if his parents were putting a crick in his sex life.

I was surprised when I reached the gate in front of my house to find Blake, the other doctor in Roark's office, on my front steps.

"Hey," I greeted as I lifted the gate latch and gazed up at him.

"Sorry to just show up," he apologized. "I tried to get you on the phone today, but every time I called, whoever answered at the station said you were out on a call."

"Okay."

"And I don't have your cell number."

Why would he? We weren't friends. "So what's going on, Blake?"

He stood and came down the steps to me. "Have you heard from Roark?"

"No, I haven't."

He nodded. "Did he tell you anything about his grandmother or the vineyard in Kentucky?"

"They have vineyards in Kentucky?" This was news. "I thought there were only vineyards in California."

"Your wine education is sorely lacking," he said condescendingly.

It was really no wonder that most people just wanted to dropkick him. "What's going on, Blake?"

He walked toward me, stopping just a few feet away. "Roark's grandmother passed last weekend, and she lived out in a vineyard in Kentucky, out in Midway, so that's where he went."

"Oh, I thought he went to Grosse Pointe."

Blake shook his head. "No, he went to Kentucky, and he's been there all this time. Normally he calls just to give me a heads-up, but not this time. And he was supposed to be back yesterday, but again, no call, e-mail, nothing."

"Okay," I said, looking at him, not sure what this had to do with me or why he was at my house at seven on a Friday night.

"I have no idea what's going on with him."

I was quiet, thinking there was more.

"Well?"

"Well, what?"

Blake threw up his hands. "Have you heard from him or not?"

"Why would I have heard from him?"

"Because he was all excited."

I was so lost. "I'm sorry?"

He seemed surprised. "You guys had a date, right?"

Fellatio on his couch could not be classified as a date. "No."

"No?"

"No," I said firmly. "There was no date."

He sighed sharply, and I could hear all the exasperation. "That makes no sense."

"I have no idea what you're talking about."

He looked annoyed.

"Blake?"

"Now I'm really lost, because last week—what was that, Tuesday— we had this pharmaceutical rep in, and normally he stays with Roark before he heads back to Panama City. But this time Roark doesn't even invite him back to his office, just says that we don't need anything and thanks him for coming by."

I crossed my arms, waiting for the point of the story.

"So after the guy leaves I tell him that he shouldn't be treating a fuck buddy that way, and he says that he's got no time for anyone anymore but you."

It was my turn to be surprised. "What?"

"Yeah. So when you tell me that you haven't heard from him, I'm wondering what the hell is going on."

"I have no idea."

His brows furrowed. "Well, could you try and call him, and if you get ahold of him, could you let him know that he needs to call me?"

"Sure."

"Thanks." He sighed, smiled, and then left, getting into the red Ferrari parked in front of my house and gunning the motor before he took off.

Inside, I immediately tried to get Roark. He answered on the second ring.

"Ess?"

Oh, the shortened name thing was kind of hot. "Yeah."

"I was wondering when you'd call."

He was? "Why didn't you call me?"

"Because I was afraid if I did, I'd ask you to come here, and I didn't want to do that."

He wanted me there with him? "What's going on?"

"My grandmother died."

"Yeah, Blake told me."

"You talked to Blake?"

"Yeah, just now. He came over because he wanted to know if I'd heard from you. And by the way, he wants you to call him when you get a chance."

"Oh… oh, I see," he said softy, and the underlying sadness was heartbreaking. "So you're just calling because—"

"What the hell is going on, Roark?" I nearly shouted.

"What do you mean?"

"I mean are we starting something or not?"

"I thought—yes. Aren't we?"

And the truth hit me. We were having our first, and hopefully last, misunderstanding.

He thought we'd already begun.

I was checking to make sure he wanted to.

Neither of us was aware of what was happening in the other person's head.

But clearly, as evidenced by the hitches in his breath as he waited for me to answer, he was already *in* the relationship. He was already *there*. I was the one who hadn't heard the ready-set-go and was waiting for some definitive word or gesture from him.

For him, allowing me close, at all, was the "Okay, I'm in this moment." He felt like he'd already said yes to me, which was why he was worried now. He wasn't sure whether we were on the same page, and there I was, waiting for a sign he'd already given me the night I drove him home. The whole letting me in was him beginning.

Christ.

Sometimes I missed what was right in front of my face.

"Yeah," I said quickly, growling at him. "So why the hell would you leave without saying anything to me?"

"I—it was too soon to ask you to go with me," he rushed out, and I heard both relief and longing in his voice.

"That's what you thought?"

Nothing.

"Roark?"

He coughed. "Yeah."

"Well, it wasn't."

"No?" he husked.

"No."

"Well, I'm glad you didn't come, because it's awful here, and my family is just insane and... I... you're the only thing."

"What?"

"Thinking about my life there, about going home, about you being there... that's been the only thing keeping my head on straight."

The thought of me was keeping him grounded, and he was looking forward to seeing me. I couldn't think of a better compliment. "Explain to me what's going on there."

"Oh, no, I don't want to bur—"

"If you say bug me or burden me with your crap or anything but how much you missed having a person in your life to share bullshit with—this could be real bad for us."

"You're serious." It was a statement, but he still sounded surprised.

"I am."

"Because why?"

"Because that's what people in a relationship do: they lean on each other."

"And if one person does like 90 percent of that?"

"Who told you life was always fair and equal?"

"Ess—"

"No, really? Who?"

He coughed. "No one."

"Then where is this everything's gotta be equal crap coming from?"

Silence.

"As long as you're in it, seriously, giving and taking and doing it as hard as you can with your whole heart, I don't see where there could ever be any problem."

After a moment he took a breath. "You're amazing, you know, and you have no idea."

"Not a saint."

"I didn't say saint—and you're not—but you're different from anybody else I know."

"Shouldn't I be, if you want to be with me?"

"Yes."

"And you do, right? Want to be with me?"

"More than you can possibly imagine."

It was good to hear. "Okay, then," I said with an exhale. "Talk to me."

"Okay, so the reading of the will happened today, and now it's a battle because my grandmother left me the winery and everyone is trying to get me to hear their side of things."

"I don't understand."

"I decide what happens to it, that's what she wanted, and my father just told me they're going to challenge me because of my illness."

"I don't understand."

"He's telling them that the cancer is affecting my mind."

"Hold up." That made no sense. "Without even waiting to hear what you'd say, he goes right to attacking your mental faculties?"

"Yes."

"That's crap!"

"Yes, it is, but if he files suit and then it goes to the state medical board, I—"

"You're telling me that something he does there can affect your practice here?"

"It could, yes."

"No," I said quickly, taking a breath. "Come home."

"What?"

"Pack your stuff, drive to the airport, and get on a plane."

"But I'm supposed to see the lawyer tomorrow and—"

"What lawyer? Your father's?"

"Well, yes, actually," he said oddly, and I could tell he was actually thinking about what he'd just said.

"No. You need your own lawyer."

"Yeah, I probably… do."

"Just come back and we'll figure everything out."

"Ess—"

"I don't mean to cut you off, honey, but I really don't think you being there is a good idea. You're too far from home and your support base and… me."

His breath caught. "You're giving me heart palpitations, and I'm trying to be so cool."

"I can't believe you left town without telling me!" I railed.

"I'm sorry, all right? I didn't want to scare you off with any more damn drama after I just told you I had fuckin' cancer!"

"I thought I didn't matter at all, because you could just leave without a word."

"What?" he gasped.

It was good, that alarmed sound, because it spoke to the truth better than any words. "It makes sense, right?"

"No. And nothing could be further from the truth."

"Oh yeah?"

"Yes, Essien, I swear I—"

"Prove it," I barked.

"Prove it?"

"Yeah."

"What are you, ten?"

"Oh, so then, this *is* bullshit you're giving me."

"No."

"Then like I said, prove it."

"How?"

"You want me?"

"I do, yes."

"Are you sure? Because you don't sound sure."

"I am, though… very sure."

"You've been thinking about me?" I pressed because I could, and he deserved the interrogation. He'd left me, after all.

"I have."

"And you're ready to show me?"

"I am," he said breathlessly.

"Then get your ass home so I know you're serious, because leaving like you did was crap. Whatever we are, we're still friends, and Blake knew what was going on when I didn't!" I finished angrily because it flared through me and out.

"I just—"

"You need to have some faith in me."

"But I do. I have all the faith in the world in you."

"Then come home. And bring your copy of the will and have either Britton or Mia look it over, and when their lawyer contacts you, you'll refer them to yours."

"That makes a lot of sense."

"I always make sense."

He chuckled softly. "Yes, you do."

"And that way you can figure out what it is you really want to do."

"Okay."

"I know you know this. I know being pressured into making a decision isn't you, and isn't something you should be made to do. But I also know that losing someone you love screws with your heart, and when that gets involved, it messes with your normal decision-making process."

"It does. Yes."

"So you need to take a breath, and the best place to do that is here at home."

"With you."

"With me."

There were several moments of silence.

"Now's the time to figure out your story," he finally said.

"I'm sorry?"

"Now, before I get home," he told me. "Before I get even more attached or excited or horny… now's the time for you to come up with a logical reason, other than the obvious, why you can't see me."

"And the purpose of that would be what?"

"Because once I get home, Essien, I'm going to want to see you. A lot. Like all the time. So if you're scared, and you're just being noble… now's the time to run."

But the thing about me was that I never ran. Not ever. "I appreciate the advice."

"You're welcome."

"Now could you get on a plane, because I need to get laid."

His throaty whimper, full of ache and need, sent a tremor of desire racing through me. "On my way."

It was good to hear.

CHAPTER FIVE

IT WAS amazing how quickly things changed. I'd spent four days thinking one way, and then because of a phone conversation on a Friday night, I was in a relationship. And it wasn't that I hadn't thought I was—I had, and then hadn't, and was now back to the go place I'd been in the evening after I'd taken Roark home.

When I'd left him that night, passed out in his own bed, exhausted, I thought he'd call me the next day. I'd been scared, worried about him and Ivy and the entirety of my life changing, but the following morning, I'd felt like I had the first time I'd ever seen the man.

Hopeful.

And now as I sat on his front steps, waiting on a Saturday afternoon, the butterflies in my stomach were actually welcome. It meant I was ready, because I was unsure, and that was something I never thought would happen again after Deanna died. Yes, I was opening myself up to hurt a second time, but the rewards outweighed the risks. I wasn't ready to marry Roark Hammond; I just wanted a chance to see what we could be. So did he. He'd said as much on the phone that morning when he called to say he'd be home around four and would I please meet him?

I sat down with Ivy on our back porch and told her that I wanted to be there when Roark got home, as we had some talking to do, and then asked if she would consider spending the night with Hutch and Mike.

Her eyebrows had lifted high. "You planning to sleep over with him?"

I groaned.

"Huh? Dad?"

"Just—"

"Good for you," she said, slapping me on the bicep. "Hutch said that he'd like to see you take advantage of the fact that you have built-in babysitters."

"You—"

"Even though, as you know, I'm not a baby."

"No, I know."

Her eyes narrowed as she looked at me. "Please tell me why you were so sad this past week."

"Was I?"

She nodded. "Hutch said it was because of Roark."

"He really needs to get out of my business."

"Yeah, I know, but you're interesting to everyone, not just him."

"Oh yeah?"

"It's because you're you."

"And what does that mean?"

She put her hand on my knee, patting me. "You're so strong, and I don't mean because of all your muscles, I mean inside where it counts."

"What do you want?" I teased. "Money? Car?"

"Stop," she scolded, whacking my stomach gently. "People don't notice you at first."

"They don't?"

"I mean, they look at you because you're tall and handsome, but then they kinda forget about you until you're there for them, and you're there for everyone."

"Do you have any idea what you're talking about?"

"Yep," she assured me. "Mom used to say, 'Your dad is a knight in shining armor. He just doesn't ride a horse or wear armor. Instead he shows up in a fire truck and wears turnout gear.'"

"Your mother said that?"

She nodded. "Yeah, so I know, right? I know you're a good man and that everyone around here adores you, so I gotta wonder how come it took my doctor so long to get with the program."

I debated what to say.

"What's wrong with him?"

"What do you mean?"

She sighed. "He's clearly not stupid, and every time you take me to the doctor, just talking to you makes him all stuttery and shaky, and last time he walked into his own door."

I couldn't stifle the chuckle.

"I mean, come on, you'd have to be blind not to see that he's into you, so I have to wonder what his deal is."

Leaning back in my chair, legs stretched out in front of me, I turned and regarded my beautiful daughter.

"Speak," she directed.

"He has leukemia."

She absorbed that news. "He doesn't seem sick to me."

"He's not, not yet. But he has it, and I'll have to live with that if I'm going to pursue a relationship with him."

"Sure."

"So now you understand both his hesitation and mine."

Her scowl was surprising. "No, I don't understand. I mean, if you like him, and he likes you—so what?"

"Ivy—"

"No," she snapped. "You're gonna do what, be scared your whole life that someone is gonna leave you or die on you? What kinda life are you gonna have? Like if Davis told me he had cancer or HIV or something else, would I just walk away from him?"

"Davis?"

"No, I wouldn't," she plowed on, answering her own question. "We would use a condom whenever we had sex and I'd watch him like a hawk to make sure if he got sick that I was right there to get him to the doctor."

"Are you planning to have sex with Davis?"

"Dad!"

Not the point she was trying to make. "I'm sorry."

"Mom would be so pissed if she knew that you were using her and her loss to keep from getting into a relationship with someone you could really see a future with."

"I just want to date him and see where it goes."

"But you were thinking maybe you wouldn't even try 'cause of the cancer, and that's awful."

"We've both been through a helluva lot."

"So have a lot of people."

"I'm not arguing with you."

"And so what, now we're just never gonna love anyone else ever again? That seems nuts to me."

"Some people don't want to risk getting hurt again."

She took hold of my hand. "But that's not us, right? We're not like that."

I squeezed gently. "No, that's not us."

Her face lit up. "So, okay, I'll stay with Hutch and Mike. You can call 'em 'cause I know you will even if I tell you I'll take care of it—"

"I have to," I told her. "It's in the parent bylaws. We have to check up."

She rolled her eyes. "But so, okay, I'll be their chaperone for tonight, and you go and have fun with the doctor."

"Chaperone?"

She giggled. "Yeah."

"Why chaperone?"

"Because Hutch says the real word he should call me is not appropriate for my age group."

And he was right, cockblock was not. "God, he's a mess."

"Oh Dad, I love Hutch so much. He's awesome, right?"

Yes, he was. "I guess," I teased.

She snorted out a laugh. "Call him now. You need to get ready."

"But I am."

"I'm sorry?" she asked, studying me. "You're what?"

"I'm ready for my date."

Second eyebrow lift of the day. "You're wearing that?"

Why jeans and work boots and a Henley were bad, I had no idea. "We're just gonna hang out at his place."

"Dad!" She was horrified. "This is a big deal!"

So now I was sitting on the steps of Roark's little Cape Cod–style cottage in a linen shirt, walking shorts, and a pair of sandals I hadn't even known I owned. I wasn't surprised that when the taxi let him out in front of the house, he just stood there at the gate, frozen, instead of coming up the walk.

"I realize I look like a tool, but my daughter dressed me," I said to break the ice.

He nodded like he was in a daze.

"I would have picked you up," I offered. "I wish you'd have let me."

"It wasn't a good idea," he explained as he came through the gate and gently closed it behind him before continuing up the path.

"And why's that?" I asked as I stood up, taking the two steps to his porch to wait for him there.

"We wouldn't have gotten home."

"Why?"

He reached the bottom of the steps and stared up at me, and I finally saw what everyone was talking about when they said they knew Roark liked me because of the way he looked at me. The man's eyes were positively worshipful.

I gestured at him. "You're crazy about me."

"Well, yes, of course," he said flatly. "And if I'd been alone with you in the car, I would have made you stop at some sleazy motel on the side of the road, and God knows what would have happened then."

"Watch a lot of thrillers, do you?"

"Oh shit, don't you?" He gasped dramatically as he came up the stairs to stand in front of me. "Awww man, I knew there had to be something wrong with you. No one could be that perfect." Heavy sigh. "You like, what, chick flicks?"

Stepping into his space, I took his face in my hands. "No, sir, I like thrillers and horror movies too, so my perfection status is safe."

"I figured," he whispered, dropping his duffel and sliding his hands around my hips. "And you nearly gave me a heart attack, just looking at you from the road."

"Oh yeah?" I asked, dipping my head to kiss his forehead and then his eyes.

"Mmmmm," he murmured, tipping his head back as I kissed his nose. "I never thought I'd have the guy I've been dreaming about for half a year on my porch waiting for me when I got home. And you look so beautiful."

"I think you're biased," I said as I brushed his lips with mine.

He trembled slightly. "I think you don't look at yourself enough, but that's okay. I like that just fine."

When I smiled before I kissed him, I heard his husky whimper and slipped my tongue between his lips, needing to taste him more than I needed to breathe. I had no idea the rules had changed until he shoved his tongue halfway down my throat to examine my tonsils.

Gone was the man who needed to be persuaded and wooed. I was seeing the real Roark now, and this guy was not inhibited or timid, not hesitant or unsure or shy. He finally trusted me enough to show me his true face.

"Come inside," he rasped between kisses, shoving me into the door, fumbling for the keys, opening it so fast that I almost fell.

He steadied me as we stumbled through the door, kicked it shut behind him, and then walked me backward until I bumped up against a wall. All the while his hands roamed everywhere, tugging and pulling, wanting my clothes off as quickly as possible.

"You don't wanna talk?" I husked, lifting his head to kiss his throat, the chiseled line of his jaw, each of his dimples, and then reclaiming his lips ravenously.

"No," he replied quickly when I let him breathe, having worked open all the buttons on my shirt and pushing it off my shoulders before sucking a nipple into his hot mouth.

I jolted in his hands, and I heard a very sinister growl of pleasure.

"Oh, I found a good spot," he said evilly before he went to his knees and deftly opened the fastener and zipper on my shorts to reach my briefs and skin.

"Roark," I groaned, hands in his thick black hair as he swallowed my cock in one fluid movement. Never had anyone taken all of me down the back of their throat, and the pressure and suction, the way he leaned back and laved and licked before repeating the maneuver, made me clutch at the wall behind me to remain vertical. "Holy fuck."

He got his hand wrapped around my leaking cock and began fondling my balls, running his fingers over my crease as he sucked and sucked until I was there, ready, shaking with the concentration that it took to keep my control and not dump onto his tongue.

"Stop," I commanded.

It took a moment for him to answer as he eased slowly off the end of my dick to lift his eyes to mine. "Why? I want to taste you."

But instead of listening, I grabbed hold of the short-sleeved T-shirt he was wearing over the long-sleeved one and hauled him to his feet.

"Ess?"

He was confused, but more than that, he was excited, and I saw it in the sudden flush, the way his pupils dilated, and the sharp catch of breath.

Spinning him around, I bent him forward over the back of the couch, loving the way he instinctively grabbed hold.

"Where's your stuff?"

"There's lube in the second drawer of the end table, way in the back."

"Really?" I teased, smacking his ass.

"Just—I wanted to be ready if you ever came over."

I scoffed.

He looked over his shoulder at me. "It's only been you for months now, ever since I realized I was living to run into you and get a smile."

"What about the pharmaceutical rep?" I asked as I reached the end table and rummaged around until I found the tube I was looking for.

He didn't answer, and when I checked to see why, I found his eyes riveted on me.

"Hello?"

"Yes?"

"God, you are very good for my ego," I said as I slipped back around the couch to him.

"Your skin is like dark sepia in the low light," he said hoarsely.

Normally I heard food descriptors attributed to me and my coloring—mocha, chocolate, caramel, and coffee—never anything else. It was never anything more descriptive. But he was a doctor, he was precise, and I liked that. "Is it?"

He nodded as I reached him.

"Big fan of all the shades of brown, are you?"

"Just you," he breathed. "Everything you."

"Pardon?" I asked, dropping the tube down onto the couch before I flicked open the button of his jeans and quickly unzipped the denim that hugged his gorgeous round ass.

"I love everything about you."

I pulled down his jeans and briefs, and when his wet cock bounced free, I took hold and slid my thumb through the pearly drops of precum dribbling out of the slit.

He shuddered in my hand.

"I don't need protection. It's been a while for me, close to a year and a half, and I've been tested since," I explained, nuzzling his hair aside to kiss the side of his neck. "And for the record, that's the only reason I care about the pharmaceutical rep."

"I've never"—he clutched at the back of the couch as I gently nibbled up his throat—"been with anyone without a... ah... ah—"

"Condom?" I offered cheerfully, squatting down behind him and helping him take off one Nike canvas sneaker and then the other before shucking down his jeans and briefs.

"Yeah, that," he barely answered, his breathing ragged right before I couldn't take it a moment longer and sank my teeth into his ass.

He bumped forward with a cry, and I grabbed hold of his hips, stilling him before I rose, kissing my way up the curve of his lower back to his spine, rucking up his T-shirt until I pulled it over his head and down to his wrists.

Curling over him, pressing my chest along his back, I breathed next to his ear as I spoke. "There won't be anyone but me, yeah?"

"Not until you say you're done."

I smiled before I turned his head so I could have his mouth.

"And I'll need a notarized letter if you plan to stop sleeping with me."

"Duly noted," I agreed before I kissed him.

I'd loved before, twice, but I'd never been *in* love, and now I got it as I felt a flutter in my chest. There had always been something not quite right in the past—wrong person, wrong time—but now, finally, I was who I wanted to be, and where, and how. I saw myself growing old in Mangrove, living a whole life here, and if I was lucky, I'd have Roark with me for most or all of that time. But I wouldn't waste any more, and I'd make sure he knew what I wanted.

Breaking the kiss, I grabbed his hips and wrenched him backward so he had to bend over to keep his balance. Forcing his legs apart, I leaned sideways and grabbed the lube, and the sound of the cap popping open made him shiver.

"I don't take any promises lightly," I said as I greased my cock before sliding a lubed finger into his ass.

"Neither do I," he mewled, pushing back, trying to get me to press in deeper.

"You have to go slow and easy."

"You don't," he ground out, his voice thick with craving. "I like slow, but not stopping. Never stopping."

"You like the stretch?" I asked as I added a second finger that he immediately rammed back on, hard and fast.

"Yes."

"You want to be filled?"

"Yes," he growled, and I heard the hunger.

Quickly I withdrew my fingers and took hold of my cock.

"Hurry."

Pushing against his entrance, I opened him slowly, gently, but as he'd asked, never hesitating, just the relentless press into his body.

"Oh Jesus, you're huge."

His ass was tight and hot, and when I shoved deep and felt him take me in, the vise of suction fisting around me, I roared his name because he felt so fucking good.

His muscles rippled and twitched, and I felt them all along my length as I eased a few inches out, only to drive back in, harder the second time, the slick lube that allowed the initial breach now making the in and out pumping a graceful, slippery pounding.

His back arched under my chest and abdomen, and as he met each short, pistoning thrust, I realized I'd never had a lover chase his own pleasure. Everyone else had expected me to pummel them to orgasm. But Roark was loud and demanding, and even when I tried to be gentle, he wouldn't let me.

"Grab your cock," I ordered, leaving no question of who was in charge and who was the one doing the submitting.

He stroked his flesh mercilessly, and I felt his muscles clamp down around me even as I reveled in being buried inside of him.

"I'm never loud," he confessed in a ragged breath, spurting over his hand, coating his fingers as the sight of his climax triggered mine. The sound of him, the feel, his taste, and his abandon wrung my orgasm from me as I used him, pumping hard, filling his channel as I held him tight, one hand gripping his hair, the other on his hip.

The aftershocks were brutal, battering, rolling through us, causing me to ease from his flesh, spin him in my arms, and crush him to my chest, enfolded and safe. He nestled against me, coiling tight, breathing with me, in and out.

"Come get in my bed," he begged me. "Please."

I knew where his bedroom was—I'd tucked him in before so I, not him, led the way down the hall.

"Are you thirsty?" he asked as I opened the door and pulled him inside.

"I just want to lie down with you," I confessed, not even bothering to switch on the lamp, the moonlight allowing me to see in the dark.

His bed was a huge California king sleigh bed with a polished mahogany finish. The first time I saw it, I'd wanted to be in it, and as I sank down onto the soft sheets amid more pillows than any one person needed, with Roark coiling around me, I wasn't sure I could ever make myself leave.

His left hand smoothed up my abdomen to my chest before settling on the side of my neck. The sounds he made, the sweet little sighs, the sharp indrawn breaths, all let me know that he appreciated the feel of my skin, of me, under his palm.

"We're a mess," I murmured as I wrapped him up in my arms and hugged him to me, allowing no wiggle room, just us plastered together, his head notched under my chin.

"Yes."

"We're going to make everything sticky."

I grunted softly.

"I don't want to date you."

"How come?" I rumbled, not worried, knowing that this was only the first part of his thought. He was getting there; sex had addled his brain.

"We're supposed to be together."

There was the rest. "Yeah, we are," I agreed.

"So let's do that."

"What is it you want?"

He took a breath, which had to be hard, since I'd only tightened my hold, not loosened it. Not that he was complaining. Apparently being bear-hugged agreed with him.

"You won't get scared."

"If the big thing didn't do it, I think you're good," I said gruffly.

"But you're okay with that, with me being sick."

"I want you to be well, but as long as you're okay with letting me take care of you and look out for you, as long as you don't get mad when I remind you to eat right and get lots of sleep and—"

"So, basically, let you be you."

"Right."

"And you'll let me be me."

"I wouldn't want you any other way, but you have to take care of yourself not just for you, but for me and for Ivy now, too, yeah?"

"Yes, of course."

"Good. We're on the same page."

"So then, I don't want you to see anyone else but me."

"And you either."

"I want us to spend as much time together as we can, until the day you say, baby, this two houses thing ain't workin' for me anymore."

"Do I have to say ain't?"

He snorted. "No, you don't."

"That's lucky," I teased, hooking a hand around the back of his head, taking hold of his hair, grasping tight and yanking so his eyes met mine. "But you could move in with me anytime you like."

His eyes fluttered as he let the obvious joy of being manhandled, of being made to hold still, wash over him.

"That little catch of breath there spoke volumes," I announced before I bent close, my lips hovering over his. "You're crazy about me."

"Oh yes," he rushed out.

"That's lucky, since I feel the same."

"I'm going to make you so happy," he whispered against my lips before I claimed his and he opened for me.

"I know," I crooned after I pulled back, and rolled him over, lying down between his parted thighs.

He wrapped his legs tight around my hips. "Don't let me go. Don't ever let me go."

"No," I promised before I kissed him again.

CHAPTER SIX

I WAS surprised when Roark came staggering out into the living room wrapped in the quilt from his bed.

"What're you doing up?" I asked quietly, even as he reached me and leaned into my side.

I myself was wrapped in the flat sheet from his bed as I stood in his living room in front of his bay window.

"I might ask the same of you," he said, groggy from sleep, his voice gravelly and low.

"Oh, it's just this thing I do." I sighed, gesturing at the pink, red, and yellow streaked sky. "I only sleep 'til sunrise."

"I'm sorry?"

"I sleep until the sun comes up, I watch it, and then I either stay up or go back to bed. Either way I'm good. I just never like to miss it."

"Even on vacation?"

"Even on vacation."

"Why?"

I shrugged. "My mother used to say that you needed to greet each and every new day so the Lord would always know you were thankful for the time you'd been given."

He lifted his gaze to mine. "I love that."

I smiled at him. "It's annoyed a lot of people over the years."

"Oh, no, it's perfect. I'll wake up every day with you from now on."

"As long as you promise to go back to sleep," I cautioned him, "because you especially can't get run down."

"Then you'll have to make sure I want to go back to bed."

"Oh, I can make sure of that," I said, bending quickly and putting him over my shoulder.

"No, wait, the sunrise!" he protested. "We have to say thank you."

I turned to look at the sky changing from dark-washed pink to bright blue. "Thank you for another day," I murmured, smiling even as I rubbed the ass of the man not squirming in my hold. I turned him so he could see too.

"Thank you for the day," he sighed.

"Okay, good, now back to bed."

"You can put me down," he said, laughing.

"I could," I agreed as I did the caveman thing and carried him back down the hall toward the bedroom.

"Though this is kind of hot."

I was laughing, too, when I threw him down on the bed and climbed in with him.

I THOUGHT it was going to be a quiet, slow Sunday, and as I sat with Roark and Ivy, Dwyer and Takeo, and Hutch and Mike on the back patio of my house, having an amazing meal everyone had pitched in to prepare, I was surprised when the doorbell rang.

"I'll get it," Mike volunteered, darting back into the house.

"Can I have a mimosa too?" Ivy asked Takeo.

"Do not ask me, ask your father. I have been drinking since I was ten. I doubt I would be the best person to put the query to."

"Yeah, no," Dwyer said kindly, taking hold of Takeo's hand.

"No," I answered her.

"Crap."

"So who had money on when Coz's sister and Chris whatshisname, the hardware store guy, would hook up?"

"Hook up?" Roark groaned. "Really, Hutch? In front of Ivy?"

"He always has a potty mouth," she told him, leaning over and patting his arm as she'd intermittently done since the two of us got to my place a few hours ago.

I had left Roark in my kitchen, then gone next door and collected Ivy from Hutch and Mike's place. When we got back, I walked her into the kitchen and told her that Roark and I were going to be seeing a lot of each other, and therefore she, too, would be around him all the time.

Instantly her eyes filled with tears, and Roark had been fast to take her hands and comfort her.

"Oh honey, I promise I'm not trying to take your daddy away from—"

"What?" she asked, before dissolving into laughter for only a moment before the hiccups began. "Ohmygod, no, not even. Pretty please take him."

"What?" I was indignant.

That was it. She doubled over laughing and hiccupping at the same time, tears running down her little pixie face.

"Explain yourself, young lady."

"Hold your breath," Roark directed.

The conflicting orders only made her laugh harder.

Once she finally had herself under control, she explained it was about time that I started dating, and she was tickled pink that it was Roark I'd chosen.

"Tickled pink?" I asked, squinting at her.

"Mrs. Evanston says that a lady's language should always be proper."

"Don't talk to that old bat, she's insane," Hutch said as he walked right into my house without knocking, with a tray full of fruit.

"Lazlo thinks she's nice, and so do I," Ivy defended her.

Hutch rolled his eyes. "She's a menace."

"Why are you in here?" I inquired, irritable. I was trying to have a private moment and he—followed by Mike—was there. "I am talking to my family, you ass."

"We are your family," he insisted, gesturing at Ivy. "Who do you think takes care of that little girl?"

"I'm not little," she replied emphatically, just as there was a knock on my screen door.

Takeo and Dwyer were there, and while I was happy to see them, I was surprised.

"Your daughter invited me to make breakfast with her," Takeo informed me before he bowed.

I bowed back, and Dwyer tossed me a roll of homemade challah bread.

"Who made this?"

He tipped his head at Takeo.

"Really?"

"Dad!"

"What?" I addressed my daughter, because she sounded like I had offended her.

"That's so racist."

"I'm sorry?"

"You don't think Takeo can make good challah bread just because he's Japanese?"

"No," I snapped. "I had no idea he had a breadmaker."

"I apologize for my ignorance," Takeo began. "But what is a breadmaker?"

Dwyer was laughing in seconds.

Takeo was confused.

Ivy began explaining to me in exacting detail not only about racial stereotypes, but gender ones as well.

Mike said someone needed to make coffee, Hutch asked me where my chopping board was, and Roark turned away from all of us, taking up position at the end of the counter.

Rushing up behind him, I leaned in and tenderly kissed the side of his neck.

"Baby, what's wrong?"

He shook his head.

"Roark?"

As he turned so he could see me, I noted the tears instantly. "What's—"

"You called me your family."

I had. I hadn't even thought about it, it had just popped out.

"I'd love to be part of your family… to belong to you."

"You already do," I insisted, easing him into my arms.

The way the room went instantly quiet made both Roark and me look up.

"You guys finally got that all figured out, huh?" Mike beamed at us. "That's awesome."

"It's about time," Hutch chimed in.

"Pot to kettle," Dwyer said snidely.

I appreciated the support.

"Hey, Dad," Ivy said, making a face. "I think you need to take a shower."

She had no idea how right she was.

Once I got cleaned up—Roark had showered and changed at his place—I met everyone outside on my back deck for brunch. I ate like I was starved and was trying to think of how I could get rid of everyone, including my kid, without being rude, when the doorbell rang and Mike darted inside.

When he reappeared, he looked odd, tense, and Hutch was the first to stand, even before we all saw the men following him.

"I need to speak to my—Roark!"

What was nice was that my new boyfriend was not scared. He was annoyed, that was clear from his frustrated groan.

Three strangers—one older, two younger, all of whom looked a lot like the man I wanted to go back to bed with—stood there. The similarities began with height, hair, and coloring, the differences evident in things like eyes and the glint in them, the dimples, the wicked smile, the chiseled features, and the mischievous eyebrows that were, at the moment, crooked rakishly. God, he was pretty.

"You don't just leave your family to—"

"*This* is my family," Roark corrected the man I suspected was his father. "This is my hometown where I'm respected and where I run a successful practice, this is my boyfriend, Essien, and his daughter and my friends, and this is where I belong."

"You—"

"So please don't throw out the word home. I haven't had one until now, since I came home my freshman year of college and came out to you and Mom."

Mr. Hammond sucked in a breath. "You don't need to air our dirty laundry; you just need to come back with us so we can work everything out."

Roark got up from the table to face the three men in suits, and all I could think was how good he looked, how calm, how grounded. "Would the three of you like to sit down and have some breakfast and meet the important people in my life?"

"We would not," Mr. Hammond said disdainfully.

One of the men cleared his throat. "I would."

All eyes turned to probably the youngest man in the bunch, maybe twenty-four, twenty-five, now that I was really looking at him.

"Crosby," Roark sighed, reaching out a hand to his brother, who darted around the table to take it.

"What the hell are you—"

"Wait," Roark ordered his father, hand on his brother's shoulder as he shook Crosby's hand. "Where are you living now?"

"This is funny," Crosby said with a grin very like Roark's. "I live in Tallahassee."

"Really?"

He nodded. "Yeah, my girl and I are expecting a baby in the fall."

"Oh." Roark was overwhelmed. The smile and the shiver told me that. "I would love to come and see you—if I could—when the baby's born or—"

"Or you and your boyfriend," Crosby said, leaning sideways to smile at me, "could come down before that and visit. Lizzie would love that."

"I would too," he assured his sibling.

"You shouldn't have any of these people near your baby!" Mr. Hammond, whose first name I still didn't know, railed at Crosby.

"These people?" Takeo asked softly.

But before Mr. Hammond could say something in my house that could never be unsaid, Roark lifted a hand to shut everyone up.

"After you and Mom threw me out," he began, releasing Crosby's hand and facing his father and his other brother, "Gran was my sole support system, and even when she had her strokes, she still knew me up until the last one."

"We know all—"

"But I didn't remember until this morning when I cleared my head about everything that she'd put a proviso in her will."

"What are you—"

"She wanted to donate either the house in Grosse Pointe or the winery in Midway, Kentucky, to the at-risk youth in those areas."

We were all silent, everyone.

"Gran said that she couldn't imagine me on the street, which was exactly where I would have been without her. So she promised me then, that when she passed she'd make sure one or the other was given to charity while the bulk of the estate would go into a trust fund that I alone would oversee."

"We know you're the trustee, that's what we're fight—"

"Oh, I see," Dwyer said quickly, looking up at Roark while the rest of us focused on him. "Whichever place your father and mother and brothers wanted, they could keep, but the other is then immediately transferred to the estate that you're responsible for and becomes yours to grant to whatever charity you see fit."

"Yes."

"No!" Mr. Hammond shouted.

Dwyer stood up and faced Roark's family. "Though I'm not a lawyer, sir, I *am* an actuary, and from a money standpoint, I can tell you that even if you try to contest the will, as Roark would receive no monetary compensation for the transferring of assets, it's doubtful that the will would even go through probate. And as you stand to inherit property, thus benefitting financially yourself… well… you see what I'm saying."

"No, I don't see."

"You and your family will be given whichever property you want, and the other is dispensed in the manner in which your mother—" Dwyer turned to Roark for confirmation, and my boyfriend nodded. "—wanted."

"This matter is between my son and—"

"Mr. Hammond," Dwyer continued, "the issue for you now is that the will grants you both the choice and assets. So because you're not cut out in any way, the best thing for you to do is not contest the will, as then it'll get tied up in probate and it could be years before anything happens."

"I—"

"But in the meantime, everything's frozen, right?" The third man, Roark's other brother, finally chimed in with a question.

"Listen." Dwyer was ready to start over with his explanation.

"That's why we plan to have Roark removed as executor if he doesn't relinquish both properties to the family," Mr. Hammond insisted.

Dwyer turned his attention from the brother back to the father. "Yes, but Roark can't do that. As executor, he's bound to the wishes of the deceased party, in this case your mother, and we're all very sorry about that," Dwyer said, glancing over at Roark and Crosby standing beside him. "She sounds like she was wonderful."

"She was delusional!" Mr. Hammond yelled.

"All the best people are a little nuts, in my opinion," Dwyer said with a grin. "So at this point, you have to ask yourself, do you want one of the pieces of property, or neither? Because any challenge to your mother's plan or Roark as executor could take years for a court to decide."

"Well, perhaps my son won't be around long enough to remain executor. He has cancer, you know."

I would have gone over the table at him, but Dwyer knew me well enough to pivot and grab, catching the brunt of my forward charge and forcing me back just enough to keep me from tearing Mr. Hammond's head off.

Dwyer missed Takeo, though, who slipped around the table and slapped Mr. Hammond sharply across the face.

"Remove yourself at once," Takeo commanded, and I, for one, had never heard that tone—dark, menacing—come out of the small, slight man. "Your words are abhorrent to all those present."

Mr. Hammond made a move like he was going to backhand Takeo.

"Rethink your intended action," Takeo warned. "It would be unwise to proceed, as I am in the employ of Aaron Sutter and therefore have an entire fleet of lawyers at my disposal."

Mr. Hammond looked murderous as he regarded Takeo, who, with an open hand, pointed toward the front door.

"It would be best to ruminate on the choice before you, accept what was granted, and do no more to harass your son, as that is counterproductive in this instance."

"You could stay, David," Roark offered to his other brother, the one who'd said barely anything the entire time he'd been in the kitchen.

"No," he replied icily. "I couldn't, not without throwing up. And you, Crosby, better leave with us right now if you expect to get any money for that little Cuban—"

"No!" Hutch yelled as Mike grabbed hold of Crosby before he went over the table like I was planning to earlier. "There is no homophobia or racism during brunch on a Sunday morning."

"Get out of my house before I call the police," I warned them as Dwyer let me go and Roark sidled up to me, slid his arms around my waist, and leaned in, squeezing tight.

"I suppose the police are gay in this town too," Mr. Hammond sneered.

"Yes," Takeo said brightly, and in the silence, we all turned to see him at the edge of the porch, and only then did I realize he was on his phone. "Good morning to you as well, Mr. Sutter. Are you enjoying Amsterdam?"

We all froze, even the Hammonds.

The way Takeo smiled and his face opened up, infused with happiness, made it impossible not to admire his beauty, but even more, the incredible warmth there on display. When I glanced at Dwyer, I saw the adoration on every line of his face.

"Excellent," Takeo said quickly with another smile. "I am so pleased to—oh, yes, I wanted to ask a favor for a friend if I might." He gave a huge shit-eating grin as his big black eyes flicked to Roark's father and brother. "Yes, thank you, sir, it's a matter of a will."

"He can't unring that bell," Dwyer explained to Mr. Hammond. "You need to go. Your son's new team of lawyers will be in touch."

And with that, Mr. Hammond and David were finally gone, charging out the same way they'd come in, Hutch following them out as Crosby stayed put with us.

I reached out and took hold of Dwyer's shoulder, turning him to me. "Takeo didn't have to do that. I'm sure we were okay."

"We," Roark repeated, sagging against me. "God, when you're in, you're all in, aren't you?"

"Of course," I said, hugging him tight.

"Takeo *did* need to do that," Dwyer insisted. "Any kind of legal issue could adversely affect Roark's practice, which could have a financial impact down the road. You don't ever want to let something small escalate when you can simply remove the threat before it becomes one."

"I'm sorry, who's Aaron Sutter?" Crosby asked, moving up beside Roark.

"What rock do you live under?" Mike asked him.

"Got your bag," Hutch announced as he walked back out onto the deck.

"Oh, thank you," Crosby said, startled. "I didn't even think to—I really appreciate that."

"That's him," Mike almost crowed, leaning over to give Hutch a quick kiss. "He's very thoughtful. It's one of the many reasons I love him."

"Pardon me."

We all turned to Takeo, who stepped into our circle.

"Mr. Sutter is arranging for a Mr. Richard Jenner, managing partner of Jenner Knox, to contact you within the next hour. His firm was just placed on retainer, and Mr. Jenner will take care of this situation moving forward. Mr. Sutter cautioned you not to speak to your father about this matter in any way, as that could prove to be problematic for your law team."

"Your law team," Crosby repeated, patting Roark on the shoulder. "Holy crap."

"Thank you, Takeo," Roark said, leaning out of my embrace so he could bow.

I moved away from everyone and took Ivy aside, hugging her before we separated and I held her hands in mine.

"All that hatred, Dad, just 'cause you're gay," she said, disgusted. "That's crazy."

"That's why you have to make sure you balance it out with lots of love."

"And action," Mike chimed in as he sat down at the table. "Like Takeo did there. You gotta stand up, too, Ivy."

She nodded and then grinned evilly. "Takeo is totally badass, right?"

"A little bit," I agreed, chuckling.

CHAPTER SEVEN

SUNRISE WAS always good, but so was sunset, because even though I still had to pull kittens out of trees and explain to senior nudists about permits for bonfires on the beach, Mangrove was my home, and everyone I loved lived there now.

At the moment I was sitting on my porch railing, waiting for Roark to get back from running over to his house for another suitcase. His brother Crosby's baby was about to be born, and we were on our way to welcome his niece or nephew. I'd met Elizabeth Savón-Hammond when she and her husband had visited us right after Roark and Crosby reconnected and had formed an almost instant attachment to the bright, loud, warm woman. Ivy had been even more smitten, and she was going with us to see the baby as well. I was looking forward to it.

"God," Ivy fumed as she came banging out of the house, dumping her packed-to-the-gills overnight bag on the porch. "Why are you guys even doing this—I want to go already."

"Roark needed—"

"Who cares, Dad? It's always something. You're driving us both nuts."

"I'm sorry?"

"Me and Roark."

"You and Roark? I'm driving you both crazy."

"Yeah," she snapped, grumbling as she flopped down in the Adirondack chair close to me. "It's ridiculous."

"I have no idea what—"

"Why're you so scared to have him move in?"

I pointed to myself.

"Yes, you. For crissakes, Dad, he—"

"Did you just take the Lord's name in vain?"

She rolled her eyes. "Whatever, ask him to move in already. It's been three months, he's had a key since day one, and now it's getting really… pathetic."

"Pathetic?"

"Yeah," she said snidely, sarcasm dripping from her tone.

"Really?"

"Yeah," she retorted with no less annoyance.

I cleared my throat. "I simply wanted us all to be comfortable with—"

"Ohmygod, he's nicer than you are, he cooks better, he lets Davis come over and study with me in my room as long as the door's open, and he got me Grover."

"Don't bring up the dog."

"Why?"

"It's not a dog, for starters."

She gasped. "Grover's my baby."

"It's a furry rat."

"He's a Pomeranian!"

"It's not a dog."

"I love him! Not only can I walk him, but I can carry him in my purse."

"Which makes him a makeup bag, not a dog."

She put up her hands. "You're impossible, and now I'm gonna go over to Hutch and Mike's and visit Grover while you wait for Roark. Call me when he gets here."

"I—"

"When you guys were up at dawn greeting the day like *The Lion King* or whatever, you should've walked over and got the extra suitcase then."

"*The Lion King?*"

"Yeah, you know, the song at the beginning when the sun comes up?"

"Go away."

She snickered as she left me.

Moments later, from up the street came Roark Hammond, waving at people as he walked by, and then, seeing me, he smiled.

It was the one he saved just for me. The one that heated his eyes, made his dimples pop, and was almost shy. It made him bright and shiny, and when I felt the familiar twinge in my chest, I sighed out the very last of my reservations.

"Hey," I greeted him.

"Sorry," he called out, jogging up to my gate. "It wasn't in the garage like I thought. It was in the attic, and I'm never home now, so my place is looking a little—"

"Hey, baby," I began, "this two houses thing ain't workin' for me anymore."

Roark froze in the middle of the path leading to my front door.

"So I think you should move in."

"I thought you didn't like the word 'ain't.'"

"I don't, but it was useful in this instance to get your undivided attention."

"Yes, it was," he said, his eyes wide as he stared at me.

I gestured for him to come closer.

"You're sure?"

"I'm sure."

"You can't take it back."

"I know."

"I would need another notarized letter with ten years' notice if you want me to move out."

"It won't be an issue."

"It won't?"

"No."

"Why not?" he prodded.

I stood up and moved to the top of the stairs. "Because I love you, and my daughter loves you, and the hamster posing as a dog you got her loves you, and so… come on. Come into my life and stay awhile."

"How long?"

"How would forever be?"

He dropped the suitcase, darted up the path, and flung himself into my arms, his own wrapping around my neck. "Forever would do nicely, Chief Dodd, thank you."

And I kissed him, hard, just to make sure we were on the same page. As though there had ever been any question.

MARY CALMES lives in Lexington, Kentucky, with her husband and two children and loves all the seasons except summer. She graduated from the University of the Pacific in Stockton, California, with a bachelor's degree in English literature. Due to the fact that it is English lit and not English grammar, do not ask her to point out a clause for you, as it will so not happen. She loves writing, becoming immersed in the process, and believes without question in happily-ever-afters, and writes those for each and every one of her characters.

TIMING

Mary Calmes

Timing: Book One

Stefan Joss just can't win. Not only does he have to go to Texas in the middle of summer to be the man of honor in his best friend Charlotte's wedding, but he's expected to negotiate a million-dollar business deal at the same time. Worst of all, he's thrown for a loop when he arrives to see the one man Charlotte promised wouldn't be there: her brother, Rand Holloway.

Stefan and Rand have been mortal enemies since the day they met, so Stefan is shocked when a temporary cease-fire sees the usual hostility replaced by instant chemistry. Though leery of the unexpected feelings, Stefan is swayed by a sincere revelation from Rand, and he decides to give Rand a chance.

But their budding romance is threatened when Stefan's business deal goes wrong: the owner of the last ranch he needs to secure for the company is murdered. Stefan's in for the surprise of his life as he finds himself in danger as well.

www.dreamspinnerpress.com

MARY CALMES

WARDERS

VOLUME ONE

HIS HEARTH

TOOTH & NAIL

HEART IN HAND

Most humans live in blissful ignorance, never dreaming of the frightening surprises and paranormal danger that lurks in the night. Most… but not all. These few who stand against the darkness are the Warders, men who fight demons and square off against all kinds of creatures from the pit with only their brothers-in-arms and their lovers—their Hearths—to strengthen them in the unending battle of good versus evil.

His Hearth
Tooth & Nail
Heart in Hand

www.dreamspinnerpress.com

MARY CALMES

WARDERS

VOLUME TWO

SINNERMAN

NEXUS

*CHERISH
YOUR NAME*

Most humans live in blissful ignorance, never dreaming of the frightening surprises and paranormal danger that lurks in the night. Most… but not all. These few who stand against the darkness are the Warders, men who fight demons and square off against all kinds of creatures from the pit with only their brothers-in-arms and their lovers—their Hearths—to strengthen them in the unending battle of good versus evil.

Sinnerman
Nexus
Cherish Your Name

www.dreamspinnerpress.com

www.ingramcontent.com/pod-product-compliance
Lightning Source LLC
Chambersburg PA
CBHW050033030726

47506CB00001B/246